EMI

He felt the bl
horror and
fluttered like

Run.

This is what he had to do now in the thickening dusk. He had to get out of here as fast as possible and pray that no one saw him enter this place or, if they'd seen him, that they would be unable to identify him. His mind spun and all he could think clearly was that he had to put as much distance as possible between himself and this poor dead creature. She was dead. It was all over for her, but no matter where she went in the afterlife, it looked as if hell on earth might be yawning just ahead for him.

Other books by Ashley Carter

Against All Gods
The Outlanders

EMBRACE THE WIND

Ashley Carter

A STAR BOOK
published by
the Paperback Division of
W. H. ALLEN & Co. PLC

A Star Book
Published in 1985
by the Paperback Division of
W. H. Allen & Co. PLC
44 Hill Street, London W1X 8LB

First published in the United States of America
by Jove Publications, Inc.
First published in Great Britain
by W. H. Allen & Co. PLC, 1984

Printed and bound in Great Britain by
Anchor Brendon Ltd, Tiptree, Essex

ISBN 0 352 31639 X

Contents

Part I—Hidden Brook
1

Part II—Freebooters' Fortress
85

Part III—Frontier Firebrand
189

Part IV—Home Is the Hunter
295

PART I

Hidden Brook

— I —

HE CAME galloping hard up Pennsylvania Avenue and headed through the White House gateway without even slowing his lathered mount. Sentries ran out to intercept him, guns bristling.

"Where the hell you think you're going?"

He jerked hard on the reins and pulled in upon his great stallion until that golden steed squatted like a dog on the pebbled drive and then flailed upward in a precarious demi-volt. Still, the rider was able to stay in his saddle, though his mount's head whipped upward, mane flying, and sweat pelted out over the guards like driven mists.

"You trying to git yourself kilt?"

The horseman grinned and eased his grip on the reins. The stallion straightened, standing as calmly now as his master. Though the animal was magnificent, its owner projected a none-too-prepossessing appearance: thin as a winter coyote, his leather jacket streaked with the red clay and grime of inclement travel, boots cracked with age, wool trousers salty and slick with wear. Only the pristine white of his collar, the lace of his shirtfront and the arrogant tilt of his slender, sun-braised features beneath the wide, limp brim of his bonnet suggested he might be anything more than a common rowdy—a type certainly not unknown in the District of Columbia these days.

"Who are you?"

"What you want here? What's your business in this place?"

The President's palace guards crowded around him and kept their guns leveled, showing taut, gray faces. He could almost see the white rims of the frightened eyes fixed on him. He sighed. Life must be dull around here for enlisted soldiers since the war. They needed a shaking up.

He tilted his squared chin and surveyed the eighteen acres

of White House grounds with the unruffled air of a prospective buyer. His calm and reasonableness plus his total disinterest in their guns and responsibilities enraged the uniformed men all the more. Among them were those who furiously favored dragging him from his saddle and clubbing him insensible with rifle butts even before they questioned him. But about this intruder there was an indefinable something which counseled caution even in the most audacious heart, unarmed and outnumbered though he was.

They hesitated.

"What's your name?" A beardless lieutenant stepped close.

"Jeremiah Newman Locke. Of Hidden Brook Plantation. Near Manassas. Rode all yesterday, getting as close as Alexandria. I have business here or I'd never have come near this infested bog. Stand aside."

The young lieutenant gripped his check reins.

"My horse bites," Locke observed in a casual tone.

The officer winced but retained his grasp, if warily. "What's your business here, Locke?"

An unarmed soldier padded out of the sentry house, carrying the log book. He caught the lieutenant's arm, face gray, eyes stricken. The lieutenant, glad for the excuse, released the check rein and stared at the register.

He read a moment, reread, forming the words with his lips. He shook his head and signaled his squad to lower rifles. "His name is here. He's to see the President." He swallowed hard. "Here's the note in Mr. Monroe's own hand—Locke is to be ushered into the President's private study as secretly, quickly and quietly as possible. . . . God's eyes, Locke, is this your idea of quiet?"

Locke bounded up the outer stairs two at a time and entered the main foyer of the newly restored mansion. He looked about, fascinated. A man didn't see a castle like this every day, and too he had seen this burned-out hulk after admiral Sir George Cockburn's men gutted it three years ago. He still recalled the throat-gripping emotion he'd felt when he'd heard that gallant Dolley Madison had returned here to find this structure fire-swept, uninhabitable.

He gazed around the high-ceilinged rooms. Thomas Jefferson had called this chateau monstrous, large enough for "two emperors, the Pope and the Grand Lama." And Jefferson was right. One couldn't credit a man's coming to live here from an ordinary house in Virginia or a slab Massachusetts cottage and remaining humbly aware of his own mortality. This was the elegance and display of royalty, though its builders swore this was the last thing they wanted. Few politicians weren't liars—lying informed their craft.

Impressed, stirred with a sense of pride and patriotism he hadn't even suspected, he felt blood racing in his veins, his heart pounding. Power and glory. That's what one sensed in all this revived splendor. Perhaps puritanical John Adams and "little" Jemmey Madison hadn't measured up to these regal surroundings. And God knew,the present occupant, Monroe, that most commonplace of all, brought nothing to its majesty. But Jefferson had, even though he did his own shopping. Locke saw the palatial White House for what it was—a monument to Washington himself, the regal president who could have been king.

The sandstone walls, quarried out at Aquia Creek, gleamed whitely, and Jefferson had added to its beauty with flowered terraces east and west of the six-floored main building which gazed south across the lawn to the Tiber.

Locke remained standing in the diplomatic reception room until a liveried black man inquired his name and then led him through high-domed, still largely unfurnished cross halls to a small private study. This room had been furnished with Monroe's personal effects from Ash Lawn Plantation.

Locke stood at the window, battered bonnet in his hands, and watched the crosshatching of sun and shadow on the parklike lawn. Somehow the truth seemed to lie more in the tidewater bog across the Tiber than in all this pomp.

He heard the door opened and he turned. President Monroe said, "Jerry. Good of you to come."

"You sent for me."

"You lost no time and I appreciate that."

"Do I curtsy?"

"A simple, unaffected groveling will suffice, my boy." The pale blue eyes lightened in the undistinguished face. Monroe appeared exhausted, though he didn't look particularly like the sovereign leader of a nation. Locke supposed after the aristocratic Washington, few men would appear hewn of true presidential timber. All of which proved how deceiving looks could be: this good and gentle man was a President to his toenails, devoting to it every breath, every thought, every drop of energy.

Monroe crossed the room smiling. They stood together in a long saffron rectangle of light from the tall window. The President was lanky, less than formidable in mien or manner. Of medium height, he seemed shorter standing before the lean six-foot stripling from Prince William County.

"To what do I owe the honor and glory of a summons to the White House?" Locke asked. "Had I been brought here in irons, there would have been no question in my mind."

Though he intentionally presented the President with the opportunity to discuss a shady region of his past, President Monroe ignored the invitation. President Monroe did not mention, nor did Locke himself press the matter further. The facts were known to the President concerning those two black and hidden years during which Locke and amassed a fortune as plunderer, privateer, pirate—operating from the infamous Amelia Island off Florida's coast. He'd departed Virginia, a boy of nineteen, and returned at twenty-one a seasoned man, hard-eyed and remote, rich enough to recoup all the losses of his father's squandering—and possessor of how much more wealth only God and gossip dared surmise.

Monroe laughed. "It's good to have you here. Your taunting laughter does a man good after all the false faces of simpering constituency. Didn't your solicitor tell you why I wished to see you?"

"Worthington Jennings is, as always, a busy man. He said only that I was to come to you in all haste."

"Assuredly, he neglected the most urgent piece of my message. You were to come quietly—even with some stealth."

"Jennings said only quickly. Or perhaps I didn't listen closely. Not every day a simple farmer is invited in to see the President."

"All your self-mockery can't conceal the fact that I and my lady came often to Hidden Brook as guests of my true friend, your father."

"That pious hypocrite." Jerry Locke shook his head. "If I hold to any doubt about you at all, Mr. President, it is that you deceived yourself that my father was a true friend. He was never a true friend to a soul alive except himself, except that it profited himself."

"Hasn't he been dead long enough for your bitterness to ebb, Jerry?"

Locke scowled, shrugged and then laughed. "I know you didn't bring me to Washington to counsel me on my father's revered memory, sir. And I don't want to waste your time."

Monroe smiled. "Still, you already may have, riding in here like a drunken banshee. Why did you come racing in like a legion of looters?"

Locke laughed, not at all abashed. "Always have enjoyed throwing eggs at high hats, Mr. President. Cato and I rode around the place earlier . . . it seemed—sort of pompous, you know. Guards at the gates. Tourists gaping from the streets. I decided if I'm to come here often at your bidding, I wanted them to know me at that gate. If I'd come, meek, hat in hand, I'd have had to beg my way in every time. Now they'll recognize me. Hell, Mr. President, from now on they'll know me on sight—and wave me right in."

Monroe smiled with him, then frowned faintly. "You're not to come back here again, Jerry. Not for a long time. Maybe never."

Locke grinned, puzzled. "Then you've called me in to tell me good-bye when I'd never have troubled you, a day's ride away at Hidden Brook."

"It's more than that, Jerry. Far more. I need your help. I've weighed men in my mind—a hundred men and more. I started with you—and I came back to you. You have every qualification for the job I have for you, and which, for the good of our poor, dear nation, I hope you will accept. But many men were as qualified—except in one way. I knew Jerry Locke's word is solid gold in worth. If you give me your word, I can go to the bank with it. If you give me your pledge, I know you'll never dishonor it. That's the extra I was looking for. I must have a man I can trust—and go on trusting. Even when, in the heat and trial of his ordeal, he may lose his faith in me—still *I'll* know that I can trust *him*. You're that man, Jerry. You're that man."

Locke glanced around the room and exhaled heavily, more displeased than flattered. "It's worse than I expected."

"What did you expect?"

"I don't know. We haven't seen you or your lovely lady at Hidden Brook in God knows how many years. I thought maybe you asked me up here to inquire about friends in Prince William. . . . No, to tell you the truth, sir, I didn't know what in hell you wanted."

"I need eyes and ears and a strong right arm, Jerry. I won't deceive you." He flung his arm, his face grave. "This White House is worthy of an English monarch. But our poor nation is war-starved, divided, in deep financial depression . . . and threatened from all sides, but as much—maybe even more—from within."

"What's the job you have for me?"

"Aye, there's the rub . . . I have a job for you. But it is so classified, of such delicate nature, that I cannot relate to you its particulars until you have agreed to accept it. And I will not ask of you that you give me such a pledge blindly."

"Being President gets conniving as hell, doesn't it?"

"It can be hell, Jerry. To mistrust the men you love. Men you respect. To fear the secret motives of the very men whose counsel you must seek. God alone knows how the Caesars of ancient Rome existed, with intrigue lurking behind every smiling mask."

"No one can doubt seriously that you want anything but the best for this nation. I know you to be truly honest, sir. Dedicated. Not the merriest rascal to be around, but the most honorable—and God, how boring that must be."

The blue eyes twinkled like wan stars. "Thank you, Jerry."

"For what?"

"For affirming that I have selected wisely. Perhaps I can offer a compromise. You do trust me. I know that. And I trust you. So, I will tell you all—or almost all—of my problem. If you decide you do not wish to serve, I will understand, and I shall not even press it. We shall shake hands and part friends. I ask only that, should you refuse, you will never—even in your sleep—murmur one word of what I say to you here."

"On that you have my vow, Mr. President. I sleep soundly, usually. And if I don't, my bed-partners do."

Monroe almost smiled through the corrosive acid of his agony. "How shocked your father would be to hear you talk like this."

"My father of cursed memory. I *have* lived recklessly. I *have* done many things less than honest. I've been called rascal, mercenary, dishonest, cruel and cunning. Not one word hurts more than to be called the son of the man I lived to hate with all my heart."

Monroe winced. "I'm thankful your poor father isn't alive to audit such bitter recrimination. I understand a great deal about you suddenly—I see you are trying to be everything in the world you believed your father was not."

"That would cleanse me inside, I can tell you."

"Yet, how he loved you! I witnessed quiet display of that affection in a hundred ways over the years. . . . And consider, Jerry, how bitterness turns our own insides to vinegar. Hate is far more detrimental to ourselves than to the object of our hatred."

"I'm still in good shape. Good digestion. Able still to laugh inside even when I must conceal it out. . . . I waste no time looking back. For hours at a time some days I no longer even recall the evil he did us—my mother, my sisters and me. . . . Well, thank God, I was able to set the wrong right. But memory of the wrongdoer rankles still and will forever, I'm afraid, no matter how deep I might wish aught."

The President sighed and indicated a high-backed Sheraton chair. He sat himself in a wicker wingback, a make-do, odd piece for this room. It did not matter. Monroe sat there less than a full sixty seconds. On his feet again, he paced the room. At last he said, "Do you know Andrew Jackson? Of Tennessee?"

"Of course I've read of him . . . I suppose next only to Washington, this country reveres General Jackson as its greatest military hero."

Monroe waved his arm. "And none can detract—except in calumny—from Jackson's exploits, his valor, his toughness. I doubt even Washington was his match in this ruggedness—as I doubt that even Washington was as ambitious as Andy Jackson. And even more, Jackson is a man of the people—accepted by them as one of them, even as he is set apart and revered by them. General Jackson did indeed defeat the British at Chalmette, outside New Orleans. Nor does it diminish one whit from his victory that armistice between the United States and Great Britain had been signed weeks earlier at Ghent.

Jackson didn't know that. The British who fought him didn't know that.

"And certainly, in all fairness, we must admit that Jackson did not suspect that the Treaty of Ghent returned all international boundaries as they were before the war, subject to decision by commissions."

For a long beat in the massive silence of this vast manse, Monroe stared down at Jerry, as though unable to decide whether to continue, or if continuing, how to choose the words for what he next felt compelled to relate. "But even in every moment of Jackson's greatest triumphs have festered foul blisters to erupt and besmirch the excellence of each of his achievements."

"I don't follow you."

"I know. I hope only that I can make the matter clear in both our minds— to remain fair to Andy Jackson while not compromising the truth as I see it, either. And also, that I do not end up the villain—of deluded, and infected mind—finding enemies in friendly shadows.

"You must trust me! The things I say in this room break my heart, choke in my throat and foul my lips to cross them. They must never go beyond these walls. If they be the imaginings of a doubting, twisted mind, prayerfully we shall determine the truth in time. If my fears be well-founded—then God help us all."

Jerry scowled, troubled. "You are talking about General Jackson?"

A wry smile. "Or trying *not* to grapple with the subject. . . . Well, to it! When Jackson won the Battle of New Orleans, he even then exceeded his authority. He acted on his own. He disobeyed War Department directives. He had been commanded to stand at Mobile. He ignored all official communiqués which did not suit his humors. He marched on New Orleans—subjecting himself to court-martial—and took the battle. Overnight, he is worshipped by the populace, and those who even whispered court-martial were swiftly and coldly silenced.

"Then, having defied the President and the War Department, at the crest of glory, cheered by a grateful nation, rather than marching his volunteer army back to the hills of Tennessee where most of them belonged, and there disband them, he insisted upon discharging and paying off—in gold—those soldiers at New Orleans. Whores and would-be prostitutes, women greedy for soldier pay, flocked by the hundreds to the Crescent City. Finally, Jackson—and most of his men—returned to their homes, but three years later, there remains and increases in New Orleans the greatest concentration of prostitutes in this nation. A sad corollary to Jackson's magnificent achievement there.

"Well, recently—while little Jemmey Madison was still President—Andy Jackson uncoiled himself from the monotony of Bible Belt, backwoods Tennessee life and gathered together his own army. He pays them, you know, from his own pocket when the U.S. refuses or cannot. And he marched south to the international border of Spanish Florida.

"Madison sent him vague orders to proceed no further south than the international line at Mobile. Florida is sovereign Spanish territory—whether we like it or not. Whether Andy Jackson likes it or not. Whether Americans living along the border like it or not. It was the call of these people—claiming murders, rape, scalping, slave stealing by thugs havened in Florida—that brought the general, brandishing his sword. Madison knew better than directly to order Jackson off that troubled frontier. If Jackson disregarded Madison's official ultimatum, only Madison could suffer in public esteem. Madison would be made to appear the fool—if not an outright traitor.

"Well, I am a prideful man, too. I don't relish being the butt of derisive laughter any more than the next man. But my pride is not my first concern anymore. The safety and security of this nation—this *entire* nation—is my priority. I have ordered Jackson and his Tennessee volunteers disbanded and returned home. So far, the hotheaded general has not even bothered to reply."

Locke felt a flaring of compassion for the bedeviled man who devoted heart and mind and soul to an overwhelming job. The sixty-four-year-old President looked gut-tired. It must indeed prove tragic that a President command where he was not to be obeyed, or where to enforce obedience would prove equal in controversy to the infamy of callous defiance. A presidential dominance once successfully flouted limps forever crippled. Before Locke could speak—if there was anything he could say!—Monroe brushed the thought aside and continued.

"In the West—out there along the Mississippi frontier—there is strong sentiment for war with Spain. I *know* war is what Jackson wants. Nothing else will serve his purpose, or fill his bucket, if I read him right.

"The Spanish closed the Mississippi to American navigation and commerce. Many in border states were ruined financially and they have not forgotten. When we were able to restore river passage for shipping of American goods, still Spain denied us the piers and facilities for shipping at New Orleans. There are legitimate grievances.

"Spain holds lax rein over the Indians, blacks and three or four thousand whites scattered along the upper coast and across the peninsula to the northern Florida panhandle. These peoples—renegades most—are satisfied with Spanish rule.

"To be awarded a land grant in Florida these days, one pledges only to rear his children in the Catholic faith. Once, he and his family and slaves had to convert to the Church. Spanish rule in Florida, under Ferdinand, is next to no rule at all. And for that reason it is a haven for criminals, fugitives, cutthroats, murderers, slave stealers and cattle rustlers.

"The complaints have come to Washington. Then they have gone to General Jackson. For years there have been daily and nightly clashes between U.S. citizens in Georgia and the Alabama territory and the runaway Indians, escaped black slaves and the fugitives who make Florida their sanctuary from our criminal justice.

"All these conditions form the basis for Jackson's overt actions. He wants to stop the black slaves from crossing the border and joining with the Seminoles—"

"Themselves runaways—"

"Right. Seminole means runaway. Those Indians are fugitive Upper and Lower Creeks, Choctaws, Cherokees and Chickasaws who've found sanctuary in the Florida wilderness. This galls Jackson most of all because it was he who decimated those very tribes in earlier confrontations with them.

"So there is huge public sentiment—in the South and West—supporting Jackson in his reckless adventuring.

"On the other side, there are facts he either refuses to face or laughs to scorn. We have American soldiers protecting our borders. As a nation, we are weakened, depleted, bled white by war. We don't need more war. We need to be let alone. We should not harass and prod and provoke *any* nation—even one as infirm as Spain is presently. The New England states would not support such an exercise.

"So this is not the mandate of an aroused majority. Far from it. Today, the center of population for the U.S. is geographically forty miles northwest by west of here—out in Virginia. Up here, in the population center of our country, the mood is one of restraint, of the need to regroup, recuperate, rebuild. But out west along the Mississippi and down on the Florida border, the wild cries are for expansion now—reaching out at all costs—even, we have reason to fear, at the expense of the Union itself. This I cannot permit."

"Are you saying that Jackson may be planning to set up a new, independent republic down there?"

"I'm not the only one prey to such anxieties. Adams, John Quincy Adams, Clay, Madison—hell, the list is long of men who doubt General Jackson's loyalties, ambitions and secret motives. Jackson's financial supporters, his backers, are certainly kingmakers—"

"Then why don't you recall him?"

"Because the men I just mentioned—the Adamses, Clay, Madison—cluck like timid hens, quailing at the thought of a public confrontation with Jackson. They fear him. They suspect his motives. But most of all they respect his terrible popularity with the people. He could wreck this Union by opposing it. They know him to be immovable, headstrong, violent-tempered. They realize that, like every zealot, Jackson is so convinced of the rightness of his cause that he regards any means to accomplish its ends as holy and justified.

"If I confront Jackson—and I shall if I am forced to it—one of us must back down. I shall not. I know that he will not. Therefore, I must know his true intent, the extent of his ambitions, the actuality of his motivations, before I move against him."

"His true intent?"

"Yes. These answers I must have: Is Jackson trying to take Florida from Spain—in order to set up a republic of his own—on American soil? I cannot permit this, anymore than if he were a foreign power. What are Jackson's true ambitions? Why has he regrouped an army and returned to Florida when he long ago won public laurels there—when he must know that the subduing of Indians in that wilderness of almost sixty thousand square miles is hopeless?"

"Do you truly suspect him of such expansionist plotting?"

"I don't *know* about him. That's the whole truth, the whole ugly problem, the whole painful situation. What *does* he want? I know *him*. Personally. As well, I suppose, as we can ever know any acquaintance. An arrogant, headstrong man. A law only onto himself. Above all law. In private life, willing to commit murder to satisfy his passions—"

"Murder. A cheap price to pay out west for a lady." Locke grinned crookedly.

Monroe sighed heavily. "I wish the weight of my fears allowed me to smile with you. As a man, knowing my own weakness, I can be tolerant of Jackson. But as President, I cannot. Is Jackson a dedicated patriot? If so—in my eyes—he is a misguided one. Is he an enemy of this central government? Is it his intention to set up the Rebublic of West Florida as an independent nation? I don't know. I've got to know. I am sworn to protect and defend this poor, depression-ridden, war-starved nation from its enemies—inside and out. Foreign or domestic.

"Does Jackson think to serve either me or this nation by fomenting trouble on the border, taunting Spain, harassing the Indians and the Spanish nationals south of the Georgia border?

"All I know for fact is that he acts without orders or authorization from me. Madison tolerated his insubordination. I cannot. Yet, if I sent him a pack of official orders, he would disobey all of them, choose those which pleased his purposes and ignore the rest, or act as he intended from the first."

Monroe paced the room, his face a gray mask. "And so, I delay sending him orders. I cannot afford to be laughed to scorn. As James Monroe, I might be fair target for his jeers and the derision of his followers. But as President of the United States, I'm goddamned if I will be."

Locke tilted his brow, admiring the aging man, deeply troubled for him. Hell, at his age, Monroe could be sipping juleps or mulled liquors on the veranda at Ash Lawn. He had nothing to gain here except what he believed best for his country. Jerry tried to smile. "And all you want is for me to find out the truth."

Monroe almost smiled at this terrible irony. "As nearly as it can be determined. Yes. No President has yet employed secret intelligence inside his own government, so far as I have been able to ascertain. So I set the precedent, as abhorrent as its prospect is to me."

"What do you want of me?"

"Follow him. Join him if you can. Trail him if you must. But in the name of God, learn his true intent—find out what in hell Andy is about this time."

Locke stood up and walked to the window. The parklike grounds gleamed in sunlight, strangely, deceptively quiet and peaceful. "From all this I gather I am acting with your blessing, but without your official sanction?"

"It's worse than that, my boy. If you are suspected, revealed, trapped, compromised, I shall have to deny you. I cannot afford you assistance except expenses placed somehow at your disposal—and my prayers."

He joined Locke at the window. His voice was low, hollow with weariness.

"If finally you return with the intelligence I need—one way or the other—on Jackson's motives, I shall, in secret, thank you, in public disavow you, if I must. However, if you bring me the truth, I shall act unhesitatingly upon it—as I would act on facts gathered by my own hands, my own mind, my own eyes and heart. The future of this poor young nation—thirty years old and threatened from all sides and perhaps from within—may well rest on the substance of your report."

"That's a hellish responsibility."

"That's why I considered a hundred men and selected one."

"Do you expect a quick answer to such an assignment?"

"I pray for one."

"Well, that's what I can't give you. My own life has only finally settled on stable ground—after a long and evil time since my father's death."

"And besides this, you're in love." The old man nodded.

"I had no idea you were so well informed."

"Miss Mary-Stuart Randolph is undoubtedly the daintiest,

loveliest flower of Virginia. I cannot lightly ask that you risk losing her—"

"And yet if I depart suddenly on an errand I cannot explain—"

"You must not explain it. Not to a soul living. As far as the public record will ever show, I invited you here on a matter concerning property owned by your father—and this property is all we discussed."

Locke winced. "Then you'll have to let me think on it. I admire and respect you, Mr. President. I've always liked you. I love my country as much as does any man. But I'm—hot-blooded . . . I have loved long—and long been denied. You ask more than you could know. . . . I'll send you my decision."

"No. Don't do that. If suddenly you're gone from Hidden Brook, I'll reckon you on my errand. With that, for now, I'll be content."

— II —

ONCE FERRIED across the dark tidewater basin of the Potomac from the town of Washington, travelers still faced a long, marshy trek out to Alexandria. The countryside itself was enchantingly attractive, but a recent air of tension, a sullen resentment of war-starved, exhausted farmers, hung like a leaden miasma in the very atmosphere.

Locke sagged in the saddle, his slouch making him almost a part of the animal, for the long ride out to Prince William County. Beside him, his Negro servant-for-life rode, stiff-backed, head erect, somehow regal in linsey-woolsey and osnaburg.

Locke glanced toward the young man and grinned faintly. Disapproval bristled like some charged aura about his body servant. Cato held himself withdrawn, silently critical.

Locke sighed and said nothing. They plodded south through rich lush foliage, massed sycamores, elms, pines; humid in the sun, they wound with the travel-gouged trail between low-hanging limbs lining the twisting trace across rolling knolls. The years faded and he was a boy again, riding this sunlit land with his father in that long-ago time when he'd trusted, loved and revered his parent—as now he despised his memory.

As Locke rode at ease, he considered the tidewater countryside in the spring sunshine and reckoned it good just to be alive. There was some hurt clinging from his past. No man finds everything as he wants it, but we encounter Jeremiah Newman Locke at that moment in his life when he felt strongest, expansive, optimistic and hopeful. He found this world good. He was young; far wealthier than anyone suspected, and most of his ill-gotten, hard-won gains had by now been laundered into tangible, respectable assets. He was in love. He could hardly remember when he had not loved Mary-Stuart Randolph. For a long time many real and imagined barriers had thwarted him there; but now most obstacles seemed removed or removable. He was in a pleasant mood and not too much troubled by his recent dialogue with the President, though his vivid memory of the way he'd left the little man, brave, alone and unbroken against a sea of ills, still haunted him.

He exhaled heavily. He'd reached no decision on the matter of the President's assignment, felt no obligation to do so: Politicians always confronted or created world-shaking crises. It went with the territory. He had his own problems.

He stretched back his shoulders. He believed himself master of his own destiny—he had proved his mettle and his mastery a dozen times on the trade routes of the Atlantic, preying on Spanish merchantmen and British warships. He felt good about himself and his prospects. He would not have believed, even if he'd been warned by some augur, that a shadow was deepening across the sunny plane of his young life.

"They didn't arrest you then?"

Locke turned and stared at Cato, his grin taunting the slave. "What'd you say, boy?"

"You heard me—mastah." The delay in stating his title was perfect timing to make the appellation an insult.

"Why should they arrest me?"

"They should have."

"You're a holier-than-thou Puritan at heart, Cato. A Salem prude with a black Edo face." Locke's grin twisted. "You're getting mighty biggety for a nigger."

He bit back a smile seeing the blood flush across Cato's cameo-perfect, brown-tinged features. Cato muttered imprecations under his breath. Cato hated being called a nigger. The slave's muttering was clear enough, slurred old-fashioned Saxon words consigning his white master to the hottest hole beyond hell. Pleased that Cato had taken the bait, and finding relief from the boredom of the hot ride south, Locke added, taunting him, "A nigger slave has just got to learn his place, boy."

"I learnt my place—mastah. I was taught my *place* by your father. But I got my dignity. My self-respect. He never took that. Nobody could. Nobody will."

"Too bad. You'd find life a hell of a lot easier without a lot of fool notions about who you are, what you are. I can tell you what you are. You're black. You're a nigger. You're my black nigger, Cato, and not a thing you can do about it."

Cato faced him levelly, black eyes flaring against Locke's. "I am black," Cato spoke with savage dignity. "A black *man*."

"A nigger." Locke swung his arm as if the matter were too trivial to discuss, a move designed to inflame his servant. "A nigger, Cato. You're a nigger slave. You're no *man* at all, boy."

"Get off that horse, mastah. I'll show you who's a man."

Locke shook his head deprecatingly. "I can't whip you a dozen times a day just to prove you're what God made you. Don't blame me. God made you black. I didn't."

"God made me black. *You* made me a nigger. You beat me just *once* on *any* day, mastah, and I calls *myself* nigger."

"Jesus, Cato. Don't be so touchy. You're haughtier than the white people down at Manticello ever could be. Who the hell you think you are? Jefferson's own son?"

Breath rasped across Cato's perfect white teeth; another unhealed scar had been ripped open. "I am Sally Heming's son," Cato answered, his patrician head tilted.

"With red tints in that black hair, for God's sake." Locke

shrugged. "Maybe you're not a nigger. No ordinary nigger, anyhow. But you are a slave. Other than that I'm damned if I know what you are."

"I am a man."

"No Hell, Cato, I didn't make the rules. I don't know who did. A man is white. A nigger is an animal—you know most people say that—an animal that can talk, that's all."

Cato's voice shook. "And you're a bastard—mastah, suh."

Locke smiled and shook his head. "No. You're wrong about that, too, Cato. I wish I were a bastard—and didn't own my father's name. But unfortunately, fate decided that, too. You're the bastard, Cato—maybe Thomas Jefferson's own bastard, but still a bastard."

"I'm legally a bastard, mastah. You is personally a bastard."

Locke laughed. "You really want to fight, don't you, Cato?"

Cato glared around helplessly. "There ought to be some payment. You flaunt all the laws and you get rich. Invited to see the President. I try to live by God's own commandments—and I live in slavery. It ain't right. It just ain't right."

"I do what I have to do, Cato. If it turns out profitably, I can't be expected to wear sackcloth and ashes. I regret nothing."

"That's what makes it all so powerful wrong. You regrets nothing. The evil you did, and you regret nothing—"

"You were beside me at every step—"

"But I regrets. I cry in my heart, where is the only place a man can cry—"

"More horse-droppings you learned from my father—"

"Yassuh. Yore daddy taught me—the hard way—that a man don't cry."

"Of course a man cries. If he hurts badly enough, he cries. God made tears—he never made them for women alone. Of course a man cries. You'll cry—when you hurt bad enough."

"No. Yore daddy taught me. A man don't cry. A man don't compromise his honor. A man don't steal and rob and murder. Yore daddy taught *me* well. Too bad he could never teach you."

"If I believed that saddle-sweat, you'd be chopping cotton on some other white man's plantation—a white man who'd never let you call him bastard, or talk back, or stand with your neck stiff and straight. I'd have had to sell you off, along with everything else."

"They is right. And they is wrong"

"My God, Cato. Don't you know yet? Need makes right. Weakness bows to wrong. I know you're all mixed up inside. How can you help it? Tom Jefferson's bastard git out of a slave girl at Monticello—a girl half-sister herself to Jefferson's own wife."

"That's all lies," Cato said. "All scandalmongering lies."

Locke grinned. That known libeler and scandalmonger James Thomas Callender in the Richmond *Recorder* as early as 1802 had published the persistent gossip that Jefferson had fathered five children by Sally Heming—three of which were sold as slaves. If any of this were true, and Cato were Jefferson's woods colt, then there were six offspring by Sally—and *four* sold into slavery.

Cato had come to the Locke estate from Monticello when he was about twelve years old and had begun to bear, according to gossip, "a striking, though dusky resemblance" to the distinguished master. Some even whispered that, "at a distance, or in the dusk, the boy Cato could even be mistaken for Mr. Jefferson."

Locke shrugged. Jefferson himself never admitted, nor, according to intimates, ever appeared to discover "the least resemblance, nor any reason for it" in any of the light-tan or yellow-skinned children sprouting upon his estate.

Still, the rumors persisted and one saw in Cato the unconscious hauteur, inner pride and seething passionate nature which was quite acceptable in the third President of the United States but intolerable in a mulatto. The caste system in which he was trapped brutally punished a black man who attempted to raise his head in any crowd or to look a white woman directly in the face. Black men were castrated or hung for less.

Cato rode straight in the saddle, still muttering maledictions whose foulness made Locke bite his lip to keep from laughing.

Cato held himself tautly, his powerful muscles bunched on his yard-wide shoulders and across the thick keglike chest. His coarse cotton and wool shirt strained and stretched against those corded tendons. Wide circles of sweat spread outward in darkening rings from his armpits. In Cato, Locke sadly recognized a furious passionate power and forceful energy too fearful to be contained within a bondaged soul. But he was as helpless as Cato to change society or the world in which they lived.

One looked at the black slave Cato and saw a massive man bigger than life itself driven by inner savagery as old as his ancient tribal fathers. There was no doubt that Cato was a Negro, yet his skin was smooth-burnished copper, his cap of black hair glinted with strange fiery highlights. One saw a man unlike all other men of his race: a sharply hewn profile, a straight high forehead, eyes as black as the Niger, aglow with intelligence, curiosity and ill-curbed lust for life. Cato often flashed a servile smile to the white men who came to Hidden Brook, but even that fawning grin set ill on the arrogant face and failed to hide the deep-rubbed anger seething close beneath the surface. Cato hated subservience, fought it involuntarily, but impotently. He forced himself to conform—because this was the only way to stay alive in the white man's world—and yet was unable to bend. His lips were full, Negroid, plum-dark; his chin was as something hewn from dark marble, his throat a thick pillar through which pulsed blue-veined arteries. He was a bitter young man, like a proud mastiff who yields under a master's firm curb yet still bristles and holds its head tilted.

"What do you want of me, Cato? Would you like to see me a simpering, church-going do-gooder like Worthington Jennings—a milksop like Harrison Randolph? What do you want, for God's sake? You ought to be a preacher. You know that? That's what you ought to be. Going around trying to get people to be better than they are."

"If I was a minister, mastah, I'd never waste my words on you. . . . Anyhow, like you say, I can't nevah be no minister, either. Law don't allow blacks to gather in any church—unless there is white people there."

"Another good law. Think of the trouble you could stir up—if you got a couple dozen blacks in a building listening to you."

"I could teach 'em right . . . even if I can't teach you nothing at all."

Locke laughed. "You're not supposed to teach me anything, boy. I'm the master, you're the slave. You'll do well to remember that—and stop trying to prod me into a fight. I'd hate to have to break your head." He grinned like a briar-eating donkey. "But you'd like to break my head, wouldn't you? Go on. Admit it."

"Why would I want to do that, mastah?"

"Hell, how do I know? Maybe because you think you could. Come on, Cato. There must be *one* kind word you can say for me. Say one. Just one."

"Why?"

"There must be one." Locke put his head back, laughing. "Think."

They traversed the six miles from the river crossing to downtown Alexandria in three hours—good travel time on the execrable ruts across what was still in those years the District of Columbia—an area which included the port village as well as the town of Washington.

Alexandria stirred with commerce, busy, compact, its eighteenth-century buildings erected hard on its walkways rising from the river, a bustling harbor which had mushroomed from a riverside warehouse and dock facilities built by Scottish merchants in 1731 and called Bellhaven by them. In 1749, the village was chartered and incorporated as Alexandria and its newspaper, the *Gazette*, was first published in 1784.

High-reaching spars and trimmed sails of seagoing ships, river crafts and fishing boats undulated at ease along its thick-logged piers. Farmers, fishermen, sailors, trappers and traders hurried along Fairfax Street in the sharp sunlight or limped upon the cobbles of Royal to Gadsby's Tavern at the corner of Cameron.

Locke headed single-mindedly toward Gadsby's Tavern too, hungry and thirsty. They rode past Christ's Church, shaded and walled, and Carlyle House, without glancing toward those celebrated landmarks, their gazes fixed inwardly upon bodily needs.

"Try to get along with the other body slaves this time," Locke told Cato. They looped their reins over leather-slicked tie rails at the cobblestoned curb. "Get something to eat and drink. And try to be one of the boys. You don't have to prove to them how brilliant you are, how righteous. Or sanctimonious."

Cato eyed him coldly. "You think I can't act like a dumb nigger when I have to, mastah?"

Laughter spewed out in humid waves around Locke. He entered the cave-dark barroom and for a moment halted, bat-blind after the eye-scorching sunlight.

Gradually, beings and fixtures took shape—men, women, roughhewn bar and thick-slab tables, sturdy oakwood chairs. The place swam blue with smoke, crowded and clamorous. As busy as the village was, this alehouse churned at the center of commerce.

Vision blurred, Locke hesitated just inside the doorway. He closed his eyes tightly for a long beat. When he opened them he could almost distinguish faces and forms floating dimly in tobacco fog and lamp-smoke.

Far across the room he recognized the round-shouldered person of his family solicitor. A pious, self-righteous, legal-minded fellow who provided the loudest basso profundo in the Episcopal choir, Worthington Jennings was nevertheless almost a kinsman, friend and executor of his father's estate. Locke smiled and called, "Squire! Jennings!"

The older man had risen abruptly from his chair and now loped, round-shouldered and in great haste past the bar and through a side exit, allowing a slash of sunlight to penetrate the darkness for a moment.

He did not look back.

Locke paused in the sea of crowded tables, frowning. There was every reason to believe Jennings hadn't heard his call, though everyone else in the hostel was aware he'd shouted. Still, the squire was an inward-turned man, committed to his own serious and weighty concerns, often abstracted,lost in self-counsel and, sometimes, rudely abrupt and discourteous. However, there was cause to give him every benefit of any doubt.

He was gone and the door slapped shut behind him.

The smile died on Locke's mouth. He was permitted no time to ponder whether Jennings had rebuffed him publicly—for no motive he could suspect—or had merely stalked out involved upon some recondite errand of his own.

A burst of wine struck Locke in the face, burning his eyes, trickling along his nose and narrowly missing his lips.

He jerked his head around, ready to strike out in anger. But his gaze struck first upon breasts so full, a bosom so hotly pink, shadowed cleavage so inviting in its depths that by the time he finally tilted his eyes to the barmaid's laughing face, his fury had abated entirely and he grinned, transforming his brooding features into a warm and wickedly handsome youthfulness.

"Welcome, handsome master," the barmaid said, her lovely face wreathed in smiles. Her manner reflected the sauciness of her frock, which showed only the toes of her shoes but just concealed the aureola of her breasts, and the dust cap tilted rakishly on red-gold curls. "Where you been all my life?"

She hefted the goatskin of wine to squirt the ruby fluid toward his mouth again but, laughing, Locke deflected her aim and she stained the shirts, coats and necks of a half-dozen unprotesting men around them.

The girl came close, insinuating her voluptuous body hard against Locke and tilting the nozzle of the hose toward his mouth. She was wondrous baggage, no more than seventeen, yet mature in breasts, hips, eyes and in the strumpet recklessness of her laughter. Though barely unfettered from childhood, her smile promised she could stoop as low as man's basest desires.

Men around them caught at the girl, but she only laughed and twisted free, intent, with blue eyes fixed hungrily on Locke's gray ones.

At the heat simmering in her gaze, the damp promise of murrey lips, Locke felt a searing twist taking a hitch deep in his loins and he was abruptly less than hungry for food, and the pious Jennings evaporated from his mind, totally forgot.

The barmaid pressed the nozzle against his lips and levered her arm upon the flagon. Wine splashed on his mouth, across his teeth, along his chin.

"Drink," she laughed. "You'll like me a lot better when you do."

Locke caught her about the waist and drew her upon the muscular hardness of his thighs, bringing her up on her toes.

"There's something I find devishly attractive about you already," he told her.

"I grow on you." She smiled impishly. "And I can feel *you* growing on me, young master."

At that moment a hand cut between them, almost as deliberately as a stroke of fate.

Locke scowled, resisting the interruption, and then he recognized young Harrison Randolph. He was little charmed by Harrison and resented his intrusion, but Harrison was, after all, sibling and spoiled darling of Mary-Stuart Randolph. One hesitated at rebuffing Harrison for fear of offending his doting sister. Locke sighed heavily and released his grip on the barmaid.

The girl sagged back, pouting, Harrison spoke to her disdainfully. "Go hawk your wares somewhere else, tramp."

The barmaid bristled, almost turned the wine-hose on the young dandy, but instead, flicked her head and turned away with one final, regretful glance toward Locke.

Young Randolph leaned rakishly upon his gold-headed cane, his flat-brimmed planter's hat pushed back on the thick rust of his curls. He was a tall, slender young aristocrat, with a spoiled, petulant face, twisted faintly with an air of hauteur. Like his sister, he was handsomely made; yet features which added up to beauty in Mary-Stuart rendered her brother only pretty. His tweed trousers and tailored jacket were the latest style arriving from London, and even his boots were British made.

Locke inclined his head in the briefest bow of civility, but Harrison misread any hint of displeasure; it never occurred to young Randolph that he could be less than enthusiastically and affectionately welcomed anywhere. He was little given to introspection; he was totally aware of the unassailable security of his position in society and he was less than sensitive toward the sensibilities of others. "I didn't see you, Harry," Locke said, adding under his breath that if he had he'd have turned and walked out.

"I was sitting with Squire Jennings," Harrison said. "I heard you call to him." His mouth twisted into a faint moue. "Even if he didn't."

Locke frowned. "Did he hear?"

Harrison shrugged. "I don't know. The squire always has a lot on his mind—a lot of devious matters."

"You sound less than cordial toward a respected friend of both our families."

Harrison's eyes darkened. "He's no friend of mine. I hate his guts. I'm no different from many who despise him, only I'm honest enough to admit it." He exhaled sharply. "Even when I go out of my way to be friendly, Jennings acts like a snapping turtle." Harrison swung his arm. "Come, let me buy you a posset."

Astonished that Harrison Randolph was actually offering to buy a drink for anyone, Locke smiled faintly and allowed himself to be piloted across the clangorous room. He sat across from young Randolph at the table Worthington Jennings had recently and hastily quitted.

Harrison's thoughts seemed for the moment turned inward to follow some convoluted skein, and then the youth shrugged coldly and said, "The pompous bastard."

Locke smiled. "Anyone I know?"

"Your good friend Worthington Jennings." Harrison made an expletive of the phrase. "He was probably hurrying off to dispossess another helpless widow or cheat orphans some where."

Locke's brow tilted. "I never heard you vent such spleen against the squire."

Young Randolph drummed his manicured fingers on the tabletop. "Maybe you never inquired as to my true feelings." He smiled sourly. "Even if you don't inquire now, I'm pleased to inform you. I don't trust Attorney Worthington Jennings. You'd be smart if you didn't."

Locke managed to smile and hide his shock. "You have good and sufficient cause for this dislike?"

"I have a dozen causes. And I said *hate*. Hate is not too strong a word for the emotion that pious hypocrite arouses in me. Why, I've heard that he goes about turning penniless people out of their homes—in these desperate times—people who have farmed the same acres for three generations. He coldly turns them out—and auctions off their pittances."

Locke shook his head. "Should you be attacking the squire's good name behind his back like this? I assure you, your accusations will go no further, but—"

"Let them!" Harrison bent forward on the thick-legged chair and took up his stein of ale as though it were a thrown gauntlet. "Let them . . . Let every word I say come back to crisp his ears—and let him come seeking redress. My God! I'd love to break my cane across his rotten back."

Locke laughed, despite himself, at the boy's malice. "Do you malign the poor man for no cause?"

"No cause? Do you find him so charming? So honorable? Do you regard him so favorably? Do you think he didn't hear you hail him from across this room?"

"I don't know. But I can't hate him just because he chooses for some private reason to show me the cold shoulder. Perhaps it's his own ill-humor. I find no personal rebuke in something which may issue from his own distemper."

Randolph braced himself on his elbow and gazed unyieldingly across the table. "Perhaps if you—discovered—evidence he'd cheated you—"

"Cheated me? Good lord, man. Jennings has been a saint toward me and my family. His largesse saw that my mother and sisters lived on at Hidden Brook in the manner they were accustomed, even though my father had squandered the last penny of the family fortune before he died. Squire Jennings didn't have to do that, and for it, I must be eternally grateful."

Harrison sneered and looked him over in good-humored contempt and condescension. "I warrant you that Worthington Jennings had *something* to gain from even that uncharacteristic display of decency."

"You are in a hellish mood."

"Jennings sank me into such a morass—and left me there! He's a dishonor to our class, to our society, to our community, profiting like a vulture on the deprivation striking the whole country, throwing proverty-injured families off ancestral property—"

"He's in business. It is his business to collect bad debts."

"How blind you are to be taken in like this by him! I warn you this: Worthington Jennings would turn you out of Hidden Brook as quickly as he would a stranger."

Locke grinned coldly. "Still. When he had his chance, he didn't. Instead, he permitted me time to recoup after my *own* father betrayed us. . . . He was better to me than my own father."

"Then count your silver when you get home. Do you know what I've just heard—?"

"Nothing good, I'll vow."

"—from people who have *evidence*. Proof. They swear that Jennings is now making a fortune buying up veteran claims to government lands and benefits—at a fraction of their value. And even from some of the poor bastards who fought in the Revolution."

"I'd have to see that proof, Harry."

"That proof exists. They say he's even forged papers of soldiers who were already dead—fallen during the last war with Britain."

Locke laughed. "Come. Let's talk about something else. You look sweated. It's none of my business but you look as if you've far exceeded your capacity for spirits."

"You're right. It's none of your business."

"My humble apology."

Harrison straightened, glanced around. "I can take care of myself."

"I'm sure you can." Locke gave him a half-taunting, yet soothing smile. "Tell me. What news of Mary-Stuart?"

Harrison shrugged. Obviously his mental faculties weighed more heavily with other matters. "She fares well. Looks forward to seeing you again, though I'm damned if I know why."

"You're not exactly my cup of ale, either."

Harrison finished off his drink, ordered another. Then he sat for long moments in the hazy maelstrom of sound, staring at a damp spot on the table as if it were the pool of knowledge for which he thirsted desperately.

At last he looked up, sweating, his brow knotted in his smooth-shaven face. "I want to borrow three hundred dollars," he said abruptly. "In fact, I'll go further. I desperately must have that amount—at once."

Locke stiffened slightly, then smiled tolerantly. It was suddenly and starkly clear why Harrison Randolph so openly and violently cursed Squire Jennings. Obviously, he'd asked the tight-fisted lawyer for the money and been rejected. Perhaps this even explained Worthington Jenning's abrupt departure from these premises. He'd been offended and repulsed by young Randolph's intemperate demands.

"You think old Jennings turned me down, don't you?" Harrison said.

Locke shrugged. "He's a hard man to borrow money from."

"Am I hearing more than you're saying aloud? Are you telling me you learned from him? Is Worthington Jennings your mentor? You find him so upright and honest, this man who was your father's friend and executor. Do you plan to emulate him?"

"In the matter of lending you three hundred while you're in your cups? Probably."

Harrison's petulantly pretty face twisted. For a tense moment he looked as if he might burst into impotent tears.

He leaned across the table, extending his hand in a beseeching gesture that Locke found somehow totally uncharacteristic and in a way disturbing, considering that Harrison Randolph was drunk, spoiled rotten by an indulgent family and accustomed to taking what he wanted.

"What's your problem?" Locke inquired in a soft, friendly tone.

Randolph sucked in a deep breath. He shook his head, unable for the moment to trust himself to speak, deeply moved to find even a concerned listener after a long day of failure. He began to hope again. Locke saw that rising expectation in the bloodshed eyes.

He expected Harrison to launch into an involved story of gambling or an illicit debt he was afraid to mention at home. Instead, after a long beat, the boy said, "Do you know Anne Stoker?"

Frowning, Locke glanced around, seeking the famous barmaid in the hazy, smoke-filled room. His gaze didn't find her. "You mean Anne Stoker the barmaid who single-handedly has made Gadsby's famous from Philadelphia to Richmond?"

Randolph winced. "That outward display is all pretense with her—it increases her gratuities to be falsely known as an artful little slut."

"Many have found her to *be* an artful little slut."

Resentment traveled like a quick cloud across Randolph's face. He spoke in a taut voice. "That is the talk. But I know better. I got to know her well . . . I fell in love with her, Jerry."

Locke was unable to restrain his laughter. "Love? Anne

Stoker? A baggage already married? Already faithless to a dozen better men than you?''

Randolph cried out as if badly and unfairly wounded. ''I won't listen to what you say of her—God help me, I can't. I've gotten her in trouble . . . pregnant.''

Locke managed to conceal his smile. ''Did she tell you that?''

''Relucantly. Yes. She's got to have three hundred at once. She knows a midwife in Washington. The woman does surgical abortions. Dangerous, but the only way out for Anne since her damnable husband has never been able to impregnate her in all the years they've been married. . . . This midwife is something of a hellion, it turns out. She knows Anne is married to a sterile, jealous and homicidally violent husband. . . . She's blackmailing Anne.''

Locke stared through wisps of smoke at Randolph, unable to credit that the youth—even at a callow nineteen—could not see that it was *he* who was being blackmailed.

Tears did well now in Harrison's pale eyes. ''Think of what a scandal would do to my family! To Mary-Stuart! And there will be a scandal unless Anne can keep the truth hidden from Stroker. He's a vile, brutish, low-class lout who cares nothing for who might be hurt. You've got to help me keep this dishonor, this scandal, from touching Mary-Stuart.''

''Do you think to buy Anne Stoker off with three hundred? Or is this just money to poke down a rat's nest—only a down-payment on your folly?''

''Hell, man! You sound like Worthinton Jennings—''

''God forbid—''

''I thought if anyone would understand, it would be you. What would *you* pay to keep the unholy truth about your own villiany from my sister? Would you want *her* to know of your piracy, the way you scuttled ships on the seas—and left innocent people to drown? Or smuggled slaves into New Orleans—though slave-traffic has been outlawed in England and here? Slaves forcefully stolen from illegal slave runners. Would you want Mary-Stuart to know that *your* money, which is to secure her place in polite society, is soaked and smeared and dripping—with the blood of murdered men?''

''My God. I had no idea you held me in such high regard,'' Locke said in a chilled and deadly irony.

"I *know* the truth! I never speak it. That doesn't mean I'm not aware. I know the truth about you. Where your money came from. I don't care. I'm a man of the world. But Mary-Stuart would care. . . . It well could turn her away from you forever."

"You'll get nowhere trying to blackmail me."

Abruptly, Harrison burst into tears. "My God, Jerry! Don't think me so low. . . . I was not threatening you! God forbid! May the holy Father strike me blind, I was merely stating why I thought that you—of all people—might understand *me*."

"I think I understand you well enough." Locke shrugged. "Maybe too well."

Locke walked in the dappling of late afternoon sunlight through the elms towering along the cobblestoned street which led down to the riverbank.

Houses crowded in close-order lines of the quiet avenue. At this hour of the afternoon all doors were closed and drapes drawn at inset windows. For this he was thankful. He found himself reacting, even unwillingly, in frustration and some self-directed aggravation, that he had undertaken this unwholesome chore for the arrogant, unprincipled, self-seeking, profligate young rounder. He felt a faint rising of choler that in marrying Mary-Stuart—and he could imagine no other future—he might well be consigning himself to a career of rescuing Harrison Randolph's charred chestnuts from continuous and unquenchable fires. In matters of the heart, young Randolph might well prove to be a self-destructive arsonist.

The sense of well-being with which he had begun this ride from Washington to Alexandria was totally dissipated. It seemed suddenly that he had come much further than six miles from the President's palace. In place of his expansive optimism, there was a disturbing stirring of dissatisfaction. A cold indignation lanced through him that Harrison Randolph would dare mouth threats, that Mary-Stuart's simpering, weak-kneed brother viewed him with such condescension and malice from behind that pretty, smiling face.

He paused outside the Stoker cottage. The three-room abode was one of the few homes set behind a small fence and courtesy throw-rug of a front yard. Most of the houses abutted on the walk, opening directly upon the street. Somehow, there seemed a sense of ironic rightness in Stoker's hut being enclosed behind a wall. This was where the man impotently hoped to imprison his lushly made wife, even while financial necessity, as well as her own restless inclinations, forced her to flaunt her not inconsiderable physical charms as the loveliest barmaid Gadsby's Tavern ever boasted.

Locke checked both ways along the silent street. For no good reason he found the texture of the silence somehow less than reassuring. Finding no one in either direction, he exhaled heavily—as if involuntarily he'd been holding his breath for ten minutes at least.

He went through the gate, his bonnet cocked low on his forehead to shade and conceal his face from Anne Stoker's neighbors. Undoubtedly, these long-abused good people were accustomed to male callers furtively entering this manse while Stoker labored at the piers or drank himself into a stupor over whist at the Old Club.

He found the door slightly ajar. Beyond it, the house sat unaccountably and mysteriously silent in the nascent dusk with the matron at home and her husband away at his work.

He lifted the heavy brass knocker and let it fall. The sound of the metal weight echoed and reverberated through the exaggerated silence. The buzzing of a bottle fly droned at the window, a hummingbird fluttered at the throat of vulnerable hibiscus.

He struck the brass plate again. The door swung silently and slowly open under his hand as though programmed to swing wide on oiled hinges to any male.

He hesitated a moment, glanced over his shoulder and then stepped inside the musty parlor, carrying his wide-brimmed hat in his hand.

He stopped as though struck without warning in the solar plexus. He stood wooden, unmoving, silence ebbing and flowing around him like thunder. His breath in his throat. He felt a sense of horror, a sense of agony. Eyes widened, anguished, he stared at Anne Stoker.

Anne lay sprawled across a hand-hooked rag rug which glittered in a widening red pattern of her own blood. Her eyes were opened, fixed, like a marble statue's eyes.

Stunned, he gazed down at her, Anne Stoker was as lovely

as she had been in life, voluptuous, full-bodied, shapely, red of hair, peach of flesh, but she was dead with all her loveliness. Someone had beaten her brutally and fatally and left her for Jeremiah Newman Locke to find.

— III —

HE FELT the blood run chilled in his veins. The horror and the pity waned and panic fluttered like wounded quail in his belly.

Run.

This was what he had to do now in the thickening dusk. He had to get out of here as fast as possible and pray that no one saw him enter this place or, if they'd seen him, that they would be unable to identify him. His mind spun and all he could think clearly was that he had to put as much distance as possible between himself and this poor dead creature. She was dead. It was all over for her, but no matter where she went in the afterlife, it looked as if hell on earth might be yawning just ahead for him. How could he explain his presence here? Who would believe him, no matter what he said, no matter how desperately he declared his innocence?

Get out. Now. If he still claimed a wisp of luck, it might be hours before poor Stoker returned and discovered his wife's battered body. He could not even spare compassion for the bereaved spouse. Into his mind flared a hundred glimpses of the future, all of them fearful.

If someone found him here, he lost Mary-Stuart through all eternity. There was no other chance—even if she forgave him, her parents and her peers would not. Whoever had killed this sad butterfly had slain as well Jerry Locke's hope for happiness with the only woman he would ever love.

And, kindly God, what of President Monroe? The little man had sent for him in desperation. What was he to think when he heard Locke had been charged with the murder of a tavern slattern?

He looked about, realizing for the first time into what jeopardy he had blithely thrust himself by agreeing to come to this hovel on a stupid errand for Harry Randolph. He'd placed his entire future on the line. And he had not even stopped to think.

Almost irrelevantly, a vivid memory of his visit with President Monroe flashed across his mind. "This is not a job for a thoughtful, contemplative, careful man. It calls for a reckless soul who'll act first and think later," the President had said. And they'd grinned at each other because each knew Monroe had found the right man for the job.

Well, he hadn't thought; look where it'd gotten him. In the street he heard a boy's voice singing lustily.

Ha, ha, ha, you and me,
Little brown jug, don't I love thee.

The carefree quality of that voice underlined the terror he'd blundered into, trapped in a hut with a murdered woman, in that quiet neighborhood. The blood seeped downward in his body. The backs of his legs felt weak and watery.

He sagged back against the door-facing, seeking support in a world gone insane. His shoulder blades touched the textured wood, but he felt no solidity, no sense of reality even when he heard the thick bolt snick into place. He could not pull his gaze from the dead woman's battered body.

He tried to ignore the persistent shattering of panic churning in his belly and numbing his brain. All that he had thought consumed less than ten seconds; the shards and fragments that charged through his mind were too random to be named thoughts. He was unable to think and that was what he had to do if he were to escape this place with the minutest hope of remaining free and unsuspected.

He looked about the room, seeing the rough, hand-tooled furnishings, the letter cloth mottoes, the artifacts of ordinary existence, without really registering any of it in his mind. He felt like a mouse in a maze looking for a way out of a walled treadmill.

Only a noise at the front gate galvanized him into action.

The agony and shock of finding this woman dead had immobilized him, but the presence of real danger shook him free of the trance.

He straightened, listening.

The sounds of boots were loud on the fieldstone walk. There was not one man out there, but two.

He strode across the small living room into the smaller, rough-walled kitchen. He heard the men rattling the lock at the front door. Thank God, he'd fallen against it and locked it, delaying them. He heard a man's rough voice cursing, yelling for Anne and at the same time shaking out his keys.

Locke ducked his head and went out the kitchen door, closing it softly and cautiously behind him.

In the walled-in back yard, he looked around—a stone-walled well, a lean-to barn with two milch cows, a few chickens, an elm tree, and that wall. He had stepped into a cul-de-sac.

He gazed at the rude fieldstone wall which Stoker must have constructed of mortar. It reared almost seven feet high. He could leap up, grasp the ledge and lever himself upward, but he had the sickening premonition of being caught, trying to clamber like a fleeing rat over that barrier.

He ran to the far side of the lean-to. The cows stirred, troubled by his presence. Great, let these animals betray him to the two men in that house.

He heard one of the men growl out in animal ulutation of anguish and horror. Hackles prickled along the nape of his neck and he widened his stride.

Grasping the sideboards he climbed up the lean-to. As he turned, braced against its eaves to grasp the rough stones of the wall top, he felt as if someone had clutched him from behind.

His heart lurched. He sighed out, cursing under his breath. A huge peg had snagged his jacket. When he jerked free of the nail he heard the fabric of his coat rip. Wonderful. Who would forget a man leaping from this accursed wall to the street beyond and running away, jacket ripped?

Sweating, breathing through his parted mouth, he pulled himself up on the foot-wide, rock-sharp ledge. He hung there a moment, checking the silent street below, then he swung around, let himself over the side and dropped to the ground.

He landed heavily, fighting to keep his balance. He didn't need to be seen sprawled in the dirt.

"Would you like me to help you up—mastah?"

Gasping, Locke jerked his head up, staring into Cato's cold black eyes.

Locked pushed himself upright and leaned for a moment against the rough wall. "What are you doing here?"

Cato shrugged. "I saw you leave the tavern."

"Did you hear me call you? Did I invite you along? Did I say I needed you here?"

Cato's voice chilled. "I followed. I saw you go into that house."

"How interesting."

"I stood outside. I saw those two men arrive, saw them go inside."

"Then what are you doing out here?"

"I heard those men yell murder. As soon as I heard that, I no longer believed you'd come out the front door."

"Your deduction is brilliant."

"I've been enslaved to you for a long time—mastah. Did you kill her?"

"Who?"

"The woman in that house. Did you kill her?"

"How do you know it was a woman who was killed?"

"Her man howled in savage loss. I've heard that heartbroken cry before. Maybe I've yelled it a time or two myself. Besides, I knew when you went in that house that there was a woman there."

"I don't have to justify myself to you."

"If there is a God you may have to justify yourself to Him—to the law. You did kill her then?"

Locke turned and strode uphill on the cobbled street. "What do you think?"

"It don't matter what I think. It does matter what the law will think."

"What makes you believe that the law will think anything—about me?"

Cato exhaled heavily. "You entered the house in broad daylight. You came running out of it like a thief—like a murderer. You believe I am the only one who saw you enter—or saw your extraordinary manner of departure?"

"If I am lucky maybe you're the only one who knows beyond reasonable doubt that I called upon the late Madame Stoker."

"If I know, that's one too many."

Locke glanced at him and laughed coldly. "A slave can't testify against a white man. That's the law."

Cato gazed at him, anguished. "Thank God they can't force me to testify for you, either."

They walked swiftly but when they came out on Royal Street, Locke forced their pace to slow. The avenue was less crowded as the supper hour approached. A late afternoon sun probed feebly among wan-lit crannies between faded old buildings.

As custom dictated, Cato fell silent and walked one pace at his master's rear, shuffling along in his wake.

Locke forced himself to walk without haste, head up, his gaze meeting or brushing briefly against those he passed. He walked with as much dignity as he could muster with a tattered shred dangling from his dirt-streaked jacket, its lining exposed.

Yelling, laughter and a clatter of mugs spewed out of Gadsby's Tavern as they rounded Cameron Street. Cato hesitated but Locke went directly to where their horses were tethered at the hitching rail.

"I think we won't stay over tonight," Locke said. "We'll ride on south. Our horses know the trail to Hidden Brook, even in the blackest night."

"It's dangerous traveling these roads at night."

"I've made up my mind."

"The animals are fatigued. They need water, a rubdown, hay and grain. They need a night's rest."

"You dare to tell me how to tend my own horses?"

"You are running away. You did kill her."

Locke's head jerked up. He stared at Cato for a taut breath, then shrugged. "Get on your horse. Let's go."

The batwing doors were thrust open at the tavern entrance and Harrison Randolph erupted through them. He strode, listing across the stoop and half fell, catching his balance against the hitching post. The horses flinched, jerking their reins, disturbed.

"You. Jerry Locke. Where are you going?"

"We're riding on home, Harry."

"Tonight? At this hour? Why? What about—my errand? What did she say? What did you do?"

"We can't talk about it now, Harry."

"We've got to talk about it now. Damn it, I've been half out of my mind, waiting for you."

"I've nothing to tell you, Harry."

Sweating, his clothing disheveled, unable to balance himself upon his gold-headed cane, Harrison gazed at Locke, wild-eyed. "You mean to run off and leave me in the lurch like this?"

Before Locke could answer, four grown men and three teenaged boys ran shouting like banshees around the corner. What they were yelling about was instantly clear.

"Where's the high sheriff?"

"Is the sheriff in there?"

Men spilled out of the doorway of the tavern upon the stoop. They caught at the gang of shouting males, trying to put sense into their babbling. "What's wrong, man? Stop yelling and tell us what's the matter?"

"It's Effrim Stoker's woman."

"Anne Stoker's been killed."

"Brutal beat to death."

"Oh, dear Jesus. Dear Jesus God," Harrison whispered. His face contorted and his chest shook violently. His knees gave way and he sagged for support upon the hitching rail, clinging to it. He sobbed, hanging over the rough railing as if he might vomit. But he did not, he sobbed brokenly.

Feeling Cato's relentless gaze fixed on him, Locke stared at Harrison without speaking.

After a moment, Harrison shook himself and straightened. He looked around emptily, as if lost, disoriented. "I must go to her," he said.

Locke caught his arm. He shook his head. "I don't think you should, Harry."

Harrison jerked his arm away, straightening, yet wavering in the land breeze like a reed. "Let me alone. I've got to go to her. My God, I've got to go to her."

"She belongs to her husband now, Harry. There's nothing you can do."

Harrison's face twisted in agony, his eyes welled with

tears. He shook his head violently and then heeled around and went reeling, half running down the street.

Locke took a step after him, but Cato's cold voice stopped him like a snubbing rope. "Let him go," Cato said.

Locke sighed and shivered slightly. "Yes. I might as well. I've done everything for him I can."

"Yes, and everything to him, too."

Locke shrugged and nodded. "That, too, I reckon."

Locke sat alone in the high-ceilinged living room of the manor house of Hidden Brook, at loose ends, lost, as if somehow caught and helpless between the world he'd always known and an existence he could not comprehend but into which he found himself hurtled helplessly.

He gazed around the graceful old house, finding none of that old sense of security and belonging he always drew from its aged and deep-felt strength of stone and mortar and loving and affection that gave it singularity.

A shadow passed across his eyes. This old house was the solid rock, the core, the center, the heart, the wellspring of his existence. From it, four generations of Locke men and women had sprung, putting back into it all their devotion and energies and essence. One almost felt their loving presence around him; they were only slightly less real than his mother and his sisters, singing and laughing in the shadowed depths of this warm manse. How he loved it! How he had dreamed upon it from Amelia Island, from the savagery of Atlantic storms, the peril of privateer attacks. He had known he would someday return to Hidden Brook and this had given him strength and hope no matter how badly his fortunes fared.

He smiled, knowing this place was different, not the kind of ordinary structure one came across every day—a stately early Colonial chateau of distempered brick, feathered with scallops and shards of light and shadow through the splendidly tall oriel windows that rose almost from base to apex of each columned flank. The front doorway was deeply inset and was overhung by an extended balcony, the whole surmounted by a pillared arch of timeless grace, which, each spring, was cloyed with matted tendrils of rain-blue creepers older than any doddering elder alive and yet fresher and brighter than the faces of laughing children. Above the black cypress shakes of the roofing, thin stone chimneys reared in reticent utility.

But the most inexpressible, unforgettable beauty of Hidden Brook lay in its antique formal gardens, tended by the unwilling sweat of slaves. To the labors of these serfs an indulgent and ungrudging nature garlanded flowered esplanades; decorated rich balustrades bordering fieldstone terraces with their fieldstone walls and steps; deepened the hues around stone fountains and granite fawns, nymphs and satyrs cavorting in frozen silence against the misty blue of velvet lawns; wreathed topiary hedges, and garnished bright espaliers and scattered tall elms to shield and shade that wide-flung messuage.

He got up from the deep old leather chair and prowled the room, scowling, his face a taut mask. Since his hasty return here from Alexandria, this beloved old homestead had offered him less than the haven and safe harbor it had always promised in the past. He scarcely slept. He ate only lightly and without appetite, and simply to quiet the concern he read in the lovely faces of his sisters and the tired depths of his mother's eyes. He hated himself as much for the hell he may well have brought thundering down on them as for his own reckless misjudgment in involving himself in the wine-sotted affairs of Harrison Randolph.

Cato hovered over him, as watchful and cold as a forbidding cyclopic conscience. When he could stand his body slave's presence no longer, he sent him on a bootless errand just to be rid of him.

Cato's departure served merely to deepen the silence in the room. He was unable to get Anne Stoker and Harrison Randolph off his mind. Mary-Stuart's dissolute brother had all the inner fortitude of a violet. Not only would he crumple under the first hint of pressures, but there was no accounting for the strange machinations of his mind. There was no way to know what the grief-stunned boy would do—one could only try to shore up defenses against the holocaust.

He strode to the window and stood braced, legs apart, staring across the gleaming blue yard. He saw nothing outside his own mind. There was little doubt that Harry Randolph would bring the stench of scandal like redolent carpetbags from Alexandria; there was small hope that he—and Hidden Brook—would be spared the odor of that affair.

Perhaps if he went away for a while, the clamor in the countryside would settle, and Harry Randolph would forget his heartbreak over his loss of Anne Stoker—whether that loss was real or not.

He winced, feeling a sense of loneliness and despair sweep over him at the idea of leaving Brook again. That two years away had been hell. He had lived in agony that, while he was gone, he might lose Mary-Stuart. If he went now, he did not deceive himself. Mary-Stuart would not be waiting for him when he returned; he would lose her forever.

He shook his head. He did not lie to himself—Mary-Stuart was the brilliant lamp-flame round which all the swains spun like incensed moths. Probably every Virginian under thirty—and all of them over forty—found Mary-Stuart Randolph haunting their nocturnal fantasies. This had been true since that moment five or six years ago when Mary-Stuart erupted from childhood into a heart-clutching beauty—a golden, fresh-faced little beauty with slender, willowy, supple, full-breasted body and laughing eyes. She wafted radiant across bright ballrooms to the quickening tempo of young male heartbeats rattling like snare drums in adoring young chests. Like some volatile vision on winged slippers she ran, laughing, into and out of new hearts every week, collecting them like oversubscribed dance cards among her souvenirs.

No. She would not wait forever and he could not ask her to. He could not walk away and forfeit all his dreams of her, either.

His fists clenched at his sides. What could he gain if he stayed? With Harry half out of his mind with grief, and set against him for real or imagined wrong, what hope for him? Her family had become increasingly less cordial to him because of rumors about his illicit activities in the two years he spent away from Hidden Brook. If he stayed and tried to fight lies and false charges, might he not lose everything?

His head tilted. The thought that he might be pressured into running put steel in his spine. He had never run away from trouble if there was reason to stand and oppose it. He would not run now. He would face the troubles that rose out of Anne Stoker's death. He would stand and face it.

Face it? Even if it proved to be a murder charge rising out of some unknown witness identifying him as the man last seen entering and leaving Anne Stoker's cottage? And what answers would he have for Mary-Stuart against Harry's brokenhearted raving? Harry was hurt and, like a wounded animal, he would likely strike out in all directions. He was not a man to suffer in silence or to bear his agony alone.

A short trip away might be the answer. For the first time since he'd blundered into Effrim Stoker's house, he put Harry Randolph and the dead girl from his mind. Without apology, explanations, self-serving justifications or varnish he could go to Spanish Florida on President Monroe's secret mission—an assignment, he suddenly realized, he had never intended until this moment to accept . . .

Glad to escape the fruitless treadmill of unanswerable fretting, he went back over in his mind his interview with the President. He admitted now that he was less than convinced of the mission's necessity, of the credibility of Monroe's suspicions against General Jackson. It went against everything he was inside, to believe the great man was a potential betrayer.

Maybe Monroe was less than a perfect judge of men and their motives. Monroe was wrong about Jerry Locke's own father, considering that defaulter and debaucher a gentleman and true friend. Monroe might well be misguided in many of his other opinions. When one got to be President maybe he found an ogre in every dissenting idea.

Jerry shook his head. He admired Jackson from the stories he'd heard about him. No one pretended Jackson was less than controversial, a violent-tempered and opinionated man. But Monroe himself had offered Jackson a place in his presidential cabinet. Had the chasm opened between these two men when Jackson coldly refused the offer?

Still, he admired and revered James Monroe, and had since boyhood. He hated letting the President down when the harried man made no secret of the fact that he depended desperately upon him. Still, to go dashing off on a wild-goose chase . . .

He reached no decision. His thoughts were shattered by the sounds of shouting at the front door, the troubled voice of the black butler and the slurred demands of an arrogant caller.

Locke heeled around and strode across the room.

He met Harrison Randolph stalking across the foyer, the wide-eyed butler quavering in his wake.

"So!" Harrison shouted, his voice echoing and reverberating in the dim cavernous upper hallways. "So, this is where you've run to, is it?"

"I live here," Locke reminded him mildly.

Harrison growled, trembling between savage rage and helpless tears. He appeared to have been drinking heavily in every ordinary between here and Alexandria. His anguished eyes were unnaturally bright, ribbed with broken red veins of sleeplessness and gilded with a kind of madness. His natural arrogance and violence, carefully leashed beneath a genteel exterior, were loosed like beasts by the liquor that washed him south, so his true nature lay baldly exposed.

"I've been hunting you down," Harrison raged so the portraits trembled on the walls, "in every tavern between here and the scene of your latest, most heinous crime."

"Come in." From the corner of his eye, Locke saw that Cato had returned from his errand and stood, watching coldly. He felt the urge to laughter but it was the mindless kind that would do none of them credit. He forced himself to lower his voice to a compassionate pitch. "Let me close the door. You're disturbing the house."

The youth shook Locke's hand roughly from his arm, but with a coldness that iced his gaze and set his lips in a gray line, Locke gripped that limb again, and propelled Harrison into the parlor. He closed the thick oak door and locked it.

Harrison watched him with bemused, condescending contempt.

"No sense trying to keep me silent any longer," Harrison said. "Every man-jack in Prince William County knows I've been looking for you—and most of them know why."

Locke winced, but bit back the rage gorging up through him. His voice remained cold, but gentle. "I'm sorry about that."

"Well you may be sorry, sir . . . I've come looking for the truth. And I'll have the truth and nothing less."

Locke's head jerked upward, his eyes flashed with steel glints. With a fearful exercise of will, he controlled his flaming anger. "You've pushed me pretty far once already, Harry. Because of love for your sister, I let you charge me with crimes I'd never have tolerated for a moment from another man. For God's sake, be warned, boy."

Harrison was too brimmed with whiskey, grief and hatred to consider the wisdom of temperance. He reacted, shouting, his voice hoarse. "I spoke then only of piracy. Of theft. Of killing strangers on the high seas. Crimes of yours well-known about you. I'm talking about *murder* now—murder of my own heart—"

"You do me great harm, Harry, with your unhinged tongue. But you do yourself no service in sinking in despair over the death of a slattern—"

Harrison hefted his cane and would have struck out with it except that the force of lifting it unsettled him. He almost fell, retreating a helpless step or two, and had to fight to keep his balance.

Locke stared at Mary-Stuart's brother, hard-torn between hatred and pity. He kept his voice tranquil, through rages quivered far beneath it.

"Go home, boy," Locke said, "before you say too much. Before you push me too far. My own temper's got a hair-trigger, and you know that. No sense trying to talk to you in your condition—it's a fool's business trying to reason with a drunk."

"Drunk? Are you such a miserable judge of men, then? Damn you, I'm sick with grief. With loss."

"You may be grieved, boy, and you may feel a loss. But the truth is, you're lucky. Without gumption enough to realize it. Go on home now. Get Anne Stoker out of your mind."

"I can do that—I can rest, sir, only when I've avenged her murder."

"What in hell are you talking about?"

"I'm talking about *you*, sir. You. You talk so blandly of Anne Stoker as a cheap slattern who knew carnally a dozen men. Well, you lie. I knew her better. I knew her purity. I knew the life she was forced into by that boor of a husband. I also have another wisdom suddenly. About you. Perhaps you were not trying to reassure me when you called Anne slut and whore. Perhaps you were consumed with jealousy!"

"Jealous? God in heaven. Of what? Of whom?" Locke gazed around helplessly, feeling as if he were mired in nightmare.

"Of me. Of my sweet and hallowed love for Anne Stoker. You had to make a mockery of it—because the truth is that you yourself sniffed around her door like a sneaking cur with the scent."

Locke's indignation was spiced with a savage desire to laugh at the mindlessness of young Randolph's charges.

Harrison's voice rose in righteous wrath. "Back in Alexandria, they are looking for Anne's killer, one 'John Doe, unknown assailant.' But I followed a bloody trail—to your door."

Locke peered at Harrison impotently. Except that the young idiot was Mary-Stuart's brother, handling him would be a simple matter of breaking his wrists and stuffing them in his mouth. Instead of taking violent reprisal, Locke said coldly, "You're out of your pickled brain."

"Am I? There are those witnesses already rounded up by the sheriff who describe a man much like you—in hat and jacket and boots like yours—of your measurements—going into Anne Stoker's house late yesterday afternoon."

"You know I went there. On *your* stupid errand."

"I *thought* you went on *my* errand. But—was it? Did you go there—incensed with jealousy because I had innocently exposed my heart to you and revealed to you my rivalry—for Anne Stoker's affections?"

Locke prowled like a caged animal. "This is too idiotic to answer."

"Is it? You were ashen when I found you outside Gadsby's Tavern, your jacket torn and dirty, sweated in your haste to get out of town."

Locke exhaled heavily. "I found myself involved in an idiot's charade. I wanted out. That is all."

"Is it? I asked you then, and I ask you now, what happened at Anne Stoker's cottage? What happened between you?"

"Nothing."

"You lie—"

Locke stared down at his clenched fists. "Don't call me a liar, boy, for God's sake. For your own sake—"

"Do you think you could hurt me now? Do you think any physical pain on God's earth could hurt me now? I repeat. I don't believe you. Something happened between you and

Anne. You quarreled. Fought. She opposed your loutish advances. You killed her. Brutally." Harrison sobbed, putting his head back as if to relieve the intolerable ache in his throat.

Locke strode to the windows. Returned. "And so now you come here in your mindless stupidity—always blaming someone else for your misfortunes. First Squire Jennings when he refused you money. And now me. You call me liar. Call me killer. Hell's eyes, you are bold—or too drunk to practice reason—I'll say that. Yesterday, you called me slave stealer, pirate, kidnapper. But now—aside with the petty stuff. Now it's killer. Don't you think you've said enough?"

Harrison shook his head stubbornly, his mouth quivering. "I loved her, damn you. She was more than just a toy to me."

"All right! I try to allow for the misguided grief of a callow boy. You made a fool of yourself over Anne Stoker. You almost got drowned in a sour mess of your own making. You were lucky. I went to Anne's shack in your stead. Thank your gods. Those men would have found you sobbing over her body and you'd be hanging soon. Thank God you're safely out of it. Go home. Sober up and think of her no more."

Harrison's face contorted, his agonized mouth pulled nervously. "You make it sound so easy."

"No. Not easy. But sensible. Go on home. Get Anne Stoker out of your mind." His voice was harsh but the arm he flung about his love's brother's shoulders and the genuine warmth of his rough hug was intended to ease the boy's passionate resentment and cool his groundless suspicions.

But it was not to be. Sobbing, the boy broke free of his brotherly embrace. "You won't see the truth, will you?"

"What truth is that, Harry?"

"How deeply I loved her. How I now pledge and consecrate my life to avenging her death. I shall find her killer. And if he resides in this house—or in some evil hut—he *will* answer to me."

Locke spoke with a patience he did not feel. "She was a doxy, boy. Her thighs swung open to men as swinging doors—for money. Face it. I'm sorry she's dead. There was much good in her. An open honesty. And a kind of laughter. But that doesn't alter what she was. She was a wanton—not worth wrecking your life—or of those you love—over."

Harrison tried to speak. He choked, a sob shook him. "I loved her. I know she loved me. I would have married her. I would have, before God."

"I am sorry."

"Sorry. But you would have me toss her out of my mind like trash—of no more consequence than an empty ale mug."

"Remember her then! But don't wreck yourself over her."

"Myself? Wreck myself? Am I your concern? Are you worried about me? Or do you quake at what will happen when Mary-Stuart finally learns *all* the truth about you. *As she will.* Before God, she shall hear every ugly scrap of it—and from my lips."

"Don't do this senseless thing, boy, in God's name."

Harrison laughed brokenly through his tears. "I have this one final thing to lay before you, *friend*. One thing. There was robbery—as well as murder—when Anne Stoker was brutally slain. No one knows this truth but me. I gave her a diamond ring. Of two carats. Of such white purity and perfection in its brilliant facets that not even the yellow of its setting stains it. She wore the ring secretly on a cheap, stout cord, concealed in the—the soft darkness between her breasts and over her heart." He shook his head violently as if to deny the tears streaking his flushed cheeks. "Her killer was greedy enough to rip that cord—and ring—from about her neck. He has it now. But I know that diamond." He looked about wildly, in mindless searching. "When I find that ring, I'll find her killer."

Locke spread his hands. "God knows, I pity you."

"Don't pity *me*. I have discovered in Anne's death a reason to go on living. I'll devote my life to finding her slayer. And it'll do you no good to piously declare how *sorry* you are. You'll be sorrier yet if you are guilty—because I'll bring you to earth with no more mercy than you showed Anne."

Locke swung his arm, voice crackling. "If I'm guilty—then do what you must. Meantime, keep your mouth shut, lest you say more than I can forgive—even for the sake of Mary-Stuart."

Harrison stared at him in pity and contempt. "Oh, you still think to pick up and go on with my sister just as always? Well, I can tell you better. That romance is over. I warn you away from her. You and your bloody hands. Stay away from Mary-Stuart—or I will kill you."

Harrison trembled visibly and ran his shaking hands through his disheveled hair. He looked about in empty grief, abandoned in his agony like some leper howling in his lair. "And to warrant that my sister is free of you, I go now to her—to tell her the whole vicious truth about you and your crimes. I shall spare you nothing—as you have spared me nothing."

When he was gone, Locke found himself restless, sweated and unable to sit still. The frustration, the indignation flared into the beginnings of rage. He raged against stupidity—Harrison Randolph's stupidity which, if allowed unchecked, could wreck them all. He raged against an apparently civilized young man so stewed in wine and debauchery and vengeance that he lost sight of reason. He raged against that indulged, self-indulgent and irresponsible young rooster who could destroy his own sister and cost Jerry Locke a price so dear he could not endure to contemplate it, much less pay it.

He wanted to run after Harrison, to beat some sense into his addled brain. But he knew better. He had to stay away from Harrison. So unsettling were his fears of his own unleashed temper after all he'd already taken from Harrison and all the boy threatened, that he saw a quick journey, however brief, away from Hidden Brook as his only hope. Where he'd go he did not even stop to consider. The urgent matter was to remove himself from the county, set a distance between himself and Harrison Randolph until one of them, or the hellish conflict between them, had time to cool. He dreaded even temporary exile from Mary-Stuart. But if a brief separation might save them in the long run, it was far preferable to some overt action against her brother which could sentence them to an eternity apart.

He yelled for Cato. When the body servant appeared, standing cold and straight, gaze unyielding, he said, "I know you stood outside the door. I know you heard everything."

"I could have heard everything if I'd been across Bull Run."

"To hell with you. I want you to ride to Elms Head. Tell Squire Jennings I desire urgently to speak with him—at his earliest convenience."

Cato's mouth twisted. "Another trumped-up errand to get me out of your sight—mastah?"

Locke laughed savagely. "I wouldn't object to having you underfoot. But I hate having you always staring over my shoulder—along your pious nose. Go. Tell the squire to come in all haste if he will."

Alone, he prowled, prey to his growing furies that would not be calmed, or moderated, or denied . . .

— *IV* —

SHE LEFT her own dinner-dance party early, retiring up the wide staircase to her bedroom on the second floor. She excused herself to her guests with a wan smile, claiming a sudden headache. That she suffered migraine was no fabrication; her head throbbed. That the indisposition was of sudden onslaught was the deception. She'd felt the first sharp pangs, like lances behind her eyes, early in the evening, precisely at that moment, in fact, when her mother regretfully announced they could wait no longer for the arrival of Harrison or for Mr. Locke. The dinner would be spoilt. They would go in and dine. Perhaps the boys had been unavoidably detained and would join them as quickly as possible.

"Hope you're soon recovered and your own sweet and lovely self again, Miss Mary-Stuart."

"The world ends when you walk out that door, Mary-Stuart. I swear it."

"I'm so sorry Jerry Locke didn't come to your party."

"They do say Mr. Locke has no more manners than—a pirate."

"I'm sure there's some good and logical excuse why neither your dear brother nor Mr. Locke could get here from Alexandria."

"Except for the sadness in your eyes, Mary-Stuart, it was a lovely party. The happiest memory of my life."

"I didn't miss Jerry Locke for one moment—even though I know you did."

"Good night, Mary-Stuart. Good night. Good night."

In her bedroom, a frilly suite fit for a princess, of pinks and tulle and pastels and tiny pillows and a fragrance neither wholly musk nor cologne, but a bewitching olio of attar, colognes and a sweet essence indefinable, yet real, Mary-Stuart stood listlessly while the serving girls undressed her and prepared her for bed. They slipped a diaphanous peach-colored gown over her head and then tied her rusty-blonde curls in pigtails on each side of her face. The oldest black woman insisted that Mary-Stuart press a scented cachet of ammonia under her nostrils.

Dutifully, Mary-Stuart held the small packet to her face until the lamps were blown out and the servants departed, then she threw the little pad across the room and pressed her face into her goosedown pillow.

"Jerry," she whispered. "Jerry."

There was no sound in the jasmine-scented night except the violins and piano from the sun-room below.

Mary-Stuart lay awake listening to the remembered string ensemble which had played for her dancing among the masses of tall candles and the clusters of flowers that had beguiled an ordinary parlor into a mythic casino of dazzling delights; all the young men who had cut in on her, commonplace young gentlemen from neighboring estates, transformed for the evening into handsome young rakes who crowded around her, swirling in her wake as she drifted, on quivering arms, through what could have been an enraptured evening. Without Jerry, it had been nothing, less than nothing. And whenever Harrison was delayed even a few hours, her mother had learned from bitter experience to ancitipcate the worst. It all could have been so lovely . . .

She rolled restlessly on her bed, disturbed by a deep and unreasoning panic, a terrible premonition of wrong.

She tried to pin down this nagging omen that roiled without shape or substance but which was painfully real nevertheless. She could not do it. The agony danced and fluttered before her eyes in the misty dark like a butterfly or a moth that would not settle and would not go away, either. What was wrong? She had every reason to be happy, didn't she?

She chewed at her full underlip. It would be hard to find much sympathy among her friends. They all saw her as the carefree belle of the countryside, famous from Washington to Richmond for her gentle and fragile beauty. One saw her in every tidewater ballroom from that moment when she'd suddenly erupted into a breathtaking full bloom of loveliness, into vivacity from a little girl's well-learned reserve. No dance or barbecue or reception was quite complete without her enchanting presence, because she provided that gossamer flare accounting for any vivid brilliance of an evening.

She felt the hot burn of tears. The truth was so different. She was not a girl who lived only to run from party to *soirée* to tea to banquet. She *needed* to be married. But not just *any* marriage would do. She'd seen girls who married the first man who asked them in the desperate fear that if they didn't take the first offer there might not be another. She could not imagine living in such durance. She could not spend her existence pretending to love some man simply because he'd rescued her from spinsterhood or some other fate worse than death. She wanted only one man; this had always been true, it had not changed.

"Oh, Jerry," she whispered aloud. She tried to conjour his face before her tear-blurred eyes. She could not. Would he keep her waiting forever? She wanted no other man, and yet she could not go on in this empty limbo, this nowhere of uncertainty. At nearly eighteen, she was almost an old maid. People would begin to smile behind their hands soon, watching her with odd leers, seeing her stay too long at parties among fresh new faces—among children. *Oh, Jerry . . .*

She could not stay in bed any longer. She got up and padded across the starlit room to the small balcony. She flung herself, into a wicker wing-back chair and huddled there, staring across the black Virginia forest toward Hidden Brook. Where was he? He'd promised to come, in a way understood if not explicit; he was to have been the guest of honor at her party tonight—the certain demonstration to peers and enemies and other neighbors that Jeremiah Newman Locke had the full approval, warmest esteem and highest regard of her loving parents. Only he had not bothered to show up to receive those honors.

Mary-Stuart sat in the darkness unmoving, her arms wrapped across her breasts. Errant night breezes tugged and riffled at the soft puffs of her sleeves and bodice. She watched small clouds drift like lacy mists across the face of the sable moon. From the sun-room below, sounds of waning laughter competed with the piano and violins and sudden fragments of shattered conversation.

There were so many reasons above and beyond courtesy and love for her why Jerry should have attended her dinner-dance in his honor tonight. Her family—as well as her father's adviser, Squire Jennings—voiced doubts about the suitability of her marriage to Jerry Locke because of his dark, hidden past.

She exhaled heavily. Recently, everyone had conspired to help convince her family and legal administrator that she should not be permitted to marry the only man she loved, or ever would love. Rural gossip spread ugly stories about the way in which Jerry Locke had recouped the family fortune and saved Hidden Brook from the auction block. Mary-Stuart told her family in all honesty that she did not care what Jerry had done—she didn't want to hear any sordid details—because she forgave him anything. Whatever crime he had committed—if indeed he had!—he had done to secure the happiness and financial safety of his mother and sisters. And, too, in a way, he had done it for her.

Harrison, her ailing father and her prideful mother could pretend otherwise, but Mary-Stuart faced the unpleasant truth that the Randolphs and Felicity Manor were in dire financial troubles. Their problems were complex—they were caused as much by her brother's gambling losses as anything else. Honor demanded that a gentleman pay his debts, even if he lost home and farm and family in the process. Harrison became violent when she or her mother or even Squire Jennings tried to make him see that he was bleeding the farm white, destroying everything her parents and their parents had accumulated over generations. But it was not only Harrison's gambling. Her father, stricken by two small "strokes" that left him slurred of speech, slow of movement and often vague, was in his own way a gambler. Squire Jennings, though solemnly advising against the investments, was obligated to make them. Most of them had been poorly chosen; none had profited. She did not have to tell them that once she was married to Jerry Locke, her own family would find itself once again "secure."

She winced. How bitter and ironic that she who loved Jerry with every fiber of her body should for one moment consider her marriage to him in the light of its financial advantages. Her faced burned.

She felt somehow cheap and dishonest that she had to consider Jerry's financial worth in marrying him. She didn't care that he had two pennies, or not even one. She would love him if he were a pauper. She would follow him to the ends of the earth in his penury if necessary. She didn't care that he was the richest man in northern Virginia. It just made it easier, that was all.

How much easier! Her parents were able to close their ears to gossip, to repulse all proffered calumny against Jerry Locke, to take him to their bosom. There might be hypocrisy in their acceptance of him, but she believed it genuine. Even Squire Jennings, sitting alone with her in the sun-room and holding her hand tightly in his boney fingers, called Jerry Locke a reckless mercenary, dishonest, unmanageable and, in the next breath, one whose word was solid gold in worth.

She felt the restlessness spreading, stinging through her body like the attacking of army ants. She could not sit still. There was not enough breath in this thick night. The very darkness seemed pressing in upon her. The music from the terminating party rose to mock her. She could not go on living unless she went at once to Jerry, unless she told him that she loved him, without money, without reputation—without reserve.

Exhaling, as if suddenly released from polite but unyielding restraints, she jumped up and ran across the room in the darkness.

Holding her breath, as if the act of respiration might betray her, she slipped the gown over her head. Fingers trembling, she loosened the pigtails and shook out her hair about her face. She did not stop to brush it. Clad only in a robe, she went stealthily along the upper hall. She heard departing guests laughing, making last minute plans, calling out, content with their stupid and empty lives.

Her father's bedroom door was ajar. Within, a saffron glow of lamplight showed him like some heavy statue on his bed, the coverlets barely disturbed. Beside the bed, sleepless and unblinking, his black body servant, matted hair cottony white, sat guard against death.

Cautiously, Mary-Stuart poised on her toes and flitted like a shadow across the opened door. Then, glancing over her shoulder, she ran into Harrison's room where servants had laid out his pajamas and robe, set a glass of milk on the bed and left a lamp turned low.

She closed the door stealthfully, found a pair of Harrison's riding pants, a rust-colored jacket and a white shirt with lace jabot. She dressed hastily. Harrison was taller, but he was slender, leanly made and his boots were only slightly outsized.

She cracked the hall doorway and checked both ways before stepping out into the corridor.

Only a lone violin made music in the sun-room below. The voices were subdued now, the laughter tired, the sad little party tattered to its lingering remnants.

She ran along the deeply shadowed upper hallway and descended the narrow black stairwell to the kitchen. As she'd prayed, black Aunt Laura and Uncle Oscar were there. These two slaves ruled the servants, administered the daily life of the estate. She had no idea how old either of them were; they had seemed ancient to her the first time she became aware of their beautiful and smiling brown faces in her infancy.

The two Negro servants had their shoes off. They sat in antique bentwood rockers before the huge old wood-burning iron stove, its fire dwindling to red coals and purple ashes.

"Good lands." Aunt Laura looked up, laughing when Mary-Stuart came off the stairs into the faintly lit room. "What you dressed up for, chile, some kind of masquerade party? You trying to win first prize for ugly?"

Uncle Oscar stirred himself. He had been dozing, though his black eyes were open. He had learned to sleep that way so that he would forever look alert, ready to leap to the bidding of the white masters.

He stared at Mary-Stuart, shaking his head. "You running away from home again, chile?"

Mary-Stuart smiled because Uncle Oscar was referring to the times when she had tried to run away from home—heading for Hidden Brook—in her distant childhood, and the way he had followed, brought her back, with honeyed words, cinnamon buns and extravagant promises.

Aunt Laura's voice sharpened. "Why ain't you in there at your party? Why ain't you sayin' good night to your guests like a genteel young lady should?"

Mary-Stuart only shook her head, dismissing this as trivial. "Uncle Oscar, I want you to hitch Amelia to the buggy—"

"This time of night, chile?"

Aunt Laura straightened, formidable, unyielding. "This time of the night? Ain't nobody hitching nuthin' to nuthin' this time of night. You goin' somewhere, you just going to wait until a decent hour in the morning."

Uncle Oscar's gentle voice was loving. "Where you wants to go this time of the night, honey-chile?"

"Ain't goin' nowhere," Aunt Laura said.

"I want to go to Hidden Brook, Uncle Oscar."

"Hidden Brook?" Uncle Oscar laughed. "You still runnin' away to Hidden Brook, honey?"

"I always will be, Uncle Oscar."

"Maybe you will. Maybe you won't." Aunt Laura stood up, a quadroon, big-girthed, statuesque, defying the ravages of time, standing as straight and taut as she ever had, a majestic black woman.

"I'm going, Aunt Laura. Don't try to stop me. If you love me, don't try to stop me."

"It's 'cause I love you that I is stoppin' you. No genteel young lady goes traipsin' out in the night like this. Goin' alone to a man's house—"

"I'm not going alone. Uncle Oscar's going with me."

"Uncle Oscar ain't goin' nowhere, 'cause you ain't goin' nowhere. Not this time of night. Now, I fix you a warm glass of milk and you go back up to bed. You still have to traipse over to Hidden Brook tomorrow sometime, you go—at a genteel calling hour."

Mary-Stuart flinched, but tilted her chin, her gaze firm. "Please, Uncle Oscar, I asked you to bring the buggy here to the kitchen door. Do I have to ask you again?"

Pained, Uncle Oscar stepped into his high-topped black

shoes and stood up, but Aunt Laura's black eyes impaled him. "Sit, nigger," she said. "Sit."

"Uncle Oscar." Mary-Stuart's voice beseeched and ordered at once.

Uncle Oscar stood wavering.

Aunt Laura said. "You want me to call your mama? You think I don't know you sneakin' out on her—dressed up in your brother's clothes. Like that ain't bad enough. Going out in the hour before midnight. On a fool errand. It ain't lady-like. It ain't seemly. It ain't right. And I ain't gonna let you do it."

Mary-Stuart's voice chilled. "I've always done everything you asked, Aunt Laura—"

"Ain't nevah ast nuthin' of you ain't best for you—"

"But I'm asking you now. Help me. I've got to know why Jerry didn't come to my party tonight."

Aunt Laura exhaled in exasperation. "Now, ain't that a pure earth-shaking question? Well, it can just wait until morning to be answered." There was terrible finality in her voice.

Mary-Stuart remained unyielding. "It may not be earth-shaking to you, Aunt Laura. It's important to me. Desperately. Something may have happened to him. I've got to know what it is."

Uncle Oscar was moving reluctantly but resignedly toward the rear door, his big shoes flapping loosely on his tired feet. "You stand where you is, nigger." Aunt Laura told him. "You a stupid black man. But you ain't helping this here girl ruin her reputation forever and final among the decent people of this here county. You ain't goin' nowhere. She ain't goin' nowhere. Now sit down."

"I'm going, Aunt Laura," Mary-Stuart said. "If I have to walk."

Her violet eyes clashed against the moist olive-black gaze of the older woman. Aunt Laura's eyes filled with tears, but she shook her head, defeated. She saw nothing but social ostracism, ruined reputation and despair ahead, but if anyone on this earth loved Mary-Stuart more than Laura, it was Oscar, and she didn't believe the old man capable of such devotion.

Uncle Oscar sighed, took up an old lantern and went out the back door.

* * *

There were still a few guests seated in the sun-room when Uncle Oscar brought the two-seated buggy around the house to the rear door. A lone black man scratched sentimental airs from his plaintive violin. Most of the remaining guests were older people, friends of Mrs. Randolph, sitting in lighthearted postmortem over the expired *soirée*.

Aunt Laura followed Mary-Stuart out the lighted back door and across the rear stoop from the kitchen. She carried a heavy afghan and insisted that the girl drape it like a shawl about her shoulders. "Lord knows what miseries you picks up in these night airs."

Mary-Stuart hesitated, then kissed the older woman lightly on her chocolate-brown cheek. "I love you, Aunt Laura," she whispered. "I love you best of all."

Laura straightened, her eyes glinting wetly in the wan shaft of light from the kitchen. "Go on. Go on. Throw 'way your reputation. Throw it away. You ain't nevah goin' to miss it noway, till it's gone."

It was almost midnight when Jerry alone, angled off the main trace, going between tall fieldstone gateposts, and headed up the long white-shelled lane toward the Randolph manor house. Myriad lamps and candles in open downstairs windows broadcast great sprays of brilliant yellow light over the terraces, the steps, the gravel, the close-cropped lawns and the fragrant shrubs. A few carriages wilted tiredly in the drive. An undercurrent of subdued music spread beneath it all.

Jerry smiled. As always, it was like seeing Felicity Manor for the first time. The baronial old mansion was beautiful, even with its graceful Georgian lines blurred and deliquescent in the obscuring dark. Small black boys with lanterns bobbling at their sides ran out of the shadows, rubbing their eyes and yawning, to greet him.

At that moment, a buggy came with speed and yet stealth around the house and rattled down the driveway.

Jerry pulled up on his horse and waited quietly, soothing his mount. He remained in the shadows until the vehicle was almost upon him. First, Jerry recognized Uncle Oscar, and then saw that it was Mary-Stuart huddled on the seat beside him.

As if by some unimagined, unimaginable miracle, Mary-Stuart found herself quickly alone with Jerry, almost before she could credit that it could have happened, in the bower formed by the obscured, unlit gazebo. She could hear the vague snuffling of Jerry's horse, ground-tied beside the carriage where Uncle Oscar waited, out of earshot. She smiled gently. Uncle Oscar probably was already asleep again—with his tired eyes somehow propped open by invisible sticks.

She gazed at her beloved in the darkness, her heart pounding wildly in her rib cage. She could see him clearly in the thick dark because she saw him behind her eyes, in her mind's eye. In her heart.

She beheld him in that vivid clarity—tall, lean, with strong rough hands and wide straight shoulders, his slender, distinctly cut features braised brown from suns of tropic seas, his high cheekbones hollowed above a cleft, squared jaw. Swarthy, with raven black hair indented deep at the temples and shaggy over his collar, he had gray eyes which chilled over abruptly, like a winter pond under tilted brows that gave him an imperious, scornful look, and often got him hated on sight.

She reached out and caressed his cheek with the backs of her fingers, needing to touch him, if only lightly. She knew him devilish, driven sometimes, and gossip tagged him dissolute. She found him impulsively generous, totally unimpressed by ancestry worship which was coin of exchange on every estate and farm around them. She'd learned him stubborn, violent when roused, passionate, an arrogant man at times when pushed, somewhat aloof, sometimes remote, sometimes lovably shy. She saw him a natural rebel, in anger ruthless, a man born to swing the world by its tail, a moral man with his own rules of ethics and conduct—a man living beyond the ken of ordinary, law-abiding citizenry. Not yet twenty-three, already he was widely infamous as a rake, a hellion and a rogue. A mocking laugh that mocked himself as much as the world, a soft heart, he stood preeminent among county men—in England he may well have been early-on knighted by his king. In fact, his grandfather had been respectfully addressed as Sir Arthur, here in democratic Virginia, until he died.

They stood close against each other in the darkness without speaking. It was almost as if static electricity sparked between them. He felt the fevered heat of her body rising against his and he responded to it, growing empty-bellied and trembling deep in his loins.

He was driven, compelled beyond any strength to resist, to hold her, to caress and fondle and love her. It was as if her very heated flesh cried out to him. He felt illness churning with the desire in his belly. He had to get away from here and yet his irresistible need to embrace her overwhelmed him. But, if he touched her, he would carry her with him forever, across every mile on his unknown odyssey, an intolerable burden that would add agony and pain of loss to every moment away from her.

He put out his hands and touched her. She quivered slightly and sank forward against the muscular tension of his body. For that moment neither spoke. How cruelly wrong it was that he must leave her. He loved her with all his heart, as all the gods must know—in their envy. If ever God Himself had intended two people to belong, Mary-Stuart was meant for him, and he for her. This must be God's plan, if God had a plan at all.

He gazed into her night-shadowed face, finding in it the startling beauty of fresh and delicate lilies. A rust-gold ringlet bobbled against her finely structured forehead. She reached out openly for love. She'd spent her life protected from evil, untouched by it, almost unaware of it beyond those tall fieldstone gates. Her world had always been a warm and protected place and he vowed to keep it ever so for her.

He felt her tremble with longing, felt fiery heat radiating from her body. Her hands clinging to him were chilled, her nipples frozen hard, pressed like small cherries against his chest. He could feel the thunderous pound of her heart, the unfettered fullness and supple symmetry of her breasts, quivering free beneath the loose shirt she wore. The night world, the distant warm-glowing house, the faint whisper of plaintive violin, everything but this tiny niche wheeled and spun away and they drifted in violent need across a misty, unpeopled cosmos.

"Oh, Jerry," she whispered. "Are you all right? I was so worried. Ill with worry. . . . I've looked for you since dusk." Even in the darkness she saw that his face changed, gray and stern. "Why—what happened, Jerry? Why didn't you come to my party—to our party?"

He kept his arms about her, kept her fevered body pressed upon his hardness, against the pound of heated blood and raging heart, but he shook his head. "I didn't think I'd be welcome here—ever again."

"What are you talking about?"

"Harry. He threatened to kill me if I came here."

She did not smile. "Since when have you been afraid of Harry's sodden threats—afraid of any man—if you really want something?"

He tried to laugh, but it was a cold and cheerless sound. "Oh, I really want you—above everything in God's world."

"You don't act like it. Letting Harry's foolish talk keep you away."

He made a wry face. "I didn't stay away on account of Harry, or even because he threatened to kill me. . . . I stayed because he ordered me away—and I didn't want to embarrass you or humiliate your family in front of your guests. God knows, things are bad enough for us now."

"Harry is such a fool."

"Still, I wouldn't want him trying to kill me, or me having to keep from killing him—before a houseful of already snobbish neighbors who are anxious to believe the worst about me. Besides, I thought after he talked to you, you would not want me here."

She drew back her head, staring at him, and he read the anguish in her eyes and the shadow of horror. He told her quickly all that Harrison might possibly retail to her of his years away from Virginia on the high seas, of the manner in which he was able to recoup the family fortune and return to live here.

"I didn't care what people said, even what they whispered so that it was certain to come back to you." He drew her closer. "I know you loved me, and felt shielded by that love. I knew the lies and half-truths that are rampant about me. I held them in contempt, as I was sure you would."

"As I would," she whispered.

"But Harry went further, Mary-Stuart. I could believe your own brother might poison your mind and heart against me where others might fail. I knew your parents ready to believe the worst about me. I was afraid you might believe Harry, when you would laugh at others."

She kissed him suddenly, fiercely. "Don't you know I love you too much to be swayed by anything—even if my own dear Harry vowed it to be true?"

He stared at her. "Hasn't he carried out his threat? He left me this afternoon, after affronting me as I'd allow no other man, vowing to end our engagement by laying before you the evils of my years as a pirate, and more than that, the news of a heinous murder two days ago in Alexandria which he is convinced I committed."

"Murder?" She shuddered.

"Aye. The murder of a tavern doxy he knew—and swears he loved."

"You mean—Harry—in love with a slattern?"

"Believing makes a thing so, I reckon. Then it's true. He loved her. I don't doubt that. In his own way, he did love her. He holds me somehow guilty of her death, though I swear to you I am innocent."

"Why would he think you guilty?"

He winced and chewed for a moment at his underlip. "I went to her house—"

"Why?" She shivered, revulsed, and tried to draw away.

"My God, Mary-Stuart, hear me out! That's why I'm here. I should have come the moment he threatened me, but I was heartsick. As soon as I could think clearly, I saw what I had to do. I came straight to you. I wanted you to hear the truth—first from me."

"Why did you go—to that girl's house?"

He laughed suddenly, mirthlessly and helplessly, seeing in brilliant clarity how easy it would have been for Harry to poison her mind and chill her heart against him. "Does it matter *why* I went there? All right, I want you to have the whole truth—and from me! I went there on an errand for Harry. No matter what he has told you—"

"Harry hasn't told me anything."

He scowled, shaking his head. "He's made no charges against me? But he accused me of murder. Refused to listen to anything I said, ordered me away from you on the pain of death, vowed to lay before you all the crimes I may have committed as well as all those laid at my door by enemy and twaddle-carrier alike."

"Harry is not at home."

He frowned, puzzled. "Didn't he come straight to you from Hidden Brook? He swore he'd carry his case against me directly to you. He left, raging, early this afternoon."

She felt ill with unnamed fears, but she kept her voice low. "Harry hasn't been home. Not since he left for Alexandria—three days ago."

He sighed heavily. "Thank God. Then I did get here in time—ahead of him. You have heard it all from me, Mary-Stuart. As God lives, I have told you all there is to tell. I don't claim it all to be pretty, or honest always, but whatever I did, it was what I believed in that moment I had to do—to stay alive, to come back to you, able to give you the life I want to give you."

"And that girl—the one Harry accuses you of—you swear she is nothing to you?"

He laughed in frustration. "Why would you need such a vow from me? Why would I want a public slattern—or any woman made by God—other than you, as long as I have you?"

She shivered and pressed her body harder upon him. "You do have me." She caressed his face. "It makes me ill that rancor exists between the two men I love most on this earth—my brother and my soul! I swear to you, I will not listen to him. I will not be turned from you. No power on earth can do that, Jerry. All I ask of you—where Harry is concerned—is that you be patient, bear with him, know he has weaknesses not hidden from me—or from my poor parents!—but that we do love him, and all his weakness. . . . He is good inside, Jerry. He has good blood. In time he will straighten out, if only you can be patient."

He sighed. "That's the other reason I came here. I came to say good-bye."

She cried out in horror. "Good-bye? Again? You would leave me—again?"

"Not for any reason under God's sun, but the hope that *time* will repair the rancor between our two houses, will ease the hatreds toward me now tormenting Harry so that he believes himself faced with a single recourse—to kill me. If I go away—for a while—on an important errand—"

"I've been too long alone now. I won't let you go!"

"If I stay, the way things are, with Harry, with all conditions, I may lose you in spite of all we can do to cling close like this—"

"The only place I want to be. Take me with you, Jerry. Now, tonight. We can elope. Run away. Nothing can ever separate us again."

He shook his head sadly. "You know better than that. Your father is ill—your eloping with me might well kill him. It would break your mother's heart. You know that. Nothing but a wedding, with flowers and music and huge receptions, and heads held high before all her friends and neighbors would satisfy her . . . and Harry. Good God, you should have seen the hatred in his face today. If I took you away, I know—raging as he is inside, and drinking as he is, bereaved already with grief which he imputes to my doing—he would come after us, with guns bristling."

"I won't let you go," she whispered.

"I've been over it a hundred times. Like a treadmill. It is the only answer. It won't be for long. You can make all plans for a wedding date that will mollify your mother and yet please you. And the errand *is* urgent—"

"What errand? What errand is so important that you can leave me now—like this?"

He winced. In his mind flared the picture of President Monroe. The little man had warned him; he could tell no one the nature of his mission, not even those he held dearest.

"Trust me," he whispered. "You've got to trust me."

"Not if you run away and leave me. Am I to believe you go without some cause? Why do you have to go—so secretly that you can tell me neither where nor why? Is Harry right? Are the things poor Squire Jennings has unwillingly told me about you—true?"

"Good God! Jennings too? What evil is he peddling against me behind my back?"

"Truths I should know, Squire Jennings says, though it pains him to retail them. I had heard much of what you confessed to me. From the squire—"

"And you loved me still?"

She kissed his eyes, the high bones of his cheeks, the heat of his lips. She clung to him, between tears and laughter. "Nothing—no one—but you yourself—ever could stop my loving you—distractedly—mindlessly—with all my heart."

She widened her thighs, coming upon his towering rigidity with an impetuosity prompted by her own quivering passions and her need to keep him close to her, with whatever weaponry the gods had made available to her—and they were formidable.

Her mouth parted over his lips, her breath sweet and fiery hot. "Stay." She stroked him. "Promise you'll stay. Nothing Harry can say now will affect me. Wait, at least until I have talked with Harry, until I make him understand how senseless it is to try to keep us apart. Please, promise that at least."

He was helpless against her. The fiery eminence at her thighs worked upon him and sanity spun and wheeled and flushed in a vortex from his mind. His hands closed on her hips, lifted her, drew her to him. Then he jerked open her loose shirt so her full breasts spilled free. He covered a breast with his mouth, suckling. Passions flared outward through her, and she put her head back, moaning.

But the fates were not through with him; they'd only begun to work their jest. A few feet from them in the darkness someone spoke his name.

"Mastah Jerry."

Jerry lunged backward, jerking his nursing mouth from Mary-Stuart's bared breast. Gasping, she clutched the jabot and closed it over her bosom. She fell away from Jerry and he heeled around, his voice lashing. "Cato. Damn it. What are you doing here?"

Cato did not flinch, nor retreat a step. His face remained cold and set. "Looking for you—mastah. . . . And I had no difficulty—finding you."

"All right, damn it. What do you want?"

"I want nothing, mastah. I come on your account. Only because you ordered me."

"All right, you pious hypocrite! I know you're enjoying yourself. Having the time of your life, eh? Why have you so generously appeared here on my behalf?"

"Upon your own command, mastah. Have you forgotten you sent me early to fetch Squire Jennings?"

Jerry sighed out heavily, fighting to keep his emotions under control. He felt Mary-Stuart trembling beside him in the darkness. He glanced around angrily. "All right, Cato. Where is he?"

Cato shrugged. "I couldn't find him, mastah. I tried his office in Winchester, the taverns and ordinaries there. His housekeeper said he left four days ago on business in Alexandria and has not yet returned home. I thought I had better let you know at once, since your business with him was so important."

Locke exhaled. "It's all right. My need to see him has lost its urgency now."

Hard against his side, he heard Mary-Stuart's joyous intake of breath. Her warm and hopeful laughter bubbled. "Then you'll stay—you'll make no further plans to leave?"

He enclosed her in his embrace. "I'm staying," he said. "Whatever the urgency of my mission—I'm afraid someone else will have to carry it out."

Mary-Stuart pressed close, clinging to him, laughing and crying at once, suddenly secure and blissful in the darkling night.

— V —

IN THE darkness after midnight, Locke returned to Hidden Brook. He spoke not one word to Cato on the ride along the ill-marked trace. The only sounds were of leather and metal gear, the slough of hooves in the mud and the snuffling sighs of tired horses.

Locke undressed and threw himself across his bed, sweated, restless, fiercely aroused as Mary-Stuart's passions, his own desires and Cato's unfortunate appearance had left him, thwarted without remedy. He winced against the strictures in his loins.

He cursed the fates and Cato and himself and the workings of the human body when only physical torment resulted from restraint, frustration or inhibition. Hell's eyes, how had those puritanical forebears existed on abstinence and prayer? They must have limped around knotted over their own bellies half the time.

Thank God, at least, for these more enlightened times. When two people loved each other, as he and Mary-Stuart did, they no longer had to lie about it, hide it or pretend it all could be assuaged with a chaste kiss on the lady's fingertips. Oh God, he hurt!

He prayed for sleep, but that didn't happen either. The long hours dragged away, the darkness deepening, the faint sounds of late night rising and falling, the baying of a hound, the crowing of an anxious cock, an unexplained shout from the slave quarters.

He rolled on the rumpled sheets, praying for sleep, praying for release. One thing this night proved. He and Mary-Stuart had waited long enough—too long—to be wed. For them, marriage, like honesty, was the best policy, and the sooner the better.

He felt sweat marble and roll in chilled lines along his ribs. He stared in the darkness, trying to see ahead to that incredible moment when Mary-Stuart would be his, all barriers, all fetters, all apparel removed. Her body and his body, as Adam and Eve must have been in Eden, what God must have intended for man and woman, and what man in his stupidity had managed to foul up through the ages.

Well, such inhibited and frustrating hypocrisy would not concern them. Thank God, theirs was a mutual desiring, a shared passion that burned hot and would not, he swore, burn out.

The purple darkness lightened, shattered with striae of pink as the first tendrils of sunlight appeared in the dark tresses of the clouds. Morning, and he hadn't slept a wink! God knew, he might never sleep again, until he was permitted to take Mary-Stuart in his arms, in his bed, in his life.

He grinned. Thank God, Mary-Stuart was wiser than he. He had promised to forget the journey away from Hidden Brook; he would stay and together he and Mary-Stuart would face their adversaries, even if their leader were her own beloved brother. Sorry, President Monroe. Whatever your differences with Andy Jackson of Tennessee, you two must settle them without the intervention of Jerry Locke. You'll have to work out your problems alone. I'll be previously engaged for the rest of my natural life—in paradise!

He lay smiling, even against the corrosive acid of need moiling in his loins. But the troubling memory of Monroe's almost pleading appeal for help haunted him. Hell's eyes! What could he do? What could he find out about Andy Jackson that Monroe didn't already know? And hadn't Monroe suggested a hundred men were qualified for the mission? Let the President get one of them. He had not promised to undertake the errand. He could not go as things were. He couldn't leave Mary-Stuart now, for untold months. And she was too delicate, too fragile to drag along with him into the hell of frontier Spanish Florida. Not even President Monroe could ask that. Nothing in Mary-Stuart's protected—even overprotected—upbringing prepared her for the hardships which were ordinary existence in that hot, wild land.

Damn it! If only Monroe were not such a quiet and admirable man, asking nothing of others he would not do himself for the country he loved and represented. He supposed that in the future—as history showed happened in most nations—the quality of leadership would deteriorate. Men would become President who'd be mere puppets of the military and monetary forces. Patriotism would become an old-fashioned, contemptible word. But at the moment, the man in the White House—the President's palace!—was honest, dedicated, old-fashioned in his *patriotic* fever to defend its hard-won freedom.

Hell, few men better than Monroe knew the price of that freedom. He had had an artery severed by the Hessians during the battle of Trenton. He had come to the very brink of death and Washington himself had commended the young soldier as a "brave, active and sensible officer." Even Thomas Jefferson had admitted himself amazed to find so much gentle goodness in one man as "I discover every day in Jimmy Monroe." And Monroe patterned himself after his longtime friend and mentor Jefferson. Monroe said he owed much to Jefferson and wanted to emulate him, wanted to earn the older man's approval and pride. When a wide rift developed between Madison and Monroe, Jefferson had been dismayed, because he found two genuinely honest and dedicated men at odds when every heart had to be devoted to the task of keeping the struggling young nation alive. Too, Monroe had said that there had been talk among hotheads like Henry Clay, John Calhoun and Andy Jackson of capturing both Canada *and* the Spanish Floridas—this as long ago as 1810. Well, someday the presidential timber of the man in the house on Pennsylvania Avenue might be a shame and an indictment of the voters who put him there, but at the moment, the sickly new republic was in unselfish, noble, large-hearted, humble hands. Tough-minded, sometimes arrogant and stubborn, but honest. How did you turn your back on such a man when he called out to you?

Locke winced. You fell in love, that's how you did it. You recognized that the President's great design could never be yours, that your own life was bound within the orderly confines of Hidden Brook, within the arms and love of Mary-Stuart. Let Monroe find some other adventurer. As the fates permitted, he would do his adventuring within the scented gates of Mary-Stuart's embrace. So be it. He had his own life, his own problems, his own existence. There was just one thing to do about James Monroe. Get tha. good and gentle man out of his mind.

He was wrenched from his reverie by the sharp, imperative knocking on his door. "Get to hell away from there, Cato," he said.

Cato opened the door, entered the room. He glanced at Lock, lying naked and miserable on the rumpled bed, eyes sleepless, mouth pulled down, nostrils flared.

Calmly, Cato went about shoving open windows and letting up blinds so the wan sunlight toppled weakly across the sills. "I trust you slept well—mastah?"

"Go to hell."

"You have a guest, mastah."

"At this hour?"

Cato lifted his wide shoulders in a shrug. His voice dripped disapprobation. "It's almost seven. Cocks crowed two hours hence. Honest men are abroad by now."

Locke's mouth twisted. "Oh, you pious son of a bitch."

Cato went to the corridor door, stood there with his hand

on its brass knob. He met Locke's gaze flatly. "Shall I tell your guest you'll be down shortly?"

Locke exhaled, tasting at the sour interior of his mouth. "Who is it?"

Cato gestured downward. "Why it's Squire Jennings, mastah. He must have gotten a dozen or so of the urgent messages I left broadcast like seed for him at every office, inn, tavern and ordinary between here and Winchester yesterday. Anyhow, he is here."

"Did you tell him my business with him was no longer of priority concern?"

"He didn't ask," Cato replied. "He said his own matters were of such urgency that he had come to you in all haste."

Locke found Worthington Jennings drinking coffee from an outsized earthenware mug in his late father's den. This had been the favorite gathering and drinking place for the two old friends in the days when the world considered the elder Locke an upright, honest citizen and not a defaulter, a dissolute and dishonest blackguard.

Locke stopped just inside the thick door, staring at the attorney.

Shock fulgurated through him at the disheveled sight of the lawyer. Jennings looked as if he had not slept in many nights, as if his best accommodations had been in somebody's haystack.

"Jennings! What's the matter? Are you all right?"

Jennings waved his long, arthritic-warped fingers. "Close the door, my boy. Lock it if you will."

Puzzled, Jerry obeyed. He watched the lawyer push the untouched dish of cinnamon buns, doughnuts and fresh pastry further from him on the old gateleg table and set down the coffee mug.

Jennings was as tall and gangly as a scarecrow—a sallow, thin gentleman of some indeterminate age between forty and sixty. He looked too ravaged by time to be forty; he was too alert, impetuous and enthusiastic by far to be sixty. Yet, the twice-widowed barrister was much nearer Jerry's father's age than his own. His hair was a muddy brown, sewn and peppered with gray, his face a mask of seamed lines, his eyes mirroring the shoddy side of ordinary existence with which he contended daily in his extensive law practice. His deep voice reverberated in the book-lined study because he was used to making himself heard in courtrooms, obeyed and respected in his dealings with defaulters and debtors. He was an unbending, unyielding man, convinced above all of his own righteousness. He knew the law—man's as well as God's—and he labored diligently to enforce these rules among his fellowmen. In Biblical times, Jennings well could have walked the deserts with the ruthless prophets like Nathan. He didn't smile easily; his upper lip was unnaturally extended over an exaggerated overbite which somehow suggested a ferret ruthlessness.

Locke warned himself he was being influenced in his view by Harrison Randolph's rancid estimate of the lawyer. After all, he owed much to Jennings. The attorney had been like a father to him—better in the long run than his own father. And one had to consider that Worthington Jennings had practiced adversary law all his professional life. He knew nothing else; there was only himself and his God on one side—and his adversaries on the other.

"First, I want to apologize for not coming yesterday when you sent for me. But I've been away more than four days from home and practice, on the unpleasant but necessary business of collecting on mortgages along the Potomac."

"I know. I glimpsed you in Alexandria two days ago."

Jenning's graying head jerked up. "Did you? Why didn't you hail me?"

Locked shrugged. "You seem deeply troubled now. Cato says you have business of your own of great urgency."

"In a way he was correct. In another wrong. The business I have is of importance, I'm afraid, to you. It is more than urgent, it is indeed a tragedy."

Locke remained standing just inside the closed door. He waited, knowing the attorney to be dramatic, an actor of no mean ability, trained on that best stage of all, the most unreal setting known to man, a court of criminal law, that place where sometimes law is the only craft not practiced.

"I have this hour come from Felicity Manor," Jennings said, watching him closely.

Locke had the amused sense that somehow Jennings had placed him, as adversary, in the docket, where, unless he exercised care and cunning, the truth might be ruled out on a technicality.

"Have you? I hope you found the Randolphs well?"

"I left them in deepest sorrow. Franklin Randolph is in shock, barely clinging to life. Rosemary has gone into seclusion. I'm afraid Mary-Stuart was on the verge of hysteria."

"What are you talking about?"

Jenning's voice chilled. "I went with that sorrying procession which carried Harrison Randolph's murdered body home—there to lie in state until the time of his burial."

Locke scowled, bracing himself, legs apart. His sleeplessness was taking its toll. The morning had a weird, nightmarish quality. "Harry Randolph dead? Murdered?"

"His body was found at dawn, by laborers on their way to the fields."

"How? Why? Who could have killed him?"

"That is under investigation. By the high sheriff. But this I can tell you. Harrison's battered body was found in a copse of elder bordering your estate—just beyond a Hidden Brook marker, in fact."

Locke drew a deep breath, held it. He was saddened by Harry Randolph's death; he saw what the shock must have done to Mary-Stuart and Harry's family. But somehow, he felt a greater tension in this room, something far beyond even the agony of tragedy.

"You have suggested that the business which brings you here—straight from Felicity Manor—concerns me. Is this the matter that concerns me—Harry's murder?"

"I make no accusations. Though I must confess others do. Many others. Scores of people within the past two days heard Harry Randolph seeking you, railing against you—"

"He was drunk. I know about that. He was here. And I assure you, quite healthy when he departed."

"I hope—for your own security, my boy, that you can document this—with witnesses."

"Oh, come on, Squire! My mother? My sisters? My servants? Will they answer as acceptable witnesses?"

"I reiterate, my boy, I have not come here to accuse you! Far from it. But I am an attorney. I do know the law. I know the demands of the law. I know as well the temper of the people who heard Harry Randolph threaten you. I want nothing more than you be acquainted with facts, able to protect yourself."

Locke stepped forward, his exhausted body trembling with tension. "What the hell are you talking about? Do you—is there anyone—who seriously charges me with causing Harry's death?"

Jennings stared at his knotted knuckles, at his long grasping hands. "More than one. Scores. I don't exaggerate, my boy. You are respected in this county. But those who know and respect you most see you as a violent-tempered man. Many know that you plied the seas off Spanish Florida on killer ships—plundering, in piracy. They don't approve of your past actions. This very disapproval makes them wary of you. And now a young hothead has made public accusations against you. There is proof that Harry headed toward Hidden Brook with the clear intent of settling a quarrel with you. They know that if he affronted you, you would have struck back."

"I might have, were he not the brother of the girl I love, whom I intend to marry."

"She—as much as any—holds you guilty of this crime against her family."

"You can't be serious. How could she? She knows I would not lift a finger to harm him—no matter how he affronted me. What lies has she been told?"

"She has not been unduly influenced by lies, my boy. Unfortunately, the high sheriff is getting a warrant, charging you with the murder of Harrison Randolph. He expressed to Harrison's aggrieved family the list of reasons why you are to be charged. They are formidable, I confess. I heard them stated coldly."

Locke clenched his fists at his side. He stared down at the gawky attorney, perched vulturelike on the rim of his chair as if ready to pounce. "What do you want, Jennings? If you too believe me guilty of this heinous crime, why are you here?"

Jennings stood up slowly, hair wild about his lean face, his clothing rumpled. "I want to help you, if I can. I came to offer my talents, my life, my very fortune to your defense if you'll have it."

Jerry winced. He felt his eyes burn and a sense of self-hatred flared through him. Worthington Jennings was only the messenger of evil: he could not, like the tyrants of antiquity, punish the bearer of bad tidings.

"I'm sorry, Worthington," he said. "I'm not worthy. I know you have been like a father—better than my own father. It was just that, in my agony, I saw that if Mary-Stuart has abandoned me, I could not believe myself left with even one friend."

"As long as you want me. As long as you need me, my boy."

Jerry Locked sighed. "They do intend to come here to Hidden Brook and arrest me?"

Jennings nodded. "That's why I came in all haste. Because you are a wealthy, landowning member of the community, part of a family which has been here for generations, the law hesitates to move precipitately against you."

Locke watched the attorney, waiting.

"I used whatever influence I have with them in urging caution and reason. I asked at least that they delay twenty-four hours in deference to your position in society."

"And they agreed to this?"

"I think they did. I believe they will give you that grace."

"What are you suggesting, Jennings? That you bought time for me—to permit me to flee?"

"How you use the time is your responsibility. Again, I merely state that we have been able to buy you that short period of grace. You see, I also happen to know something which may be brought to the attention of the sheriff within the next few hours—the law enforcement people in Alexandria are seeking a man answering to your description—not your name, yet, but your description—as the last person to have seen Anne Stoker alive."

"I won't lie to you. I was there. I found her dead."

"And you fled?"

"I saw no reason to hang around—and hang. I'm not being facetious, Worthington. I happened to know, and I'm sure you know, that Harry Randolph was deeply involved in an affair with Anne Stoker. Had he lived, the law may well have come to his door."

Jennings stared at him, face starkly cold. "I'm sorry. I don't follow you. I have *no* knowledge of Harrison's involvement with the Stoker woman. Oh, I don't pretend he didn't drink too much, gamble too much. But I never heard a whisper as to his involvement with that—that woman."

Locke stared at the attorney for a moment, ready to call him liar. Then he shrugged, shaking the thought away. It did not matter. He had trouble enough; no sense fighting with Jennings too.

"What is your advice to me?"

"As your attorney, an officer of the court, my advice is to surrender to the sheriff when he arrives with his warrant and trust to the law to protect you—if you are innocent."

"Damn it. I am innocent. I didn't kill Anne Stoker. I certainly did not harm Harry Randolph. I deeply regret both their deaths but I feel no responsibility, no obligation to submit myself to the vagaries of law. I'd hang just as high—innocent or guilty."

"I might be able—because of your name, position and wealth—to make some plea bargain. Perhaps a year or two in jail. This would clear all charges against you, permit you to return one day to Hidden Brook a free man."

"A free, ruined, disgraced and empty man. A man without friends—a man hated by his fiancée and her family. For crimes I did not commit. You'll have to do better than that. I will confess to nothing."

"The very workings of the law itself may uncover the real criminals, if you are guiltless—"

"Damn it! Stop saying that. No matter what so-called *evidence* you've heard, no matter how strongly you are moved by it, I am not guilty."

"The sheriff's people may find the true killers—of Anne Stoker, and of Harrison Randolph. Harrison was, after all, killed on the open road. He may have fallen victim to road agents, thugs, an escaped slave. There are many ways he may have died. . . . It is only unfortunate that he was found at the edge of *your* property, brutally beaten, after dozens of people heard him making violent threats against you."

Locke's mouth twisted. "How long might that take—in the present state of police procedure and competence?"

"I would not deceive you. It might be years. If the truth came out, it might come only through accident. Or it may never be known."

"In the meantime, I have been elected the quarry?"

"On very persuasive evidence, my boy. I heard that evidence, and my faith was shaken, I must confess. I saw Mary-Stuart Randolph cry out in agony, turned against you."

"Then what chance have I in the view of disinterested citizens?" Locke said. "Have you another suggestion, other than confession and plea bargaining, to which I will never agree?"

"As your attorney, I have little else to offer. One takes his chances with the law. One hires the best defense possible and one takes his chances. . . . I cannot make such a suggestion, but having been over all this a hundred times in my own agonized mind, I know what I would do."

"Run." Locke spat the word.

"You protest your innocence. The evidence is strong against you. If you disappeared for a while, perhaps the law might locate the truth—and exonerate you. It's the only alternative I see."

"What about my mother and sisters?"

Jennings looked pained. "I protected them with all my substance, will and energies once before when you were away for two years, when none knew if you'd ever come back alive. I would not abandon them now."

"Thank you, Squire. I sometimes overlook my deep debt to you, but I never forget it. . . . My mind is chaos. My heart is broken. If I leave here—accused of murdering Mary-Stuart's brother—I'll never see her again on this earth."

"I bring you a sad truth from Felicity Manor, my boy. As deeply as it grieves me to retail it, I can tell you the coin of Mary-Stuart's deep devotion to you has been reversed—she views you now only in hatred and revulsion."

"I cannot go away letting her believe—"

"Again, I must counsel caution. You must trust to palliative time. Only the *proof* of your innocence in her brother's death would release Mary-Stuart from her present malevolence toward you. . . . Go. Give her time. Time is your only hope."

"God help me. You make me see. I have no hope."

"I shall not be idle while you're away, my boy. If there is truth, we shall find it. I shall prod and spur and urge the law forces to relentless pursuit of the truth. The truth will set you free. If you are behind bars, the same lawmen may not work as diligently to find another culprit."

Locke sank against the door. "How much time have I?"

"None at all. As I say, when the charges and description arrive in the Anne Stoker murder, the high sheriff of Prince William County may well refuse to delay longer in serving his warrant on you. I can tell you, it would appear to him—to all disinterested ones—that you killed Anne Stoker, and when confronted by young Randolph with some irrefutable evidence, you slew him and left his body hidden in a copse of elders."

"And whille I am gone, you would see to the safety and comfort of my mother and sisters?"

"Do you need to hear me swear that? I will protect them as if they were my own dear family—as I consider them. . . . A power of attorney signed over to me by you will make it possible for me to administer their affairs, as well as your own, to your very best interests."

Locke left Cato holding their horses, two mounts and a beast of burden, carrying a sack of gold and a few changes of clothing, guns and ammunition, concealed in a pine hammock near the fieldstone gates at Felicity Manor.

As if reading his mind, Worthington Jennings had counseled strongly against his intruding upon the grief, heartbreak and rancor overwhelming the Randolph home. "You'll find only hatred there. They are convinced of your guilt. They are mindless with loss. Do not intrude upon their grief. Don't waste time which could see you far south of here. It is worse to run if you are to permit yourself to be caught. Flight is almost tantamount to a confession of crime and as brutally punished by the law."

Locke had remained silent, knowing that he was not about to depart Virginia without one mighty effort to convince Mary-Stuart of his innocence. If he were able to change her heart from hatred, her mind from accusation, he would not even leave this place, though they dug a hole beneath the prison and dropped him into it. He had to make her see he was innocent. It was a straw but he grasped at it, hoping it might be the one fiber fierce enough to support him.

— VI —

LOCKE PROWLED the vaguely lit veranda. After a long time the front door was reopened. Locke crossed the stone flooring to face Claro, the solemn-miened butler who had bade him wait. For the first time in his memory he had been left cooling his heels outside.

"The family deep in grief, mastah," the butler had said. He was a lean reed of a man, no more than medium height, but appearing taller because of his string-slender form and pipestem legs. His father and grandfather had been butlers in this house, and even though they had been slaves, treated like domesticated animals, they drew great pride from their position and place of trust. They were trained to high excellence.

Claro stepped almost undetected to bar the doorway. The black man who had pretended innumerable times with guile and simpering smiles to welcome Locke in almost distracted delight to Felicity Manor, now seemed chilled, gray with distress, but nonetheless adamant. "Miss Mary-Stuart say she sorry. She won't see you, suh."

He moved as if to close the door. "I must see her, Claro."

He did not smile. "I'm sorry, mastah. They terrible grief in this heah house. They seen' nobody." His black eyes fixed on Locke's. "Young Mastah Randolph is dead."

"I know that, Claro. If it were not urgent—"

"I'm sorry." Claro's voice was dead, but icy with authority. He retreated a step to close the door.

Suddenly raging inward, the blood rushing upward across his face and pounding in his temples, Locke caught the door and wrenched it from the butler's grasp.

Shocked, Claro fell back a step. "Please, suh," he said. "Don't do this."

Locke gave him a glance as he strode past him. "I'm sorry, Claro. It's too damned late for etiquette."

"Yassuh."

"You get back to the kitchen. Or whenever in hell you go. I'll call you if I need you."

Claro nodded but followed Locke silently across the foyer. Locke opened the closed door to the sun-room and thrust it open. The three people inside the room looked up at him. The Episcopal minister, a slight man in rust suit and turned collar, leaped to his feet. Rosemary Randolph sat holding her hands to her face. Tears streaked her cheeks. She looked as if she had been crying for a long time, might cry the rest of her life.

Mary-Stuart came up from her wing-backed chair set in a long shaft of lamplight. She had never looked lovelier, never more lost to him. Her lips were swollen with her crying, her eyes red and puffed. Her body slumped in upon itself. The kind of grief he had wanted always to shield her from, she believed he had heaped upon her. She shook her head, her face as cold as marble.

"Have you no decency?" Her voice was filled with a contempt that answered her own question. "Haven't you hurt us enough?"

"I have not hurt you at all. I never would."

Mary-Stuart shuddered, revulsed. "We don't need your lies here. My mother is ill. My poor dear brother lies dead in the room yonder. Can't you leave us in peace?"

"I must ask you, in the name of God, out of respect to these dear people and their grief, to leave," the minister said.

Locke didn't even glance toward the clergyman. He did not take his gaze from Mary-Stuart's wet-violet eyes. "I'll go, Mary-Stuart. But not before you've listened to me."

She tilted her head, cold to him. "I listened too long already. I don't care what more you have to say. I don't want to hear it."

"You will hear it. I'll stay here until you do."

"Does it mean anything to you that my mother is prostrate with grief, my father on the verge of death—and my brother in a casket?"

"I share your grief."

"Spare us any more of your pretense and evil hypocrisy. You have done to us all you can do. My brother is dead—"

"But I'm fighting for my life. More than my life. I must have your love—your understanding—or I am dead though I live a hundred years."

"If I did not know the truth, the entire ugly truth about you, your words would break my heart. They do not—they ring with falsity—with emptiness."

"All right! You've judged me. Found me guilty. Condemned me. But you'll have me here—until the law itself drags me away in irons—until you hear the truth from me."

Mary-Stuart exhaled heavily, twisting a tear-wet handkerchief in her fists. She shook her head. "Not here. This is not the place."

"Nor is it the time," the minister said.

Rosemary Randolph looked up. Her voice was choked. "You killed my son. You killed my son."

His eyes suddenly filled with tears, Locke fell to his knees before Mary-Stuart's mother. "Mrs. Randolph. In the name of God, look at me—"

"I cannot look in your face—"

"You've known me all my life. You must know I would not harm your son, or knowingly cause you one second's grief."

Rosemary withdrew, staring at him coldly. "Please go away. Please go away. I have known you all your life. But I know you went away from here—to a life of crime. I know you to be hard inside, and evil. I know you capable of murder. I know you killed my son."

She spoke the words in a terrible empty, flat tone, like rote, like something imperfectly remembered. She stared at him, but she looked through him. She did not see him. She saw nothing but her own grief.

Sighing, Locke stood up. With a contempt that chilled him, Mary-Stuart said, "if you vow to leave quietly, and at once, I'll talk with you—for five minutes, though it sickens me to hear your lying voice."

Holding his breath, Locke followed Mary-Stuart from the sun-room. She crossed the foyer and opened the door to the formal living room. He waited for her to enter ahead of him, but when she remained stiffly waiting for him to precede her, he stepped across the threshold and stopped as if poled.

The large room was banked with flowers. The casket had

been set in the center of the darkly designed Persian rug and Harrison's body placed in it by the mortician.

Locke felt as if he'd been struck viciously in the solar plexus. If he had doubted before the depth of Mary-Stuart's hatred for him, it was now manifest.

Locke's gaze returned to the body in the bier and held it, anguished. The undertaker had worked on the dead boy, but the contusions, abrasions and purpled welts were barely and poorly concealed and disguised. Harrison had been beaten to death furiously and without human pity.

"Is there nowhere else?" he said.

He heard her moving wraithlike beside him. "You can't hurt him anymore," she said. Her low voice quavered with her hatred. "Or are you afraid to stay in the room with your handiwork?"

He heeled around, caught her arms. "I know you are in torment, Mary-Stuart. I know you are mindless with grief. But does this erase the love you swore for me—just last night?"

"I despise and regret every moment I've spent with you in my thoughts." She tried to break away from his grasp but he would not release her. "Let me go."

His voice was muted, but vibrating with helpless fury. "Is this the faith you had in me that could not be swayed by anything on earth—even by Harry himself?"

She shuddered. "Harry is dead."

"And I regret his death as much as you. But I am not guilty of it. I have no guilt—"

"Or is it you feel no *sense* of guilt? Because you are incapable of it?" She laughed in a dead tone. "You've lied to me enough, Jerry. You said you were not a rival of the slattern Harry was obsessed with—and yet Squire Jennings himself, reluctantly, told me Harry was sickly jealous of you."

Locke winced, feeling as if he'd been struck across the face. "And the son of a bitch told *me* he didn't even have knowledge that Harry was involved at all with Anne Stoker."

Her mouth twisted bitterly. "Oh, how like you. Strike out at the one man who tried—in vain—to defend you in this house. He may be your last friend. Go ahead, destroy him too."

Locke stared down at her pale, masklike face. She had been ready in jealousy last night to believe the worst—that he had gone to Anne Stoker's shack in passion and need. Now, in her grief, she was as cold against his entreaties, as dead to his touch.

He felt helpless to reach her at all.

"My God, Mary-Stuart. You swore no power on earth could turn you against me. . . . Yet, the first accusations that are leveled upon me—by men without evidence—"

Her low voice shook. "I believe only the unanswerable evidence against you—my brother's body."

She broke free and swung her arm toward the casket, sobbing brokenly, her knotted fist pressed against her aching throat. "Please. In God's name. Go. Leave me in peace."

"I did not kill your brother, Mary-Stuart."

"Stop, Jerry! They said this morning you were a conscienceless killer. You don't have to prove it."

He stared down into her eyes. They were tear-streaked, shadowed, swirling with sickness. "They said much. But one thing they could not say. That I killed Harry, that I would touch him in rage—"

"I begged you. I pleaded that you be patient with him in his weakness. But you would not. When he stood in your way—with a barroom slut—you killed her. When he confronted you with proof of your crime, you killed him. Now you come brazenly here—"

"I came here to make you see the truth. But the truth is the last thing you want to hear. You are sick that your brother has been slain, and I understand that. But, before God, I did not kill him. Think, Mary-Stuart. Don't destroy us like this. Think, Mary-Stuart, I came last night to tell you I would go away. The last thing on earth I wanted. But I believed it best—that I leave until Harry's violent hatred for me waned—"

"Yes. That's the *reason* you gave for leaving—"

"Damn it. It was the reason."

"Was it? Wasn't there some kind of nebulous mission you were going on? Some errand you refused to explain—"

"I could not. Or I thought then—last night—that I could not—"

"I don't want to hear your explanations now!" She pressed

her hands over her ears, trembling, her face contorted with her anguish. "No more of your lies. Spare me."

"I could not tell you—"

"And now you need not. Only go."

"Listen to me."

"I don't have to listen to you. The evidence of my poor brother's body, the charges of the sheriff, have told me more than I'll ever want to know. Do you think I don't know why you were so anxious to get away last night—on that trumped-up mission? You were so anxious to leave. Just for a little while, you said. Had you killed poor Harry already? Was he already lying dead in that ditch? And you came to me—with blood on your hands?"

He stared down at her face, set against him, her lips gray, her eyes flat with hatred.

"All right. There is nothing I can say. Nothing that will convince you of my innocence. No way to make you know I love you more than life."

"I don't want to know it. It does not matter now.It sickens me. There is only one thing you can do for me." Her mouth twisted. "One way to atone for your wrong. Go to the sheriff. Surrender to him. Confess to your crimes. Pay for them. Then—and then only will we be quits. Only when I never have to see you again will I live in peace."

He caught her arms again, helpless. "How could you have turned so quickly—so violently—against me?"

Her eyes glittered with hatred that bordered on madness. But her voice remained lów—brokenhearted, but savage. "I loved with all my heart. And with all my heart I hate you."

He stood a moment, gripping her arms. The pressure increased in his lungs though he was unaware he was not breathing. At last he nodded, the chill in his own voice matching hers. "All right. You won't see me again. I'm sorry as hell I cannot grant your last request of me. I won't go to the sheriff. I won't ćonfess to crimes I have not committed. I will never say anything but the truth. And that truth is simple. I love you. With all my heart."

She turned her head away, writhing in his grip. His fists tightened. He pulled her closer, up on her toes. He bent over the flawless beauty of her cheeks, her eyes wide under his. He closed his lips over her mouth. The sweet scent of her body attacked him, overwhelming him. He wanted to weep, but instead he laughed, an angry growl.

She fought, trying to get free. "Have you gone totally mad?" Her voice slashed at him, her breasts heaving. "If you care nothing for death—have no respect for the dead—consider the living. At any moment someone could come through that door."

"The hell with them," he muttered against her face. "They think me a killer—they can hang me no higher as a rapist."

The color drained from her cheeks. "You have go insane," she stammered.

"If I have, girl, take all the credit to yourself. Your brother is dead. Your love is dead. But I am alive, goddamn it. And as long as I live you'll never forget me."

Her eyes closed for a moment and then opened wide. She was unafraid, but infuriated, cold with fury. "I can't believe this." Her voice was dull. "Even of you."

"Believe it." His voice mocked her cruelly. "You may marry another, go to his bed, but you'll take me with you as long as you live. You'll lie in another man's arms maybe. . . . I can't stop that. But before God, you'll dream of me."

She seemed not even to hear him. Her head sagged back and she stared up at him, a look of resignation and contempt swirling in her shadowed eyes. Though he pulled her closer, his hand seeking her breast, she remained cold, distant, unattainable, unreachable.

His mouth covered hers again. His hand caressed her breast with a fierce, helpless abandon. Her nipples hardened, the supple flesh grew heated at his touch, and he felt her heart pounding wildly.

She did not fight him. She sagged, lifeless, in his arms. But her hatred had not stopped him, nor would her contemptuous resignation. Nothing would stop him because he could not stop. He lifted her feet from the floor and moved with her to the deep couch. He sank down upon it, holding her.

"Don't do this," she said in a dead flat tone. "I'll scream. The servants will come—you can only make me hate you worse."

"Hate is hate," he said. His voice rasped against her face. "You despise me for crimes I have not committed. Now hate me for this—for loving you above heaven."

She stared up past him as he tore away her clothing. "If you loved me you would leave me in my agony."

In answer, he pulled her clothing from her. She struggled, but only managed to fall with his body pressed between her thighs. Enraged, she whimpered and struggled, but he only thrust himself harder upon her.

"Don't," she begged. "If you have no respect for me—have respect for the dead."

"Too late for that. He has none for me. He has killed your love for me."

Her knotted fists beat at his face, but every time she struggled, her writhing body was twisted harder against him. He could feel the heat of her femininity—the fevered burn rising against him.

He ripped aside his own clothing. She fought, trying to roll away, but he pressed himself against her. She gasped, crying out. He thrust himself forward. She closed her eyes and her head rolled back and forth, but she was no longer able to oppose him.

When she opened her eyes, they were pained, with a delicious agony that betrayed her. Tears brimmed to her lids but did not spill. She chewed at her mouth. Her fists battered at his shoulders, then clawed, and then dug into them, the nails ripping his skin. His hands closed furiously upon her breasts. Their mouths struck hard, held fastened. Her lips parted, opened wide and he thrust his tongue deeply between her teeth.

For some mindless moments—a few seconds, a prolonged eternity—they struggled feverishly as if trying to meld their bodies as one. Her hips moved, at first slowly and reluctantly, and then with abandon.

"Oh God, do it, damn you." She panted against his mouth. "Do it! Do it and be damned!" Her fingers clawed at him, her silken legs went about his waist, locked tightly at the ankles as if to hold him imprisoned forever to her. "Do it, damn you," she moaned. "Do it to me as you did it to that poor girl Harry loved! Do it, you rotten lying killer! Ruin me and run away—leave me—ruined—my brother dead. . . . That's really what you want, isn't it? Isn't it?"

Her voice rose into a keening cry. He was unable to speak, crippled by a towering passion and overwhelmed by sweetness he had never expected to encounter on this sad earth. He tried to pull away, sickened by his attack upon her, but she would not release him. She worked her body faster, and he found himself unable to withdraw, her body burning down there, searing him. He moved faster, feeling her rise against him. A sudden frenzy attacked him. He shuddered upward from his toes and then sagged, with her, drained at the instant she found release and completion . . .

She sagged under him then and lay still. For a long time he did not move away. Her body remained fiery and wetly hot, though she was crying softly. He was overwhelmed by compassion, by love, but when he tried to speak to her, she only shook her head, flinching against the sound of his voice. He let her cry. He knew she loved him. But her hatred would always be between them, even as it was in this moment when she lay, clinging to him, closed upon him, face averted, and trembling violently.

PART II
Freebooters' Fortress

— VII —

THEY RODE south on the post road toward Richmond. Locke sagged in his saddle, silent, forlorn and bereft. Already he yearned back to Hidden Brook as an Eden from which he'd been exiled, which he would never see again on this earth. But his agonizing loss was Mary-Stuart, more than ever now that he knew how totally they were meant one for the other, in every way. She had wanted to fight him, oppose him, hate him, but she could not because she belonged to him, she was part of him. With all his heart he wanted to turn back and race to Mary-Stuart. Even if she would have received him, returning to Prince William County with a price on his head was the surest way to lose her, the direct route to prison—maybe even the gallows.

"Do you have any idea where we're going, mastah?" Cato rode slightly behind him on his gray Morgan, slack-leading their pack horse.

For some moments, struggling and drowning his own agony, Locke did not answer his slave. When he did, his voice was brusque. "What the hell you care?"

"I care. Why shouldn't I?"

"Why should you? You have one duty in this life, Cato. Go where I travel. Serve me. You're a slave, Cato. I don't give a damn who your mother was or who your father might be. You've got to stop asking so damn many questions."

Cato grinned tautly. "Why?"

"Because, damn you, it's none of your business where we're going. We are headed south. That's all you need to know."

"Don't snarl at me, mastah . . . I didn't cause you to lose your home and family and fiancée . . . I didn't swear warrants against you for murder."

Locke glanced coldly across his shoulder. "One more murder won't get me hung any higher."

Cato laughed, taunting. "Consider yourself fortunate, mastah . . . all the crimes you have committed and got away with."

"You think it's some kind of justice that I be charged with murder, don't you?"

Cato shrugged. "I just wonder what delayed them."

"For one thing, I'm not guilty, damn you."

"A technicality—mastah."

Locke swung in his saddle, leather creaking. Torn between savage laughter and agonized rage, he stared at his body servant. "Don't be so all-fired anxious to see me hung, my self-righteous dawplucker. I've stipulated in my will that my personal slave be slain along with me, or put to death when I die, and buried at my feet."

"And no headstone?"

"Of course, no marker at all. They don't mark the graves of animals."

"Yet there is a marble memorial marking the grave of your father's horse."

"Hell, that's different. He was a remarkable animal. Faithful. Fleet-footed. And he never talked back."

"You know what I think, mastah?"

"I could not care less."

"I think maybe we're all born again and again. Not our physical selves, but our spirit, our minds—"

"Don't say soul. Niggers don't have souls."

"—and souls. We all belong to an ever-flowing river—of energy, of knowledge, of accumulated wisdom."

"Then why aren't we smart the second or third time around?"

"Some of us are. That's why I am certain we are our own ancestors! We do bring with us something from another age, another incarnation."

"That doesn't make sense. We're born stupid, almost without instincts, and we die whimpering in second childhood—"

"Some of us do. Some of us die violently—because we live violently."

"If you're going to start preaching, I'm not going to listen to you."

"We are not born with the wisdom accumulated in an early existence because of two traumas—the terrible shock of birth, the ordeal of death."

"Where'd you ever hear a word like trauma?"

"At Monticello. They used words there. It means a wounding, an injury, Trauma is a German word."

"My God. What did you do, listen at doors? No wonder they sold you off before you were ripe."

"Think about it, mastah. What might we know if we carried wisdom from former existences, facts one can never know without sad experience. What visions of past existence fade, blacked out in the terror of birth?"

"Did you know you're a boring individual?"

Cato shrugged. "At least, mastah, I took your mind off your own woes."

Richmond crouched along the banks of its swollen river, sending streets, roads and cow paths on aimless bias through the flavescent belly of the encroaching swampland. The streets rang with shouts, creaking of dry wheels,rumbling of wagons, pound of leather bootheels on plank walkways. Two-wheeled carts, loaded with cotton bales, tobacco or short logs, lumbered through the muddy thoroughfares. Riverboats rocked at anchor at its jack-built piers. It was a dank and somber town, its solemn people and its rude buildings were unprepossessing, ungracious toward outsiders, a phobia which would grow over the years. But Locke reminded himself emptily that in his jaundiced view it would be ugly were its streets paved with gold. It was not home.

"If it's all the same with you, mastah," Cato said as they threaded through the teeming main street, "let's find something to eat."

"I'm not hungry."

"Maybe you're not, mastah. But I ain't got my own grief to munch on. I got no broken heart to ruin my appetite. You've managed to go almost two days now without eating. I'm hungry."

"All right, damn you. Anything to stop your complaining." He turned his mount in before the Richmond Hotel. They swung down and loop-tied their mounts. "Stay here. I'll bring you out something."

"Sorry, mastah. I got a two-day hungery gnawing at my gizzard. I've waited for you before. I'll just go along with you."

Locke grinned coldly. "What makes you think they'll serve you in here?"

"I'm your body slave, mastah. I can go anywhere you can go. If you stand up for me."

Lock jerked his head, motioning Cato to follow him across the walk and into the hotel. The tavern room was crowded in the late morning. Many other guests had their body slaves in attendance, but these young blacks sat respectfully on a bench at the rear of the room.

Locked pushed his way to the bar, with Cato at his shoulder. Locke ordered two beers.

"We can't serve niggers, suh," the bartender said; men along the bar hesitated, waiting.

Locke ignored them. "Cato's not a nigger. He's my body servant. I want him served. I expect him to be served."

The bartender hesitated, then nodded. "We got only home-brewed beer and whiskey, suh."

Locke shrugged. "That's all right. It's wet, isn't it?"

"Wet and kicks like a mule. Just thought I ought to tell you. Every Virginian with any spine makes his own booze, suh."

"To sell unstamped, eh?"

The bartender smiled. "That's right. To sell. Untaxed. Taxes on a man's libations are an abomination, suh, not to be borne by self-respecting free men."

He pushed the two steins of beer across the damp bar. Locke handed the first mug to Cato, who took it and drank thirstily. The bartender watched him.

"Come a far piece, have you?" the bartender asked.

Locke shrugged. "Far enough to work up a thirst." He still had not touched the beer before him. "And a gut-aching hunger. Serve us two meals at one of those tables."

The bartender winced. "Yes, suh. But sit over in a corner with your nigger, will you? And close to a window? No sense offending my regular customers."

Locke met his eyes levelly. "Any of your customers get offended, friend, you direct them to me."

Cato sighed and grinned, satisfied . . .

* * *

He could never afterward say why he lingered in Richmond, loitering over brandy in the Richmond Hotel tavern, bored and finding nothing in common with those other plantation owners, secure in their God-granted elitism, and faithful to their gospel of misoneism. They lived, suspicious of strangers, intolerant of anything new, resisting all change, civil only to members of their own caste.

He was listless; unable to turn back, unwilling to put more miles between himself and Hidden Brook, though reason dictated early and unbroken flight. Perhaps unconsciously, he willed himself captured, arrested and returned home—even in irons. Home, that was the magic word; this was the malady robbing him of the will to pick up his existence.

He sat, glum and wordless at the table, while Cato wolfed down both their suppers.

They retired before nine to their room where a pallet had been thrown on the floor at the foot of his bed for Cato. The wide windows overlooked the barnyard, the stables and outhouse, but Locke stood unmoving there, as though the view looked out on Eden, long after Cato was snoring on the straw mattress.

He could not get Mary-Stuart out of his mind. He saw her enduring the tensions and sadness of her brother's funeral; he saw her heart hardening toward him; but most of all he saw her as she had been in his arms, her body opened to him, frantic with passion and desire and taut with hatred. She trailed after him in the darkness, like a faint trace of perfume, not quite tangible and yet inescapable.

He fixed his melancholy gaze on a bleak star winking against the damask dome of heaven. A remote pianist in some tavern exhumed the last wisps of sentiment from trivial ballads that belonged to everybody's yesterdays. The music ripped at him like talons, with every note pregnant with meaning and memory and melancholy nostalgia. He wished to hell that sound would cease, and yet he knew he'd be more lost than ever when it did.

He tilted back his head to keep the deep-welled tears from spilling along his drawn cheeks. Knowing it useless, he prayed silently, begging God and Satan together, and separately, for one word from Mary-Stuart, a sigh, a sign, a note, a message.

There was none. There would not be anything of her. He realized it could never be the same again, he would never have her anymore. Their love had burned hot, with a white-heat fierceness, but it was over, chilled, like the glint of some long-dead star.

He had seen that in her eyes, even as she clung most furiously to him.

He must have groaned slightly, or sobbed deep in his throat. Cato was instantly awake, levering himself up from his pallet with the corded muscles of his calves and thighs. "What's the mattah, suh?"

"Nothing. Go to sleep. I don't want to talk to you."

Cato padded barefoot across the thick, planed-oak flooring. He stood at Locke's shoulder a moment, staring out at the mists on the distant river. "What's wrong?"

"Nothing's wrong, you bastard. Everything's lovely." Locke's taut throat ached with such spasms of pain that he could hardly speak. His voice forced itself upward through choked-back grief; it sounded odd, as if he had *la grippe*, as if timbered with tears. "Go back to sleep."

"You can't keep running backward in your thoughts."

"When I can throw off my agony, I will. And without counsel from you."

Cato's voice raked him with scorn and reproach. "A grown man does not cry—even hidden in the dark."

"What the hell do you know?"

"I know what your father taught me—with a whip—when I wept in loneliness for Monticello: a man does not cry. A man takes what life hands him. He does what he must with what life gives him. Or takes from him. But he does not cry. Your father would be ashamed of you."

"Would he? Then the old man and I are quits. I'm ashamed of him. Disgraced by his memory."

"At least he didn't cry, no matter how badly he was hurt."

"He was like you, you bastard. He didn't cry for one good reason. He had no tears . . ."

They had breakfast the next morning in the hotel tavern around seven. Cato ate ravenously, uncertain when he'd get his feet under a table again. He consumed three slices of sugar-cured ham, three eggs, a stack of six pancakes and three mugs of coffee. Locke sipped his coffee black and, with some mild revulsion, watched his slave eat.

As Cato mopped up the last oozing of cane syrup from his plate, the stableboy appeared, hat in hand. "I brung your animals around front like you say, mastah-suh." He bobbed his head, staring at the scuffed tops of Locke's boots. "All fed, watered and rubbed down. Like you say. Yassuh."

Locke flipped the boy four bits and the black youth retreated, backing away, grinning.

"You trying to spoil that nigger, giving him real money?" Cato asked.

Locke stood up. He pulled his bonnet down on the side of his head in the rakish angle he wore it from old habit; he did not feel rakish.

Cato leaped to his feet, grabbing up four warm soda biscuits in his fists as he went. He belched loudly, glanced around guiltily and hurried out of the room behind Locke, his flat-brimmed hat, an ancient discard of Locke's father's, sitting back on his crimson-tinted black-matted head.

He smiled inwardly with some satisfaction, seeing the envy and admiration unwillingly heaped on him by the other black servants-for-life; they had eaten, without utensils, from tin plates at the kitchen door. They envied Cato; he had a master who stood up for him.

Cato put his shoulders back and widened his stride, walking out in Locke's wake.

The sun glittered hotly at eight in the morning. The street teemed with people, astir with commerce. As they crossed the board walk toward the hitching rail, both Locke and Cato hesitated, reacting as if they'd sensed, rather than heard, the whirring whistle of a rattlesnake.

A glint of reflected sunlight grabbed at them from across the street, a reflection and an unwarranted sense of wrong.

Gasping, Cato lunged forward, throwing himself in front of Locke as a flint-lock rifle exploded from a niche between buildings at a long angle across the street.

The thunder of the rifle stopped every man on the street. Some froze where they stood, others leaped for cover. A dray animal reared in its traces and the cartage driver stood up, whipping him frenetically.

Cato's shoulder caught Locke in the small of the back, sending him sprawling behind a watering trough at the curb.

The bullet struck like an incensed wasp, knocking Cato's hat ten feet along the walk. A man, stunned with fright, picked up the hat and simply stood holding it as if in a catatonic trance.

Cato caught his balance, swinging for a moment beneath the milling horses leashed to the slicked pole. He was already running toward the middle of the street by the time he gained his equilibrium.

The glinting reflection of sunlight was gone, but Cato did not slow down. He was almost in the middle of the rutted, hole-pocked street when Locke's yell stopped him, like a stone striking him in the back.

Cato stood poised in the middle of the road, bareheaded, legs apart.

"You damn fool!" Locke shouted. "Where the hell you think you're going—you're unarmed."

Cato winced, looking around, so filled with fury that he had not even hesitated long enough to realize he was chasing down an armed man with nothing more than his bare fists.

Across his shoulder, he saw Locke fighting a rifle from his saddle scabbard. Locke jerked the gun loose and ran out into the street, joining Cato.

Around them, life had not picked up its ordinary tempo yet. The onlookers remained where they'd stopped when the rifle exploded, but now they watched, withdrawn, curious.

Locke and Cato ran past drays and carts halted in the roadway and up on the boardwalk. The air-space between the two buildings was empty. There was no sign of the attacker.

Cato pushed between the buildings and ran to the rear of the alleyway. He hesitated there between the two stores and cautiously checked both ways. There was no one to be seen. The morning was suddenly exaggeratedly quiet and serene.

When Cato returned to the main street, he found Locke trying to get some description of the gunman.

"Didn't see nothin', mister."

"Didn't see, hear, or suspect nothin'—till that gun went off. . . . Hell's sake, mighty nigh kilt your nigger."

By the time they'd questioned a dozen bystanders on both sides of the street, Locke was seething with fury. A man had tried to kill him in broad morning sunlight, on the busiest street in the town, and not a living being had caught a glimpse of the assailant. The bastard walked among them carrying a flint-lock rifle—not an easy weapon to conceal!—and nobody had noticed or remarked him. Somewhere among these bland faces the killer padded, undetected, unsuspected, awaiting his next chance.

Swearing under his breath, Locke strode back to where his horses and pack animal awaited him. Cato followed quietly, looking around warily, searching the street, the windows, the alleyways.

Cato's voice raked at Locke. "And now somebody's been sent to kill you, mastah."

"Somebody who walks around unseen," Locke said in mocking disbelief.

Cato grinned. "Maybe an angel of God."

"With a long rifle?"

"God moves in mysterious ways, mastah." Cato plodded along, moving his horse almost even with Locke's. The slave rode at a respectful pace and yet close enough to shield him.

Locke glanced both ways along the street, watching the walks as they headed toward the town limits, going south.

"A man lives by the sword—" Cato began.

"Listen, Cato. Don't make me hate you this early in the morning. I have a warm feeling toward you. Let's leave it that way for a few miles, anyhow. I am in your debt."

"Of course you are—mastah."

"You saved my life. I can't forget that."

"I do hope not—mastah."

Locke half turned in the saddle, staring at him. Cato's black hat sported a ragged hole in brim and crown. He exhaled heavily but did not mention it. "All right. You saved my life. Now you're doing your damnedest to turn it all to clabber. I suppose you think I owe you something."

Cato grinned. "You could set me free."

"Set you free? What in hell would you do if you were a freed black man in Virginia?"

"I don't know. Why don't we try to find out?"

"You might as well forget it, Cato. You're my slave for life. And forget the notion I owe you anything. I don't owe you a damned farthing."

Cato shrugged. "It's your life—mastah."

"Hell, boy, you did nothing more than any other faithful nigger slave ought to do. I'll thank you, for whatever inconvenience or discomfort you suffered. I might even buy you a new hat. But as for anything else, forget it. I owe you nothing."

This settled satisfactorily, the slave silenced, Locke sank his heels into the shanks of his horse, speeding it south toward Charleston. He did glance around just once in a while to check his back trail.

— VIII —

THEY RODE warily. They could sense the unseen presence of that mysterious assassin trailing them. Days seemed breathless in the mosquito-infested lowlands. The nights were haunted by unexplained, inexplicable sounds. They passed few travelers on the deep-ribbed traces; those they encountered they watched suspiciously, spoke with guardedly, departed from quickly. They turned often, drawn around by a sudden sound only to find an empty road stretching behind them. Indian summer blazed through the forests and put its torch to the trees, singeing leaves and foliage, spreading cerise and tan and magenta like molten flame across the hammocks.

The killer crept silently behind them. Though they never saw him, they knew he was there, relentless on their trail. No matter how clever their ruses, they found no sign, caught no trace of him. But he stalked them and they paused often, holding their breath, to listen. A sudden noise cracked loudly in the pastoral silence, but when they drew rein, all activity, all sound seemed to cease. No fowl or wild animals stirred in the thickets. They could discern no telltale throb of horses' hooves behind them. But the hired slayer was there, watching, waiting, chosing his own moment to strike.

They spurred their horses, riding fast, then slowed suddenly. Nothing. They set traps, with Cato plodding forward leading the pack animal, Locke concealed in an obscuring copse beside the trail.

Alone, Locke slumped in his saddle and listened. He heard nothing but the odd throb of his own heart, the erratic tempo of his own breathing. No sound, no shadow of movement showed on the twisting trail. It was as if the world of the swamps held its breath with him.

He was devoured by clouds of mosquitoes, attacked by deer flies, but though he sat patiently, with insects stinging him, sweated, aching with tension, no one appeared on the back trail. If that slayer were back there, the very undergrowth had swallowed him.

Locke exhaled heavily. The troubling sense of imminent danger persisted.

He was back there, all right.

He gave up at last, urged the horse up on the trail and galloped full-tilt until he overtook Cato on the road. Cato looked at him questioningly.

Locke swung his arm in defeat. "Found no sign of him."

"He's back there."

"He's smarter than we are."

As he did every question, Cato had been giving this matter much thought, deep cerebration. "Maybe. Maybe not. So far, he has proved only one thing. He is a paid assassin. A hired killer. He has trailed his quarry many times before. He is not going to be panicked into making a mistake."

"That doesn't make me feel a hell of a lot better."

"Still, you know you are dealing with a professional."

"Hell, I knew that the first time he shot at me."

They could not rest and in the next eternal days and nights the whole silent world became a haunted place.

It was as if their own minds played tricks on them. Suddenly, both would hear horses' hooves behind them, but admitted ruefully they were spooked because when they drew rein and listened, breathless, any sound ceased on that back trail.

Locke shivered in the oppressive heat, sweat forming in marbles at his armpits and then running in icy trickles along his ribs. One thing, the threat of danger, his own wariness, kept Mary-Stuart from his mind—sometimes he went as long as twenty minutes without thinking back to her.

They kept plodding forward cautiously, letting their horses follow the tortuous twists of the ill-defined trace.

"We keep looking back," Locke said with a sour smile. "He could easily go around us in the night and ambush us from ahead."

Cato considered this, then shrugged. "You encourage a conniving, unforgiving type enemy—mastah."

Locke exhaled. "Somebody wants me dead, all right. But who?"

"Why don't you pick a name from the Virginia tax rolls?"

Locke smiled tautly. "Why don't you go to hell?"

"You mean this ain't hell—mastah?"

"Who hired that killer? A professional like that wouldn't come cheap. Might even work for the government. Who sent him? Who wants me out of the way bad enough to pay so dear for it?"

Cato shrugged. "We'll find that out when we find your friend back there."

"Unless he finds us first."

"Even so."

At the first glimpse of Charleston, sprawled along the rim of its own mammoth natural harbor, Locke felt a sense of exultance. He had won a victory of sorts. He hadn't settled the war of nerves between him and the man stalking him, but he had won a battle, temporarily at least. He had triumped over that skulking wraith who pursued them with such diabolical cleverness; he had defeated the days and nights of watchful tensions and broken, restless sleep, the swamplands, the forests, the wild nightmares plaguing his own mind. Charleston. Even though that assassin had struck in Richmond, Locke felt a vague safety among other people. He and Cato must remain vigilant, but they had outwitted the killer out there in the dark wilderness.

Charleston stood in its urban glory, already almost 150 years old, a haughtily regal aging dowager of a city, with the spice and variety of Irish, French and English towns about her. Her streets were paved, her markets clearly defined, her mansions snobbishly walled, her great oaks dripping moss older than the republic. Named for King Charles II of England, the community had reigned as capital of South Carolina until about forty years ago. Unlike many seaboard towns settled by sects and zealously guarded against outside intrusion, Charleston was—if reluctantly—a melting pot. Ten years after the English established the port at the confluence of the Cooper and Ashley rivers as a port of call for its man-of-wars and trading vessels, French Huguenots arrived, followed in the middle of the next century by thousands of Acadian refugees. During the Revolutionary War, captured by the British, with the Union Jack flying in defiant regalness everywhere, the site became home for Irish-impressed seamen who jumped ship, Italian fishermen, homeless Indians, enslaved and freed blacks. Each race, each nationality, each group engraved its own ethnic imprint, erecting magnificent edifices honoring its own gods—St. Michael's, the Huguenot church, the colonists' powder magazine.

They found the narrow streets crowded with carriages, black vendors, carts loaded with cotton and wagons piled high with truck crops. People hurried in the mild sunlight, entering and leaving buildings, loitering along the walks. Locke suddenly found himself suffering a stifling sense of being hemmed in, trapped, vulnerable. Among these stranger's faces he would never recognize the killer's—until it was too late.

"We'll go down to the docks," he said across his shoulder. "Book passage on the first southbound ship out of here."

Cato shrugged. "My only duty on this earth. Go where you command, mastah."

An open cabriolet clattered by, a sparklingly polished vehicle, drawn by two smartly brushed and high-stepping horses and driven by a high-hatted Negro coachman in rust-black suit, his chin tilted toward the sky. In facing seats of the carriage tonneau was gathered a bouquet of lovely young girls, their laughter as bright as their pastel frocks, their faces fresh and enchanting, their bodies supplely rounded and graceful, under their dainty parasols.

Locke stared as the carriage approached. The girls glanced at him, looked again briefly, giggled and lowered their gazes becomingly. Then shyly they looked up once more in a game stylized and conventional. Ignoring custom which demanded that he remain formally civil, Locke grinned mockingly and bowed deeply. They caught their breath and looked away, as if shocked by his crude behavior. He grinned after them.

"Well, it's good to see your heart is mended," Cato said. "You're well enough at least to ogle the women again."

Locke smiled. "I'd never go to the Louvre and not pay humblest homage to its masterworks of art on display, Cato."

"Anyway, you're recovering."

"You're not as wise as you think, boy. No matter what happens inside me, life goes on. That's all. I've lived long enough to learn that."

In the busy downtown, Locke reined in and tied his horse at a metal hitching post. He jerked his head, ordering Cato to follow.

They crossed the walk and entered a quietly aloof hat shop. The store smelled of new and imported fabrics, furs, and old money. Shelves of stylish male chapeaux lined both sides of the narrow rectangular space. Hats were advantageously placed on glass-top cases, on racks and on tables. A middle-aged man in frock coat, striped trousers, highly polished boots and four-in-hand tie, crossed the deep carpeting to greet them.

"Looking to buy a new hat," Locke said.

The clerk smiled obsequiously. Though Locke's jacket and trousers were travel-streaked, rumpled and fading, there was about him an indefinable air of the gentry. The clerk knew his clientele. Travel was an uncomfortable, unpleasant affair at best and few arrived in Charleston looking better than bedraggled.

"Of course, sir. Your head size, sir?"

"It's not for me." Locke jerked his head toward his body slave. "It's for him."

The clerk's face flushed red to the roots of his hair. "Your slave, sir?"

"That's right. Something nice. Something with flair."

"But, sir. It's none of my business. A new hat—our style—you'll forgive me, our prices—for a nigger?"

"I didn't ask the price, did I?"

"No, sir. You didn't. But I must remind you. This is a very exclusive shop. Patronized by the very best people of Charleston."

"I'm sure it is. Now, if you'll help me pick out a hat—"

"Sir. I apologize for presuming. But one does not buy new hats for his slave. One gives him cast-offs—"

"He's got one of those." Locke indicated the bullet-torn hat in Cato's hands.

"Perhaps you'd care to buy something nice and give him yours—"

"It wouldn't fit him."

"Pardon me, sir, but is that important, whether it fits him or not?"

"It is to me. Now, let's look at something."

"Sir, if you insist upon wasting your money—after all, it is your own substance, and I would not presume to tell you how to spend it—"

"I appreciate that."

"Still, sir, we don't sell hats to niggers."

"*I'm* buying the hat."

"Still, if he wears one of our hats on the streets of Charleston. It could—harm our impeccable reputation, sir."

"You'd rather pass up a sale than see a black wear one of your hats?"

"We have our reputation to think about, sir. And, too, there is the matter of cost. . . . It would be a waste of money when you could buy your man a perfectly suitable work hat at the general store down the block."

"If that's what I'd wanted, I'd have gone there." Coldly, Locke glanced toward Cato. "What sort of bonnet you think you'd fancy, Cato?"

The clerk breathed sharply, as if in pain. "I'll sell him a hat, sir. But he can't try them on . . . I can't permit that."

"Then you better measure his head and be sure the one he selects is right," Locke said. "He's going to have a good-looking hat when we leave here, even if it ruins your whole goddamn day."

The clerk winced, tried to smile. He glanced toward the front door as if praying no other customers would enter during this trying transaction. "Have your boy pick out the style," the clerk said. "I'll see if we have it in his size."

"You'll have his size," Locke said negligently. "Because we'll keep looking until you do."

"Always fancied one of them Panama planter's hats,

mastah,'' Cato said, gazing on the flat-crowned, wide-brimmed hat gleaming on the glass-top counter. The chapeau sported a small bright green feather. Locke grinned and nodded.

The clerk looked ill. ''Your man would endanger his life striding around this town in a planter's hat. Not even freed niggers dare do that. Why white people would stone him for his haughty airs.''

Locke gestured downward lazily. ''Maybe not. Cato's a good-looking man. He may make your hat look good. Business might improve. Except he's much bigger, he bears some resemblance to the former President Jefferson, don't you think?''

The clerk's face went pale. ''Please, sir, I must ask you not to be so disrespectful to that great man.'' Hands trembling, the clerk extended a gleaming new planter's hat toward Cato. Cato set his shabby headpiece on the glass-top case. Accidentally, the clerk knocked it to the floor with his elbow.

Cato did not notice. He set the white hat at an angle on his head and strode toward the mirror. He gazed at himself for a long time.

Locke counted out gold eagles on the counter. ''I think he likes it,'' he said to the clerk.

Cato swung around, laughing. ''Lawsy, it's beautiful. Truly beautiful. I'll turn the head of every woman I see . . . mastah.''

Locke and Cato left their horses and gear at a livery stable. They walked along the street to the nearest tavern, conscious of people reacting to Cato's new hat. Negroes grinned, showing the whites of their eyes and glittering teeth. White men winced, as if their teeth were set suddenly on edge. Locke ignored them and Cato strode as his shadow, shoulders erect, handsome head back, the tiny green feather winking in his hatband.

He removed his hat and held it in his hands when they entered the saloon. Locke bought each of them a drink. Cato downed his, but Locke left his glass untouched. He motioned with his head and Cato followed him out a rear exit.

They headed via side streets and alleyways toward the docks. Locke felt reasonably certain that he had managed to depart the saloon undetected by the paid assassin who stalked them, no matter how closely the killer kept them under surveillance. No new customers had entered the tavern in the time between their ordering drinks and their hasty departure out a rear entrance. Nevertheless, as they approached the harbor, he found himself unable to resist glancing across his shoulder.

Along the heavy-beamed piers, seagoing vessels from every port laid to, or stood in the roads, riding at anchor. Beyond them, strung together like cheap beads, keelboats, flatboats and river craft of every description bobbled like floats where they'd unloaded their cargo. The smell of the sea struck Locke on a blustery east wind and mixed with the stink of decaying fish, fresh paints and naval stores added to the aromas of high-piled merchandise waiting to be loaded—tobacco, cotton, lumber, raw hides, salted meats, rums and tars.

With Cato at his shoulder, Locke inquired about immediate sailings, found many brigantines, three-masters and schooners bound with the next tide for Europe, Morocco, South Africa, the Scandanavian waters, but none calling at Florida ports.

"Business is bad down that way. And there's danger from the freebooters still operating out of Amelia Island. Every time the British or us Americans hangs a slave-stealer or a pirate, a dozen more slip out to take his place. A man needs a cargo bad to take a consignment south of Savannah," the port master said. "You'll find most honest captains sailing wide of the Spanish Floridas, the Bermudas and the Keys."

"Hell, I don't need an honest skipper, so much as one going my way," Locke said. "I've no interest in his cargo or his destination and I'm willing to pay a fair price to get me and my man to Florida."

The balding official nodded. "Then your man is Captain Alexander Arbuthnot."

Some old warning memory flickered across Locke's mind. "Arbuthnot, eh? Is he in port?"

"You know Arbuthnot, do you?"

Locke shrugged. He was well-enough informed about the aging Scotsman to refuse to acknowledge any acquaintance in law-abiding society. "You said he might be sailing for Florida," he said noncommittally.

The harbor master agreed. "Arbuthnot is the skipper of the

Chance." The man waved his arm toward the wide windows overlooking the harbor. "A fine schooner, standing in the roads yonder. You can see her plain from the window. Myself, I'd go overland to Florida before I'd sail with Arbuthnot. They say he don't hire sailors, but cutthroats. A desperate adventurer and, they also say, not only a freebooter and trader in anything from gold to slaves, but a friend of them runaway Indians down there in Spanish Florida. They tell me he trafficks with them red men down there. I wouldn't trust his oath. But I'm sure he'd sell you passage on the *Chance* south to Florida. An' if he don't decide to have your throat cut for your valuables, you should make it—sooner or later. He's an excellent skipper. None can say he ain't. So there is your ship, Spanish Florida-bound . . . for the rest I can say no more."

Locke laughed. "You know all the ills there are to know about Alexander Arbuthnot—"

"Not all! I doubt any man—alive—knows all his evil."

"Do you happen to know also where we might find the gentleman?"

"At this hour? Aye. You'll find Captain Arbuthnot at any of the groghouses along the piers. He loves his libations, but he hates to walk very far on dry land."

Within the hour, Locke sat face to face with Alexander Arbuthnot in a small, beer-sodden groghouse a short stroll from the brink of the sea where his dinghy bobbed, strung to a post. Locke introduced himself, and Arbuthnot, after giving him a glance with some puzzlement in it, or the vagary of ill-served memory, shrugged and invited him to sit down.

Arbuthnot offered him a cool drink of peach brandy which was too sweet for Locke's appetite and a "chaw of real old Virginy cake." But Locke declined this also; he had never developed a taste for chewing tobacco.

Arbuthnot spat expertly, ringing the inner rim of the nearest brass spittoon. The skipper of the *Chance* slumped, like lard melting over both sides of his chair, an enormous-bellied man, short of breath, with decaying red hair, splotched scalp, sun-bleached blue eyes and a thick red beard, carefully and lovingly trimmed. His burring voice came right off the high crags and wild moors of heather-brushed Scotland. He looked as if he'd been drinking for hours; his shirt waist was sweated and sour, sweat glistened on his thick red neck and in the graying hairs of his chest. A battered officer's cap crouched beside his elbow on the table, looking like a greasy dead cat. When a waiter brought new rounds for them both, Arbuthnot insisted on pledging allegiance to the United States, respect to George Washington and hope for the prosperity of the American commonwealth.

"You've not sought me out to exchange pleasantries," Arbuthnot said finally. "I vow you've come to me with a business deal of some sort. Out with it, my fine young man, you'll never find one more reasonable to deal with, nor a man more understanding of the vagaries of this here life."

"I wish to book passage aboard your ship to Spanish Florida, Captain. For me and my servant."

"What servant is that?"

Locke gestured toward Cato, where he slouched on a bench along the smoke-blackened wall, his white planter's hat held delicately before him in both hands. Arbuthnot studied the black man a long moment, seemed entirely and secretly pleased about something. "Your slave, eh? So I'm dealing with the gentry, am I?"

"Will that affect your decision to sell us passage?"

"Nothing affects that decision, lad, but the price. I set a price. You are willing—and able—to pay it, you got a cabin, clean and comfortable, good food and a safe passage."

"I'll pay it."

Arbuthnot's head came up. "Like that, eh? Without even a hesitation to hear the price? What's the matter—you kilt somebody? You on the run?"

Locke breathed deeply. It wasn't that Arbuthnot was suspicious; the skipper of the *Chance* seldom dealt with ordinary tourists. "Let's just say I'm anxious enough to get to Florida to meet any reasonable price."

"Aye! Let's just say that." Arbuthnot tossed off the remains of his brandy, slapped down the mug on the table and, in the reverberating thunder, ordered more. "Your servant, at your biding, Mister Locke."

"When are you planning to sail?"

Arbuthnot grinned widely. "You are in a shove, aren't you? Huh? Out with it, sir. You're among friends here, no matter what you've done."

"Let's just say I want to go quietly—without being listed on your roll of passengers, without being seen boarding your ship if that is at all possible."

"That can be arranged, too." Then the officer hesitated. "Though it'll cost you extra. You can't fault me. You're the one buyin' stealth, ain't you? Can't complain that I make whatever profit from it I can, eh? A man has to git along in this hard world, eh, Mister Locke?"

"I'll pay extra."

"Ah." The captain laughed. "To be sure. No haggling. A man that makes his decisions clean and open. To be sure! A man after my own tastes. A man with more in his heart and mind than he's willing to trust on his tongue."

"I'll be honest with you, Captain Arbuthnot. Not enough that you might want to turn me in for a reward. If there were such a reward—"

"I see you think me a rogue. And a man who makes a bargain with a rogue proves only himself the fool, eh?"

"Some man, or men, are on my trail and I want to travel swiftly and quietly beyond their reach. And I would like them not even to know I was headed south."

"And you think to be safe in Florida?"

Locke exhaled. "Safe enough. Who's ever safe in this life? Anyway, I have business there."

"Do you now?" Arbuthnot narrowed his sun-braised eyes and peered closely at Locke. "Did I never meet you before, mate?"

"Not that I recall."

"At sea maybe?"

"I have been to sea."

"Aye! I'll wager you have. Maybe we've met—on Amelia Island?"

"I would remember you."

"Aye! I'm not an easy man to forget, eh? Well, it's settled then . . . three hundred in gold for you. A hundred for your nigger—he'll eat scraps from the galley and bunk in a hammock along with the cabin boys."

"He can sleep in my cabin."

Arbuthnot drew his tongue along his teeth, nodding. "That's your own taste, sir. I ask no questions . . . I make no judgments. Been a long time at sea . . . met every oddity in this life, I'd wager—a time or two at least."

"All right. Four hundred."

"In gold."

"In gold. When can we come aboard?"

"How say you to the hour around dawn? We sail on the high tide, promised for eight hundred hours in the morning. You and your nigger come to the landing there—I'll have a boat on hand to meet you."

"I'll pay you when we come aboard," Locke said.

"Aye! We can stand that. Want to make certain we don't forget and sail without you, eh? You sure you never sailed in Florida waters?"

Locke shrugged, and with that the bargain was struck, their passage assured. Arbuthnot reached out and touched the fabric of Locke's sleeve. "There's this one last thing. Mister Locke. You named no port in Florida. Nor did I. Say this. I'll put you off in a Florida port. A reasonable place, but a site of my own choosing." He laughed. "You ain't the only one, lad, with more in his heart than his tongue can say. Eh? Eh? Huh? God bless America. Eh?"

Locke found lodging for himself and Cato in the seamen's inn upstairs over the same alehouse where Captain Arbuthnot remained, drinking at his table. The room was small, dingy, a fleabag, though Cato doubted a self-respecting flea would be caught dead in it. "The bedbugs would chase the fleas."

"It's just for the night," Locke said. He had sunk into a fearful lassitude. "I want a room where I can watch the *Chance*. Captain Arbuthnot looks the nervous sort who might change his plans quicker than his shirt."

Yawning with fatigue induced by inner distress, Locke sagged into a chair beside the single window which overlooked the cobbled street, the piers and the sea lanes beyond. The *Chance* rode quietly at anchor, her running lights glowing warmly in the darkness and reflected in the sea. Locke found himself studying the men who strolled that street below him, entered its buildings or left them.

He didn't know what he sought. A man who'd tried to kill him. This was all he knew. An unknown man. A man he wouldn't recognize if he met him face to face. A man hired by someone who hated him furiously enough to want him dead? Who?

Locke shuddered visibly at the answer he was adducing inside his own mind, an answer that was spreading like a virus, infecting and debilitating him. From the moment that assassin had fired from across that Richmond street, a terrible conviction, too heartbreaking to face, too fearful to dismiss, had been building in his mind. He began to believe—through a process of elimination—that Mary-Stuart hated him enough to want him dead. She could have—perhaps through friends of her father—sent this man to kill him. This heartbreaking thought made no sense, but it was the only answer, as agonizing and horrible as it was. Mary-Stuart believed he had killed her brother. He had violated her in the very room where her beloved brother's body lay in its casket. Wasn't this enough to unhinge even the most stable-minded of beings? Was Mary-Stuart not mindless with grief, with hatred, with the need to strike out? She knew he had headed south. She could have sent a man to kill him, to even the desperate score between them.

The horror of this conviction was bitter and repellent to him, hardly to be borne. It could not be that Mary-Stuart, even in madness, could swing from protected, angelic young girl to a woman with murder in her heart. The thought stunned his senses, broke his heart. But only in her hatred—that terrible reverse side of the coin of her passionate love for him—could he find a reasonable motive for anyone's sending a man hired to track him down and kill him without a word.

He shuddered, unwilling to believe, and doubting, yet unable to deny the savage logic of it. Mary-Stuart's emotions were volatile—she loved passionately and she would hate as violently, with all her mind and heart and body and soul. She believed him guilty of murdering her brother. To her grieved mind he had showed himself callous enough to stride in and rape her in the very room where her brother lay dead. He may be by now such an object of violent hatred that it must gall her like wormwood to think he lived and walked abroad while her beloved brother lay dead—at his hands.

Cato complained of hunger. Locke stirred himself from lethargy and sick, paralyzing horror, long enough to plod down the steps and bring his slave hot food from the alehouse below.

Then, fully dressed, too agonized to sleep, too exhausted with the debilitating fever of horror and regret and loss to endure the ugly whirling of his own thoughts, he fell across the bed. The sounds of the alehouse ebbed sometime after midnight, and the sounds from the docks died, and finally he slept.

He never afterward knew how long he slept, or what woke him. He slept fitfully, woke for long hurting moments and then slipped into unconscious depths again. Once, he was aware that Cato had curled up on a pad on the floor at the foot of his bed, that the dark street was empty, that he cried out deep inside to Mary-Stuart, and then plunged into sleep again, like a man escaping himself when he can no longer exist inside his own skin, live with his own thoughts, endure his own loss and self-hatred.

He stirred on the mattress. What wakened him? A mouse whispering in the wall, the tide breeze stirring curtains at the window, a sick and terrible premonition of horror?

He bit his lip to keep from crying out. He swam up from the numbing depths of sleep as if through thick green slime that choked him and held him down.

Chilled, terrorized without knowing why, he opened his eyes and stared upward at the masked face of the black-hatted man bent over him, long-bladed hunting knife poised to rip upward into him.

— IX —

THE MASKED man drew his arm to plunge the knife upward into Locke's belly.

Locke gasped. He bit back a yell of terror, as if mired in a nightmare, and tried to roll away on the bed. His attacker caught his belt buckle in an oversized left fist, lifting him in a stunningly easy motion.

At that instant, Cato sprang up from the mat at the foot of the bed. Cato growled, in atavistic roar that evoked the avenging spirits of his ancestors from ancient tamarisks, kraals and baobabs.

The killer stopped. He jerked his head around. His sharp intake of breath tightened the fabric of his mask across his mouth. For that instant, stunned, he stared at Cato.

Locke acted in that providential second of respite. He had one chance to stay alive. He clutched at it. Rather than trying to break free of the big man's viselike grasp, Locke lunged toward him. He drove the extended fingers of his left hand toward the eyes glittering between hat brim and mask. When the man's head lunged backward instinctively, Locke struck him across the throat with the side of his hand. A fearful rupturing sound rasped from the man's parted lips.

The fist loosened on Locke's buckle. As the man retreated, Cato snagged his wrist and twisted with mindless strength—a hatred building through frustrating days and sleepless nights on that trail south—and the man dropped the long-bladed knife and gurgled in helpless agony, as if trying to cry out but unable to force air through his crippled windpipe.

Almost as the knife clattered on the floor, Cato caught it up in his fist.

The man staggered backward, striking the wall so heavily that everything in the room shook. Off balance, he turned, trying to claw his way through the open window.

Cato was on him like a cat.

As Locke came off the bed, he paused, wincing. He stood, poised, as Cato drove the knife blade into the man's side—once, twice, three times.

The man sagged like a croker sack of potatoes against the wall. Cato waited, but he slumped unmoving.

"I'll light a lamp," Locke said.

He struck a long sulphur-headed match and lit the wick of the lamp. When he turned, holding the light in his hand, Cato groaned.

The slave hurled the knife so it struck the wall, imbedded and quivering there. Cato stood, round-shouldered, staring down at the masked man crouched like a clump of clay.

Cato's voice shook with self-hatred. "Now I've—killed a man," he said.

Locke exhaled. "Welcome to the club."

"I never killed a man. Up close like that before."

"He meant to kill me, Cato. He would have killed you. If he'd known you were sleeping on the floor down there."

"That's what man is—a vicious animal. He can kill another man, but he can't give back life."

Locke spoke gently. "You didn't make the rules, Cato."

Cato remained standing for a long time, sick with anguish. Locke held the lamp so the light sprayed across the dead man. "Wonder who he is?"

"He's the man I killed."

"Put it out of your mind, Cato. God will forgive you."

"How do you know?"

"If there is a God, He will forgive you."

"I can't believe God can forgive—taking another man's life."

"You didn't invite him up here to kill him, Cato. He came around."

"I went insane. I couldn't stop. I was like an animal—"

"Sure. You were no better than any other man. No better than I am, Cato. . . . Hell, we're all tarred with the same stick. All of us. He pushed us until we killed him, Cato. We didn't want to. We had to. Somebody sent him to kill us." Locke shuddered at the thought of who must have hired this assassin. "Let's find out who he is."

Cato remained standing where he was, round-shouldered, empty-bellied, sick inside. He had killed a man and he would not recover from the horror of it for a long time.

Locke bent over the dead man. A thorough search revealed nothing except two gold eagles, a pouch of cigarette tobacco and paper. The man carried no wallet, no identification, no letters, no scrap of self. There was not a clue as to who he was, where he came from.

Locke exhaled heavily, relieved, almost glad that he did not know who had hired this slayer; perhaps would never know now.

He remained on his knees. "I've heard about these hired assassins before," he said in a low, musing tone. "Men who belong nowhere, to no one. Governments secretly hire them to rid themselves of unmanageable rivals, or to assassinate uncooperative heads of alien and even allied states. . . . I've heard about them. I never saw one before."

Cato sighed. "Only thing we know about him—maybe all we'll ever know—he's a Yankee."

"A Yankee?"

"Only a Yankee wouldn't know a Southerner's slave sleeps at the foot of his bed. When he saw me he thought he was looking at the devil himself."

"I know the feeling." Locke pulled down the mask from the slayer's broad nose, but he had never, that he recalled, seen that grayed, swarthy face before. The eyes, as empty as a church on Tuesday, glittered flatly in the lamplight.

Cato said, "What will we do with him?"

Locke straightened, standing. He placed the lamp on the table beside him. He was aware he was sweating, trembling, as reaction set in. He shrugged. "We'll leave him here."

Cato hefted the man's ankles, Locke lifted him by the shoulders and they heaved the corpse upon the bed, rolled him on his back, fixed the covers over him. Locke even folded the man's arms across his chest. "Sleep well, you son of a bitch."

He blew out the lamp. They stood for a moment in the darkness and then went out into the dimly lit corridor and down the steps to the street.

A longboat from the *Chance* glided into the dockside a little after five that morning. Two oarsmen and a helmsman spoke to them in hushed voices, helping them from barnacled ladder into the belly of the dinghy. Slapping of water against pilings was the loudest sound in the deep darkness before dawn.

The sea, from which Locke had escaped with a sense of relief and determination never to return, welcomed him like an alluring mistress. The smell of open water, the sharp stink of tar and paint, the heated smell of the food simmering in the galley, it was as if he were coming home again. He stood for a long moment on the deck, his legs apart, his wide shoulders back.

A cabin boy touched his arm. "If you and your man will follow me, sir. Captain Arbuthnot says welcome aboard the

Chance. He hopes you have a pleasant voyage, sir, and enjoy your elegant accommodations."

They pursued the skinny youth down a ladder into a breathless companionway. The boy opened a door upon a crib about six feet wide and no more than eight feet deep. A single porthole opened upon the sea. There was room for two stacked bunks, a straight chair, a table lashed to the bulkhead.

"My God." Cato whispered.

Locke laughed. He tossed the cabin boy a silver dollar. "Is this Captain Arbuthnot's idea of elegant quarters?"

The boy grinned, showing dark gaping places in his discolored teeth. "Elegant quarters. Them's the captain's words, sir. Not mine. But this I can vouch for. They are as good as any aboard this here schooner. Not even the captain's quarters is much roomier."

Locke nodded. He hadn't anticipated that the *Chance* wasted much thought or space to the niceties of life. The schooner was a trader's vessel, and every inch was set aside for cargo—whatever fate dictated that might be!—to return money to her owners. "My compliments to the captain. These quarters are indeed luxurious. They will do fine."

"Better than being in jail," Cato said. "Yet much like it in many ways."

When the boy was gone, Cato lapsed into silence. He sagged upon the chair and stared at the floor. Locke started to speak to him, then changed his mind. He went out on deck.

He found little to reassure him in the sullen faces of the crew. They did not speak to him, glanced toward him only when it was unavoidable. He shook his head. Captain Arbuthnot had recruited from the ratholes of this universe for his able seamen. He asked a great deal more of them than manning helms, jibbing the sprit staysails, running out lines or tying off the halyards.

As the tide crested and began its outward run, the anchor was pulled in and washed down, the fore, main and mizzen masts were hoisted less than two points off wind to give the sleek ship a smooth run out of the harbor and beyond the shoals.

Locke stood at the railing. He watched the land drift away behind him. A sense of terrible melancholy enveloped him. He could not escape the fearful suspicion that Mary-Stuart, deranged by grief and hatred, had dispatched that killer to track him down. The thought of it made him ill, yet he admitted all was forever over and dead between them.

Nevertheless, Locke thought of Mary-Stuart, even when he was certain he was fated not to see her again. He remembered her beautiful body, fiery with passion, in his arms. He recalled the gentle music in her laughther. He thought of the tears he'd left her to shed, for a dead brother, for a blighted romance that had informed their lives since they were children. She had often run away from Felicity Manor to come to him at Hidden Brook. And he had repaid her by breaking her heart, attacking her, and running away like some scurrilous sneak in the night. He clenched his fists at his sides, felt his eyes brim with tears, his throat choke and ache.

Beside him the sea seemed to run past in a swift bright current against the plankings of the sleek vessel. Far ahead, thick cumulus clouds boiled, like rusted tubs against a gray sky. The ocean darkened and the swells rolled higher. The *Chance* continued to plough across the cresting waves, headed east.

From the deck above him, Captain Arbuthnot's voice hailed him. "Find your quarters comfortable?"

Locke stared up at the captain and grinned. "As long as I don't try to turn around with the door closed."

"You won't spend much time in there," the captain shouted against the wind and the slapping of the sails. "Plenty of room to sleep in or die comfortably in. Eh?"

Locke nodded, watching the sea darken around them. The captain laughed. "Knew you'd spent time at sea. Minute I laid eyes on you. Beat me if I ain't seen you someplace before. . . . Got your sea legs in a hurry, eh?"

Within three hours they were shuddering under the violent pitching and tossing of the sea. Locke returned to his cabin to find Cato violently ill. The slave had tried to vomit in the thunder chamber, but as the vessel yawed and rolled, as the stench rose from the pot, his own sour stinking discharge increased his agony and his wish to die. He was certain the ships timbers would buckle under pressures of storm winds and high water, and the ship would flounder and sink. He hoped so.

Locke stayed on deck as much as possible, but with the

rough seas and the screaming of the wind, he had to fight to keep his footing, grip tightly to keep from being swept overboard.

The *Chance* continued outward bound. The cook was unable to prepare food in the galley; they existed on cold side meat and fruit for the first two days. Gradually, the weather subsided. Cabin boys swabbed the stateroom and Cato got weakly to his feet. He still hated the sea with all his heart, but he always had, he always would. At least he could stand up like a man, even if he felt weaker than a mewling child.

He fell asleep at last, oblivious to the shouts and cries going on outside, the clatter of untensils in the galley, the creak and groan of square-rigged sails and their sheets. He curled up on the top bunk, praying that when he wakened they would be in Florida waters. He vowed aloud that if he ever got off this ship, they'd have to burn the world and sift the ashes to find him and bring him aboard again.

On the third day, Cato awoke ravenously hungry. He needed a bath, he needed fresh clothing, he needed dry land, but his hunger was most immediate.

Laughing at him, Locke brought him a tray of food from the galley, and sagged on the chair, watching him wolf down the eggs and pancakes.

Suddenly the door was thrown open. Both Locke and Cato looked up, taut. The memory of the man who'd trailed them from Richmond was still hot in their minds.

The man in the open doorway stopped, his eyes widening. "You got this cabin, man?" The voice was clipped, British, and so accented the words were less than clear. "They didn't tell me the other passenger was a black."

Locke stood up from the chair. "I'm the other passenger. This is my servant Cato." He met the laughing blue-gray eyes levelly. "Who are you?"

"Just told you, old chum. I'm the other passenger. There's two of us this trip. Well, three, counting him." He inclined his head toward Cato.

The young man remained unmoving for the moment in the open hatchway, carefully inventorying Cato and his master. After a moment he smiled, warmly and engagingly. "Robert Harmbrister here, fellows," he said.

Harmbrister appeared to be about Locke's age, and equal in

height. He was even thinner than Jerry, with fair wavy hair; he appeared cultured, good-looking, patrician in bearing, a rakehell by inclination with sharp-hewn features, tilted head and a go-to-hell smile.

When Locke didn't speak at once, Harmbrister laughed. "And you're Jeremiah Locke, of Virginia."

"How did you know that? I've not even told the captain my name."

"Oh? Didn't you? Forgive me, chap. It's downright bloody habit, finding out whatever I have to know. My training. One can't go against his training very well, eh?"

"I don't know." Locke watched his guest narrowly. "What is your training?"

"Now that's a good question, Mr. Locke. A downright pertinent and sharp-minded question, that is. I've had training in so many things—"

"You mentioned snooping to learn what you had to know."

Harmbrister grinned. "Did I say snooping? I didn't mean to pry. At least, I meant no harm in prying. I heard you were about my age, headed my way. I thought, what ho, we might find something in common. So, I came to pay my respects. Do hope I haven't gotten off on the wrong foot. I have a way of doing that, you know."

Locke didn't reply at once. He sank back in his chair. Cato hurriedly finished off his meal and eased past Harmbrister, going through the hatchway to the deck. Harmbrister remained where he was. Finally, Locke smiled and indicated the bunk or the table. "Sit," he invited. "Or lean somewhere."

He extended his hand and Harmbrister shook it enthusiastically. "So you're one of those Southern gentlemen, are you? With your own estate and all, eh? And your own body servant. Slave for life, I suppose? Opposed as all hell to slavery, myself. Nothing personal, you understand."

Locke laughed. "The hell with it. I don't care what you like or dislike. You have to do what you have to do. As long as you don't try to make me live by your rules, I don't give a damn."

"But don't you people try to make others live by *your* rules? I mean, the slave states do attempt to force every state which comes into your Union to be admitted as a slave state, does it not?"

Locke shrugged. "I don't know."

"That isn't quite right, is it, old fellow? What you really mean is you don't care. You have your way of life. That you live on the sweat and misery of the enslaved doesn't bother you?"

"I sleep pretty well."

Harmbrister laughed. "Old sensitive me, I perceive you growing quite bored by the trend of this conversation. . . . Forgive me. I don't go around making enemies—unless I have to. I hope we can be friends. . . ." His smile warmed. "What's your business in Florida?"

Locke did not smile. "I'm sorry. I can't say."

"There you go. It's the same with me, lad. If you'd asked me, I'd have told you something. Polite as hell, you know. But all a lie." He grinned, leaning forward and peering at Locke from narrowed gray-green eyes. Those were changeling eyes—from shadowy blue to a wan green as the lights changed, as his face changed. Locke sighed. This was a complex fellow, for all his easy smiling and puppylike friendliness.

Robert said, "Well, go ahead. What are you then? Besides a gentleman farmer back home? Are you a spy, lad, on your way to Spanish Florida? An agent for your President?"

Locke's head jerked up. Something tripped in his chest. It was as if his heart skipped a beat. "Why did you ask that?"

"Just logic, old lad. Deduction. From habit again. That's all. No harm meant. No offense intended, but no one ships with Captain Arbuthnot on ordinary business."

Locke shrugged. "I suppose not. . . . For a skipper taking his ship to the Floridas, he's heading hard east for Brest."

"When you ship with Arbuthnot, you sail his pattern." He stuck his tongue in his cheek. "Now I have no idea why Captain Alexander Arbuthnot swings so wide east to travel south, but this I can warrant you: He has his own good and sufficient reasons."

"He could be planning to sell you and me—and Cato—as slaves in Barbary."

"No. Three of us. Fine specimens that we are, we'd never bring that kind of price. No, he'll likely deposit us in Florida—when and if it suits his plans. . . . I like the old boy myself. He and I have a lot in common. He can drink me under the table. But what the hell, so can a healthy ten year old. But we have many of the same passions, the same obsessions, the same hatreds, the same crooked streaks. I don't trust a man who's too honest, huh?"

"How about you—what are you—a spy for the king?"

Robert laughed. "I might be. But I'm not. But if I were, I could no more reveal my true self to you than you to me, old sport. We can be honest with one another. To a point. Just let us not believe we deceive each other. As long as we hoodwink the rest of the world, eh? I can tell you this much. I'm not a bad fellow at heart. I get my inordinate male beauty and endearing charm from a royal father. Unfortunately, he didn't see fit to bequeath me his name. For the last two years I've been free of entanglements. I fought against you chaps—with all my energies, heart and vigor—and now I feel not a trace of animosity toward the most aggressive of you. Weird, eh? We people are trained to turn hatred on and off at the command of our leaders."

"You must have been a child to have fought in the War of 1812."

"I was there. Five years ago. Well, four really; I came in as a beardless young noncom of seventeen. Distinguished myself. Got sent to officers' training. Ended a lieutenant, by God, but by that time the unpleasantries were over. And here I was a soldier trained to violence—and no wars to fight. A man brought up to hate—and nobody to hate." His smile broadened. "I looked about—and I found Florida. I do say—there's hate enough down there for the best—and the worst of us."

Shipboard days dragged slowly. Locke found himself almost constantly in young Robert Harmbrister's company. He was unsure whether or not he trusted the young Englishman, but it was impossible to dislike him. If one cared for puppies or kittens or an outgoing, laughing youngster full of energy and drive, one had to like Harmbrister. Anyhow, the debonair young ex-lieutenant gave Locke no choice. He arrived before breakfast, challenging Locke to ten laps around the deck, to a climb to the crow's nest. He talked and laughed constantly and gradually Locke began to like him above any other friend he'd ever had.

He told Harmbrister about Mary-Stuart, finding some balm, some strange release in talking about her.

Harmbrister was enchanted by the verbal picture Locke painted of the girl he loved above all else in the world. "She's super, chap. She sounds extraordinary, the sort of lovely creature every man should love once in this lifetime, but seldom is so fortunate. How I envy you! How I pity you. To have had a love like that and see it turn to wormwood. I never loved anybody like that myself—only me. The love affair with my mirror and my fist are worthy of Shakespeare's passionate prose."

Locke grinned, shaking his head. He had never met another man quite like Harmbrister. Perhaps the former soldier was one of a kind. He laughed at danger and yet Locke knew, without being told, that Harmbrister was headed toward some kind of extreme peril in Florida, but he would go to it laughing, he would plunge into it, with all his heart, and his laughter intact.

"You know what you need, old friend? You need another woman. I learned early that the best cure for one skirt—is another skirt. What a hell of a place to find yourself, trying to recover from the loss of your woman. A ship full of ugly men! God's hat. I would have brought a woman along—shared her gladly, you know—you in your need and all—had I known we'd be so long at sea."

"Well, at least Arbuthnot has finally turned south."

"Don't count on it. He may just be tacking—to catch the wind."

Locke learned that though Harmbrister spent his days and early evenings with him and Cato, he drank, sometimes until dawn, with Arbuthnot in the captain's cabin.

Despite the rigors of his heavy drinking the night before, Robert would show up each morning, freshly shaven, his lean face glowing with that bright pink healthy glow peculiar to the British, his clothing impeccable, his boots shining and polished. No matter that he'd been yelling and talking and drinking with Arbuthnot till daylight, he was up running ten laps around the deck, challenging able seamen to race up the halyards into the rigging and back, the loser to stand for the grog. He did betray one slight concession to his riotous nightlife. He drank heavily sweetened limeaid by the quart. He would strip down to the waist and fence with Locke all over the main deck, sweat marbling his lean body. Sometimes he swung his épée in his right hand and balanced a quart mason jar of limeaid in the other, and never spilt a drop.

One morning, carrying his quart of limeaid, Robert said. "Got the old man roaring drunk last night. He told me what the cannon was all about."

"What cannon?" Locke stared at Harmbrister.

Harmbrister gazed at him, eyes wide with disbelief. "Maybe you're not an agent after all; maybe, be-God, you're an escaped murderer. You've got no curiosity, no snooping eye for a detective or an agent. . . . No, you don't see half enough to keep you alive, you don't. I'll fair worry about you down there in the Spanish Floridas by yourself, I will."

Robert led Locke conspiratorially aft along the decks. Then he pulled away a weathered canvas and revealed a small cannon. But what a cannon. It looked as it were cast from solid gold.

A sudden voice blasted from behind and above them, amplified by a megaphone and carrying the authority of God Himself. "This here is the captain. Get to bloody hell away from that cannon, Mister Harmbrister."

Harmbrister did not take his eyes from the fieldpiece. He waved his arm negligently. "Pay no attention to the old man. He's too fat and too short of breath to come down here himself. If he sends somebody, we'll whip the shit out of 'em. I'm just in the mood to hit somebody after this cramped voyage."

"Is that stuff real gold?"

"Not likely. But by God, it is gold-plated. Looks like a good clean inch of pure gold over the metal casting." He took a small knife from his pocket and scraped at the exposed surface.

Arbuthnot's voice roared like thunder. "You scar that there cannon, mister, and I'll put you in irons. In irons you'll stay until you leave this ship."

"Why would anybody want a gold cannon?" Locke said. He drew his hand along its scrolled, gleaming surface.

"Aye. That's what I asked myself—until I couldn't stand it

anymore. Then I asked the captain. He was a bit reluctant. A bit vague at first, but some smiling, a bit of flattery and heavy on the grog, I got it out of him. It's a gift—from the skipper himself and his owners—to the governor of Spanish Florida."

"For what?"

"For an expression of the esteem of the shipowners and the skipper of the *Chance*, that's what."

"Does Arbuthnot do a lot of business with the Spanish—and the Indians in Florida?"

Harmbrister jerked his handsome head up, laughing. "Ah, ha! You are an agent, aren't you? For the President? God, don't let Arbuthnot know. You'll end up as breakfast for the barracuda."

"I just asked a perfectly natural question."

"Sure you did, old son. And I hope you'll find somebody who'll give you a perfectly natural answer."

"But you won't?"

Robert stared at him, grinning, tongue firmly in his cheek. "How could I, old friend? I'm a stranger here myself."

— X —

THE SEA lay lime-blue and milk-green, fringed with gray and scalloped with thunderheads along the horizon. Locke and Harmbrister sprawled high on the forward deck, getting the blaze of the threatened sun. They wore only white duck pants hacked off at the knees; their bodies were sweated, oily. The *Chance* ran lazily before the wind, sailing a fixed course to leeward, the wind coming from directly astern or no more than a point or two off of it. They were somewhere south and east of Savannah and the near-tropic sun blistered Robert's fair British skin, but he would not complain, move to the fringes of shade nor admit to agony. "The darker skinned I am, the better they'll like me, the more they'll trust me, where I'm going,'' was all he said. The he added, ''Hope you're not looking for ease, or even a hell of a lot of civilization down here in Florida, old fellow.''

''I've been down here before.''

''Sure you have, but Florida, if you don't mind my saying it, mate, is a man-made hell—made a hell by your countrymen.''

Locke shrugged and lay listening, his arms under his head. ''They've got troubles in Florida,'' Harmbrister was saying, almost as if talking to himself. ''It's the wildest country there is in the new world. The West— the land beyond the Mississippi—ain't the hell that the Floridas are, because you Yankees ain't tried to civilize it out there yet.''

''Do you loathe Yankees in particular, or is it just people in general you hate behind your sweet smile?'' Locke inquired.

''Don't hate Yanks, mate. Ones I've met personal seem likable enough. But dumb. A lot of you are ignorant—not stupid particularly, but ignorant, kept ignorant about a lot that goes on under your own noses. Like you now, a privileged land and slave owner of Virginia, what do you know of General Andrew Jackson?''

Locke felt something stir deep inside him; his interest pricked up. He sad, ''He's a revered general. Maybe most loved next to Washington.''

''He's a bloody murderer, that's what he is. But have you read of his murders in your newspapers? A free press! Protected by the First Amendment to your Constitution, and what truth do you know about Andrew Jackson?''

''What *truth* do you know about him?''

''You can't joke with me on this here subject, old friend. Him and his atrocities, I know all about. Because I was there, and I seen him. A revered and beloved general! My ass. Attila the Hun was a darling lad beside your Mr. Jackson. He was in Florida in 1813. So was I. What did you read of his exploits in Florida?''

''He subdued the Indians who had been raiding the border towns. He—''

''Jesus. The fairy tales you people get as news! Jackson led his band of bloodthirsty vandals across Florida. He killed Indian women and children, hacked their heads off and left them to rot in the sun. He killed all Indian livestock and either burned or trampled their gardens and corn fields. He razed every tepee and every red village he marched through."

"He was carrying out a military campaign—"

"The hell he was. He was decimating a race, a people he considers lower than beasts. Carnage. Slaughter. But warfare? If it were not so horrible, I could laugh. I might smile anyhow, but now the bastard and his bloody murderers have returned, to finish what they left undone four years ago. God help the Indian children born in the past four years, or any of those who escaped his butchery before."

Locke exhaled heavily, but kept his voice light. "To look at you, one would never suspect you carry such hatred."

"Listen to me! There is no justice before God in what that man is doing. He turned Florida into a bloody slaughter-pen, and now he's back to do it again. . . . That poor damned territory. . . . While England was fighting its colonies, it returned Florida to Spain in exchange for the Bahamas and Gibraltar. Then, when the colonies became the United States and feeling their cock, they claimed West Florida—whatever in hell that comprised—land all the way to Mexico, or maybe even the Pacific. I know it included Louisiana because there was a rebellion in what they called West Florida when Napoleon's brother Joseph took the Spanish throne. The Republic of West Florida was proclaimed and Baton Rouge was captured. Indians and niggers lived pretty good in the wild country down on the Florida peninsula for a few years. Hell, I've heard the bloody abolitionists and the Quakers talking about helping escaped black slaves run north. Horseshit. This was a money-making scheme for the Quakers and their ilk. Smart blacks ran south to Florida, joined the Indians and reverted to the bush, wilder than any red man what ever took a scalp.

"Them Negroes even set up a black nation of their own along the Apalachicola River—their own country about forty miles long. Then old Jackson came along—that rednecked backwoodsman who hated Indians just slightly less than he hated niggers. Carnage.

"But it ain't just Jackson, evil and vicious as he is. It's all the landgrabbers posing as patriotic Americans—"

"Maybe they learned from the British."

"Maybe. But because another man rapes a woman don't

make rape right for you. Because evil was done before don't make it right now, or in the future or ever. West Florida's flag—a lone star on a white field—was ripped down. Then your President Madison told a General Matthews of Georgia that if he captured Amelia Island, off Florida, the United States would accept it as sovereign territory. On what justification, I never heard from nobody. Then Madison was trapped before the world and had to repudiate Matthews's invasion.

"By that time the colonies were back at war with us British. And old Jackson got his chance to slaughter in Florida and claim territory that the Treaty of Ghent would take away from him. Instead of being hung as a war criminal and bloody murderer, he was revered as Old Hickory! Oh, my kindly God. America is not the first nation to revere its generals, but it has made some mighty statesmen from some sows' ears, I can tell you."

"I've heard of hating a renowned man, but it's a disease with you."

Harmbrister sat up, nodding vigorously.

"You're right, you know! Bloody right. It is a disease. That's what it is. I am sick with my hatred. Obsessed. I just realized it, talking to you. I'm more than a little insane on the subject. And you've touched on it exactly. I can tell you this. I'd like to join Old Hickory and his bloodthirsty mob—because that's what it is, it's no army. He knows nothing of warfare, or war or military tactics. . . ."

"Why would you want to join him?"

"Like the old wooden horse of Troy, lad! Wouldn't that be beautiful? To infiltrate. To march among them and secretly and stealthily eliminate his redneck beasts one by one—and looked sorrowed and shocked when the news was announced. Oh God, that I could!"

Locke turned his head, watching the young ex-soldier. "How would you join him?"

"A man like Jackson? Easy. Turn up at his camp with a small company of mercenary cutthroats, recruited from ratholes and outfitted as soldiers. Might even go so far as to teach 'em discipline and close-order drill. Impress the hell out of Old Hickory—he'd welcome me!" He laughed. "He'd welcome anybody, if the newcomer was bloodthirsty—or if he came to Jackson literally with blood on his hands."

The sun was gone, the wind freshened to twenty knots, the thick clouds reflected in the disturbed surface of the sea. The first inkling of trouble came in a cry from the crow's nest. "Ship! Hard to larbard."

Already a shabby gang of seamen clustered at the larboard railings, gazing at the approaching vessel. Aft and forward other men dropped their duties and stared at the ship coming between them and landfall and cutting at a long angle clearly calculated to bring her dead across the bow of the *Chance*. There was a sense of urgency in the oncoming craft, its canvas filled; it was no ordinary brig passing casually in the trade lanes. As it neared one saw it was the sort of raider that lay in wait—a tall-masted brigantine sporting topgallants and every foot of sails bellied to the wind.

Close-hauled as Arbuthnot ran his schooner, the *Chance*, with sprit staysails trimmed and mizzen-reefed, appeared to lay almost at anchor before the approaching windjammer.

Without a word, Harmbrister levered himself to his feet and ran to the nearest ladder going upward toward the wheelhouse. Locke joined him, running with him across the poop deck.

When Harmbrister flung open the door, both the captain and the helmsman heeled around, the sailor gray-faced, the master flushed and raging. "What ye lubbers a-doing in my presence half naked like this? Get out of here, Mister Harmbrister and take your friend with you."

Harmbrister ignored the order. "You're letting that blackbirder overtake you without a trace of a protest."

"You lubbin' idiot. I got my canvas out full. What you ask of me?"

"That you don't endanger my life—at least without making a run for it."

"I see no blackbirder in the first place. I see another freighter, with as much right to the lanes as I have. An' if it was a raider as you imagine, Mr. Harmbrister, what makes you think I could outrun her—if I were of the nervous-Nelly disposition like you?"

"You could try," Locke shouted, staring off toward the hard-running ship coming across the wind, reaching for her highest speeds. "You're close-hauled and at least four-points off the wind."

"Ah, a seasoned seaman suddenly, are you, Mister Locke?"

"Put up all your canvas," Locke said, without taking his eyes from the ship closing in on the port side. "Tack! Fill the sails. You can still outrun her if you reach broad to windward."

"Aye! Only this be my ship. This be my responsibility. Its crew and its cargo and its safety. I run her as I see. . . . I say, even if you're right that we're facin' a blackbirder, we'll only be sunk if we try to run."

Harmbrister cursed him, yelling. "You stupid Scot. You'll be sunk anyhow. Or sold to some sultan as slave to be sodomized if you let them take you. Them heathens love fat asses like yours. And you can stop playing coy. That's a blackbirder on our port. I've seen craft like her before."

"And I," Locke said.

"I got my ship and my cargo to think about."

"I've got my skin," Robert said. "And I mean to fight to keep it. If your owners ever learn the truth about how you let yourself be taken—"

"Get out of here," the skipper shouted, his face flushed and his vast body quaking.

"Let them take you," Locke said. "That's your decision, Captain. But I'll fight them. I won't be taken—to be sold into slavery—or impressed to duty on some British warship."

"Nor will I," Robert said.

"You're passengers aboard my ship," the captain panted, short of breath and gasping. "You make one move to disobey my orders and I'll put you both in irons. You make a move to disturb the tranquility or to endanger the safety of this here ship and I'll order ye shot."

"Start bellowing your orders, Captain. The quicker you let your crew know your intent, the sooner I'll have men to fight with me," Harmbrister said.

Locke laughed. "As for your irons, Captain, I'd as soon be in yours as theirs."

As if the *Chance* stood anchored on the rising swells, the brig sailed in upon her like a mastiff after a terrier. Big guns bristled and snouts were visible along the top plankings of the square-rigger.

Robert gave Arbuthnot one last beseeching glance. When the captain glared up at him from narrowed eyes in their puffs of fat, Harmbrister heeled and ran from the wheelhouse. Locke followed, with the skipper roaring curses in their wake.

"Arm yourselves, men," Harmbrister yelled from the poop deck. "The captain means to let us be boarded. You got one chance. Fight for your lives or be taken."

Men sprang from the railings and bulwarks to obey him, arming themselves with cutlasses and small arms which somehow made them look pathetic as the cannons sent salvos across the main deck.

Robert glanced toward the captain on the poop deck and then shouted across his shoulder at Locke. "I think we put the fear of God—or of his owners—into old Arbuthnot! The old bastard is afraid one of us just might live to talk. . . . He's ordered the *Chance* turned down the wind and he's ordered up more canvas."

"Hell! It's too late for that."

"Aye. But you don't read him right, old son. This here last-minute run ain't nothing but window-dressing. . . . Now nobody can't never say he didn't *try* to run for his life."

As new canvas spanked upward on the four masts and bellied out reaching across the wind, the schooner lunged, leaped and plunged like a sailfish through the high-rising waves, racing at a hard tack out to sea to fill every unfurling sail.

The blackbirder showed no colors, whatever flag she may have been flaunting earlier. The brig veered a few points to intercept the schooner.

Harmbrister and Locke could see the skipper, slumped like some sullen Buddha against the railings, watching the end of the unequal race, coldly seeing his ship run down, overtaken and entrapped.

Around them, seamen ran to stations with musketry, as effective as toys against the cannons belching fire and death from the privateer.

"The gold cannon," Locke shouted.

Harmbrister stared at him a long beat, then put his head back, laughing. "You think it's meant to be fired in anger?"

"If it's got a hole in its end and a lanyard; we'll fire it."

Harmbrister led the way at a run, roaring with laughter. He ripped away the protective covering, exposing the golden cannon, scrolled and polished and gleaming.

Harmbrister patted her polished surface. "We might as well blow it to smithereens—if those pirates get their paws on it, Governor Castillo won't ever glimpse it nohow."

A skinny seaman, naked to the belt and barefooted, threw aside his musket and leaped to help them roll the golden carronade into place and snub it down. "Be a gunner by profession," he shouted. A second fellow brought cannon-balls and powder. Another stood with linstock ready.

All this time, in an agony of frustration and rage, Captain Arbuthnot screamed in impotent fury from the poop deck, his voice fragmented on the wind, lost in the blackbirder's cannoning.

Thunder sounded from the attackers' ship and a cannonball sailed close across the bow of the *Chance*.

This warning was all Abruthnot required of his adversary. "Heave to!" the skipper roared from the poop deck.

Harmbrister raged with laughter. "Listen to the treacherous old bastard. He fights and surrenders fast—if in no way furious."

Locke was yelling for Cato. As if attuned to the thinking of his master, the slave appeared with a bucket of nails, bolts, and screws. "Personnel killer," Locke said.

"You savage bastard," Harmbrister said admiringly. "We'll give 'em grapeshot as well as the cannonball, eh, mate? You been in these fights before, my lad."

"I know we've got one chance and just one. We fire this baby once. They'll blow us out of the sea before we can fire her again. We're dead unless we make our one shot count." Locke jerked his head. The seaman lashed down the cannon, blocking and tying it off as securely as possible on the pitching and yawing deck.

The gunner stood with linstock at the ready.

"We're only going to make them mad anyhow," Harmbrister agreed. "Your personnel killer is our only hope. A few well-placed killings might take the heart out of them."

Locke drew a deep breath, held his hand aloft. "That and a well-placed cannonade."

The others stood, breath bated. Another roar sounded and a splintering crash meant a mast had been struck. The brig tacked in boldly now, guns bristling, crew waiting along the railings.

Locke waited as the *Chance* rode upward with the swells and then plunged downward into the trough.

"Be ready," Locke told the gunner.

The *Chance* tilted, rode high and crested on a wave. Another fusillade and the deafening thunder of a direct, close-at-hand cannonade.

Locke seemed unaware of what was happening around him. As the *Chance* plunged, nose down, he slashed downward with his arm and yelled, "Now!"

Incredibly the brig shuddered under the suddenness and crippling fury of the blow. The shot struck the superstructure which blazed instantaneously with fire. Along the bulwarks men screamed in mortal agony, their bodies ripped and torn by metal. Some staggered and fell, bloody on the decks, a few pitched between the railings, carried dead out to sea.

While men aboard the *Chance* yelled in snarling triumph, and brief chaos halted all aggression from the attacker, its officers roaring orders and its company wandering hurt and dying in the flare of fires on her blood-wet deck, Locke concentrated only on the small gold cannon.

His gunner loaded the piece once more with powder and ball. Cato poured in the nails, screws and metal. As they worked intently, in obsessed silence, the blackbirder renewed its attack, firing its cannons in brutal retaliation, her hasty shots going wide.

Locke signaled his men to be ready for his order. Again the *Chance* crested a churning wave and once more plunged downward toward the trough. On this falling motion of the ship, Locke ordered the cannon fired again.

The lanyard sizzled, the cannon roared, acrid smoke clouding over them. The weapon shook, rocking back against its lashings.

It was all over that quickly. The second shot from the gold cannon was a direct hit. The personnel-killing metal took a fearful toll of the men left standing on the brig's open deck. The cannonball ripped into a powder magazine. An explosion shook the brig to her pegs. Her gun crews went into panic. They abandoned the great guns lined facing the *Chance*. Officers screamed at them and beat at them with belaying pins and musket butts, trying to get them back to their posts, but the seamen ran in agonized circles, some of them mortally wounded, the others filled with dread at what was happening around them. They leaped for any cover. The brave among them abandoned everything else to fight the spreading fires in the superstructure.

In that brief moment of delay, as if caught up on some driving wind from her stern, the *Chance* glided away from the fire-blasted, bloody-decked brigantine.

The big ship seemed to wallow helplessly, drifting. Yells, screams and agonized cries trailed across the rising seas to the running *Chance*.

As the *Chance* rode away on the wind from the black-smoking brig, Locke ran to the fantail. He stood there, far aft, staring back at the other ship, watching the brig quiver and blaze, the conflict forgot.

Around him, and along the open decks, the *Chance*'s company roared with savage triumph.

Locke remained where he was. Astonished and relieved, he saw that the brigantine had abandoned the chase, quit the fight and luffed alee to fight the flames on deck. Her fires ebbed and then rose and flames licked upward through vast-spread shrouds, doing a final damage. Smoke curled up black from her and she seemed to drift in circles like some mindless wounded animal.

From the bridge, Captain Arbuthnot's voice roared through a megaphone, summoning Locke and Harmbrister to the wheel-house, on the double.

Locke turned to obey. For the first time he saw that Harmbrister stood, devil-may-care, smoke-streaked, eyes wild with laughter, bared to the chopped-off shorts, at his side.

Harmbrister touched Locke's arm. "Just a second, old mate. We can't go into the captain's august presence in this state. What say we bathe and dress formal?"

Locke laughed, again admiring the convoluted workings of the soldier's steel-trap mind. He returned to his cabin, washed up as well as he could and, with Cato's assistance, dressed in his best.

Harmbrister knocked on his door. The British soldier was shaven, brushed and polished in a red and drab uniform with high heeled boots. "Helps me look down on the fat bastard," he said.

They walked along the decks, going up to the bridge and

into the wheelhouse where the sweated Arbuthnot awaited them in a state verging on apoplexy. "You two bastards," he roared. "You not only countermand my orders; even when you obey, you mock them."

"You have this here way of bringing out the best in us, Captain," Robert said.

"You son of a bitch. I'm putting you two in irons."

"For what?" Harmbrister's voice lashed back. "For saving your hide?"

"For going against my orders, mister. For endangering my ship and my men."

"Oh, for hell's sake, skipper. I know you love your ship. But your men? You'd feed 'em to the sharks and sleep soundly that night."

"Next, you'll be telling me I ought to thank you." Arbuthnot's voice trembled.

Harmbrister stuck his tongue in his cheek and winked at Locke. "Exactly the reason why we come all dressed up to see you, skipper. To be proper received as proper heroes. To be thanked—Mister Locke especial—for a job well done."

"A job well done." Captain Arbuthnot looked as if he might cry in helpless frustration. "And now I recollect ye, Mister Locke! Knowed I'd seen that face afore. . . . You sailed the *Pegasus* out of Amelia Island after Captain Harper was killed . . . and not more than two years ago."

Locke shrugged. "Two years is a lifetime—in our business, Captain."

Captain Arbuthnot glared at him, his jowls quivering, his eyes red in their sockets, blood throbbing in great blue veins at his temples. "Ah, you confess it then. You. Nothing but a blackbirder yourself. A goddamn pirate. A freebooter. Mincing around respectable with a black slave at your beck and call!"

"You better thank your gods that you had aboard a man that knew how to fight the blackbirders trying to board you," Harmbrister's voice lashed him.

The captain swung his fat arm. He prowled the small room, sweated and quivering. "Thanks, is it? Ye be waiting for me to thank you, be you? Well, let me tell you this, me lubbers. You'll be standing there with a beard to the floor, your backs bent and hell froze over before you hear a word of thanks from me."

— XI —

TO LOCKE'S astonishment, Harmbrister was returned enough into Captain Arbuthnot's good graces to be drinking with the skipper in the master's cabin that very night. It was as if no tensions, no mistrusts, no ill-feelings, existed between them.

And Harmbrister did get drunk, so soddenly and totally that, by midnight, seamen carried him to his own stateroom. He slumped in upon himself, helpless, as if the liquor had liquefied his bones and turned his tendons to jelly. He sang filthy songs from long-lost barracks. He laughed without reason and giggled like a girl. When the sailors tried to set him on his feet, he was unable to stand alone.

However, he was up and on deck ahead of Locke the next morning. In fact, both Locke and Cato still slept when Harmbrister banged on the stateroom door. Cato swung down sleepily from the top bunk and padded across the narrow cell in a state of semiconsciousness and opened the hatch.

"Wake up, Locke!" Robert yelled, sticking his head in the open doorway. "No time to loll around in your bunk. Meet me on deck in five minutes, old mate. May be the most important moment of your life."

Locke sat up, yawning. Harmbrister grinned at him, nodding in a conspiratorial way, and winked. Then Robert withdrew, slamming the door behind him. Puzzled, Locke swung his legs over the side of his bunk, still yawning and scratching at his ribs.

Within ten minutes, he was beside Harmbrister on the port side. He found the Englishman leaning against the railing and staring into the hard-running water as if the sea held the secret of existence for him.

"There you are, old hunt-stumper." Harmbrister heeled

around. He jerked his head, motioning Locke to follow, and set off striding briskly aft.

Locke fell into step beside him. "What's this all about?"

Robert grinned at him. "About you and me, mate. And what the skipper has in store for us. What his plans must have been. What they are and what we can do about it."

"What are you talking about?"

"Us. You listen quick and you listen well. I can say it only once. The bulkheads has got ears. We walk all the way aft to the very point of fantail. Won't nothing look amiss in that, as long as we look like we're a-laughing and joking, and nothing on our minds. Laugh a lot. Makes no difference if what I say ain't nothing to laugh about, you laugh anyhow. Laugh big and put your head back with your laughing. Look like your enjoying yourself before breakfast."

"I seldom laugh out loud before breakfast."

Harmbrister roared with laughter at this and clapped Locke on the back. But he said, in a desperate tone, "I reckon you have guessed already that Captain Arbuthnot had a deal on with that blackbirder, whoever he was, to let him board the *Chance*? Laugh it up."

Locke put his head back, laughing. He said, "I know he didn't exactly thank us for upsetting his plans—whatever they were."

Harmbrister laughed and nodded. "His plans included letting the blackbirder make off with something aboard this ship, something of such value that it's hidden—under lock and key."

Locke laughed. "The cannon maybe?"

"Oh, hell no. I'm talking about riches, man. I got no idea what value. Got no idea what it is. Only that Arbuthnot's deal was to let the blackbirder steal it—and somewhere they'd divide the take."

"Only we fouled it up."

"That's right. I don't know his plans for us. Maybe you and me and your slave were meant as a bonus. But we had no importance like whatever is hidden on this ship."

"And he hates us worse than ever that we ruined his deal?"

"That's right. And only part of it. That blackbirder came in expecting not even a token protest from the *Chance*. That's why I believe the skipper meant you and me and your boy to be taken. If there was an inquiry, we might have spoke against him. But his crew are such criminals that not one of them would be allowed to testify. So he meant to get rid of us, too."

Robert laughed uproariously and prodded Locke, urging him to laughter.

"That's all past. The old boy is not one to carry a grudge—especially when he's got bigger sharks a-bitin' at his ass."

"The blackbirder thinks Arbuthnot double-crossed him?"

"Aye, lad! And he can't run far enough or fast enough to escape his former partners. They'll be after his heart and his hide now. They'll cut out his heart and strip away his hide. He's sick in his guts with what he knows now. There ain't a rathole deep enough for him to crawl into. . . . Oh, they're after him. He told them they could come in on him without a shot fired, and when they edged close to us, we filled their decks with shrapnel and grapeshot, we put a ball into a powder keg, we set their ship to flames . . ."

"And they think it's his doing—his betrayal?"

"Aye. Captain Arbuthnot's life is forfeit—from this minute. Oh, that blackbirder is back there—limping slightly, crippled a little, but on Arbuthnot's trail now with a savage madness. . . . Nothing more righteous than another criminal who thinks you've choused him."

"Does Arbuthnot mean to kill us?"

Robert laughed, but shook his head in his laughter. They were far out on the fantail now, the wind fresh and chill about them, a new sun spattering the wake with silver. "That wouldn't buy him nothing now, I think. . . . No, the captain's got but one thing on his mind now. He hates us both, but killing us wouldn't profit him. He wants to be rid of us. I know he means to put us off at the first port ahead. He means to stay no longer in that port than necessary to take on fresh water and provisions—and then to run again, to buy himself some time."

"Then we're safe enough for the time being."

"I think so. But it's not safe that I'm studying now with all my heart, mate."

Locke forced a broad laugh for the benefit of any watching

eyes, but he stared into Robert's face, puzzled. "What are you thinking?"

"About that treasure. That hidden riches aboard this here ship. . . . It must be a fortune beyond your wildest imagination. Enough so that if Arbuthnot split it with the blackbirder, he'd still live like a fancy king to the end of his days, no matter if his owners wrested the *Chance* from him and denied him his papers as a skipper for the rest of his natural life . . . and that well could have happened. Arbuthnot had to figure that in the possible cost. Whatever the odds against him in this matter, he went into it—and only you and me messed up his plans."

"We got our skins. I say we debark this ship as the captain permits and thank the gods we're alive and out of slavery."

"That's all very well for you to say, because you ain't given it no thought. Them same gods that helped to keep you out of slavery and alive, you think they wouldn't be most happy to see you rich as a king, as well?"

Now Locke did laugh honestly and openly.

"Them gods help them what helps themselves," Harmbrister said. "I say we take that treasure—whatever it is. We relieve the captain of it. He meant to lose it to undeserving blackbirders—"

"Who would split it with him."

"Who *might* have split it with him. I never seen no blackbirder I'd trust as far as I could spit—excepting you, present company. They might of split with him. We'll never know. And I could not care less. I know I won't."

"You mean to take it from him—and leave him a ruined man—with his owners, with his ex-partners that he still might buy off, if he had the treasure—with whoever the stuff is consigned to?"

Harmbrister shrugged. "This here is business we're talking, old mate. And there ain't no place in business for sentiment. Arbuthnot had nothing against you and me—yet he meant to see us taken by that blackbirder, just to insure the safety of his own fat hide. Is that very sentimental? Maybe you don't need no money. But I do. I need all I can get my claws into. If you want to help me take that treasure—what Arbuthnot would of lost anyway—I'll vow you my equal partner. Fifty-fifty, though I thought of it myself and have done already much of the spadework."

Locke laughed loudly and slapped Robert on the shoulder. "Now what are you talking about?"

"About last night. I got the skipper passed-out drunk. And that ain't easy, because I got no tolerance for alcohol myself. It acts on my system just like poison, it does. But I got a real formidable willpower I have, and I put it to work last night—along with a few drops of laudanum to help lull the captain to sleep. . . . I made the first hunt for whatever it was the captain planned to turn over to the blackbirder. . . . It ain't in his cabin, I swear to that."

"You got any idea where it is?"

"Not the foggiest, mate. That's where you come in. That's why you are worth a two-way split of the fortune. You got to find it. You got to steal it. That's all you got to do."

Locke put his head back and laughed loudly. "Is that all? And what will you be doing?"

"The hardest part, mate, that's what. Drinking wi' the captain . . . keeping the old skipper occupied and suspecting nothing while you find the treasure."

Locke shook his head. "You make it sound so easy."

"It is easy when you compare it to out-drinking the captain when alcohol is a poison to your brain and your liver and your guts. . . . But there's just one other little matter."

"Yes?"

"Time. Time is what we got nothing of. We stand somewhere off the Florida coast now. And the captain will be putting into port within the next day or two. Time is what's against us, mate. Time's our enemy. Time is what is running out on us."

Locke spent the day prowling the ship. There was little in his casual actions to arouse the suspicions of even a naturally mistrusting man like Captain Arbuthnot. The crew, scurvy derelicts though they undoubtedly were, honed and scarred in the meanest ports of the seven seas, cheered Locke on sight. They gripped his hand, excessive in their approbation as they thanked him for saving their lives.

Arbuthnot would have had to be a doubting man indeed to conclude other than that Locke was unwillingly being showered with due homage, and that he wandered the decks and companionways and even the holds belowdecks to escape embarrassing displays of blessings and commendations from rough, godless villains who'd long forgotten how to pay deference or reverential respect to anything or anybody.

All Locke gained from his prowling was the sure knowledge that no treasure existed on the ship, or that the captain had concealed it so cleverly that only he could have led the blackbirders to it had they succeeded in boarding the *Chance*.

The afternoon waned. The *Chance* sailed toward land, going west by south across the warming waters.

Locke stood at the railings watching the sea, the first gulls, the thunderheads on the horizon. Occasionally, he glanced aft, almost expecting the brigantine to have regrouped and come in deadly pursuit. The sea lay calm and empty.

How cleverly could Arbuthnot have hidden a chest of any dimensions large enough to contain a fortune in anything? Or was the hidden fortune merely a figment of Robert Harmbrister's fevered imagination? As Robert had said, he needed money—all he could get his hands upon. Was his need the mother of his invention? Did he believe a fortune existed because he wanted it with such obsession?

Then he considered himself. Was he perhaps giving Arbuthnot credit for too much cleverness? There was not the slightest doubt that the skipper was a clever, maliciously smart and dangerously knowing man. But suppose he had a large chest to conceal? Would he stop to be clever about it? Or would he be merely practical?

Smiling, suddenly coldly calm, Locke went down a hatchway to the corridor along which his own stateroom and those of Harmbrister and any other potential passengers were situated, lined up like cells in a row.

He strolled the length of the companionway without slowing. He located what he sought, four doors from his own and on the inside, across the corridor. All the staterooms were closed, probably all of them were locked, but only one was extra-bolted with heavy metal hasps and bulky lock.

He sighed and returned to the deck. He spent the afternoon lazing in the sun, though Robert braised him with scowls whenever they met. Locke ignored the soldier's grimaced messages. That night he and Robert ate dinner as last-night-out guests of the captain. The skipper appeared totally at ease and apparently in good spirits. Only Robert seemed sweated with anxiety.

"At heart I reckon you're not bad lads," Arbuthnot said. He grinned sweatily across the linen-covered table at Locke. He insisted he had forgiven them both for trespassing against him, for disobeying his direct orders, even for endangering his ship and his cargo and his crew.

"You're right, Captain." Harmbrister made a terrible effort to conceal his anxiety. "Both me and Locke here. We're both just young, high-spirited lads—sorry for any inconvenience we caused you—and anxious now to make port."

"Aye." The captain drank lustily. "And you'll be making port safely—and soon. We should come in on Amelia Island with daybreak tomorrow. We get a favorable tide, you lubbers should be kissin' dry land long before noon."

"It can't be too soon for me." Robert tried to keep his voice level, but it quavered, exposing his tormented suspense. His hand trembled on his wineglass. He dabbed at perspiration beading his upper lip and his forehead. Though he laughed and said he couldn't drink at all, he looked harried, nervous, driven, and kept stealing meaningful glances toward Locke. But Jerry ignored his fretting.

The meal dragged on, long past dark.

Locke left Robert and Captain Arbuthnot somewhere around nine o'clock. When the ship's bell sounded, he got up and excused himself, leaving the two men drinking together at table. Robert was deep in some story of a night he had spent in a whorehouse with three women vying to please him and rouse him with new delights. Stories such as this titillated, excited and increased the rate of drinking of the captain. Erotic adventures, described in rawest terms, made the fat skipper sweat and reach often for his bottle, drinking, spilling the liquid from the corners of his fat lips, and urging Harmbrister on.

Locke went directly to his own cabin. He had picked up a thin metal blade in the afternoon and he fashioned it into a hook, with Cato watching him silently. Then he sent Cato to stand in the hatchway and watch for anyone who might enter their corridor. No one except Harmbrister should be coming into the area, but they had to be on watch for stewards or cabin boys on night errands.

Cato leaned heavily against the top step. Behind him, Locke worked on the heavy lock with the makeshift hook. He was sweated down; it seemed as if hours raced past, but it was really only a matter of minutes when something clicked inside the metal lock and it sagged open in his fist.

"Cato."

The slave came quickly to him, along the corridor as lithe as a panther—and as stealthy.

Locke removed the brass fastener from its metal hook. "Replace this but don't snap it shut, for God's sake. Then lean against the wall as if you're waiting for me, like you don't know what you're doing."

"That'll be easy."

Locke grinned and patted his servant's arm. "Don't worry, Cato, your gods will protect you."

"But my gods are not your gods—mastah."

Locke shrugged, stepping through the doorway. "Maybe they have reciprocal arrangements." He closed the door behind him and lit a candle. He stood unmoving for long seconds, holding his breath. He felt like Ali Baba in the cave of the thieves.

Kegs, hogsheads, caskets and boxes of rare vintage wines, expensive fabrics and precious metals lined the bulkheads. But despite the cash value of these materials, Locke shook his head. Too bulky. He still had not found the treasure Robert Harmbrister sought so eagerly.

A small cedar chest, a couple of feet wide and deep, lay where it had been casually shoved against a case of French Bordeaux wine.

Locke's heart quickened. Before he even opened the chest, he knew instinctively he'd uncovered the riches Harmbrister coveted, the treasure Captain Arbuthnot had meant to split with the raiding blackbirders.

A sharp rap of knuckles on the door facing brought him up, tense. He blew out the candle and stood, eyes closed in the darkness until white moonlight, filtered through the porthole, illumined the room in misty purple.

He heard voices outside in the corridor. Cato spoke loudly, as if addressing the deaf. Locke could not distinguish the other voice; he prayed it was a man of dim perceptions, because Cato sounded as innocent and casual as a confessed murderer on the gallows.

He grinned despite the sweat burning his eyes. Poor Cato. Life had cast him in a role he was constitutionally incapable of playing: first as a slave, and then as a party to crime.

Locke lit the candle again when it was quiet in the companionway. Opening the lock on the chest proved more difficult and took longer because it was smaller and he had to be careful not to leave incriminating scratches on its pristine surface.

He lifted the lid of the chest carefully and sank back on his haunches, stunned. The chest gleamed with the riches of plundered people, stacked with tall columns of what, through the laundering of possession, had come to be known as Spanish gold. He saw the coins had been minted in Madrid, all Incan blood totally laved away in the process.

He went across the room, lithely, and spoke to Cato through the facing. "Bring a duffel bag filled with cannon balls, metal bars, anything heavy."

He returned to the chest and sank to his knees before it in reverential genuflexion. He remained like that until Cato's tap on the door brought him up and across the narrow cell.

The deed was quickly accomplished then. He filled the thick-napped bag of coarse wool with the gold and placed as many pieces of metal as could be crammed into the chest. Then he locked it and dragged the seaman's sack across the deck. With Cato standing watch at the hatchway, Locke moved the pouch into his own cabin.

He sagged on the lower bunk then, his heart slugging in his rib cage. He was assailed by doubts. He had stolen the gold, had it in his cabin. All he had to do now was remove it from this ship, under Captain Arbuthnot's suspicious, watchful eyes. Hell, Harmbrister, you're not so clever after all, and I'm even more stupid for going along with you.

Unable to sleep he prowled the cabin as the ship's bell tolled off the hours. Cato climbed into the upper bunk, but the slave did not sleep either. Locke did not speak but paced in the cramped cage, to and fro.

After a sweated eternity he heard Harmbrister stumbling

down the gangway, abusive, snarling at the seamen assigned to see him safely in his cabin.

Locke pressed his ear against the door facing, listening. Harmbrister went on singing, cursing, raging. Then the seamen, muttering under their breath, departed up the ladder and the companionway drifted into a taut, listening silence.

As Locke touched the knob to open the door, a sharp rap told him Harmbrister was there. The ex-soldier was sweated, red of face, his hair disheveled, clothing wrinkled, but he looked sober. He looked as if, despite the captain's best peach brandy, he had never been so coldly lucid in his life.

Locke cracked the door enough to face Robert. Harmbrister looked ready to weep helplessly if the answer went against his prayers. "Did you find it?"

Locke nodded. "It's everything you thought. And more."

"Aye, God." Harmbrister looked as if he might crumple sobbing in relief and exultance.

"You want to see it? You want to divide it now?"

Harmbrister laughed, checking over his shoulder. "I don't want to touch it yet. I trust you. You keep it. Throw it around casual going ashore. I'll come to your hotel room and we'll divvy the spoils—and live like sybarites ever after."

— *XII* —

LOCKE STOOD on the forward deck, feeling excitement churn in his mind, while doubt caused his belly to tighten and spin emptily. He watched as men in longboats maneuvered the schooner to a berth at the piers.

His heart lurched as Amelia Island closed around him. This subtropical land was like a paradise unknown, something few men had ever seen west of Eden.

He'd stood unmoving, entranced, as they crossed the approach to the wild land he'd called home for two barbarous years. Perhaps it was a strange sense of homecoming, or only the pleasure of anticipation after eternal days at sea, but the island had never looked so beautiful, so inviting. Somehow, the place intrigued one's mind, inflaming it like a lovely but faithless woman; one knew he'd seen her before, loved her and owned her body before, but did he really know her, would he *ever* really know her?

The green land spilled out onto sandy beaches ringing a natural harbor with the St. Mary's River estuary to the north, the river curling north and east of the wicked old port town sprawled out like a prostrate whore on the northwestern spit of Amelia Island.

From the sea, this reef flared like some riotous garland of flowers and shrubs with all evil artfully concealed in its rotting underbelly—drooping willows, wild hibiscus in brilliant scarlet clusters, sour-orange trees, lush elders, white with blossoms in the spring, heavy with acrid fruit each fall.

The longboats guided the *Chance* three miles through a narrow channel of sound and river to the dock facilities. The beaches glittered with virginal whiteness, and beyond them the salt marshes, the curdled sodden swamps.

The old town lazed in the sun, unchanged as far as Locke could see. Its weathered buildings—ships, chandlers, taverns, rum shops, gambling houses, boot makers, blacksmiths and brothels—fringed the quays. The town tiered up from the harbor, a patchwork of careless huts and neglected shacks, tar kilns, cane and indigo fields, small gardens. It crouched, a place of pirates, slave dealers and renegades. It had not changed. The transporting of slaves had been outlawed by England since 1805, and now importation of slaves was prohibited by the United States. The only change these laws effected on Amelia Island was an improved and profitable new traffic in human beings.

The settlement exuded that stale odor of all ancient places. The first Spanish port had been established here in 1686 when this island had been called Santa Maria. In 1702, South Carolinian forces of English and Indians captured the fort and destroyed its Catholic mission as a first order of Protestant Christian business. Without Spanish commerce to keep the place alive, it waned, withered and died. By 1730, the island was deserted to the herons, gulls and pelicans. It remained so until a new port was erected and manned by fifty English soldiers. At this time, this garden spot was renamed in honor of Princess Amelia, sister of George II of England. The Spanish owned it again now and made not even a token effort to patrol or quell its lawlessness.

Below him and around him, hurrying men shouted as lines were cast ashore and looped, securing the *Chance* alongside the black cypress docking. The gangplank was lowered and Locke sensed the tensions building in him.

Sweat boiled out of his pores in a way not even related to the ninety-degree heat. Perspiration bubbled from his hairline, across his forehead, along his cheeks, beaded on his chin and stung his neck. His clothing grew damp and rivulets coursed down from his armpits. His whole body itched, moist and scorched. His hair lay plastered to his scalp, his clothing adhered clammily to his flesh.

He saw Cato standing near the railing with the duffel bag and their own meager pouches. That coarse woolen sack stood out in Locke's eyes like some fire-struck cross.

He glanced toward the bridge from which, moments earlier, Captain Alexander Arbuthnot had been directing the berthing of his ship. Arbuthnot was no longer up there.

Locke's heart sank. Was this a good omen, or had the old reprobate spied the duffel bag?

Locke inhaled deeply, his chest tight. Where was Harmbrister? He had not even glimpsed the ex-lieutenant since last night at his door. He strode across the deck. "We won't wait any longer, Cato."

Cato nodded. The slave looked as if he were being devoured by tensions. His eyes glittered with ill-suppressed panic, his lips were drawn in a taut line. He looked ready to explode.

Locke winced, certain the slave would try to struggle down the gangplank under the unmanageable weight of the duffel bag. For him to offer assistance to his slave would only draw undue attention to them, exacerbate an already touchy situation. There was no reason Arbuthnot could not demand to inspect their bags before they departed his ship.

Cato jerked his head toward the bags as if they contained nothing more valuable than soiled shirts, and they were hefted by grunting, sweating seamen who staggered toward the gangplank. One of the cabin boys, gasping under the weight, said to Cato, "What you got in this bag, nigger?"

"Gold," Cato said. "Don't it feel like it?"

The boy sneered in contempt and called a fellow to help him down the gangplank. Cato walked with dignity, unhurried, ahead of them and crossed the plankings to engage a hack.

"Glad to be going ashore, be you?"

Locke caught his breath and heeled around, feeling his face go gray as the blood seeped downward in his body. Captain Arbuthnot stood in a shaft of shade from an overhang, red-faced, his small eyes glittering like beads in sockets of fat.

"Aye," Locke said. "And thankful."

Arbuthnot gave him a cold smile. "Knowed I knew you. . . . You didn't bamboozle me, mate. Want you to know. I was on to you from the first. And then when I seen you turn that cannon on the blackbirder, it all struck me clear who you was, all right."

"I know you were wise to me, Captain." Locke grinned at the stout man. It was easy to smile. The duffel bag lay on the dock, the cabin boys who'd borne it were returned up the ladder. And he was relieved to be safely departing Captain Arbuthnot's company. He found no reason to mention this. He merely bowed slightly and started down the gangplank, wanting to run but forcing himself to move with at least as much dignity as Cato had demonstrated.

"Just a minute, mister." Captain Arbuthnot's voice impaled him.

Locke winced. He stopped as if pinned to the ladder. His fist gripped the rough rope. He glanced over his shoulder, keeping his face expressionless.

Captain Arbuthnot smiled coldly. "Ain't you going to wait for your partner in crime?"

"Partner, Captain? What crime?"

"You know what crime. I could have throwed you and Harmbrister in irons for the way you took over my ship. I could have delivered you to the Alcalde here at Amelia—in irons—to hold for legal action by my ship's owners."

"Someday you'll forgive us for saving your hide, Captain."

Arbuthnot cursed. "You and Harmbrister is fortunate I do

feel kindly toward you. All I ask is that you git him as well as yourself off my ship.''

Locke exhaled. ''I think Mr. Harmbrister can find his way off your ship, Captain. And I assure you, he'll be even happier than I am to debark.''

Arbuthnot shook his head. ''Can't understand why you'd be so happy to go ashore in a cesspool like this.'' He made a sour face. ''God almighty, how it stinks.''

Cato had found them transportation—a rickety hack, a spavined horse, a senile black coachman. He returned, walking ahead of the quavering, rattling conveyance. He made far better time on foot across the sun-seared plankings than the open cab.

Before Cato and his battered trap could cross from the cobbled street, an ornate barouche of deep mahogany, with red upholstery and iron-rimmed wheels, cut directly across their path, almost running Cato down.

Cato stopped and retreated a step to save himself. He cried out, angered and shocked, yelling at the occupants and waving his arm threateningly toward the high-hatted coachman and the two women in the open tonneau.

Locke paused halfway down the gangplank and stared, openmouthed, at what he saw, more a vision than reality. Assuredly two of the most beautiful women he'd ever beheld, and one so excruciatingly lovely she may as well have been alone in the carriage for all the attention she permitted her companion.

A dainty green parasol almost shaded her face, which was faintly shadowed beneath the wide floppy brim of a large tailored straw hat. She sat slightly apart and aloof from the woman beside her. She rode, totally heedless of her companion, the noisy, staring rabble in her path, the blaze of white sun, the stench of fish, tar and refuse.

Locke's first reaction to her self-possessed beauty was *royalty*. She'd been born to the purple, and existed in a rarified, tyrannical world of authority nowhere more cultivated than among the ruling Spanish. In the first moment of being suffered to behold her in person, one recognized that she accepted her exalted position, her rank, even her ethereal loveliness as a divine right. She afforded immediacy to that cliché, blueblood of Castile. She *was* a blueblood of Castile. This is in no way to suggest that Locke resented her aristocratic *hauteur*. In no way! He enjoyed it. He appreciated it. In her, he applauded and approved that imperious manner. It lent the final crowning touch to a magnificent elegance.

From her unadorned sun hat to her fragile slippers she was as lovely as she was out of place in this foul fortress of freebooters.

Locke joined the unwashed rabble in staring at her in admiring deference. Her hair glowed blondely—but what a blondeness. Not the soft, girlish, rust-tined texture he found captivating in Mary-Stuart, but the *old* gold of *ancien régime*. A Castilian blonde! Until this moment he had never realized the true, breathless significance of this description.

Her parasol and sun hat lay a pale gray shadow across the cameo-perfection of her features, darkened the Spanish-black of her large, wide-set eyes. Her full, soft crimson (if there be such a dilution!) lips seemed curved to laughter and only temporarily restrained. Her throat, an insolent scepter, with more gold spilling to the high mounds rising at the laced, low-cut bodice of her pale green dress.

A shudder unlike anything he'd ever experienced before fulgurated through Locke's fevered body, an ache and exultance compounded of longing, of loss, of regret, of wonder, of anticipation and, most of all, an electric shock of desire, a violent need for something out of reach, something he would never have, but which he would never stop wanting to the core of his soul.

He stared at her with such unyielding intentness that some inexplicable communication passed between them. For one brief moment, her gaze touched his, and held. It was for less than the space of a breath in eternity. But she *had* looked at him. More importantly, she had *seen* him, was aware of him as someone apart from everyone else on the crowded piers, and something static flickered in her eyes before she coolly looked beyond him to where Captain Arbuthnot stood, practically genuflecting, at the head of the gangplank.

It was then that Locke saw trunks and bags lashed to the rear of the barouche.

He remained unmoving as the second woman stepped out

of the carriage, assisted to the plankings by the tall black coachman, splendid in glittering livery and highly polished boots. This woman, like her mistress, was not to be found in ordinary existence—unfortunately for those of us destined there to pass our days and nights.

She stood regally tall and slender; in her shone a pride and dignity which had nothing to do with royal birth—obviously denied her—but which germinated and flowered from a deep-felt self-respect, sense of self-worth and hard-earned position. She was young—surely still in her teens—but a mature, ripened, fully developed female. Her skin gleamed moistly, a light mauve color; she was a mixed breed, a mulatto—called a Morisco in the Latin countries: the offspring of a Moor and a mestizo.

Locke was aware that he stared like a yokel and that Cato, who somehow had wandered to the foot of the gangplank, stood rooted, even more stupefied by the Morisco beauty. His eyes showed white rims, his lips sagged so the sun glistened on his dry teeth.

Locke smiled inwardly. One had to forgive him and Cato for gaping like flycatchers. They'd been a long time at sea. And even had they come straight from the local brothel, they still would have paid wide-eyed homage here. One seldom encountered two women of such exquisite grace in a month of Sundays—certainly not in the same hour in a pit of iniquity such as these Fernandina docks.

The incredibly lovely maidservant strode imperially, under her own dainty parasol, clearing a path, almost spreading an invisible red carpeting for her mistress. Most of the population of Fernandina had gathered on the piers at the arrival of the merchant schooner. The entire pier stirred, a writhing mass of black and white humanity in bright degrees of undress. They loudly hawked their wares—indigo, tobacco, Indian relics, live chickens, voodoo charms, steamed oysters, crabs, boiled shrimp, fresh-fried fish. But they fell away, parting like the Red Sea as the Morisco girl approached.

Her passage was disputed—all unintentionally!—at the foot of the gangplank where Cato sagged, abstracted by her unreal loveliness.

"Out of my way, you nigger." The words were harsh,

stunning, from that lovely red mouth. Rather than spurring Cato to leap aside, they further befuddled and incapacitated him, shocking him into a helpless immobility. "I said move!" the girl cried. "Get out of my way."

Before Cato could move, she slapped him hard with the back of her hand across his cheek.

Cato staggered back, more in sorrow and surprise than any pain. He fell against the support bar of the gangplank and hung there, his hand against his face.

"What the hell do you mean, hitting my man like that?" Locke spoke to the maidservant but his gaze was fixed on her mistress. Inside he was laughing, thinking, *maybe we can go lie down somewhere and discuss this*. The Castilian blonde did not bother to look at him.

The Morisco girl merely seared him with a glance. The two regal females swept past, fragrant as flowers, going to the deck of the *Chance* where Captain Arbuthnot awaited them, smiling and bowing and sweating.

Locke did not forget that unearthly beauty in the next hours. Ruefully, he admitted he would never forget her after this briefest encounter—strangers passing. In fact, no matter where he went now, he would not forget her, and whatever woman loved him would share his bed with the vivid recollection of this golden nymph.

He got into the battered cab, the duffel bag at his feet, unnoticed. He leaned forward. "Tell me," he said to the cabbie. "Was that a vision—or was she real?"

"Señorita Castillo y Martiz?" The aged cabby kissed the tips of his fingers. "Señorita Yolanda Castillo y Martiz is more than real, senor. The daughter of the Spanish governor of Florida."

"I wonder what he wants with a gold cannon?" Locke said, sighing.

"What? Eh? I beg your pardon, senor?"

"Nothing. The governor's daughter, eh? What's she doing in a place like this?"

"Señorita Yolanda is returning from Spain. Her ship had an evil encounter with a privateer. They managed to fight off the sea devil, but only barely made it here to port. She was forced to wait here for new accommodations to Pensacola. Her father has arranged for her passage on the *Chance*."

Cato said, "And her servant girl? What is her name?"

The cabbie laughed. "That one? Her name is Isabella, sir. She is a mulatto. They call her a Morisco—but it is still mixed blood."

Cato nodded. He lifted his hand to his cheek again, barely aware he did so.

— *XIII* —

THE FERDINAND HOTEL was not far enough removed from the piers to escape the smells, the flotsam and jetsam of the sea, flung ashore on its tides to rot and stink in the sun and to ride inland on every east wind.

The hotel was very nearly the most pretentious edifice in town. It gathered the elite—the man with money enough to afford reasonably comfortable, but unreasonably priced lodgings. Wide stairs with many steps—a Spanish obsession—led to long upper corridors, rooms with sixteen-foot ceilings and many narrow but extremely tall windows gaping open to any errant breeze.

The owner, behind the desk in the lobby, looked up and then peered, puzzled, almost recognizing Locke. It was only when Jerry signed the register that the name clicked in the inkeeper's memory.

"Ah, *El Capitán Veneno!* The hotheaded one! I was sure I recognized you, señor! It has been a long time. Such a long time."

"Two years." Locke nodded. "A lifetime in my trade."

"*Sí*! Many come—many die—many forgotten within two years down here." He grinned and nodded. "But you—you made your mark—a hard man to forget, *Capitán*."

Locke turned the register and studied it. Robert Harmbrister's name was not there. A faint fluttering of panic stirred like troubled moths in his belly, a sense of wrong that he could not put a name to.

He described Harmbrister but the manager, listening, smiled and kept shaking his head. "I've seen no one to meet your description, señor . . . this I promise. I shall let you know the moment he arrives."

Locke gave him a gold piece. "I'd deeply appreciate it if you did."

Already awed that the famed—and infamous—*Capitán Veneno*, who had dominated this area and its sea lanes briefly but memorably, who had suddenly and completely disappeared so one might have thought him dead, now returned, and ingratiated and indebted by the generous gratuity, the hotel owner nodded, smiling widely, his moustache wriggling. "I have a most elegant suite for you and your servant, *Capitán*—eh, Mister Locke. . . . Just this morning vacated by royalty—my best accommodations."

The high-ceiling second-floor rooms had been newly swept and straightened, but the wan scent of flowers remained—that fragrance which had struck him forcibly as Yolanda Castillo y Martiz and her handmaid swept so imperiously past to the deck of the *Chance*. How sad that she should walk out of his life before she barely entered it!

Locke stood at the window staring at the *Chance*, idle, warped to the piers. Except that he and Harmbrister had stolen a royal fortune from Arbuthnot, he was strongly tempted to return down there and proceed with the *Chance* to Pensacola, or any other port chosen by the governor's daughter. He knew better. Neither he nor Harmbrister could draw a full breath until the *Chance* was out of sight on the sea—if then. And where in the hell was Harmbrister? What sort of game was being played out there?

He shook away his apprehension, turned and grinned over his shoulder. "Anyhow, Cato, we'll sleep tonight in their beds—still warm with the memory and imprint of their bodies."

Cato exhaled heavily, distracted.

Locke laughed. "I never saw you so taken with a woman before, Cato."

"I'm not like you, mastah. To pant after every female. My head and my heart turned with every pretty skirt that swishes past. No. But in my heart I know when I find the woman meant for me." He sighed. "I saw that one today."

"And I saw her backhand you and call you nigger."

Cato's head tilted. "I'll have her on her knees to me—and calling me master—if I live."

"If you live that long."

The mysterious and ravishing beauty of Yolanda Castillo y Martiz did not drive Mary-Stuart from Locke's mind. Far from it. Despite what Cato said and believed about him, he had been faithful to Mary-Stuart—in his fashion. No one had ever displaced her for an hour from his mind and heart. He thought about her now, but somehow her rust-tinted gold hair was like rich and thickly spun old gold . . .

He prowled the room, unable to relax. He kept waiting for the sound of Harmbrister's boots on the corridor flooring, the rap of his fist on that door facing. Rather than risk missing Robert, Locke sent Cato to bring their lunch on trays.

Cato was gone for a long time. He returned with boiled shrimp and fresh lettuce, with boiled eggs and plantains. They ate ravenously, washing it down with wine.

For Locke, even this pungent meal was tasteless. Not even the sauce, hot with cayenne and piquant with herbs, satisfied him. He could not believe any ill had befallen Harmbrister, and yet at the same time he could not believe the ex-soldier would remain this long away from a fortune in gold. Or had Harmbrister learned something he didn't know? Or was Harmbrister framing some sort of charade in which he had already been elected to play the goat?

The sun was westering, the breezes waning from the sea, the hotel growing humid. Locke prowled his room. He admitted he had never met a man quite like Harmbrister. He had dealt with killers, thieves, confidence men, liars, cheats, kidnappers, dishonest politicians and conniving priests, but Harmbrister was something new for him—a handsome, sharp-minded young rascal who lived by his wits, who achieved by outmaneuvering his fellows. He was certain by now that Harmbrister was planning some skulduggery, but what?

A knock on his door brought him heeling around from his window. He was sweated, his shirt uncomfortably clinging to his body. He strode across the room, signaling to Cato that he would admit their caller. A sense of relief flooded through him and he was smiling as he pulled open the corridor door.

His heart sank. He stared at the fat, moustached innkeeper. The stout man looked as if he might cry. "*Capitán,*" he said, "a thousand pardons. But I must ask a favor of you—and if you will grant it, you will find me eternally grateful."

"Yes?" Locke waited, watching the unhappy man.

"This suite, señor—"

"Yes. What about it?"

The man swallowed through a taut throat. "I fear, *Capitán,* I have rented you this suite in error."

Locke shrugged. "It's all right. It's quite satisfactory. We are settled nicely here."

Now the fat man's eyes did fill with tears. "But you don't understand, señor. This suite belongs to her majesty, her highness, the daughter of Governor Castillo of Florida."

"She moved out."

"No. I *thought* she moved out, señor. A thousand pardons. I am an ass. The third son of a jackass. I believed the señorita sailed on the ship *Chance*. However, I was mistaken. She did not go. She is downstairs. In the lobby. Furious. Waiting for her room."

Locke grinned. "So she didn't sail, eh?"

"Señor, some sort of mix-up. Forgive me. She did not sail. I acted in haste. Please, if I may remove you and your man to other quarters—equally as fine, perhaps a mite smaller?"

"You may tell her serene highness that my man and I will *share* this suite with her and her maidservant. That is the only way I could accommodate her."

"Oh, please, *Capitán*. You make a joke. But it is the kind of joke that could lose me my hotel—cost me my life. Her father—the governor—is totally without any sense of humor. Please, sir. This night, free to you and your servant, if you will permit me to exchange your rooms."

By now, Yolanda and Isabella had entered the corridor from the stairwell. They stood waiting, heads tilted and coldly set.

Tongue implanted in his cheek, Locke glanced toward the two women. They refused to face him. He spoke loudly. "You mean they would throw me and my servant out of these rooms—and not even thank me?"

The innkeeper trembled. "Oh, I am sure they will thank you. A million thanks, señor, and my undying gratitude—"

"I know, but you're not my type." Locke saw a whisper of a smile pull at Yolanda's lips. But her head tilted higher. He shrugged, surrendering. "What do you bet, they don't even thank us?"

Before Locke's belongings could be removed from the suite along the corridor to a single room with large window overlooking the harbor, black men were entering with Yolanda's trunks and suitcases. The scent of flowers multiplied in the room.

At last, Locke was entirely relocated, and when he bowed toward Yolanda going through the door into the corridor, she merely tossed him the briefest glance.

He was right. She did not thank him.

Darkness settled in from the sea. The air was cleaner, the winds fresher. Palms rattled at the casement windows. Songs flared from the nearby whorehouse, along with laughter and curses and unexplained screams. Business as usual in Fernandina, Locke knew, from old memory. But there was a change: He could not forget that Yolanda occupied a room a few doors from his. She had looked back at him. She had seen him. She had met his gaze—a matter of extreme flirtation in a woman of her rank. The smell of flowers was strong in his nostrils and it did not come in on the sea breeze.

He and Cato had dinner in their room by candlelight. Cato was abstracted and silent. "You act like you're in heat," Locke said.

"Females get in heat," Cato said. "The male has her scent—and the madness. I have the madness."

They both tried to laugh. But Locke found little laughter in this strange subtropical night. The *Chance* had disappeared from the harbor; one moment she lay warped to the pier, the next she was gone, as if she had vanished on the incoming mists. And there was no word, no sign from Harmbrister. The innkeeper had seen no trace of the gentleman.

"Perhaps Captain Arbuthnot suspected Mr. Harmbrister of stealing the gold—and slew him," Cato suggested.

"Or maybe they were in this deal together somehow. Though I can't figure how in hell that might be. Did we find that chest too easily? Did we take it without obstacle? Did they want us to take it? Are we marked men, holding a fortune for them?''

''Captain Arbuthnot is gone with his ship,'' Cato said.

''But where in hell is Harmbrister?''

''I don't know. But perhaps we had better sleep in relays. One of us will watch while the other sleeps,'' Cato suggested.

''You keep forgetting you're a nigger slave—born to take orders, not to give them—don't you?''

''Yes.'' Cato nodded with quiet dignity, and unabashed honesty.

''Since it's your idea, I'll let you sleep first.''

Locke prowled the room, unable to sleep anyhow. He thought about Yolanda in that bed a few doors from him. He wondered if she were asleep, or did she lie awake, troubled? He yearned back to Virginia, and Hidden Brook and to Mary-Stuart. He closed his eyes, summoning the image of her into his mind. She came to him across time and space, but the hell of it was she had deep gold hair and Spanish eyes.

Damn his eyes! What was wrong with him? Why couldn't he be faithful to one woman? God knew, he loved only Mary-Stuart. But this did not blind him to the incredible beauty of the Spanish señorita. He could not get her out of his mind even when he knew her to be unobtainable. What would it profit him to spend his life yearning after her? Nothing. And yet he could not expel her from his mind, banish her from his thoughts, simply because it was meet and right to do so. He loved Mary-Stuart, but fate denied her to him. And no matter how faithfully he loved Mary-Stuart, he admitted to God and the darkness that he would tear down that thick door to get to Yolanda Castillo y Martiz, if only he thought she would put out her arms to welcome him. Damn it! He admitted what he was, but he couldn't help it.

He was sweated and miserable. Somewhere in the black island night, Robert Harmbrister stalked, or lay dead, or waited, plotting. Which? God only knew. But it was the worst kind of waiting, locked in this room with no idea what was going on outside it, what was in that ex-soldier's mind. One fact alone was irrefutable: Robert Harmbrister would do anything for money. And there was a hell of a lot of money in this room.

A sharp, insistent rap at his door brought him to his feet and across the room.

Once more he confronted the fat, sad face of the innkeeper. He exhaled, feeling as if he had not breathed for some tense moments. "What in hell is it now?"

"It is past midnight, señor."

"I know that. Did I ask you the hour?"

"I am only following your request, señor. I wish only to report to you. I close the hotel doors now. The man you sought—your friend Mr. Harmbrister—he has not yet arrived." The innkeeper smiled uncertainly and stood waiting with his fat paw trembling, ready to spring out to receive a tip.

Locke shook his head, frustrated. He tossed the man a coin. "Try to get some sleep."

"Thank you, *Capitán*. The same good wish to you."

The noise at the door had wakened Cato, who slept only lightly anyhow. Neither of them slept much the rest of that night. The wild sounds of the town ebbed and quieted at last. It grew so quiet one heard the mullet striking in the bay. Locke and Cato were up with the first fissures of dawn, pink and yellow and cerise across the harbor. They abandoned all hope of rest until they found Harmbrister or somehow learned what had happened to him. Cato went out to find breakfast. He returned with coffee, scrambled eggs, fried chicken and hot sour-milk biscuits.

Locke ate, trying to fill the empty void spreading in his belly. Cato sat silently. His usual ravenous appetite seemed thwarted, stilled. Locke smiled. "Do you keep smelling flowers?"

Cato looked up, face solemn, and nodded. "Violets, I think."

Locke could stay no longer in the room. He went out a little after eight seeking Harmbrister, or some word of him. The places of business along the harbor opened, proprietors dull-eyed and yawning. They listened politely to Locke, some of them recalling him from that other lifetime of two years ago. But none could help him. None had seen a man answering to Robert's description.

At the whorehouse across the cobblestone street from the piers, the madam got out of her rocking chair, tossed aside her fan and picked her way to him on tender feet. She remembered him with pleasure and welcomed him warmly. "My God, we thought you were dead. Such a pity! A beautiful man built like you!"

She regretted she had not seen Harmbrister. "He sounds handsome. And clean. And young. We don't always get such clientele as you and your friend." She smiled and stroked Locke's face. "We have some prize new virgins—hardly used. White girls in their teens. Would you be interested?"

Locke smiled and shook his head. "I need release, Madame. I admit this. It's been a long time. Too long. But unfortunately, you don't have either of the two women I want in this world."

He returned along the redolent, crowded street to the hotel. The owner's wife sat in the lobby. She bowed and smiled with her broken teeth. Locke hurried up the wide stairs to the second floor.

The image of Yolanda smote him as he came off the landing. He saw neither her nor her maidservant in the corridor. But the scent of violets haunted him its entire length.

He found his own door unlocked. He opened it and stepped inside to bedlam.

Cato lay in the middle of the floor, trussed up like a hog on its way to market.

Locke knelt beside him, removed the gag from his mouth, the ropes brutally tight on his wrists and ankles.

"I see Harmbrister was here," he said.

Cato nodded. He sat, trying to rub circulation back into his wrists.

Locke swore. "Did he hurt you? I'll kill him if he harmed you."

"Only my dignity." Cato exhaled heavily. "He took me by surprise. One moment he smiled, friendly as always, the next he showed me the long snout of a handgun. And he no longer smiled. I give him only that he looked terribly unhappy about what he did—"

"I could look unhappy too—for millions in gold."

Cato sighed. "He tied me up. He was gentle enough. Quite gentlemanly. But thorough. Oh, he was thorough. If you had not come back, I'd have been another hour getting out of these knots."

"He meant business."

"He said he had to have time to get away, to get off the island. He kept apologizing—for everything he did—and for what he was doing—to both of us."

"The bastard. Apologies come cheap—by the mouthful."

"He said to tell you how sorry he was about this. He said to tell you he was sorry, but his need was twice as great as yours."

"I can see how he would believe that."

"He said to thank you for all you did to help him. He was most friendly, really. And apologizing. And he seemed truly regretful."

"But he took it all?"

Cato nodded. "That's what it all adds up to. He took it all."

Locke got up. He went to the bed and pulled a woolen duffel bag from beneath it. "Not quite all. I thought he might want it all. So I divided it. I did it while you were out so there'd be no chance for him to beat you to make you reveal if there was more. I figured he never had seen the first duffel bag full, so I left him one to find—and be satisfied with. After all, he told me himself, he never did trust a man who was too honest."

— XIV —

NOWHERE ON earth does each new day begin with more promise and then burn itself more quickly to a sweated crisp than in Florida. A pristine sun, rising moist and chaste from the sea, wipes away all darkness and dark memories. Langorous dawn breezes stir one's curtains and gently rouse the sleeper, inviting him to the cool, invigorating beauty of this untouched morning world. The streets of the town lie clean and empty, like brooks running clear between rocky banks. The beaches glisten clean and uncluttered and freshly cool like fresh-turned white sheets. A strange clarity intensifies the air, sharpening the sight and honing all the other senses. Palm fronds rattle like castanets, and newly opened buds of roses, jasmine, gardenias, jacaranda and hibiscus perfume the dankest alley and grow brightly rampant along the fences and the walls. But by ten o'clock men are yelling, fighting and arguing in the fouled streets, the accumulated trash begins to litter the beaches and the pitiless sun blisters every living thing, drawing off the last ounce of sap, energy, pleasure and good will. One staggers into the nearest shard or fragment of shade, too exhausted, too depleted by the sun, even to despise the heat . . .

The morning still possessed a scintilla of silver clarity, a last wisp of cool breeze fingered the curtains, a soft kiss of flowery perfume yet overrode the smells of wood smoke, fried fish and donkey dung. Locke lingered over his coffee. Someone rapped lightly but persistently at the corridor door.

Cato left the seat by the window where he sat watching the sun on the harbor. He crossed the room and opened the door. Then he stood silent, as if caught and paralyzed in a catatonic trance. Still rankled and edgy over Harmbrister's sneak assault on Cato, Locke instantly feared the worst. He lunged to his feet and strode across the faded carpeting.

The Morisco girl stood there, slender and breathtakingly lovely out of her mistress's overwhelming orbit.

"Yes," Locke said. "What is it?"

Isabella gave Cato a glance charged and prickled with contempt. "I've come from my mistress, her serene highness Señorita Castillo y Martiz. I have a message, but your nigger is too stupid to speak, open his mouth or to listen."

"Cato is entranced, señorita. Struck dumb by your beauty. As all men must be."

The Morisco girl's expression did not alter, but a faint touch of blood reddened her cheeks and one saw she was less than displeased.

"I'll take the message," Cato managed to croak.

Both Locke and Isabella laughed at him . . .

By seven-thirty that night, Locke, attired in the finest lightweight suit he could buy at the general store which provided any merchandise taken from merchantmen, warships and traders, presented himself at the door of the suite occupied by Yolanda Castillo y Martiz.

Isabella answered the door. She wore a peasant blouse and slippers. She smiled, curtsied and invited him in. Somehow she then withdrew, or vanished from the face of the earth, and Locke found himself left alone in the candlelit room with the loveliest creature gracing the Western Hemisphere. Explorers dared unchartered seas, invader and aborigine died violently, flags were struck in the names of long-dead kings, colonists starved, wars were fought and treaties abrogated to clear a wilderness for a backdrop worthy of her gemlike elegance. Now the barbarian lances were rusted and barber poles hung in their places. Insuring a civilized setting for her had cost a pretty penny and she was worth every exorbitant peso of it.

She gazed at him for a long beat from across the saffron-lit room. She was so elegantly made! She looked as if her lovely head had been set upon that exquisitely fragile perfection of her lithe young body after every precise consideration of effect, shock-value and symmetry. She appeared regal and cool, but in her olive-black eyes glinted promise of inward fire.

"Your serene highness," he bowed.

Yolanda stood near one of the windows, bathed in the delicate afterglow of the sun. Her pale, sequined dinner dress winked, glittered and sputtered wanly in the candlelight as it slithered over the curves of her body. Her low-cut bodice revealed the creamy perfection of her full breasts almost to their pink aureolae. She remained for that discourteous extra moment, unmoving, her bearing regal, her beauty accented by the careful plait of *oro de España* hair piled like a tiara upon her perfect head. When she spoke, her voice was low, faintly imperious and, at the same time, hypnotically warm and sensuous.

"So you are Señor Locke, *sí*?" She gave a small wave of her flawless hand. "The brave and reckless *El Capitán Veneno*? We have not been formally introduced. I hope you don't think me bold inviting you here under such conditions. Still, I felt a certain *obligación*, no?"

"Obligation, your highness?"

"After all, we did inconvenience you, did we not? Forcing you from your rightful quarters, as we did? And not even bothering to thank you?"

"Divine right, your highness."

Seeing he was teasing her, but politely, Yolanda smiled. "Allow me to introduce myself. I am Yolanda Castillo y Martiz. My father is Hernando Maria Flores Castillo, the governor of the Spanish Floridas. . . . If my *Ingles* is less than perfect, forgive, and remember please—*Ingles* is my second language, no?"

"It never sounded lovelier than crossing your lips," Locke said. He gazed at her, fascinated. The warm olive tones in her fair skin enchanted him. In her he saw the dreams, the conquests, the treacheries, the cruelties, the pride and the magnificence of a majestic people. He stood, entranced. But far more than deference stirred within him. He wanted her. Savagely. Fiercely. Furiously. Immediately. Deep in the vaults of his mind, ancient recall showed him lunging upon her, ripping away her clothes, ravishing her, suckling at her breasts, driving himself into her until he found release and surcease from the furies raging inside him. Good God! The daughter of the governor, a protected offspring of nobility, a gentle and civilized lady of high position . . . he would have to be on strictest guard against his own most primitive instincts.

With a deliberate, feline grace, Yolanda came to him and took his hand. He felt the cool pressure of her fingers but was keenly aware also of the faintest trembling in her touch.

She poured a Spanish wine, a rich Madeira, into two glasses and they drank to the fates.

The wine burned sweet on his lips, hot in his throat and devastating on the taut-wound nerves in his belly. Sounds from the street seemed muted as if by some royal edict. Everything outside this room faded, remote, removed. He could see a slice of distant turquoise sky through a tall narrow window, hear the faint castanet rattling of palm fronds.

Yolanda was outwardly totally at ease. He had little reason to doubt she was less than serene inside. She could hardly want him with the seething passion with which he desired her. He had seen a stallion almost kill itself, squealing and fighting to get to a dam in heat. He believed that mangled stud far less possessed than he in this quiet moment. He wanted Yolanda with a desiring unknown before—even for Mary-Stuart—because his desire for Yolanda was mindless, immediate, bound within the heady perimeters of this candlelit room, this langorous night, this static-charged moment in time. He could never hope to have her. His being permitted this near to her could almost be perceived as another hellish prank of fiendish gods, laughing hysterically at his discomfort. He could think only one thing: He would go straight from Yolanda's fiery presence to Madame Clara's whorehouse at the piers. He could not get there what he wanted, but some prostitute would find her wildest fantasies played out in every heart-stopping aspect.

Yolanda's aristocratic, modulated voice, quietly and condescendingly played on his nerves as if upon drawn strings.

She spoke of his interests, asked about his home, his plans, his family, his ambitions. Her voice faded in and out of his consciousness, battling against his own overpowering thoughts. He kept a polite smile on his lips, he hoped he nodded in all the right places, but sometimes he lost whole phrases, whole fragments of her conversation, yet he was able to draw one certain conclusion despite his inability to concentrate clearly on anything except the rise and fall of her breasts, the clear imprint of her hardened nipples under the diaphanous fabric: She wanted something from him.

She said nothing of herself and yet he slowly came to realize that some kind of bargain was being proffered here as in any commercial bazaar of the world. She wanted something.

He bit back ironic laughter., aware and somehow shocked as he discovered for the first time the determined little tilt of her chin, the taut line of her mouth at certain moments, the way her black eyes narrowed thin sometimes, even when she smiled. She was royalty, all right, performing for a commoner, feeding him baked duck and Indian rice and plantains and Spanish wine and sweet smiling. She declared she only wanted to express her gratitude for a past favor. But she wanted something. Oh, she wanted something all right.

He grinned inwardly. And that made two of them, driven by hidden desires . . .

He looked down at himself. Perhaps his own desiring was not too hidden, at that.

"They do say that you came to be the most feared man in

this port,'' she was saying. ''Such strength. Such cleverness. Such reckless courage—''

''Who have you been talking to?''

''They all say this. All who remember you. And who can forget such wild and gallant exploits as achieved by the fiery *Capitán Veneno*? Why did you suddenly walk away from all you had conquered? Or do you not wish to talk about it?''

He shrugged his shoulders.''I don't mind talking about it. I just got fed up. A bellyful. I quit and went home.''

''And yet you have come back? You do not wish to say why?''

He exhaled heavily. ''I don't really know why.''

''Perhaps you are—looking for something?''

''Perhaps.'' They exchanged words and yet they said nothing of what seethed inside them just under the surface. He was afraid that what the lady of noble birth wanted was probably mundane. He wanted the heavenly warmth and exultance of her body. At this moment he wanted her above all else. He saw with a harsh, inward laughing at his own vulnerability that he would live for Mary-Stuart, but he would die to possess Yolanda's fragrant loveliness. He saw his affections for Mary-Stuart as a lasting, reverential, gentle love, compared to the fire and storm and holocaust of his desire for this woman across the wan-lit table from him. He would always love the calm beauty of Mary-Stuart but he wanted Yolanda's supple, fiery body with a lecherous driving obsession that unhinged him and left him shaken inside.

He was aware she was laughing lightly, saying something he had missed entirely. How much had he missed, mesmerized and confused inside his own thoughts?

''I beg your pardon, señorita?''

''I only said I saw you. Yesterday. Coming out of Madame Clara's.''

His head jerked up. At first, he could not recall, then he remembered; he had gone to Madame Clara's seeking Harmbrister. He merely shrugged. ''Perhaps men have desires unknown to women, señorita.''

Her smile twisted her lips and her dark eyes swam with changeling shadows. ''I doubt that,'' she said. His heart lurched. Was this a royal command? An aristocratic flirtation? "But I cannot believe—a handsome, virile man like you would be forced to find—pleasure?—in such a place."

He exhaled heavily. "There are all kinds of men, all kinds of pleasures, señorita."

"I'm sure of it, Jeremiah—*mío*. But I do not see you in such a place. It is somehow less than one thinks of the infamous—and famous—*Capitán Veneno*."

He laughed. "You sound jealous. How I wish I could presume to believe that were true . . ."

"I am jealous, *caballero*. I despise waste—of any kind."

His heart quickened. Surely, if God were kind, there was invitation couched somewhere in these throaty words? Please, God?

She filled his wineglass to the brim. He held her gaze, his brow tilted. "You'll make me drunk."

"Perhaps that is what I want, *caballero*. You are so serious. So polite. So formal! What is it they say? Wine dilutes the will and washes away the inhibitions?"

He laughed. "And sometimes spoils the performance."

She gazed levelly into his eyes. "I doubt this would be true of you, *caballero-mío*."

Yolanda finished off her wine. She set down her glass and walked to the window. Beyond her, the night deepened through a silvery sheen. He remained a moment in his chair. Then, as if attracted by irresistible forces, he got up and crossed to her. He stood at her shoulders, close against her so that both of them were unmistakably aware of the rigidity bulging at his belt.

When she did not draw away, he pressed closer, insinuating his pulsing verticality into the heated part of her fevered hips. He felt her shiver like a dove.

Emboldened, he slipped his arms about the narrows of her waist, drawing her back, hard and demanding, upon that colossus tempered and inflamed by her fragrance, her nearness, her loveliness.

He held her pinioned there for a long time. The breathless moments ticked away and neither spoke. Beyond the narrow rectangular windows the harbor, the river, the sea and the town spun away into the cosmos, lost.

She spoke only once. She whispered, "Jeremiah-*mío*."

This seemed to call for no response, and he made none.

She held herself rigid, as if recalling her training, her years in the convents with the nuns, her vows, her position in royal society, her dreams, as if counting the beads of her rosary, and fighting a losing battle inside her own conscience. And then, as if everything before this moment, and beyond this night, melted and lost all reality, she turned slowly and pressed in with her hips upon him. She tilted her pelvis and parted her thighs slightly, standing on her tiptoes to fashion her fiery femininity precisely upon his quivering eminence.

Her eyes closed sleepily, her voluptuous mouth parted, her heated breath, sweet enough to drink, seared him.

He slipped the straps of her sequined gown down over her shoulders. She trembled, her whole body quivered, but she did not protest.

Her bodice slipped and her taut, high-standing breasts spilled free of their last fetters. He stared, enchanted at their golden loveliness, and then bent his head as if in homage, suckling her.

She cried out, her head falling back. She trembled in unalloyed ecstasy, clutching the crown of his head and holding him with fierce strength to her breast.

She slumped against him, her thighs parted wantonly wider so that only the sheer lustrous fabric of the silk dress lay between his bristling blade and the hot chalice opening to him.

"Oh, don't," she whispered. "Please don't." And yet her hips undulated upon him, moving in abandon as if to some savage, unheard rhythm. Her arms went up his back and her fingers clawed into his wide shoulders, dragging him down to her.

"*Yo sabo jamás*!" she whispered, voice taut, "I never knew. I never knew."

She trembled with such violence under his nursing lips on her swollen breast that her hair shook loose from its braids and fell down, like golden damasks, fragrant about her shoulders and to the small of her arched back.

Her lips searched hungrily for his and he pulled her closer, his hands like talons, gripping her hips, working her body upon his.

"Jeremiah-*mío*," she gasped. "Please! Wait! Wait! Please! . . . I have never felt such agonized delight before. . . . I have lost my head. . . . In the name of God, be strong for both of us."

He spoke, breathless, against her parted mouth. "I want you . . . as I never wanted anyone."

"And I you, *corazón-mío*, truly." She struggled, frantic. "And I you. . . . Perhaps I intended a little flirtation, but you are too forceful, too exciting for me. . . . Oh God, I am helpless. . . . I am undone."

He suckled her breasts again as his answer. He could feel her shivering in ecstasy as the thrilling electricity surged inside her from his nursing lips nuzzling at her nipples.

Suddenly, she cried out and broke away from him.

She stopped against the wall, mussed, her hair rich in torrents about her shoulders and bared breasts. She did not look like a marquis's daughter. She looked like a wanton, glittering and wild-eyed with desire. But she was shaking her head from side to side.

"We cannot. We must not. . . . Please, Jeremiah-*mío*, listen to me! Am I nothing but a whore, to be taken—on the first night—on the first night?"

He shook his head as if trying to clear it. She pushed her hair back from her face. "Please, Jeremiah-*mío*, forgive me if I tempted you—if I led you on past that place where I could laugh and put you off."

A shudder wracked him; he did not answer.

Her eyes brimmed with tears. "Say you forgive me," she begged. "I am at fault. I am sorry. But we must not—not here—on the first night when we meet—as if I am a common slut. Don't you see? I know now I want more for us, Jeremiah-*mío*. More than even I suspected the first time I saw you and felt my heart ache with pleasure. . . . Don't hate me, Jeremiah-*mío*. Be patient. We may yet know ecstasy that not even heaven holds."

He felt a chill go through him. Despite her tears, despite the way she had shivered in his arms, bared her breasts and parted her mouth wide to him, he felt a warning shock. This was contrived. Even this weeping, this pleading for forgiveness, this begging him to be strong for both of them—all contrived. She wanted something from him—something that had nothing to do with surrendering her body to his.

Rage gorged up through him. Perhaps her perfidy came too

close on the heels of Robert Harmbrister's betrayal, too soon after his loss of Mary-Stuart who refused to believe his vows, but he stared down at her and saw only one more mendacious human being.

He growled. "I quite understand."

But she was sensitive to his suffering; perhaps she had not escaped totally unscathed. She cried out, "But you don't understand! I don't want you to hate me."

"I don't know you well enough to hate you."

"Please! Don't take that cruel, cold tone. If you won't believe me honest and sincere, then take it—and be damned. Do it, and walk out of here and I spit on you. I never want to see you again. . . . But wait, love me . . . be gentle . . . only God knows then what can happen between us."

He bowed, turned and walked out. She followed him to the door, reached out after him, then closed it and sank against its facing, shivering.

He headed toward the whorehouse, changed his mind, decided to get drunk in the nearest tavern and abandoned that idea, too. Would God he could find the answer to his needs in the bottom of a bottle, and release from his agony in the clutches of a whore. But he could not. It was not that easy for him.

Sick with desire, aching with frustration, he walked along the corridor to his own room. He found his key, unlocked the door.

He stopped in the doorway, staring. Cato and Isabella shared pillows and a pad from Cato's cot in the middle of the floor. Her peasant's dress was thrust above her naked hips and pulled down from her outthrusting saffron-colored breasts. Unhurriedly she covered herself. Before them was a pot of at least four pounds of boiled shrimp they had peeled and eaten in hot sauce and washed down with wine. Discarded bottles rolled on the floor.

Locke felt a little better. Cato, at least, looked happy.

Cato grinned weakly up at him from his pillow. "Like mastah, like slave—eh, mastah?"

"You look a lot happier than your master," Locke said.

Cato smiled, caressing Isabella's flushed cheeks and swollen lips with the backs of his fingers. "Isabella does things—with her mouth—you would never dream."

Locke winced. "Just don't tell me about it."

Isabella straightened her dress and stood up. "I better go. My mistress will be looking for me." She parted her mouth and kissed Cato furiously. "Don't forget what I told you, Cato."

Cato laughed up at Locke. "She wants me to kill you, mastah. Or leave you. She says I am not a slave here in Florida and that I should leave you—or kill you."

"She's probably right," Locke said, smiling at Isabella's guilty flushed face. "I think you'd have more fun killing me."

"Exactly what I told her," Cato said. She drew in her breath raspingly and started from the room. "But she feels very strongly. She has no sense of humor about such things."

"Many women don't," Locke said. The door slammed behind Isabella. "Hell hath no fury like a noncombatant."

He prowled the room for a long time, unable to sleep. Blood still boiled fevered in his veins. He still saw Yolanda's full breasts bared and open to him, the sweetness of her breath, the depth of her surrender.

The depth of her surrender? He stood at the darkened window long after Cato had cleared away the remains of his party with Isabella and lay asleep across his cot.

Had she surrendered at all? Or had she been like some master military strategist planning a campaign? And a campaign to what end?

She held him at arm's length; she drew his lips to her fragrant breasts. She dragged him closer, she pushed him away. After all, it was their first night, she was royalty; they were strangers, and yet it all seemed calculated. She drew him as the moon draws the tides; she repelled him with the faint, inviting smile of the coquette. She teased, she promised, she used the coin of her golden body to lure him as with the molten gold of her smile. But despite the promissory notes in her eyes, the hot breath sweet and fragrant across her parted lips, it was still all a matter of a trade. She wanted something from him, and, like any strumpet, she bargained for it with her body.

— XV —

AN HOUR before dawn the next morning, Locke was out stalking alone on the beach. He found no answers at the water's edge. Wryly, he decided that if he walked two miles on the beach every morning, it would not help. His heart would not mend, he would not forget, or resolve anything, but he might soon become proficient in skipping stones across the surface of the water.

Wattled-beaked pelicans eyed him warily. He watched the sea lap, tireless tides upon a warm and patient shore. He tried to keep his mind blank, but he thought of every hurtful thing he'd ever experienced. He walked for a long time. The sun came up, crimson across the harbor, and the foaming spume, lapping high, pursued him south along the sodden shore.

His mind chased itself upon the same unavailing treadmill: He had to stay away from Yolanda. He knew he could not, as long as he remained anywhere near her. He saw that stallion ripping its belly trying to get to its dam. He loved Mary-Stuart but, having lost her, he looked for the excitement, the desolation, the fascination he was aware one always found in new romances. But any affair with Yolanda Castillo y Martiz would be costly. She wanted something from him and she wanted it badly enough to dangle her charms before him, like a carrot hung out on a stick in front of a plodding jackass.

The hell of it was, she was coldly calculating about it. She meant to strike a bargain with him.

God knew she was lovely enough to justify any sacrifice she might ask of him. There was no sense pretending she found him irresistible—she found him at hand, useful, necessary for something she wanted accomplished. Perhaps she had gotten slightly carried away last night. For a few moments she had lost control of the situation; she'd lain helpless, her breasts bared, her will diffused. It's easy to get emotional about the one man you believe can help you out of jeopardy.

He didn't want to be used—even by a vessel as lovely as Yolanda, the Marquis Castillo's daughter. It all came too soon after his loss of Mary-Stuart, that mysterious and unwarranted attack on his life by a hired, unknown assassin, the betrayal by Robert Harmbrister. He had reached that low place where he believed in nobody—himself least of all.

Since he'd fled Virginia—a fugitive hiding in shadows—abandoning everything he loved, all he held dear, any chance of finding the truth or of clearing his name—he'd been firmly determined to join Andrew Jackson's forces on the Spanish Florida border and make an attempt anyhow to carry out Monroe's assignment. He couldn't go on forever failing everybody who trusted him.

Now, he was less than certain about even this mission. Jackson stood tall, head and shoulders above ordinary men, renowned, admired—even revered. He was a military man sacrificing life, health, time and fortune to secure the frontier. He was doing something he believed in. He had his detractors, but who were they, and of what quality? Robert Harmbrister, thief, scoundrel, betrayer, was one.

What proof had he—what proof had Monroe provided—of any perfidy on the part of General Jackson? President Monroe suspected the Tennessee general—because Monroe's advisers suspected him, because as President, Monroe had to be extra-alert, sensitive to any threat of betrayal. He admitted he had no proof.

Harmbrister had been violent and vocal in his accusations against Jackson. But Harmbrister was a renegade. He regretted his lost faith in Robert equally as much as the loss of the gold. He had come to feel friendly affection for the rakehell; he'd never had a friend he cared for as much. And he'd lost his faith in him. What did this do to Robert's estimation of Jackson as general, soldier, human being?

He laughed coldly. It left it empty, counterfeit, worthless . . .

He had very little—nothing—to sustain his investigation of a celebrated war hero.

He had lost all heart, he did not want to go forward with Monroe's mission. It seemed to him everything he touched crumbled like wormwood in his hands. He was tired—sick and tired—of dealing in the dishonesty and trickery and mendacity of human beings.

He wanted to escape Yolanda before he was helplessly enslaved and could never leave her, even if he were doomed to trail after her as low and unnoticed as her shadow. And Yolanda, too, proved herself last night far less than honest. She spoke with the elegance, diction and élan of the nobility, but in order to get what she wanted, she was willing to behave like a wanton.

It was not that he made love to her and then prudishly faulted her for giving in to his advances. Far from it. He hated only her being so coldly calculating in her surrender!

If he became more deeply involved with her, he could sink into a hell on earth of his own making, because he did not deceive himself: He was beyond the pale as far as her royal family was concerned. He was totally unsuitable—a Protestant, an American, a commoner. And no matter if Yolanda returned his love for a little while—as she swore. Her own conscience and lifelong habits and training—once sanity restored itself inside her—would mitigate against him, against them. To think otherwise was to fool no one but himself.

Hell, what could he do? He could loiter here, stay in Yolanda's lustrous orbit, abandon everything else, provide Yolanda whatever goods or services or blood she required in this bargain she wanted to strike with him. He could stay until she surrendered to him. If she ever did.

He could clear out. Though he'd lost all heart for the mission, he could find Andrew Jackson, at least be faithful to Monroe's trust in him, carry out the assignment, even if it proved totally fruitless—as he was convinced it must.

Or, he could do what he wanted deep in his heart to do, down where emotions overruled common sense. He could return to Virginia, go home to Hidden Brook. He could go back to Mary-Stuart. He could face the music—the false charges of murder. Perhaps he would lose everything. Maybe he could not clear himself. But he had heaped disgrace upon his family by running like a jackal in the night. He could make amends to them, no matter what it cost him, and in doing so, he could live with himself again.

As if magnetically attracted by the intent, unyielding gaze

of someone fixed on him, he jerked up his head and looked around. At first, the beach seemed deserted, bearded with sea oats and wind-bent pines and sand-scarred cabbage palms, with snipes, gulls and herons feeding in the shallows. Then he caught the flickering of a shadow, the substance of a form, crossing the deep white sand.

It was Yolanda.

His heart pounding in his chest, he stood unmoving. She came directly to him. She smiled faintly, reached out and took his hand.

They walked together along the somnolent shore. The world shone lush, as green and empty and morning-clear as Eden. They did not speak. She moved against him, so her slender hip brushed his, tormenting, the friction like static charges. He put his arm about her and they moved slowly, with her head against his shoulder. It was as if they were lost in time and space, with an eternity to spend like this, and yet, even here at this moment, he was aware of tension in her, anxiety.

His doubting was thrust out of his mind by the scent of her, the warmth and nearness of her. He felt himself spinning and wheeling helplessly into that mindless and passionate need of her. She had only to come near him and it was as if she carried him downward with her to the breathless depths of some fiery pool where he could only sink deeper, no matter how fiercely he struggled, unable to breathe, unable to withstand the pressure building inside his lungs.

He drew her down upon a mat of sea oats and wild grass. She lay in his arms and opened her lips to his kiss. She tasted so good! An ache of need shivered through him. He pressed himself upon her, feeling the heat rising from her thighs as if from a bubbling cauldron. His hands closed on her breasts. For a long, mindless time, he nursed and caressed and fondled them as if he could never love her enough. With his finger he traced her lips and then slipped it between her teeth. She sucked frantically on his finger, breathing raggedly and writhing against him.

His other hand touched the twisted hem of her cotton skirt, moving it aside. She wore no petticoat, her golden legs lay revealed to him. His hand caressed upward along her inner thighs and closed on that fiery triangle, and he pressed his fingers deep into the fevered liquidity.

"Oh, don't," she said.

He shuddered. "You're driving me insane. You'll make a chattering idiot of me. Don't you know that?"

"Jeremiah-*mío*. Can't you understand me?" she whispered, frantic. "I want you, Jeremiah, as no woman ever wanted any man. As I did not even know a woman could desire. . . . But—oh, Jeremiah-*mío,* so much is spoilt if you take me like this."

"I see only heaven."

"And I—only ruin. For me. I am a virgin, Jeremiah. I *am* a virgin. Chaste. It is expected of me. Demanded of me. It goes with what I am, what I was born to be. Don't you see? Chastity—was never even a problem—until last night . . . until now in your arms."

Slowly, he forced himself to retreat from Eden, to return to reality. He collected the fragmented pieces of his taut-strung nerves and by sheer will came all the way back to cold and aching sanity. He raised himself from her, replaced her skirt over her golden legs, lifted her bodice over the tight, swollen rise of her breasts.

He felt as if he might vomit.

Yolanda clung to him. Her eyes brimmed with tears and suddenly she wept, violently, inconsolably, clinging to him.

"Oh God, Jeremiah-*mío,* I am in hell. I am in hell."

"Welcome home."

They sat in the patio of the hotel under a large striped parasol, because it was a public place and less demanding upon them. They sat at the small oakwood table, but neither touched the drinks before them.

"Just think," Yolanda mused. "How nearly it came—we almost did not meet at all."

"My stomach would feel better if we'd never met—more than that moment at the *Chance*."

"Oh, my beautiful," she said. "Don't you know? It was already too late as I walked past you on that gangplank. I had *already* looked at you. I had already *seen* you."

"And I you."

"Did I excite you? Did you think me lovely? Did you want

me?'' She glanced down boldly toward his belt. ''Like that? The moment you saw me?''

He grinned. ''The very first moment. You don't have to ask that.''

''But I do! A woman loves to hear she is lovely—''

''From a safe distance she loves to hear it.''

''Do you understand me then so little, *corazón-mío?* If you will tell me that you loved me, that you wanted me with a fearful passion, I will confess to you a secret I could tell no one else on this earth.''

''I loved you.''

''With a fearful passion,'' she prompted.

''I shook inside, wanting you. As I shake now.''

''I got all hot—and wet—down there—when I looked at you,'' she whispered, her face fiery red. ''The first moment. There. I share with you my truest secret—I could not tell Isabella, my duenna, my priest or my father—oh God, especially not my father! I can tell only you.'' She reached out and pressed his arm with icy fingers.

''Don't touch me,'' he said. He grinned wanly.

''And to think, only but for the fates and an unreliable Captain Arbuthnot, I would be gone, and I would never have known what desire can do to a woman's insides—make her ill and exultant and hot and cold and sick and happy—all in the same moment.''

''What happened with Arbuthnot?''

''My father arranged with the owners of the *Chance*, and with the captain himself, that I would be picked up here and carried to my father's palace in Pensacola. I have been here a month—since our ship was almost destroyed by pirates.''

''Your passage aboard the *Chance* was all arranged, and Arbuthnot wouldn't take you?''

''Arranged by my *father*! The governor. A man with whom Captain Arbuthnot must stay in very best graces if he is to trade with the Indians and Negroes and others in Florida—and that is the source of the captain's income, the business he does with Spanish subjects in Florida.''

''What did Arbuthnot say?''

''That he regretted it a thousand times. That he, sickened by what had happened to him, begged my forgiveness, but he could not endanger my life by allowing me aboard the *Chance* at this time.''

Locke laughed. ''So he left you here. And to think I thought I hated the old knave.'' He gazed at her. ''I am eternally in his debt.''

''Why would he dare to put me off his ship?''

''I think I can tell you that. Arbuthnot truly *was* afraid to take you with him. He left here running for his life. He may well not make Pensacola . . . he may not make it alive to the Keys. He knew the governor would be furious if he did not allow you on board the *Chance*, but that the governor might hang him if he took you aboard knowing your life was in danger . . . as it would have been. There is a blackbirder out there hunting down Captain Arbuthnot. And they mean to blow his schooner out of the water. So at least the old boy didn't lie to you about the danger.''

She smiled. ''At first, I was enraged. I hated him. But now, I feel much better about it. Like you, I am eternally in his debt. He sent me back to you.''

''You keep talking like that and I'm going to rape you right on the downtown plaza.''

She exhaled heavily. ''Oh God, if you only would. Rape me, I mean. It would make it all so simple.''

''Sure. And the waiters would probably get a hell of a kick out of it.''

She put her head back laughing, exultant, pleased with herself, happy with her world in this moment. ''Oh, Jeremiah-*mío*,'' she cried, ''how can it be that I could love anyone so helplessly?''

Sudden shouting in the sun-braised streets shook the glassware on the patio tables, fragmented the lazy silences under the banyan tree. Waiters and guests leaped up from the table and ran across the cobbles to the portico overlooking the crowded avenue.

Yolanda and Locke hesitated, taut, at their table. The shouting did not recede, it intensified. The people who had knotted at the gate muttered at each other, looked ill. They seemed to want to turn away, but were sickly fascinated by what they saw.

''I must go,'' Yolanda said.

"Why?"

"Because I know what it is. I know without seeing what it is. . . . I don't want to see, and yet I am drawn to it." She stood looking down at him. "You need not come with me."

He grinned up at her, tongue in cheek. "Now you've made it impossible for me to do anything else."

She gave him a wan smile and took his hand, clinging to it almost like a little girl. Even before they reached the street, he saw her face had grayed and her eyes looked stricken.

They sidled through the silent knot of people at the arched exit of the patio. A few yards away a growing crowd of people gathered. They came from everywhere, the boats, the piers, the shops, the gardens, the indigo fields. They came running.

Yolanda did not hesitate. When they reached the outer perimeter of the onlookers, she pushed her way through, clinging to him, her grip tightening on him as if she gained strength and security from him.

At the inner ring of silent, gaping people, they stopped.

Locke felt bile gorge up through his throat. He looked on a fearful sight he had never seen before, a hideous terror he had not expected to see this side the seventh ring of hell.

A couple of white men, three Negroes and four Indians had staggered, crawled and clawed their way up from the river and from the wilderness beyond it. Not one was a whole man, all were mutilated, some with their scalp locks sliced away, some with eyes hacked out with knives, some with their bellies ripped open—with bayonets or swords, he reckoned. Some had been shot, their kneecaps blown away.

He swallowed back the sickness, staring at them. It was not that they lived despite their wounds; it would have been too easy for them to die quickly. They had been mutilated purposely, so they died slowly, in agony.

The lone doctor on the island did what he could for the men, but there was little to do but stanch the blood, bandage the open wounds and give them laudanum against the pain so they died in peace.

Staring at the mutilated men, the witnesses growled like animals, their rage boiling up in them, too terrible for words.

Her legs apart, bent forward at the hips, Yolanda saw it all. She looked as if she might faint. Her eyes dilated, her mouth pulled taut and white and her cheeks went pallid and rigid. But she did not look away. It was as if by some command that she must witness it all, and though it sickened her, she did it.

Suddenly she cried out, almost an animal ululation of agony and rage. She jerked her hand free from Locke's grasp. She thrust people aside and pushed her way through the crowd. Locke followed and the crowd closed in behind him like the underbrush in a thick forest.

"Yolanda."

She did not pause nor look back. She ran, along the cobbles, across the walk and into the hotel. He caught her inside the lobby. He snagged her arm. She looked at him, her eyes glitterig like a lynx's eyes, madness swirling deep inside them.

"What is it, Yolanda? For God's sake, what's the matter?"

She stared up at him, her taut mouth pulled, her whole body tense. When he relaxed for a moment, expecting her to answer him, she broke free and heeled around, running again.

She did not go far. She reached the foot of the side staircase and fell across it, her head on her arms, sobbing.

Locke sank beside her, agonized for her, filled with compassion. He gently touched her shoulder, but she shook free, weeping inconsolably. "Tell me," he begged. "What is it? What's the matter?"

After a long time, gasping for breath, she straightened and looked at him. "Do you say you don't know?" Her mouth twisted savagely.

"I swear I don't. I never saw anything like that in my life."

"How fortunate you are. . . . If you lived here—in Florida—among my poor people, you would see it all the time." She swung her arm, sobbing. "You would never grow accustomed to the slaughter, the butchery, but you would see. Oh God, you would see it."

He sank to the wide slab steps beside her. His hand on her shoulder shook with the violent trembling of her body.

"It's the Americans," she whispered in a savagery that threatened to unhinge her. She was talking as if to herself; she seemed hardly aware of him; she stared around her, her tear-reddened eyes focused on nothing, disoriented. "The

American slaughterers. The thieves. Killers. Liars. . . . My God, how I hate them. How I'd like to kill them all."

"Who did it, Yolanda? Who?"

She shook her head with a terrible, unthinking impatience. "I told you. Won't *you* have the truth, either? It is not the first time they have marched in and burned and mutilated our people. No, not by a hundred! And not the last . . . until God Himself can stop that murderer."

"What are you talking about?"

She stared at him, her face twisted with her hatred.

"About you! You, you filthy godless American, with your pious chaplains invoking God's blessings on massacres and mutilations and murders! With your flags and your hymns and your brutality. It's not enough to chase frightened, half-mad Indians and runaway blacks across our borders and deep into our sovereign territory—and shoot them down like animals. That's not enough—mutilate them. Chop off the hands of little children. Hoist the severed heads of Indian women on tall poles for their men to find when they creep back out of hiding in the swamps."

"Who does this?"

She waved her arm, distracted. "It's my father's fault. He is to blame for every mutilated Spanish subject your butchers leave bloody on our ground. He should stop them! But he talks of treaties with the Americans—the Americans who haven't honored a treaty since their first one, unless it profited them. He talks compromise when he should be talking war. He advocates making concessions—one more concession—and one more. He thinks only of peace—peace at any price. Well, before God, peace at the price of those poor mutilated devils on that street out there—that price is too high."

Locke drew her against him. She lay passive upon him, trembling, hardly aware of where she was.

Her voice quavered. "There is no peace. There will be no peace in Spanish Florida until that slaughtering butcher has killed us all. When he has slain the last Negro, beheaded the last loyal Spaniard, driven the last homeless Indian into the sea, then this slaughter will stop. Ask him . . . ask him if it will stop then . . . ask that slaughtering bastard."

A Spanish general, with several aides in his wake, strode into the hotel lobby. He started across it, then saw Yolanda weeping at the foot of the stairs. He stopped, drawing himself up. "Your highness. I was just coming to see you."

"I'm sorry, General Morales. I don't want to talk to you," Yolanda said. She shook her head. "I'm too ill."

Francisco Morales shook his head. "How unfortunate that you should witness such mutilation. I would not have had such a fearful thing happen for any price."

"Do you think I've not seen mutilated Spanish subjects before, General Morales? Oh, I forget. I am able to smile, even to laugh, to eat, and then it all happens again."

"Our garrison here is so weak, your highness. With the pirate Luis Aury claiming Amelia Island for the Republic of Mexico, we know an attack by the Americans is imminent. I am here to plead with you to ask your father to send reinforcements. Well as we fight, we are helpless to stop such attacks by bands of Americans. We won't be able to withstand an attack in force."

"You tell him," she whispered. "I have talked until my heart is broken. I cannot talk anymore."

— XVI —

HE DID not see Yolanda again for a week. He went a dozen times a day to her door in the Ferdinand Hotel, but she sent Isabella with the same message each time. She could not see him. She would not see him again. Isabella volunteered the information, in a taut tearful whisper, that the Doña Yolanda suffered deep melancholy. She had been so stricken before. She must somehow recover alone from her stress; she would have it no other way. In the meantime, Isabella shrugged . . .

He wanted to obey Yolanda's edict and stay away from her, but he could not resist the magnetic attraction she held for him. He had kissed her, touched her, held her pliant and liquid-hot in his hands. He could not forget such painful ecstasy. And he could not live in memory.

His resolve to action—born with the sight of those mutilated men in the streets and hardened with Yolanda's agony—congealed like a bad case of indigestion in his solar plexus, so that when he breathed, he breathed in sharp discomfort around that constant pain. He determined to cross Florida seeking General Jackson's forces, though he did not see how he could depart Amelia Island until Yolanda at least spoke to him again, recognized his existence on the same unhappy planet.

At last he sent a brief note to her by Isabella. He wrote simply, "I know you have from the first wanted me to perform some task for you. Will you see me to tell me what it is you want of me? I promise, if I can, to carry it out for you."

Isabella was gone even a shorter interval than usual. She returned to the corridor door, eyes sad, disconsolate. "The señorita says to tell you only that she wants nothing of you. Now or ever."

Walking around with an empty sense of insufficiency and loss moiling in his belly, Locke tried to occupy his mind with mundane matters, anything to deny it truant flights to Yolanda, and the memory of Yolanda and his helpless desire for her.

Cato was infrequently underfoot these days. Isabella spent every moment she could steal from her royal mistress with her mustee lover. When Cato managed physically to be in Locke's presence, he was abstracted, dreamy, absentminded.

"Isabella," Cato said, "she is made of fiery love. Her body is hot lava. She gives herself to me—a hundred times a day if I am able . . . but what she really loves above all else is to do things with her mouth and her tongue . . ." He shivered in recalled delight. "Things that have me yelling in sweet anguish."

"For Christ's sake, spare me," Locke said. "Don't you two talk about killing me anymore?"

"Sometimes." Cato shrugged. "But not as frequently as before."

Forced to some kind of diversionary action, Locke discovered a Fernandina in mourning, paralyzed with fear, a place he'd never suspected, an Amelia Island totally and incomprehensibly changed in the two years he'd been away.

Three years ago there'd been a vibrant air about the town, as if it celebrated an unending, almost nightmarishly persistent fiesta. Always some new ship—merchantman, privateer or trader—put into port for one reason or another, bringing more rum, more treasures, more loot and booty. There seemed always something to celebrate, even if it were no more than staying alive through another frantic and violent night.

Walking through the streets now, Locke found little festivity. Few people smiled except the whores who'd taught their lips to lie. In the past two years a dozen adventurers had led forays against the island and its ineffectual Spanish rulers. Some came in the name of the United States. Many of these hotheads claimed vast regions of Florida for the U.S., because there was total confusion about boundaries and the Spanish government based in St. Augustine and Pensacola sat impotently awaiting edicts that never came from Madrid, while fights and battles boiled around them.

One tough old frontiersman, General Matthews, an ex-governor of Georgia, convinced he had the support of the U.S. Congress and assurances from President Madison, came into the harbor with guns blazing, captured the island with the help of mobs calling themselves "American patriots" and proclaimed the "Republic of East Florida," which he assumed would then be claimed as territory of the United States. He was able to promise each patriot two hundred acres of Florida land. Nine American gunboats sailed into the estuary and—under orders from *somebody* in Washington—aimed their cannon at the fort.

As General Matthews, and his patriots advanced on Fernandina, the Spanish major hauled down his country's flag. The patriots rushed ashore. For a year, the island remained under their heel. The patriots stole everything or demanded reparations and taxes, and they plundered plantations along the St. Mary's River and on the coast. When Great Britain protested in behalf of Spain, President Madison declared in shocked tones that he'd neither encouraged, supported nor had prior knowledge of the invasion. For a while, Amelia Island lay weakly in the sun, licking its wounds, recuperating, the Spanish once more in nominal command.

Now the streets were crowded with dour-faced people who lived in frantic dread of doomsday. It was only a matter of time, they said, before new invaders appeared on the horizon. Who forgot that Great Britain, for all her ill-fated adventures against the States, still coveted soil south of Canada? And who better than Great Britain knew the impotence and vascillating nature of Spain's King Ferdinand? British agents fomented an Indian war on the upper Mississippi. Tecumseh's Indian raids were a long way off and his rebellion had been silenced by William Henry Harrison at the battle of Tippecanoe. But every attempted land-grab, every broken treaty, every ambitious adventurer, was a threat to the vulnerable island.

Great Britain continued at least a covert search of American ships, seizing men to serve her navy. And so, even after the British had been defeated by Americans under Jackson and pirates under Laffite at New Orleans, Amelia Island remained a plum for picking. Fernandina became wilder, more chaotic, a center of smuggling, slave traffic, every vice conceived in the fertile brain of man, and a harbor for renegades. Its taverns reverberated and stunk, crowded now with onimous clientele, suspicious, deadly felons who had forgotten how to laugh except at another being's suffering. The town smelled, a slum of shacks and lean-tos and temporary shelters. Across the river the town of St. Mary's provided an outpost much like Fernandina where pirates, freebooters and renegades exchanged flour and gunpowder for smoked meat, beef, potatoes, indigo and runaway slaves chained and captured in Spanish Florida by bounty hunters. Amelia Island was in hell.

In every tavern where Locke tried to recruit men, he was listened to with derision and hooted with scorn. "You gettin' together a company of men? Why? For what?"

Locke shrugged. He admitted he wanted a better class of rascal than he found in the alehouses, but he didn't bother to tell them why he was trying to recruit a company of men. He remembered that when he'd asked Robert Harmbrister how he'd join forces with General Jackson, Harmbrister had told him arrogantly that he'd recruit a company of thugs, train them and offer them to the general as soldiers. Locke had no better plan; it was worth an effort. The half of that Spanish gold he'd stolen would adequately provision, clothe, arm and pay a company of militia. Beyond that, at the moment, he had no plans. He would get together his company of men and head west across the panhandle of Spanish Florida.

It was in one of these taverns that he found a solution to his recruitment problem. An underling of the town's mayor moaned in his rum about the unrelenting overcrowding of the squalid town jail. "Soon it will have more inmates than the fort. In case of attack it will be one of our greatest dangers. A riot in the jail would cripple us—and tie up our army. It grows every night. Already it stinks to heaven like a giant slop jar."

Locke hesitated only a few seconds. He left the tavern, pushed his way through the busy street to the command post of General Francisco Morales.

The fort, like the town and the island, lay in chaos and disarray, with everything looking as if it were stacked, ready for immediate and total retreat. The walls of the edifice reared over six feet, erected of an olio of dried mudbricks, coquina and other shells mixed and hardened with clay and hay. A gate of heavy oak swung back on ropes and pulleys operated by two barechested men grunting at wheels.

A noncommissioned officer barred Locke's way, musket across his chest.

"I want to see General Francisco Morales," Locke said.

"The general is too busy to see every one who comes here."

"You tell the general I have a plan that may help him with his prisoner problem. Tell him also that I met him in the presence of Governor Castillo's daughter."

"Why didn't you say so?"

The general lounged behind an ornate desk in a room of rich artifacts and heavy furnishings. He appeared an imposing, handsome man. He glanced up impatiently, recalling Locke with no great display of pleasure or warmth. "What's this about my prisoners, señor?"

"How would you like to get rid of some of them?"

Morales laughed without mirth, without any overt friendliness. His voice remained cold and businesslike. "I would dearly love to get rid of *all* of them, señor. But I should be severely reprimanded for wholesale murder."

"But if I took them—some of them—off your hands?"

Morales leaned forward. "How many of them?"

"Enough for a company of militia."

"A company of militia? What militia? What do you consider a company?"

"A company is any damned thing I say it is—"

"A platoon."

"As you say. I'm a sailor. Not a soldier. The company I see is a couple of squads."

"Eight men."

"Still, eight men out of your overcrowded cells. Eight men removed as troublemakers in case of attack."

"Attack?" Morales's head jerked up and he went gray around his moustache. "What do you know of an attack?"

He's yellow and scared, Locke thought. Aloud, he said, "Nothing. No more than I hear as common talk in the taverns."

Morales's dark eyes remained agonized. "Oh, there is an attack coming. We have our spies. Our military intelligence. We know these things. You are an American. I don't know if I trust you."

"What difference does it make if you trust me or not—if I take my company of felons from your prison and get out of here?"

"Get out? Where do you plan to go?"

"West across Florida. I swear to be no threat to you or anyone on the east coast."

"I don't know that I should be the one to provide you men for some adventure—likely against the Spanish crown." They argued back and forth. Locke became angry, but controlled his temper. An outburst would avail him nothing. He saw that Morales actually was weighing it all in his mind, thrashing it out. At last, he nodded, and invited Locke to dinner with his senior officers.

Though the food was delicious, gourmet seafood prepared by excellent Spanish chefs, and wine was continually poured to refill glasses, the dinner with Morales and his senior officers was a dour affair. These men believed they existed on a powder keg and they could think, or discuss, little else. No matter where a conversation started, it twisted back upon itself and the threat against Spanish Florida, against Spanish rule and, more urgently, against the garrison on Amelia Island.

"We have tried to be friendly with the Americans who want to homestead in Spanish Florida," Morales said. "Gracious King Ferdinand allows Americans to emigrate into this beautiful land. He grants to each head of family fifty *fanegadas*—almost two of your American acres to each fanegada. He allows an additional twenty fanegadas for each family member or slave. And your immigrants are no longer required to convert to Catholicism. They now swear only allegiance to the king and allow their children to be baptized in the Church. For all our kindness and generosity, I fear East Florida is being settled by Americans eager to bring Florida into the United States."

"Why do you believe they are not simply looking for new homes in a warm, pleasant climate?"

Morales laughed without mirth. "God knows, I might wish that! But every evidence denies it! Even when they accept the land grants, they question whether or not the American-Florida border is adequately defined. Are they not, perhaps, actually on American soil?

"And Amelia Island remains a prize that makes the American mouth water all the way up to your presidents. Half a million each year in profit passes through Fernandina. The Americans can hardly sit still and keep their hands off such a bonanza. Now, intelligence tells us of some kind of northern division of East Florida. As if such a division could possibly exist. Yet, our king says we must permit among us this man MacGregor—who has come here with almost two hundred outlaws and buccaneers from the wars of liberation in South America. Are we to believe MacGregor intends suddenly to *stop* fighting the Spanish, and to live in peace with us. You think he does not covet Amelia Island as well?"

"You have your problems."

Morales blanched; it was no joking matter with him. "We are trapped here. Between MacGregor and his cutthroats and Luis Aury, that pirate flying the flag of Mexico. Ah, no, it is only a matter of time, señor."

Locke smiled. "Perhaps then I am doing you a favor to take even eight prisoners out of your jail and off your hands."

The wine had mellowed the general's mood. He swung his arm and nodded. "Take . Take them, as long as you vow not to let them come back here to Amelia Island. We've got enough rats without them? Sí? Sí?"

The bureaucrat who said the jail stunk like a giant slopjar had not exaggerated; he had erred on the side of moderation. Locke's head spun when he entered the place. He wanted to retch at the odors. He managed not to cover his nose, to keep his face expressionless.

The men gathered in the small oval exercise pen. The section was enclosed with metal fencing, and soldiers stood, armed along the walls.

"I want eight men," Locke told the sullen, bearded faces. "Eight men who want to get out of here."

"Get out of here and do what, mate?"

"Enlist in my army."

A roar of laughter went up. "An army of eight men? What do you plan, to invade Russia?"

"What do you care? Is it better to stay in this stinking cesspool or to get out of here where there's clean clothes, good food and fresh air?"

"Fresh air might kill us."

"What is good food, mate?"

A lean man in filfhy pants stood up. "Listen. I know this man. He was my captain on a ship. A good man, I say. I'll join you, Mister Locke."

The matter was not quickly settled. The pen rattled with threatened riot. Much bickering, bargaining and threats followed, along with questions about pay, length of service and foul jokes about men who would join the army just to escape prison. But Locke recruited his company of thugs. There were, finally, so many applicants that he could pick and chose, forcing them to submit to a basic health check as he tried to find the least diseased, the men with the best teeth, no ruptured hemorrhoids or misshapen toes.

He was satisfied with his eight recruits. The remaining prisoners yelled and taunted his army as he marched them out of the prison compound. He paraded them under guard to the garrison where General Morales had agreed to accommodate them in outdoor pens until Locke was ready to move them out.

The entire next day was spent delousing, shaving and washing the recruits in hot lye-soap water. They began to look better already, to resemble human beings again. They ate well at the stockade, food purchased in gold from Morales's kitchen. Once Morales found that Locke was able to pay in gold, a subtle alteration appeared in the general's attitude toward the American. Morales set an exorbitant price on every piece of goods, every service. Locke paid uncomplainingly. He knew the gold went directly into Morales's own pocket. But it did not matter. It was a cynical business at best. Morales knew he knew.

On the third day, Locke arrived at the fort in an open-bed supply wagon drawn by two dray horses and driven by Cato. In its bed were stacked two dozen drill-green fatigue uniforms of cotton—intended, said the proprietor of the thieves' market where Locke bought clothing, hats, shoes, ammunition and weapons, for a liberator's army in South America. The goods themselves had been appropriated by a privateer en route.

Locke was especially proud of the cocky hats. Of light material, they would be ideal in the humid Florida heat, and each bore a bright little cocarde, designed for some lighthearted military group, and which he accepted as his own distinguishing status mark.

Locke's band knew nothing yet of close-order drill. But among the prisoners Locke had located an ex-army drill sergeant named Halstead. The soldier had been arrested for double murder, with an axe. He put Halstead in command as first noncom officer.

He was astonished, and he saw veiled surprise in the faces of Morales and his officers, when Halstead marched the uniformed company—in two squads—out of the compound to a hard-voiced cadence.

"Well, I'm damned," Morales said. "So he has his company."

For Locke there arrived the moment of no return. There no longer remained any reason to delay. If he tried to linger, even overnight, on Amelia Island, his agreement with Morales might be abrogated and his men returned to jail. He had his supplies, his horses, his wagon, his men. The time had come to cross the St. Mary's River and start south and west. He delayed, watching the hotel doorway like a lovesick schoolboy.

He had gone to Yolanda's door. There had been no answer. Neither Yolanda nor her maid were inside. Emptily, lost, he turned away.

Cato was noncommittal. He had parted tearfully with Isabella, he said, promising to come to her when he had garroted his hateful American master. No, he had not seen her serene highness Yolanda, nor heard from her.

The river lay broad and flat, the land green and forested beyond. The crowds gathered along the shaded walls, waiting for the departure of this strange little army.

There remained nothing but for Locke to give the order to head for the boats which would transport them across river to St. Mary's.

Agonized, Locke delayed. He could not believe that Yolanda, distressed as she was, deep in melancholy as she must be, would let him walk out of her life without even a farewell.

A carriage rattled along the street, stopping near the edge of the crowd. What appeared to be two small men got out of the tonneau and walked in the sun toward where Locke stood beside his horse.

Shocked, his eyes widened; he recognized Yolanda. She wore a blue shirt of denim, men's lightweight work trousers and boots. Her straw hat was handmade. She still looked beautiful, and not like a man. The blouse accented the thrust of her breasts; the suppleness of her hips were accented by the cotton trousers. Even wearing boots, she walked with the light, hip-writhing movement that was in itself upsetting and mind-bending. Dressed to match her mistress, Isabella walked just behind her.

"Yolanda," Locke said. He stepped toward her. "Thank God. After all, you came to say good-bye."

Yolanda did not smile. She met his gaze levelly. He saw that she was still pale, that distress still clouded her lovely eyes. But she had put the horror of that mutilation behind her—for this moment at least. She said, "We have not come to say *adiós*. We are going with you."

"What?"

"You are headed to West Florida. That is where I must go. Isabella and I and my coachman—we will go with you."

"You can't." Locke spread his hands helplessly. "This is no trip for a woman."

She shrugged and still did not smile. "Then don't think of me as a woman. Look on me as a man. A man like any of the others in your company. Forget I am a woman." Now she laughed, a biting taunting sound. "Forget I'm a woman, if you can, *caballero*."

PART III

Frontier Firebrand

— XVII —

THE FIRST night they made camp a few miles south of St. Mary's settlement on the west bank of the river. A well-defined trail twisted inland linking the plantations along the coast. The British had fostered the citrus industry and the cleared groves spread out all the way to St. Augustine and along the St. John's River.

When they entered the forests, they found the underbrush and thick canopy of trees so clotted as to be stifling.

Cato walked beside the open supply wagon with Isabella. They seemed to have unnumbered matters of vital importance to say to each other. It was as if they believed time too was their enemy and anything left unspoken between them now would never be said.

Locke smiled grimly, watching them. He saw that while Cato spoke often in that quiet, firm and solemn tone of the premature sage, it was Isabella who chattered constantly. She walked beside him, vibrant with life, swinging her arms for emphasis, lapsing often into Spanish.

Locke saw little of Yolanda on the first days out. She stayed in her carriage, remote, removed, distant. When she did emerge, at meal times or rest stops, she was incredibly changed in a sad way that disheartened Locke and made him want to promise to protect her from all agony, even when he knew he was as helpless as she facing the horrors that distressed and plagued her.

Yolanda stood unsmiling at these stops, her dark eyes fixed on some inner turmoil he could neither see nor share. The exuberant Latin effervescence, the seething passions and delight in life boiling always just beneath the lustrous surface of her skin, ebbed and died. When she did speak, her lovely voice was subdued, sober, calm and passive. But her stillness was a chastened quiet, a resignation and retreat from ugliness and terror she could not endure.

He tried every trick he knew to draw her out of her desolation. Her tone remained gentle, but she appeared preoccupied, all her thoughts and concerns turned inward.

He walked beside her carriage, his hand on the window frame in the vehicle door. "Won't you even talk with me?"

"Of course." Her voice was deadly polite. "What do you wish to say?"

He laughed helplessly. "It is not that *I* wish to say anything particularly. I want *you* to talk to me."

"I'm sorry. There is nothing to say. Nothing you would care to hear."

"How do you know? Look. You wanted something from me. From the first. I was not fooled about that. The wine. The vivacity—even the first kiss—all of it was calculated to soften me for some bargain you wanted to strike between us."

"I'm sorry."

"About what?"

"That I was so transparent. I can say only that I was in panic. Terrified. Desperate."

"And now you're not?"

She almost smiled, a wan fleeting lift of her lovely lips. "Not in the same way. No."

"But you wanted *something* of me. Won't you at least tell me what it was?"

She sighed and sat gazing at her hands for some moments. The carriage bumped and rattled over the deep-chewed ruts. "It was this—I wanted you to agree to take me overland to my father in Pensacola. . . . But I gave it up. I determined not to ask you."

"Why?"

She gazed at him, chewing at her underlip, her eyes bleak. "Because the cost of our—bargain—was too high. For you. And, I found—for me. I thought I could buy your help for the price of a harmless flirtation. I soon learned better. Nothing could be harmless between us. We could not be casual, either of us."

He laughed. "I was never casual about you from the first moment I saw you."

"I know. And I soon found that I would be enslaved by

you. I would fall in love with you—as I did not know a woman ever loved a man. As I had read about in romantic books but did not believe. And that could not be. We could never become—so involved. It is impossible."

"My God. Why? Because Americans kill your people down here—you hate me because you hate Americans?"

"It has nothing to do with the Americans. Or the slaughter. They invade us. But we are not at war with them. We try to keep peace, but they butcher our subjects. My king should stop this, my country should stop it, my father should stop it . . . but that, sad as it is, has nothing to do with you and me—except that it sickens and depresses me."

"You can't let this evil destroy you."

She spread her fragile hands. "But it has. It will . . ."

"You can't let it come between us."

She laid her hand on his side of the window frame. Her eyes brimmed with tears. "Oh, my poor Jeremiah-*mío*. You don't understand at all, do you?"

"No. I'm pretty stupid."

"You're not stupid at all. If a *caballero* can to said to be *muy grande hermoso,* you are beautiful, Jeremiah-*mío*—in your face, your body, and most of all, in your dear heart."

"If I'm so wonderful, why are you so cold to me?"

"Please, Jeremiah-*mío*. We have already gone too far! It cannot be. Between us there can be nothing. It cannot ever be. Oh, *corazón-mío*, I am not *free* . . . I have been betrothed by my family to the Duque de Castile since I was a little girl—no more than six years old."

He plodded, empty-hearted, bereft, along the narrow trail, watching Leonard Halsted harry his eight-man army into a disciplined unit.

Halsted assigned chores at rest stops. He had the men occupied with military matters, no matter how inconsequential, at all times. He allowed one squad to rest, sprawling and complaining in the shade, while the other marched, presented arms, learned drill commands and hand-signal communication.

Halsted's voice lashed them, rasping: "An army has got to have discipline first. First over everything. You learn to obey orders 'cause it's your *instinct* to obey orders. Obeying orders means not only saving the lives of men around you, but more important to you, saving your own skin. Discipline alone does that. God knows what military man first realized that. Joshua maybe. Or one of his noncoms. Or Saul. Or the early Greeks. Rules. Laws. Orders. Discipline. It's the only way to train men to work together—by instinct!—to be able to trust each other under fire."

"Under fire?" Clemmons, a towheaded boy from Georgia, imprisoned for unspecified crimes against the Spanish state, shook his head. "What fire? Nobody said nothing to me about being under fire."

"You're in the army, ain't you?" Halsted yelled at him.

"I'm gettin' empty-bellied hungry too, Sarge. We do one hell of a lot more drilling than eating."

"We'll buy fresh eggs, vegetables, smoked meat and fruit," Locke said, "at the first farm we reach."

A youth named Tavares spoke up. He'd been jailed for a rape-murder on Amelia Island. He was a pale, quiet-looking boy, nearsighted and reticent. "I been this trail lots of times. We ran niggers across here after we rounded them up in Indian camps. There's a plantation owned by a man named Starke—" He hesitated and glanced around, squinting in his nearsighted way, as if trying to orient himself in the thick forest. "Can't be more than four or five miles on ahead."

Halsted glanced questioningly toward Locke who nodded. "On your feet," Halsted commanded. "We'll cover that five miles double-time."

"Jesus, Tavares," Clemmons said. "You and your big mouth."

The little company moved at an unrelenting pace. Halsted had forced his soldiers to carry their muskets. "Want you men to get used to 'em," he said. "Got to be part of your arm. Like your hand. Get so it's part of you." But in the interests of speed and arriving at the Starke plantation before nightfall, he allowed the squads to stack their guns in the flatbed of the supply wagon.

Isabella returned to the carriage with her mistress. Cato drove the supply cart. The soldiers marched at double-time, Halsted's raucous voice rattling and reverberating the cadence among the walls of trees.

A muttering arose among the men before they reached the

plantation. The troops slowed and when they came out into the clearing, they stopped and stared at the charred remains of the manor house, barns, slave cabins and outbuildings. Everything was burned to the ground, the fields trampled, the groves destroyed.

For no good reason the company advanced up the narrow drive through the water oaks to where the chateau had stood. Tavares whispered, stunned, "One of the prettiest big old houses in this here part of the state."

"Indians," Clemmons said. "Them goddamn Seminoles."

Isabella heard him and her voice rose, scathing. "Americans! Oh, they would like the world to believe it was the Seminoles . . . but places like this fed them. They begged at places like this. They don't burn them."

The soldiers found a couple of bodies of dead military men which appeared to substantiate what Isabella said. Clemmons shook his head. "It don't make sense. Why would Americans want to burn places like this—owned by an Englisher?"

"That is simple enough," Isabella said, her face gray. "These people supported the Indians—gave them food—and were loyal to the Spanish government."

Tavares straightened from bending over the body of a soldier. "Somebody has stripped these fellows of anything valuable, but here's a letter this fellow had written to somebody."

Tavares could not read. He handed the letter to Halsted who passed it on to Locke. Halsted jerked his head toward the decomposing bodies. "Bury them," he said.

Locke read the unfinished letter written by the slain soldier.

Dear Mom,

To think I'd of never seen land like this if I hadn't of joined with General Jackson's forces. This Florida is like land nobody ever saw before! The sun shines all the time. I can't wait until I'm out of the army, we'll come down here, get some acreage and live—on oranges and alligator pears and everything good that you want to grow, why it grows in this sunshine and rain. Why these here hammocks are so thick you can hardly walk through them without hacking your way. There is every kind of small bushes, most of them covered with berries, and shrubs, and then spreading over all of this are sweet bays and water oaks and wild magnolias and more kinds of pine trees that you would even believe. Wild game is so abundant no one would have to go hungry and fish strike in every lake and river, and . . ."

The letter ended. There was no address, no way that Locke could hope to forward even this scrap of missive.

"Move out," he said to Halsted. "We'll make camp beside the river."

They reached the St. John's River at the ferry landing in the deep narrows known to the Indians as Wacca Pilatka—a place where the cows could swim over. The whites called the settlement Cows Ford, a site of British land grants as early as 1765—two especially large grants were those of the Marquis of Hastings and the Marquis of Waterford. Within ten years a ferry was in operation, transporting fruit, cotton and indigo from the plantations south along the river and the coast. When the Floridas were returned to the Spanish, the English estates were abandoned, but the Kings Road was developed through Cows Ford and the ferry remained in existence.

At Cows Ford, Locke's company met a wagon train headed for Virginia. He wrote a hasty letter to his mother and asked the wagon master to see that it was delivered to Manassas. This was agreeable. His company was entrusted with mail and money secured in pelts tied with leather string for destinations in the panhandle. He found amazing the guileless, blind trust of people who turned over thick packets of treasure or savings to strangers in the hope it would reach its destination safely.

"I think most people are good, mastah," Cato said.

Locke nodded. "I suppose so. There is a kind of faith working here that says, let me trust you this time, because there may come a turn when you'll have to trust me. I suppose you're right. I suppose most people are decent."

Yolanda shook her head. "Ordinary people only are decent. They are trustworthy and good to each other only until they are given—or take—power enough to make them ambitious, or money enough to make them greedy, or sink low enough to make them vicious."

* * *

They headed northwest toward Suwannee, a town controlled by the Indian leader Billy Boleck—called Billy Bowlegs.

The platoon under Halsted was looking better by the hour. Halsted no longer called cadence, this was done by the men in the squads, taking turns. They marched as if toward some rendezvous with glory.

Only Locke found little to raise his spirits on the long trek west. The country was higher, pine forests and hammocks. He wanted to stay away from Yolanda, but knowing she was there in that carriage was an impossible temptation. He longed to look at her, the olive eyes, the rich old gold of her hair. She had said all there was to say. She was pledged, a vow taken with deadly seriousness in her Catholic country; she was betrothed in a marriage arranged between families. She could not betray that trust. Looking at her, he knew it was even sadder than that: No matter how much she loved him, she would not betray her vows.

By the third day out, the tensions between himself and Yolanda were brutal—on both of them. She tried to be her natural self when they faced each other at breakfast, at rest stops or around the evening campfires. She failed miserably. She was conscious of his nearness. Her eyes strayed to him no matter what she was doing. Her hands shook when she handed something to him, took something from him. When she asked him the simplest question, her voice quavered, her eyes touched bravely against his and then fell away. Under the golden-tinted flesh, a pallor etched itself and deepened. He tried to put her at ease. He was resigned to her betrothal; he had never believed he could have her; all his life he had heard of vows between families, especially among the very wealthy, the nobility and certain faiths. But his kindliness unnerved her and she wept. "Oh, what a stupid, insensitive fool you must think me," she said.

At a rest stop on the second day west of Cows Ford, he came upon her alone at a creek, her blouse removed, her breasts creamy against the lace bodice of her chemise. She stood up from the clear pool where she'd been bathing her face. Locke apologized and turned to retreat. She said, "I know how terrible it is for you, Jeremiah-*mío,* because it is terrible for me—to want so deeply and be denied! I know I am the fool—living by old standards that are not mine, by old patterns of life, trying to deny the truth between us."

He tried to smile lightly, knew he failed. "Don't worry about me—until I start beating my head against the iron rims of your carriage."

"Poor Jeremiah." She laughed, a sad heartbroken little sound with mirth drowned in her tears.

Impulsively, she reached out and touched his arm. Her fingers burned against his arm. As if without volition on either side, they came together, her lips parted, thirsty for his kiss. His hands moved on her bared arms and he drew her roughly against him.

She caught her breath but did not struggle. His hand on the small of her back pressed her in upon him. He felt the arhythmic pound of her heart through the cushion of her full breasts, the remembered fever at her thighs. For a long beat she melted against that abrupt throbbing tower at his belt. Her hands clung to him and then, trembling, she drew away.

Locke released her instantly. He stood breathing raggedly through his parted lips as if he had run all the way west from Wacca Pilatka.

"Oh, God forgive me, I'm sorry," Yolanda wept. "This is not fair—to you."

"I've long ago quit thinking about fair." He grinned. "I'm down now to where I'll take what I can get."

She smiled gently, sadly. "I am evil, leading you on like this. Weak and evil."

"Why don't you wait until I complain?"

She clutched his arm. "Oh, Jeremiah-*mío*, as good as you are, as kind as you are, I owe you more than that—"

"I'll drink to that."

She sighed heavily. "i owe you decency to keep my own emotions severely under control. To keep my place. Not to torment you . . . I promise you it won't happen again."

He gazed down at her and smiled crookedly. "I'm sure you're trying to make me feel better, but somehow it's not working. I'll try to make it easier on both of us. I'll try to stay away from you." He bowed, smiling, turned and walked away, rock-hard, empty-bellied, his gut aching . . .

* * *

Resolving to stay away from Yolanda was much easier vowed than carried out; it reckoned without the fates.

Her scream broke the deep afternoon stillness of the forest the next day. Lying in the shade of a loblolly pine, Locke had been dreaming about her. At first, the sound of her cries were unreal, remote shards of his dreaming.

He came up on his feet. His small army leaped up, alert. Cato came running from some secret bower where he'd hidden himself and Isabella. Halsted came across the camp, gun in his hands, running.

But as swiftly as the others reacted, Locke broke through the underbrush around a creek well ahead of them.

Her hair loose and wild about her face, Yolanda lay sprawled on the ground. Tavares had leaped upon her from the brush and now held one hand clamped over her mouth while he tore at her clothing with the other.

Locke didn't even hesitate. His boot caught Tavares in the groin as he crouched vulnerably over Yolanda. The kick lifted the boy off of her. The convicted rapist moaned and tried to turn over. Locke caught him at the crotch and by his shock of black hair. He lifted the youth bodily and hurled him headfirst into the rocky creekbed.

He did not even look to see how the boy landed. He didn't even hear the splash of water over the thundering inside his own temples.

Locke caught Yolanda up in his arms. She was shaking badly, her lips trembling. Her face was pallid and her cheeks rigid. She clung to Locke, her nails digging into him. Holding her, he did not even glance toward the creek.

Halsted ran past them and out into the water without slowing.

Tavares lay sprawled, buttocks up, head down in two feet of fast-moving water. Halsted caught him by the belt and dragged him from the creek. He half threw him on the bank.

Tavares lay unconscious on the grassy incline. He looked young and harmless, like a choirboy, sensitive and slender, lying there. One had to know his criminal record to suspect the fury of the passions that spurred him.

Halsted said. "What you want me to do, Captain? Run him away?"

Locke looked down at the boy for the first time. He wanted

to kill Tavares, but he shook his head. "No. He wouldn't live long."

Halsted shrugged. "No loss."

"Except to us."

"This kid ain't going to change, Captain. You'll forgive me, ma'am," Halsted looked at Yolanda, his bearded face flushing slightly. "No offense. But it wasn't you as stirred Tavares up. Wantin' a woman ain't got anything to do with what he feels—he hates women; he wants to debase 'em, degrade 'em and hurt 'em. He's just a born rapist, and that's the way he'll die, I'm afraid. When we was in jail, he tole me just how he feels."

Locke sighed. "He'll hurt in the groin for a long time. And by the time he gets well, maybe he'll have sense enough to realize that we're all watching him."

Halsted gestured, resigned. "Whatever you say, Captain . . . but don't never say I didn't warn you. It's a sickness with this here kid. When he gets the drive, he don't no way care that anybody's watchin' him."

Locke lay sleepless in the wagon bed that night. A canvas flat had been stretched on four poles over the wagon and mosquito netting draped beneath it. He watched the stars glitter whitely against the black sable sky. He was empty-bellied with longing. He had driven himself all day, but he was unable to get Yolanda out of his mind.

He lay restless, unable to sleep. Whether he wanted to or not, he conjured up the heated image of Yolanda's naked body in his mind—the full, shapely breasts, golden and tipped with rubies, the long sculpted legs, the fevered thighs, a treasure of beauty untouched.

He tried to think of something else but there was nothing else to think about in the langorous night. The faint breeze did not even dry the sweat marbled across his forehead.

His eyes burned, but he could not sleep. Still, he thought he had drifted into restless dreaming when the netting parted and Yolanda crawled into the wagon bed with him. He stared, eyes wide, as she closed the netting behind her, moving as if she held her breath. She crept across the flat pad toward him. She wore a lightweight robe, buttoned from the base of her throat to her ankles. She lay beside him, touching him gently, as a butterfly might settle for a moment upon a flower. He was almost afraid to move for fear she would disappear.

Holding his breath, Locke stared at her, his heart slugging wildly. Her old-gold hair spilled loosely about her face and shoulders. He could smell the faint, yet inescapable scent of flowers—violets?—about her. He tried to control his emotions, but he was powerless against the desire surging through him, the boiling blood engorging him. He felt an immediate bristling erection, a savage need that made him at once weak and invincible.

"Jeremiah," she whispered. "Are you awake?"

"God knows I hope not."

She waited. When he said nothing more, she whispered. "I have come to you. . . . I have come—as I've known from the first I must. But I've come for so many reasons . . . to thank you, to make you see how it is with me. But only one reason matters . . . I could not stay away. Not anymore."

"Jesus. Don't ask *me* to be strong for both of us."

"I've not come to ask anything of you, except that you love me. I have come to you, Jeremiah—if you want me."

"If I want you?" His voice struggled up through his throat. "I want you—but I know better. You are promised to someone else. . . . God knows, I'd want *him* to keep *his* hands off if you were promised to me—"

"I was only a little girl. Vows were made in my name. No one asked me. It doesn't make sense—in the world today—to cheat myself of the only true passion I'll ever know on this earth, in order to keep some empty promise made in my name. I'll go to him. I'm vowed to do that. But I'll be empty for him—as likely he'll be empty for me."

"Oh God, Yolanda—"

"At least, if the rest of my life is empty without you, I'll have—this time with you. Anyway, it doesn't matter. I want you. I've been insane with need for you—since that—since you charged in and threw that—that man off of me. You would have killed him! I saw it in your face. Casually, you would have killed him because he touched me. . . . I never saw anyone so strong. So good. So beautiful. *Muy grande hermoso!* I knew in that moment that despite all vows—I belonged to you." She shuddered and laughed at the same time. "Or, don't they say that violence is a powerful aphrodisiac—didn't the gladiator fights prove that to the Romans? I don't know. I don't care. . . . I only know I am yours—if you want me—to use—as you wish. . . . What you want—whatever you want of me—that is what I must have."

His hands shaking, he slowly loosened the large buttons of her robe and removed the garment, slipping it down over her supple shoulders and tossing it from them. She lay naked in the wan starlight. She reached out and caught his pulsing rigidity in her hands, caressing him, stroking him. "You have not been for one moment out of my mind," she whispered in a frantic breathlessness. "How would I live with myself—if I did not have you?"

He drew her down beside him, her eyes fixed on him filled with tears of pleasure and anticipation. He kissed her soft mouth with a gentleness that ignited and flared into fury. Her lips parted and he thrust his tongue probing deep into the sweetness between her teeth. She opened her mouth as wide as she could to him, as if trying to take him deeply into her throat. She moaned and thrust herself upward to him as if to devour him.

His hands caressed the resilient warmth of her breasts. Her nipples hardened under his touch and her bust engorged with fevered blood. She writhed against him on the pad. She panted as if unable to grasp a full breath, but when he moved his hand down over the flat planes of her golden stomach into the fiery chalice at her thighs, she exhaled heavily, sighing out, and then breathed deeply, passionately. Her hips writhed helplessly under his touch.

She tried to lie quietly while he fondled and caressed her, but he roused her beyond endurance. She whispered against his mouth, "Do it now. Please. I want you. In me. In me. In me."

She opened her body to him—fresh and new and untouched—and mindless with desire. He thrust himself into her and she cried out in exquisite agony.

She struggled upward, feverish with passion. He came down close to her in the violet darkness, found her black eyes and her red mouth parted wide. She was holding her breath, but when he drove himself into her, she gasped aloud, closing her arms, her hands, her fingernails, her ankles, her body, upon him.

Those clasping hands drew him greedily to her. She whispered frantically and mindlessly against his face, into his ears, her breath unendurably hot and sweet against his skin. He felt their hearts pounding in a savage tempo, as one organ.

He laughed inwardly, feeling stronger than any god. He moved faster, driving himself into her. She thrust upward. She whimpered and cried out, sobbed in ecstasy, but he heard her only through the thunder erupting inside his own temples. He did not know what she was saying.

But this did not matter; neither did she . . .

— *XVIII* —

IN THE days that followed on the trail west, caught up in the enchantment of Yolanda's passionate love, Locke's life took on new meaning and a rapture he'd never anticipated on this sad globe. No longer was Yolanda content to look ahead in passive resignation to the hateful role that life, her family and tradition had designed for her. Now, in a burst of exultant excitement, she clung to Jerry's hand, kept him constantly by her side, dreamed aloud about what their life together could and must be. As she had existed in the depths of desolation after the mutilation at Amelia Island, she now spun at a crest of delight. The nights were not long enough, the days sweet enough, to satisfy her passionately awakened taste for life. All she could think, all she would countenance when they talked, was keeping Jerry Locke forever at her side. As he could not make her listen to any recital of the insurmountable obstacles he foresaw ahead of them, he smiled and found his hours with Yolanda on this wilderness trail the embodiment of his most fevered fantasies—this hot, wild frontier a place of perfection—as long as he held her in his arms. However, unlike Yolanda, he did not believe their romance could persist. He wanted to harvest all the joy from this present that he could by shutting out the world and what he knew to be its ugliness.

"You'll see. I'll change my father," Yolanda cried, nodding, convinced the depth of her passion could drown all dissent.

"Aren't you afraid he believes with all his heart in his way of life?"

She shrugged her lovely shoulders. "Once he sees you—with my eyes—he will agree with me. I have only one life—and I must spend it with you—as your slave. He'll see that." She laughed. "I'll make him see that."

Locke tried gently to prepare her for that cold day when this trek ended, when they walked out of paradise into that pragmatic world of laws and tradition and compromise. There was little he could say, less he could force her to hear.

"I was asleep. A sleepwalker." She sighed. "I slept through life until you woke me up—there in the bed of that wagon—"

"Or are you dreaming now?"

"I was never more wide awake. Never more sure of what I must do, what my life—what our life—must be. Father will see it as I do. Despite his training and his attitudes, he loves me. He wants me to be happy. I know this. When he sees my only hope for happiness is with you—"

"Hadn't you better plan what will happen if he refuses to see that?"

She laughed. "I have. Oh, I have. In that sad case, if he opposes us, you and I will go down to the harbor in Pensacola and sail away—on the first ship bound for some island where the only laws will be those we make—you and I."

Locke realized that Yolanda existed on daydreams, lived in a fool's paradise, that she could be plunged into despair, into that dark and bleak vault of desolation that sometimes claimed her, if she insisted upon defying all the codes and customs by which she'd been reared. Her entire happiness depended on their finding some way to establish their own world, with no contact with her former existence, her royal family and those unbending vows awaiting her at Pensacola. He saw no such hope, no firm foundation for her fantasies. At the moment of his supreme happiness, he felt the chill premonition of what unhappiness lay ahead for them. Yolanda had already shown she could not compromise with evil, adapt to hurt, accommodate herself to pain—she could only retreat, inside herself, damaged and despairing. He had seen at Amelia Island what agony did to her. How often could she face these destructive situations—without shattering completely inside?

He held her close, wanting to protect her, to make her least dream come true, but feeling helpless and fearful.

He neglected everything else on this trek, concentrating on making Yolanda as happy as possible—for as long as he had that power. She saw no end for their paradise; he saw small hope for any permanence.

Halsted kept the two squads of soldiers under an unyielding discipline. At first, the ex-thugs rebelled, openly preferring the rigors of a stinking, overcrowded prison to Halsted's petty tyranny. Gradually, his training paid dividends. The ex-convicts even saw the motivation behind their learning to obey orders at once, to respond instantly to commands. They now kept their rifles cleaned and oiled without Halsted's prodding. They challenged each other in target practice. Not even Tavares revolted. He walked bent over, like an eighty-year-old man, but he obeyed every command Halsted barked at him; somehow he managed to keep pace with his company. He avoided Locke whenever possible; he carefully kept his gaze on the ground when either Isabella or Yolanda passed near him.

Abruptly, the quiet of the lonely trail was shattered. On the fifth day west of Cows Ford, the outside world intruded itself with a vengeance upon Locke's mobile Eden, fate took another savage twist in the disorderly pattern of Jeremiah Locke's existence.

The pound of fast-ridden horses thundered in the earth. Halsted threw up his arm. His company ceased marching and stepped out into the deep brush at both sides of the trail. Locke felt a sense of pride in the perfectly executed maneuver. It didn't seem like much, yet he knew it could save their lives. He was proud of Halsted, proud of his company of felons.

Five soldiers, wearing the uniform of the Spanish Army, rode lathered horses at a gallop. They slowed when they saw

Locke's supply wagon, the dust-covered, yet impressive carriage in which Yolanda rode with Isabella.

None of the soldiers spoke English. Isabella came out of the carriage. The soldiers dismounted, sweated and desperate. Locke ordered food and water and rations for their horses while they talked with Isabella.

They spoke rapidly in Spanish, with much gesturing of arms, sudden bursts of tears and equally inexplicable savage laughter that had no mirth, only heartbreak in it. The leader, a young lieutenant, agreed to allow his horses to rest, drink and eat grain. When he saw the food the soldiers and Cato set out, he nodded his appreciation and ordered his tired men to eat.

Isabella explained to Locke that the adventurer Gregor MacGregor had arrived in Fernandina's port with five vessels—an expedition out of Savannah and financed by American money. One Georgia firm agreed to purchase thirty thousand acres of Florida land at a dollar an acre from MacGregor if his expedition succeeded. Though he had only a hundred and fifty men, rumor had raced ahead of him, placing that number at more than one thousand. When he'd attacked Amelia Island, two days after Locke and his company departed, the fort had capitulated without resistance. The garrison, which could have beaten off the invader, retreated across the river and fled to St. Augustine where the commander, Francisco Morales, was court-martialed and sentenced to death. The lieutenant and his men were on their way to the other seat of Spanish government, four hundred miles from the east coast, at Pensacola.

Exhausted, dispirited and overcome with fatigue, the Spanish soldiers slept that night with the Locke company encampment. They were up before dawn and, after a breakfast of cornmeal cakes and coffee, they rode away at full gallop.

The rest of that day Yolanda was silent, withdrawn, though she refused to leave Locke's side. Without fully understanding why, he felt a desolate sense of loss, as if this sad moment on the trail were the beginning of the end for them . . .

When they first heard shots in the hammocks rising to the south of the Tallahassi trail, Locke thought emptily that the Spanish soldiers had run into some kind of ambush.

"We'd better investigate," he told Halsted.

The soldier agreed. He yelled commands. Four of the marchers took guns and ammunition and fell in with him. The others made a camp in a hammock, sitting armed guard around the wagon and carriage. Yolanda did not want Locke to accompany Halsted and the squad.

He kissed her lightly, but left guns for her, Isabella and the black coachman. "We've got to investigate," Locke said. "We're getting near the Suwannee—and that means Andrew Jackson and it means the Micosuki Indians."

She clung to him. Then she stood beside the wagon, taut-drawn as he marched, carrying a long rifle at his side, with Halsted and the squad.

The shooting came from a clearing less than a quarter of a mile from the trail. The gun battle claimed the minds, attention and total energies of the combatants. Locke and his men were able to creep stealthily to a knoll from which, concealed by willows and elders, they watched the strange encounter.

They counted six Indians who had made a camp near a sinkhole in which there was water. From the protection of trees ringing the clearing, men in American Army uniforms fired upon them. The Indians, caught in the open, and ill-armed, returned the fire from prone positions on the ground, but by the time Locke and his men reached the knoll, the Indians were throwing down their weapons and surrendering by standing up with their arms high over their heads.

The soldiers—there were twelve of them under command of a lieutenant mounted on a cavalry horse—strode out into the clearing, guns ready. They came in from every side and the Indians stood, immobile, in panic.

The lieutenant deployed his men around the encampment. With five soldiers standing with guns fixed on the Indians, the others gathered up the weapons the red men had thrown on the ground. Then these same soldiers ripped open the Indian packs with bayonets. The soldiers called to the lieutenant. They'd found what they sought. They held up large chunks of bloody beef as some kind of evidence.

When one of the Indians protested, a soldier struck him in the face with the butt of his gun. The Indian sagged bleeding to the ground. He lay unconscious, ignored except by swarms of flies.

A second Indian, staring at the fallen youth beside him, heeled around in panic and ran toward the forest. One of the soldiers took careful aim and shot the fugitive in the back of the knee. The Indian stumbled and fell, crying out in pain. At a sign from the lieutenant, two soldiers ran across the clearing, caught the bleeding brave under the arms and dragged him back into the center of the encampment.

The Indians were quickly tied, their wrists bound behind them with leather strips. Even the unconscious youth was revived with water and sand thrown in his face until he rolled over on his back, protesting, his face battered and blood leaking from his eyes, nostrils and torn lips.

The lieutenant gave an order and the captives were lined up. The wounded one was forced to stand, blood running down his calf, over his ankle and foot. The youth with the gun-whipped face was forced to stand, wavering reedlike, in the line. The soldiers retreated a few yards to where the lieutenant sat on his horse.

"Reckon these murderin' reds is going to learn to stop stealing cows from decent white folks?" The lieutenant's voice rang with wrath, as thick and accented as peppered grits.

If the Indians understood him, their faces revealed nothing. They stood, hopeless, trembling.

"Maybe if we teach them, they'll know. And the rest of their thievin' people will know." The lieutenant nodded, gesturing with his arm, his neck red, his face flushed.

At the lieutenant's signal, the soldiers raised their Kentucky long rifles to their shoulders. The Indians screamed, mindless.

The guns fired, the sounds reverberated in the silent forest and set the birds to screeching and putting wild turkeys into flight.

Each Indian buckled, shot in the kneecap. They fell, agonized and writhing, in the dirt. Taking his time, one of the soldiers forced each of them to stand up again.

One more, the soldiers reloaded and placed the long rifles to their shoulders. This time the second kneecap was torn from the legs of their captives. The Indians fell to the ground and flopped helplessly there. The soldiers watched them but did not try to make them stand up.

"I've seen enough," Locke said.

Halsted nodded his head, agreeing. He deployed his four men in a wide circle of concealment about the clearing. They moved out silently, slipping through the underbrush. Halsted's order was simple: Shoot once over the heads of the soldiers when he fired and then reload as swiftly as possible.

Halsted waited, giving his men time to spread out. Then he lifted his gun, ready to fire. Locke knelt beside him, musket thrust against his shoulder.

Halsted fired. Around the clearing the other men fired. Locke took careful aim at the head of the lieutenant's horse and pressed the trigger. The animal lurched upward and then fell dead. The lieutenant, screaming in fright, tried to leap clear. One leg was caught under the falling horse.

Halsted stared at Locke, astounded. Locke was reloading. His killing the lieutenant's horse bought them the precious time they needed. The element of panic now mixed with shock at this attack from all sides, and even the seasoned Tennessee volunteers were thrown for that instant into chaos.

The lieutenant, yelling more with rage than pain, was unable to shout orders.

Halsted leaped to his feet. His voice rode like a clarion across that clearing: "Drop your guns. Back six paces from them and stand firm. Do as you're told and you won't be killed. You're surrounded on all sides."

The soldiers hesitated, then obeyed that stentorian voice, the cold command. They had laid down their guns and backed away from them by the time the lieutenant could extricate his leg from beneath the leather and sinew of his dead horse.

The lieutenant yelled, his voice raging at his men. "Damn you, you lily-livered bastards. Did I tell you to lay down your guns?"

He jerked his own handgun from its holster. His leg was bent and he was in agony, but he waved the gun, trying to rally his men.

Locke took careful aim and put a bullet in the sand inches from the officer's toes. The dirt leaped up between his boots.

The lieutenant was brave, but he was also intelligent enough to know that bullet between his boots was only a message, and put there as a warning. That shot acted like an incredible sedative upon his emotions.

He backed away a few feet, stared at the handgun in his fist as if he detested the sight of it and tossed it without another word into the collection of long rifles. With his head up, his face gray, he joined his men. He stood unmoving, rigid, looking ready to explode, but cautious enough in his valor to stay alive.

Halsted and Locke walked out into the clearing, holding their guns on the line of soldiers. Across the clearing two of his men stepped out, holding their guns fixed on the army men.

From the ground, the wounded Indians, though agonized, watched in awe as if the great spirits had answered unspoken prayers.

Letting the lieutenant and his company see the armed men behind them, Halsted yelled in that stentor's voice: "All right, the rest of you men. Hold your places. Shoot the first man that moves."

Something happened in the lieutenant's face. This trick of yelling to unseen men was as old as military maneuvers, and yet it was like the equally old bluff of being warned about someone behind you—you had a fifty-fifty chance of being wrong.

Again the lieutenant, recalling that bullet between his boots and the fact that he could at this moment be dead, remained unmoving.

While Halsted and Locke held their guns fixed on the company, Clemmons and Masters gathered up all weapons, including those of the Indians. Clemmons found leather thongs and metal shackles in the lieutenant's saddlebags.

"Shackle them," Locke ordered.

Clemmons went as swiftly as possible behind the line of men, first securing their wrists with leather thongs and then linking them with shackles. When the twelve men were shackled, Halsted shouted, "All right, the rest of you men. Come on in here."

From the concealment the other two men came, with guns ready. For a long beat the lieutenant waited, his face slowly growing redder. Fires crackled in his eyes. He glared at Locke. "Is this all the men you have?"

Locke shrugged. "How many did we need?"

The lieutenant trembled in rage. "I don't know your uniforms. Who are you?"

"I don't know your uniforms," Locke said. "Who are you?"

"You son of a bitch. We're the United States Army. We're General Jackson's soldiers."

"What are you doing down here on the Tallahassi trail. This is Spanish Florida."

"This is army business, you bastard."

Locke stared at the lieutenant. "Just watch your tongue, mister, and maybe nobody will get hurt."

The lieutenant's voice crackled with savage laughter. "You'll get hurt. General Jackson himself will twist your balls until your eyes bug out."

Locke stepped closer. "Maybe I ought to finish you off then, so you don't have to see it." He glanced toward the Indians. "I know how you hate to look on cruelty."

He brought the rifle up negligently. The lieutenant's face grayed out and he retreated a step. Something in Locke's face turned his fortitude to clabber. He shook his head. "Don't do that. Goddamn it, that's murder."

Locke continued to stare into his face. "Then you order your men to march out of here. Order them to obey our commands. The first one of your men that makes trouble, I put a bullet in *your* head, Lieutenant." He glanced toward the Indians again. "And I won't hesitate over it."

The twelve men marched silently, shackled, with their arms secured behind them, across the clearing and through the hammock toward where the rest of the company and the carriages waited.

When Locke came out on the rutted trail, he saw Yolanda standing alone at the edge of the encampment. She did not have the handgun he had left with her. She looked as if she had been standing, taut and straight, for a long time.

She saw him and the breath exhaled out of her. She came running along the clotted trail and threw herself in his arms. She was pale and trembling fiercely. He held her gently while Halsted marched his prisoners past them. He went on standing there, holding Yolanda in his arms.

— XIX —

YOLANDA CAME to Locke in his makeshift night quarters in the bed of the supply wagon. It was after midnight. She was tense, her lovely face unhappy. She had been waiting a long time. He could not tell her, but he had spent an hour writing the first of his reports to President Monroe. He still had no idea what kind of report he would write, or what he would be able to do with it once he completed it. But he wrote slowly, telling exactly what he had come upon on the Tallahassi trail, precisely what he and his men had seen. He did not allow his own feelings to discolor what he wrote. He stated cold facts and nothing else. He folded the paper then and sat for a long time, staring beyond his flickering candle into the deep Florida night.

"Jeremiah," Yolanda whispered. He smiled and pushed back the netting. She came in upon the pad with him, breathless.

He half rose, supporting his weight on one hand, and gazed into her face, gentle and warm—and hurt. He saw in her eyes she wanted him to tell her what he had been writing, what he had been doing that was important enough to keep him from her all these hours. Her insecurity only enhanced the sensual enchantment of her golden face. He loosened her hair and slipped his hands into its rich and fragrant beauty. Some electricity in her hair, the heat of her skull, something he had no name for, swept through him and possessed him. He shuddered suddenly, overwhelmed with his desire for her. He whispered her name over and over and the thrill of it added to his sense of exultant excitement. His tender voice affected her too and as he spoke her name she breathed faster and pressed closer to him. He felt her hands move over him, reaching for him, caressing him, thrusting her palms deeply between his thighs to heft him, panting. She pressed her face against the rough hairs of his chest, nursing his paps, running her tongue along the hard tendons of his muscles. Her hands closed frantically upon him as if she somehow feared losing him. His own hands tightened on each side of her head, holding her hard against his chest, his fingers moving in the warm texture of her hair. Her breath burned his flesh. He reached down and removed the silks and laces of her night garments. Her tongue worked faster, flicking across his bared skin, inflaming him. He put his hands under her armpits and lifted her head to his, her mouth to his. Her hand gripped the columnal tumescence rising in response to her caressing, his need for her body. Somewhere in the night sounds rose from the sleeping prisoners, from the soldiers, from the horses, from the animals creeping in the primeval forest, but no sound outside this wagon could penetrate his conscious mind now.

He lifted himself and came down upon her. Her eyes had been closed and she opened them. Her legs opened wide and closed about his waist. She drew him to her in frantic need. He lost himself in the black depths of those soft eyes, in the fevered heat and liquidity of her body. He felt a surge of pleasure and delight he knew came to a few human beings on this inhibited planet, a glory of two people caught up in a moment of mutual desiring and loving.

He rose to a fevered apex of sensual pleasure, spun there, wheeling and skidding across a cosmos of blinding explosions and then plunged downward into darkness. Slowly, he drifted up to reality. He was aware she clung to him, sated, pleased, transported out of herself.

He felt a strange, inexplicable shiver of cold. In this moment of perfectly shared bliss, the chill of loss swept across him. In a fearful lucidity, he saw that he would lose Yolanda, that he was helpless to keep her. Though she pressed close to him, clinging to him and whispering his name in pleasure, he had already lost her . . .

He did not mention his premonition of loss, the chilling omen of wrong, to Yolanda. In the next days on the trail, she was happy. "I love you so," she cried. "I am so proud of you. My heart feels as if it will burst."

But even in her joy, she found Locke preoccupied, and

able to spend less time with her. At first, she merely smiled, confident of her young charms, sure that he loved her as deeply as she loved him.

She saw that the prisoners made travel slow and difficult. The eight soldiers of Halsted's squads were kept on constant alert. Locke learned that the only safe way to permit Jackson's soldiers to eat was to unshackle them two at a time and allow them to dine, under guard. This was a slow process, time-consuming.

The lieutenant watched with a sour smile. He was a lean, tall man from eastern Tennessee. His name was Lester Catchpole. He had been at Chalmette with Jackson.

"What you going to do, Locke, when you come on a company of our American soldiers?" Catchpole taunted.

Locke shrugged. "First thing I'm going to do is put a bullet in your head."

Catchpole grayed. He did not doubt this; there was nothing in Locke's cold eyes to doubt. "That won't keep Old Hickory from hanging you high for murder."

"Then I'll see you in hell, Catchpole."

Catchpole laughed. "Jesus. I can't wait to see what General Jackson's going to do when he learns what you did to his men." His laugh raked at Locke. "He's mighty jealous about the safety of his men."

"He'll have his chance to do what he will, Catchpole, once we report to him what we caught you doing."

"Doing? What was we doing? You think we wasn't carrying out orders?"

"I don't know. You tell us where General Jackson is camped, and we'll march there now."

Catchpole stared at him. "I might just do that, Locke. . . . First, I advise you, make your will."

Yolanda caught Locke's arm and drew him away from the company, walking with him into the cool hammock alongside the trail. "Did you mean that?" she said, staring into his face as if trying to read hidden secrets in the depths of his gray eyes.

He frowned, gazing into her troubled eyes. "Did I mean what?"

"I heard you tell that Lieutenant Catchpole that you would take him to General Jackson's camp. Did you mean that?"

Locke breathed in deeply. He winced because he realized that his resolve to undertake President Monroe's assignment had hardened into an inflexible determination. He could not say when it happened—that day at the White House, that later day on Amelia Island when he saw the first mutilated Indians, or when he came upon Catchpole's men. Clearly, Catchpole figured he was at war—with renegade Indians, fugitive blacks and any Spanish who got in his path. Obviously, this was General Jackson's clear understanding. Whatever he did down here was done as open warfare. The only thing wrong with all this was that Spain was not at war with the United States; Jackson's men were invading Spanish territory. Was this simply a maneuver in the name of securing U.S. borders—or did Jackson mean this time to conquer and claim Spanish Florida? For the first time, he understood the doubts assailing Monroe in Washington.

He stared down at Yolanda, holding her close to him. Except that he had come into Spanish Florida through Amelia Island and saw Jackson's attack across the international border through Yolanda's eyes, he would never have fully appreciated the monstrous wrong in what Jackson was doing. He saw that Monroe was not as concerned about Jackson's wrongdoing down here, as he was about the motives behind it.

He could not say any of this to Yolanda. Monroe had pledged him to secrecy. And yet, his promise to the President was not the reason he refrained from explaining the mission to Yolanda. What anybody knew about him from this moment could endanger that person's life. He wanted to protect Yolanda, not to place her in jeopardy.

He snarled back at Catchpole when the shackled lieutenant warned him that any moment, around any bend in this trail, he might come upon Jackson's men. He had no illusions about his capability of resisting a force of the Tennessee soldiers.

A thousand times a day he tried to figure some way to insure Yolanda's safety. If an avenging company of Jackson's cavalry rode in on them, he doubted that any of them, men or women, would be spared. But he did not speak aloud of this; he did not want to infect Yolanda with the panic that roiled inside him. There would be time to tell her of the peril when he could also describe a way out of danger for her.

"Listen to me," she said, gazing up at him intently, as if she'd been following the involved skein of his thoughts, "get rid of those men."

He laughed emptily. "How?"

"Leave them beside the trail," she said. Her eyes went as cold as spilt blood. Passion seethed close under the low tones of her voice. "Shackle them to trees and leave them. Somebody will find them. Maybe Jackson's own men. If God is kind, maybe Micosuki Indians will find them, unarmed and chained. Maybe wild animals will find them. You cannot say from your heart that you care."

He shook his head. "Hell hath no fury like a woman's—"

"These vicious men are invading my land," she said. "Land my father was sent here to govern—by my king. Land ceded to us in the Treaty of Ghent. This land is ours! The Spanish Floridas belong to Spain—in the eyes of civilized people, and before God Himself. This is not some whim of mine. Civilized men met at Ghent—and this land was returned to Spain—which rightfully owned it. What right have these butchers to come down here and slay our people, burn their villages, mutilate and rape them?"

"I don't know."

"You do know, Jeremiah-*mío*! I felt helpless until I met you. I saw no way for my poor country to defend itself from ruthless, heartless invaders. I dreamed of uniting the blacks who have fled the cruelty of the Americans, the Indians who have been dispossessed by them, left homeless, betrayed and driven out by them, along with the Spanish who live here and the Spanish nationals who have sworn allegiance to Ferdinand. My own father is too weak. Men like Francisco Morales lack the guts for anything but petty graft and political theft. But you are not too weak. They would rally around you, Jeremiah-*mío*. You could lead them."

He shook his head, staring at her. "There is one thing you forget, my violent little Joan of Arc. I am an American. As much as Lester Catchpole, as much as General Jackson. I don't agree with what they are doing, but I am as loyal to my country—I am not disloyal in dissent. I see wrong. I want to change it. I see evil, I want to repair it. That doesn't mean I love my country any less. . . . You must know that Spain has been wrong a thousand times—and yet you love her no less."

Her eyes filled with tears but she could not surrender her dream. She clutched his arm tightly. "Oh, Jerry, help me! Join me. Leave these men on the trail and come with me to Pensacola. From your little army of eight we will build one of a thousand—red, black, Spanish—fighting together under your leadership."

"You know I can't."

She trembled violently. "I know you must. I know if you love me—you *will!* It's the only way we can be together. My father could not deny us if you rallied an army for him. We could force my father—as governor—to spend Spanish taxes and Spanish treasure to support our army. He would back your army. He would back you. He could not deny us."

She wept suddenly, clinging to him. He held her gently, pressing his face into the rich fragrance of her hair. The sun lay dappled about them in the hammock, a hot and humid Florida afternoon, and yet Locke shuddered with cold . . .

The next morning they came upon an Indian village which had been destroyed, left in ashes. The gardens of the women had been trampled, the fields of maize uprooted or burned. Every hut or tepee had been razed. The dead women and children had been left to rot. On long, peeled pine poles the severed heads of two Indian women looked down on the ruin of their lives, the slaughter of their animals, the extinction of their tribe.

Ill, Yolanda threw herself into her carriage, weeping in rage and anguish.

Lester Catchpole's voice raked at Locke. "You want to take off these here shackles and give us back our guns now, Locke?" His cold laugh struck Jerry like spittle in the face. "We'll give you an hour head start. You got my word on that."

"I wouldn't take your word on who your mother was."

Catchpole laughed. "Easy to insult a man when his hands is shackled, ain't it, traitor? Look around you, Locke. See this here village. Ain't two days old. That means Jackson's men are nearby. Hell, they may be watching you now from that forest. Sure as hell you're a-going to come up on them—around a bend."

"Be sure if they attack, you'll die first, Catchpole."

Catchpole laughed. "That ain't going to save your skin, Locke, or your greasy Spic bitch, either. When them fellows git through with her, you'll wish to God you'd accepted my kindly offer to stay alive and run."

Locke turned away, fists gripped at his sides. He had to get away from Catchpole or kick his teeth in. He started away, but Catchpole's voice stopped him, like something thrown against the small of his back.

"Got yourself up shit creek and no paddle, ain't you, traitor?"

Locke glanced over his shoulder. "Maybe. But I'm the one walking around free, while you're tied up."

"Sure. You got us," Catchpole taunted. "Got us tied up and chained. What you going to do with us? Looks like you got yourself a mess of trouble and no way out. Yes, suh. Sure does. Looks like you done catched yo'self a tiger by the tail . . . don't it, *Mister* Locke?"

Locke stared at the lean, bearded backwoodsman, hating him. But his fears for Yolanda multiplied a hundred times. If Jackson loosed his soldiers like ravening dogs on the Indians, what would they do to a Spanish noblewoman?

The caravan moved slowly forward. Jerry felt as if it approached the outskirts of doom. He wanted to turn and run and yet there was nowhere to run. He could devise no plan to insure Yolanda's safety, to guarantee against a surprise attack—or a frontal assault by superior forces—of Jackson's army. Catchpole had not lied. The very evidence of Jackson's men disarmed and shackled was his own death warrant.

He winced, thinking he could face this with some resignation if he could devise some way to assure Yolanda's escape to safety. This was all he thought, all he could think, and it was an endless circle, over and over the same ground. There was no way out, for either of them.

For half an hour before they reached the site, they heard the forest-rattling sounds of a large encampment ahead.

Catchpole heard the noises and put his head back, raging with laughter. "Locke," he yelled. "Unchain me and my men and run for your life, traitor. Can't promise you no head start no more—but I can vow you a hangrope when my general and his men git you."

Catchpole's soldiers stirred, infected by their lieutenant's insolent defiance. They yelled, hoo-rawed, their voices carrying ahead of them like trumpets in the forest.

Halsted's men marched among them, threatening them, but the prisoners were unruly, certain that their guards were now the captives.

Whatever contingency plan Locke might have effected, whatever ruse he may have devised for circling the encampment or avoiding it, was negated by the noisy soldiers.

There remained only one course open to him: to move relentlessly forward, straight ahead on the trail. By now the encampment up there was well aware of their approach.

His eight-man company marched warily, guns loaded and held ready on their shoulders. The soft unbroken cadence moved them forward as a unit. Halsted marched beside them, head up, shoulders back, but his eyes searched for any flash of movement from the thick woods on each side of the trail.

They came out upon the plains of Tallahassi. This ancient clearing had seen the gathering of Indian tribes for untold hundreds of years. It was ringed by great oaks and flowering magnolias, by sweet bay and short-leaf pines.

In the clearing was grouped a large and ostentatious caravan. But with a sick sense of relief, Locke saw it was not a company of Jackson's men. There were dozens of ornate carriages, with silk fringes, scrollwork, high polish and glittering metal. Even the supply wagons were highly painted and covered with rich-textured fabrics. A contingent of soldiers, wearing plumed hats and the gaudy uniforms of palace guards and mounted on Arabian horses, had ridden to the brink of the camp and stood awaiting the approach of Locke's wagon, carriage and marching men. Staring at this display of opulence, Locke ordered his men slowly forward. The guards, with guns ready, parted and let them enter the outer perimeter of the encampment.

The waning afternoon sunlight flamed radiant, reflected in the brilliance of conveyance, artillery, uniform and insignia of nobility. The bright sheen of the deep reds, the opulence of gold, the luster of silver, designated the cavalcade Spanish, and more than that, Spanish royalty. The pomp and glory, the color of flying pendants, the legion of mounted cavalry, the gaily bedecked animals, the platoons of uniformed foot soldiers celebrated an insolent aristocracy totally unaware of the real world around them.

In the center of the vast camp, linen-covered tables with gold candelabra and silver service had been set out and were attended by formally attired servants.

Locke moved forward at the head of his company, feeling as if he had walked into the past, into the mindless elegance of Marie Antoinette's France. This magnificent caravan paraded across this bloody, ravaged land and saw only its own reflection, smelled only its own imported colognes, heard only its own laughter.

Isabella leaped out of the carriage as soon as the company entered the outskirts of the encampment. She ran forward, greeting some of the guards, surveying the people eating and drinking at the tables under the soothing music of string ensembles. She stared for a moment and then ran back, calling out to Yolanda in excited Spanish.

At a signal from a gold-braided officer in high hat, Locke held up his hand, signaling his company to halt.

He stared around him at the camp, stirring like a small, temporary city. There was no way to ascertain the number of people in this place, civilians, servants, soldiers and the service personnel required to keep these hundreds of animals and dozens of bright vehicles moving.

A man arose from the head of the largest, most elaborately set table. Of medium height, he wore sparkling polished, burgundy, high-heeled boots. He was somewhere between forty and sixty; one could not be sure. His eyes looked tired, but his face was oddly unlined. He was balding but the fringe of hair on his pate and curling over his ears and collar was deep black and glistening with oil. His travel suit, formal, with laced jabot and string tie, gold vest and burgundy jacket, gleamed in the sun. He walked with the arrogance of authority.

He carried a wineglass, brimmed with chablis, but when he saw Yolanda, he threw the gold-monogrammed goblet from him and it shattered on the ground.

"*Padre*!" Yolanda cried. "*Mío padre*!"

She ran forward and flung herself into her father's arms.

He laughed and cried at once, petting her and smoothing her hair.

Watching them, Locke felt that chill spread deep in his empty belly.

Governor Castillo was unfailingly polite toward Locke. He invited him, along with Yolanda, into his private tent—a mammoth covering of canvas with heavy furnishings, Persian rugs and a fourposter bed turned back with fresh sheets and embroidered gold spread.

Governor Castillo smiled warmly every time his gaze touched against Locke's. He listened, with an attentive, indulgent smile, as Yolanda extolled Locke's virtues, his bravery, fortitude and incredible charm. He nodded and smiled his approbation and approval, remarking over and over that he did not know where Yolanda could have found such a "paragon of virtue." But Locke was not deceived, nor did Yolanda's father intend that he should be misled by his smiling. Locke and Yolanda's father understood each other. The invisible barriers between them could not be removed or scaled. Governor Castillo would not tolerate it if they could.

Locke was far less than surprised when Governor Castillo dismissed the subject of Yolanda's new friend and turned to a topic nearer and dearer to the governor's own heart: himself.

Governor Castillo and his entourage, advisers and guards were returning from a conference on the Georgia border with General Andrew Jackson, representatives from the State Department, and several generals and senior officers under Jackson. They had, upon reaching the plains of Tallahassi, intercepted the soldiers from Amelia Island bringing the distressing news of MacGregor's invasion of the island. Also, the soldiers had apprised the governor that his daughter—that very apple of his eye whom he had not seen in months—was only a day or so behind the soldiers on the trail. He determined then to await her arrival so she could accompany him the rest of the way to Pensacola.

"Your holding soldiers of General Jackson's army as prisoners creates an unhappy problem," Castillo told Locke, smiling. "It would cause an incident between the general and myself. I would be distressed if that happened."

"I am sure that Jeremiah will release the prisoners when

we leave this camp, Father, if that is your wish. Though I must tell you that they should be tried as criminals for their inhuman attack on Spanish subjects.''

Yolanda covered Locke's hand fiercely with her icy fingers. But he did not reply to her suggestion, nor even have the opportunity. Governor Castillo lapsed into a detailed version of his meeting with Jackson.

''I do want the delicate balance between the general and myself maintained.'' Castillo said, smiling. ''I have worked too hard to smooth matters between us to have it destroyed by an incident—even prisoners taken on our lands. General Jackson and I had a very rewarding conference, Yolanda, my dear. Most profitable. We were stern at times, and yet always affable. The general always was most polite. He let me understand his problems and seemed to understand mine. I told him I was helpless to do anything until I received instructions from Havana.

''There was only one point on which the general was bitter and adamant. His claim is that a Negro fort has been established on the Apalachicola River—here in Spanish Florida—equipped with arms and munitions supplied by the British. He insists that a Captain Arbuthnot is one of the suppliers of the fort's arms and munitions and demands Arbuthnot be turned over to him as a criminal, conspiring with the blacks against the United States. Again, I had to tell him I was helpless without direct orders concerning our relations with British subjects.

''General Jackson argued for some time, but remained calm. He declared that from this fort Negroes who are runaway slaves from United States plantations—and therefore American subjects and property of American citizens—under a leader called Garcon—are plundering the countryside and firing on boats passing up and down the river. General Jackson says he must protect American interests—the boats and lives of American traders and sailors.

''Again, as politely as possible, I explained that I could do nothing without direct instructions from Havana. I told him, as politely as I could, that until I received such word, there was no action I could take on any of the matters so distressing to him.

''The general remained coldly polite, but he said America

could not and would not sit idly by and allow renegade blacks to harass and kill their people. The slaves, he insists, are rightful property of United States citizens and must be returned to their rightful owners."

Locke saw that the final impression the polite and smiling governor had left with the Americans was one of wavering, irresolution, indecision and total timidity. Jackson threatened to attack the Negro fort unless the Spanish agreed to destroy it and return United States property—the runaway slaves. All Castillo had actually said in the end was that he remained unprepared to take any action at this time. And so the conference had ended . . .

Locke stared at Yolanda's father. This hesitant, weak and cowardly man had knowingly or unknowingly given General Jackson *carte blanche* to act across the international border. He had given Jackson the answer the U.S. general wanted. Castillo was going to take no action. This suggested to all the Americans present at the conference that the Spanish authority would not be too upset if the United States meted out summary justice on its own, recovered its own property, even if this meant destroying the Negro fort. Jackson must have read this as an invitation to march into Florida . . .

Yolanda cried out in protest. If her father permitted American forces into Spanish Florida on any pretext, nothing but open warfare would ever dislodge them.

"Compromise, my dear. Diplomacy," her father said.

"They don't see it as compromise. They see it as weakness. As cowardice."

Her father merely smiled that indulgent smile and patted her hand reassuringly. "You should leave matters of state to me, my dear," he said. "I'm sure I'm capable of handling them better than you."

"They're killing our people." Yolanda's voice was empty.

"This is hardly a matter to discuss with a lady," Castillo said. "Even a warlike young Amazon like my daughter, eh, Señor Locke?"

Locke felt Yolanda's black eyes burning on him, begging him to speak, but he sat silently. Yolanda leaped to her feet and ran weeping from the room.

Governor Castillo smiled and waved his hand negligently. "She is only upset. Very high-strung. She always has been.

By heaven, if she'd been a son—she'd have been a fiery warrior, eh?" He smiled again. "She doesn't take after me, eh? I know the long-term value of diplomacy. Compromise. Poor Yolanda. She never will."

Locke spread his hands. He also didn't know where in hell Yolanda had gotten her beauty from, either . . .

Despite Locke's evaluation of Governor Castillo and his entourage as a gathering of self-indulgent, morally atrophied, and decadent elite, the royal caravan had broken camp by dawn the next morning and noisily prepared to march west with the first full daybreak.

Yolanda ran through the busy camp to him. When she saw that he remained with his company and his prisoners and had made no arrangements to join her father's train, her eyes darkened and her cheeks paled.

She gestured helplessly. "Are you going to let me go on without you?"

For a long beat Locke didn't answer. The dust-powdered sunlight spilled gold tints across her face and slashed faint shadows in the depths of her eyes. Her dress was mussed, her hair danced in flighty, confessional disarray. But it was the strange timbre in her voice that agonized him, made it impossible for him to speak through the sudden tautness in his throat, made him want to look away from her.

At last he said, "There's nothing else I can do."

She looked about, not seeing the busy preparations of the breaking camp, the forming caravan. With him, whether he wanted to or not, she saw the beautiful nights and the quiet days along the trail; the discovery of a love she had not even suspected existed, and which now lay crumbled and lost for reasons she couldn't understand, or refused to face.

"What's to happen to us?" she said.

But she knew the answer to this, too, maybe even better than he did, and for that moment he could find no words to answer her.

And then, as she stood before him, bleak and unhappy, her full breast rising and falling, her eyes empty and frantic, Locke realized with a shock that they *were* truly parting, and likely it was forever. Perhaps until this moment he had not believed it, maybe prayed for a miracle. There was to be no miracle. Horse wranglers and coachmen shouted around them in the erupting billows of dust and carriages moved into protocol-dictated places in the growing line.

He swallowed hard. The sense of loss that he had not faced until now staggered him. He could not let her go without reassuring her, reassuring himself. "I'll come to you, Yolanda. You know that. As soon as I can—"

"Come with me now." Her voice quavered. "Make your life my life—"

"My life is your life."

Her chin tilted, her black eyes glittered. "You lie. If you leave me now, I'll never see you again. Do you think I don't know that?"

He held her gaze, kept his voice level. "I'll come to you."

"No. And anyway, it would never be the same. My father will be set against you. It won't be the same."

She did not mention that unknown man to whom she'd been plighted since childhood, but the lost tone of her voice evoked his image between them.

"Your father is already dead set against me. But that does not keep me from you. I have a job to do . . . when it is done, I will come to you. You may not want me then, but I will come."

She shook her head, eyes brimming with chilled tears. She looked about, distracted. "If you let me go now—with them—I have lost you."

"No. Not if you love me."

She laughed emptily. "Love does not mean much in their world. Vows. Family. Tradition. Custom. Religion. Nationality."

"Yes. Those are a few of our obstacles."

"They are not important. What on this earth is more important for us—than you and I?"

He held her arms tightly in his chilled fingers. He shook his head. "Nothing. But . . . you must go with your father now. He would not go without you."

"You can come with us."

"No . . . I'll come to you. Soon. As soon as I can. It's all we can do."

She withdrew from him, the light in her black eyes as chilled as a shard of starlight in a frozen river. She exhaled heavily. "It's over. You've chosen, haven't you? I've lost you."

He caught her hand but she pulled free. The camp reverberated with a hundred sounds, loud around them; dust swirled across them from the hooves of prancing cavalry horses. She let her gaze touch briefly against his face, then she turned and walked away from him slowly, her head down, her skirts dragging in the dust. She did not look back. She wandered between the rows of soldiers, the nervous horses, the laughing nobles. She was helped into her carriage by two liveried footmen.

He stood unmoving, desolated, as the wagons, animals and carriages lurched forward, moving west. The gray dust clouded back across him.

— XX —

LOCKE STOOD as if rooted to the ground of the Tallahassi plains until the tail end of the Castillo caravan disappeared in the lush green West Florida forest, and he was still there when the last wisp of dust drifted back across him and dissipated on the wind.

Halsted's hoarse voice woke him from his reverie of loss. He looked about, unsure where he was, disoriented. He found Halsted's laughing face an affront. He saw little reason for laughter left in this empty planet.

"Think you got a little trouble," Halsted said.

A little trouble; this meant only that life went on; your heart broke, your life crumbled, but life went on apace: You had a little trouble. Locke wanted to rage at his sergeant, but his anger was not directed at Halsted, rather at himself. He had let worldly concerns and obstacles intrude between himself and Yolanda—he was a coward who deserved to lose her—and yet he was not prepared to accept it. Inside he felt shattered, unable to pick up the pieces, to go on, to face even a little trouble. He managed to speak in a level tone. "What's the matter now?"

Halsted grinned again. He squinted against the sun. "You best come see."

Locke nodded; life went on.

Taut, Locke followed Halsted across the tortured, recently cleared campgrounds. Bits of paper fluttered on the breeze; distantly, a blue jay scolded from a gum tree. Before they reached the supply wagon, Locke heard Cato's anguished baritone, wailing, sobbing, laughing, singing and whimpering.

With Halsted laughing beside him, Locke peered over the walls of the wagon bed.

Cato sprawled in its sump on his back. He lay, almost helpless, unable to rise. He held a half-filled bottle of Spanish wine in his fist. Beside him half a dozen empties littered the wagon bed.

"What the hell's the matter with you, Cato?"

Cato opened his eyes slowly, painfully, letting them focus as much as possible. He stared upward, pupils glassy, white-rimmed. "Oh, there you are—mastah. . . . Thank your god I am drunk. If I were not drunk you would be dead—mastah. At my hands, and I—I would be on my way to Pensacola."

Cato let his head sink back and he reared his body upward, fighting invisible fetters. His mouth opened wide in anguish and he sobbed helplessly.

"You think he's dangerous?" Halsted asked.

Locke glanced at the sergeant. "In that condition? Do you?"

"He's a hell of a big nigger. He might be dangerous when he sobers up." Halsted laughed again and shook his head. "Poor bastard. He's talked about nothing except killing you and going with his Morisco bitch to Pensacola with the Spanish."

Locke shrugged. "That's the price she has set for herself. He must prove his worth—his right to be free—his worthiness of her—by killing me."

"I'll kill you—mastah. . . . I'll kill you yet."

"Sure you will."

Cato raged, weeping helplessly, his nose leaking, tears streaming down his face. "You don't know. . . . I've got to. I've got to! She requires it and she is my soul! My soul. I cannot live without my soul." Cato rocked, rolling his head back and forth on the rough boards.

Halsted laughed. "So you're all that stands between this big nigger and true happiness?"

Locke shrugged his shoulders again. "I always have been."

Halsted whistled between his teeth. "Maybe I best chain him—until he sobers up. Until he comes to his senses."

Locke shook his head. "No. Leave him alone. He'll sober up—sooner or later. But he'll never come to his senses. How can he? He's a true disciple, an Old Testament prophet, a conjure man, an oracle, a sage, a white man's woods colt. Asking him to come to his senses is just asking too much."

"God forgive me—for the way I hate you, mastah," Cato bawled. He struggled like an upturned beetle, helpless. "God forgive me."

"Let him sleep it off," Locke said to Halsted.

Halsted shook his head, amazed. "I've never yet seen another nigger treated so much like an equal."

Locke held up his hand, warningly. "Be careful. If Cato hears you call me *his* equal, he may want to kill you too."

Fleeing Indians crossing the Tallahassi trail brought Locke his first actual knowledge of General Jackson's whereabouts. Catchpole coldly refused to tell him anything about locating the general's headquarters. Catchpole said only, "Jackson's men will find *you*, renegade. Don't you fret it."

This frantic exodus of Indians out of the north shocked Locke. He learned from an Indian prophet who spoke English that the Indians he saw in flight were those who had been living in peace on reservations set aside since the Treaty of Fort Jackson on the American side of the international boundary, within lands claimed by the United States after Jackson defeated the Creeks at Horseshoe Bend.

"Why are they running if they live on land ceded them by the treaty?"

The prophet looked ill. The drums had brought word that the Father in Washington had loosed Sharp Knife to "chastise" the Indians once more. President Monroe's appointment of Jackson as commander of forces earlier authorized by the

Secretary of War to "pursue the Indians and, if necessary, to cross into Florida and attack them if they shelter themselves under Spanish protection," threw the Indians into panic and a frenzy. They were terrified of remaining in Jackson's path.

The prophet who spoke with Locke kept glancing around nervously; his eyes glittered with a look of wildness, of helpless insanity, of terror beyond human endurance.

This same look of bewildered frenzy marked the faces of all the Indians he saw. Their eyes were distracted. Even in repose, their faces betrayed the inner anxiety and terror that Andrew Jackson's name struck in their hearts. To some he was the evil spirit incarnate. His hawklike eyes fixed on them along his falcate nose was enough to unman the bravest of them. And he had, again and again, uprooted them from their homes, closed their hunting grounds to them, displaced them to new regions only to attack and force them out later on, razed their property and slaughtered their livestock. He had starved them into submission. They had been tricked, deceived, lied to, cheated and harangued by this man who actually referred to himself as their "benevolent protector, friend and brother," until they trembled, unhinged, overcome by physical weakness, lassitude and illness at the mention of his name.

Now they were fleeing ahead of him again. The word that Sharp Knife was on the march once more sent Indians running into Spanish Florida, forsaking whatever possessions had been left to them. They were addled and deranged, running from terror into madness.

"Sharp Knife and a million warriors camp yonder," the prophet said. "He sweeps forward into Florida like a wild fire in the forest—scourging everything before him."

Locke told Catchpole that he had information that Jackson was moving into Florida and was encamped only a few miles away.

Catchpole's mouth twisted. "I say you listen to lies. Indians don't know the truth. They'll tell you anything they think will delay you or get you in trouble."

"Where do you think General Jackson is?"

"I know where he is, bub. We started out for Fort Scott

from Nashville with one thousand troops. We covered the 450 miles in forty-six days. But it was hell. Cold and rain and mud made the roads ditches and the ditches rivers. We fought them baggage wagons every damned foot of the way. We was met by General Gaines outside Hartford, Georgia. Unfortunately he didn't have any more supplies than we did—him just coming from Amelia Island and just being told he was being replaced in command by Old Hickory. We'd been through forty-six days of unadulterated hell, and we was half starved by the time we reached Fort Scott.

"Things wasn't much better at the fort as far as supplies was concerned, but we rested, we ate some and we regrouped. General Gaines's men had burned Fowltown, an Indian place under a Seminole chief named Neamathla. General Gaines ran the Seminoles out. Then them thieving Seminoles ambushed a big open boat that was conveying forty American soldiers, seven gentle white ladies and four little children up the Apalachicola River toward Fort Scott. It was a bloodbath. Them Indians killed all but one woman what they took captive and four men what managed to escape to shore. Them red devils took them innocent children by their heels and bashed their brains out against the side of the boat.

"General Jackson at Fort Scott mapped out the way he meant to punish and chastise them Indians for what they done to American property, American people.

"Whilst we was there, that party of red devils you come upon us punishing back there had attacked a white man's farm in Georgia, slaughtered his beef and burned his house and barn. The general sent me and this company to run them down. We was to report back to the general at Fort Scott. So I know that's where he's at."

In the middle of the afternoon Halsted and Tavares returned from a scouting trip. Halsted looked gray. He nodded. "General Jackson is bivouacked upriver all right. And it's just like that Indian said. You never saw so many goddamn troops in your life."

Locke glanced toward the shackled lieutenant. "I thought you said General Jackson had a thousand men?"

Catchpole gazed up at him in contempt. "That's right. We

left Nashville with one thousand regulars and volunteers. The governor was going to send new recruits. General Gaines added his forces. And almost two thousand Creeks have joined the general to fight with us."

"Creeks? I thought they were the nation he almost decimated at Horseshoe Bend?"

Catchpole shrugged. "Right. I was there. But that's all past. The general told them that since he's punished them, he's forgiven them and he'll protect them as long as they obey him and close their ears to false prophets and—" he glared at Locke, "white renegades stirring up trouble."

"That means he has nearly three thousand troops," Locke said.

Halsted shook his head. "You ain't figurin' to fight *them*, be you?"

Locke shook his head. "There's an old saying in my family, Halsted. When you can't lick 'em, join 'em."

Halsted looked at the shackled men lined behind the supply wagon. "You hopin' to join General Jackson now?"

Catchpole roared with laughter. "That's the goddamn day I'm livin' to see. The day you ragtails join Old Hickory."

Locke had learned his lesson from the raging yells of Catchpole's company when they'd last approached an encampment. This time he gagged the soldiers and their lieutenant, removed their boots and kept them away from anything with which they might raise a racket.

They marched slowly toward the Jackson bivouac. Locke was aware that outposts of the camp had spied them. When he reached the edge of the huge arena, he halted his company.

With leather thongs, he secured a long rifle with its mouth pressed under Catchpole's jaw and its butt tied to his own hand and wrist. Even if he were shot, his rifle would blow Catchpole's head off.

Cato still lay sprawled in the bed of the supply wagon. One of the soldiers handled its dray horses; it was followed by the shackled Tennessee soldiers, with Halsted's men, unarmed, behind them. Halsted himself brought up the rear of the company.

Walking slowly, Locke entered the encampment with Lt.

Lester Catchpole, barefooted, and thonged to his rifle, angled beside him. Catchpole's face flared red to the roots of his hair. His eyes glittered murderously. His body trembled visibly.

Locke ignored him. Getting his first glimpse of this camp, Locke was overwhelmed, as Halsted had been. For the first time he encountered the might and pomp and military glory of the United States war machine. This place was a bivouac—an overnight camp. Yet, like the *castra* of the ancient Roman legions, it was laid out like a temporary city, with a flagpole and the American flag, along with Jackson's pennants and the Tennessee insignia flying in the breeze. At the perimeter of the camp were laid out the horse corrals, the grounds for the Indians, the supply wagon areas. The tents of the enlisted men and junior officers lined the camp streets, like spokes from the flagpole. Deep within the camp, the large tents of Jackson and his senior officers dominated the site. Men worked or marched on all sides. Three thousand men in a temporary camp could look like uncounted legions.

Locke guided Catchpole and led his company and prisoners along the main street toward the huge tents of the senior officers. Every activity in the camp ceased, an intense silence settled everywhere. They walked past the Indians first, and these bronze-skinned men stared silently and filtered out into the street. Soldiers flowed in from all sides. By the time Locke had walked to the center of the camp, the roadway was lined with silent, watching troops.

A major came striding from the headquarters area and met Locke at the flagpole.

The major stared, incredulous, at Locke. Then, recognizing the young lieutenant, the major addressed him. "In the name of God, Catchpole, what goes on here?"

Catchpole looked ready to burst with rage, ready to weep in anger, but gagged, he was unable to reply.

The major jerked his head around, staring at Locke as if to burn his image into his brain. "Who are you, sir? What in hell is this?"

"My name is Jeremiah Locke, Hidden Brook, Virginia, sir," Locke said respectfully, but with a chill.

"What are you doing with my officer trussed up in this way?" The major's voice shook.

"It's an involved story, sir. But I would like you to hear it."

The major looked ready to erupt. "Oh, I want to hear it. And now." His voice rasped. "First, you better loose that contraption and remove that gag from the mouth of an officer of the United States Army."

"No, sir. You can see the hammer is tied back, too. Any sudden moves, the lieutenant will probably be killed. . . . I'll regret that."

"You'll hang for murder."

"Not if you'll listen to me," Locke said. "Then, we can slowly let down the firing pin and Lieutenant Catchpole will be perfectly safe."

The major sweated. "I'm listening, Locke."

"I wanted to join General Jackson. When I heard he had been placed in command of an army down here, I brought my company of men south to Cows Ford on Kings Road and started west. A week or so west, I came upon Lieutenant Catchpole and his men." Locke jerked his head toward the barefooted troops shackled behind them. "They had surrounded a camp of six Indians."

"They were sent on a mission to overtake some murdering Seminoles."

"Yes, sir. And they overtook them. But they did not take them prisoners. They did not even kill them outright. They mutilated them, sir."

"Mutilated?"

"Shot off their kneecaps. I could not believe that they had such orders from a civilized army—and not from a man like General Jackson that this whole country reveres. I took them prisoner and brought them with me—for whatever you see fit to do."

The major trembled. His face was gray. Though he was in his forties and obviously had dedicated his life to the military, he had never before encountered a situation to parallel this one.

He gazed for a long beat into Locke's face. Locke kept his eyes level, expressionless; he did not blink or look away. A hint of weakness in this place was signing one's own death sentence.

The major moved his gaze to Lt. Catchpole, to the cocked rifle fixed against his throat and thonged to Locke's hand and wrist. Then he surveyed the barefooted soldiers and Locke's company of felons beyond.

He brought his gaze back to Locke's face. "You stand where you are, Locke. I am Major Reade. As of this moment, you can consider youself a prisoner of the United States Army."

Locke's tone matched Major Reade's precisely. "I had hoped for a better welcome than this. I came to join you. I thought you, and your other officers, would want to know about mutilation—"

"That's enough." Major Reade's voice shook. "That's just a goddamn enough. What happens to you is out of my hands. You just stand where you are. General Gaines and General Jackson will have to hear about this." He inhaled deeply, staring at the long rifle. "If anything happens to my lieutenant in the meantime, I'll see you hang for murder."

Locke held his gaze. "You better warn your soldiers. They can't kill me without killing Catchpole. You can't even remove that gag without setting off this gun."

Reade managed to keep himself under control. He jerked his head around, seeing the armed men who stood undecided at the fringe of the onlookers. Reade lifted his voice. "Nobody makes a move without the command from me. That means nobody. You men. All of you. Stand as you are."

— XXI —

LOCKE'S FIRST glimpse of the hero of New Orleans was as unsettling as his initial impression of the Tennessee general's splendid bivouac on the river.

Jackson was fifty years old at this time. He stood tall, vulture thin, wracked with a persistent cough, a lingering lung fever and a pain in his side which caused him to spit blood and which had reduced him to a skeleton. A constant "crick in the neck" forced him to cock his head at an odd, hostile angle as if he withdrew from everything and everyone he faced. He was a fanatic, a ruthless man of military authority accustomed to total command and respect equaled nowhere in the upper echelons of the armed forces. He accepted and demanded deference from anyone in his presence, and this included congressmen, judiciary and presidents. He was constantly surrounded by aides and hangers-on. His wild, uncontrolled and uncontrollable demeanor had intensified in the past few years since his unfortunate clash with civil authorities who opposed his military rule in New Orleans after the last war. He would brook no interference or opposition on any level. He became daily more high-handed, convinced sincerely that the honorable ends he sought justified any means in accomplishing them. His shrill voice and deep-set, falcon-bead eyes made him a conscious master at terrorizing his opponents, victims and enemies—which comprised a majority of most groups outside his immediate army, cronies and backers. Anyone who opposed him or the expansion of his nation according to his design was disloyal, a renegade and a traitor no better than an egg-sucking hound. He had that xenophobic prejudice native to all backwoodsmen against strangers and outsiders, and his cruel experiences with civilian politicians and opposition newspapers had deepened and congealed that mistrust into a strident hatred.

Major Reade was gone from the center of the arena for a long time. The onlookers lining the streets grew restive and sweated, but none departed, none made any overt move toward Locke or his men.

The two unequal foes stood stalemated.

Locke waited. A kind of exultant madness glittered in Lester Catchpole's pale eyes. The back of his red neck deepened to a fiery crimson. He had reached that place where maddened need for vengeance unhinged his reason. He also found himself supported and encouraged by the rage he had seen burning in Major Reade's eyes. Locke was going to be filleted, the skin peeled off his hide in bloody strips. Catchpole was almost willing to die violently if only he lived long enough to witness Locke's final defeat, degradation and crucifixion.

The minutes dragged past in the westering Florida sun. The sky itself was bleached cloudless. Flies buzzed around Locke's head and gnats crusted Catchpole's nostrils and eyelids, since the shackled officer was unable to brush them away. This discomfort and nagging indignity outraged him as much as the larger crimes committed against him in these past days. Sweat coursed down his face.

Locke's anger flared as the minutes stretched into an hour. Then, with the heat and tension of waiting, a clarity burned into his mind. The authorities here would deal with him on their terms, in their own good time. This waiting in the sun was part of the treatment he could expect from them. They wanted him to think for a long time about what was in store for him. When he understood this, he relaxed, sighed out and stood at ease, watching the thousands of red warriors and white Tennessee regulars watch him.

Finally, almost two hours from the time Reade strode away, two lieutenants and a captain, with three master sergeants, appeared from the command area. They walked out into the street. For the moment they ignored Locke and his prisoner. They inspected the supply wagon. Cato had recovered slightly, enough to sit sweating out his hangover on the boot of the wagon with the soldier who handled the dray horses.

When the inspection was completed, the knot of officers and noncoms returned to where Locke and Catchpole stood.

The sergeants cautiously inspected the contraption Locke had rigged with the rifle barrel fixed against Catchpole's throat. One of the sergeants said, "I can let down the firing hammer, Captain. No danger to the lieutenant, sir."

The captain nodded. Only then did he address Locke. His voice was low, but level and vibrant with authority, pristinely pure of any hint of compromise. "The general is willing to talk to you. Despite your criminal action against this military authority, we will overlook such actions for the time being. But if you want to see General Jackson, you'll have to agree to certain conditions in advance."

"I came all the way from Virginia to join the general," Locke said.

"We've taken that into our considerations. Now, we've got to undo some of the crimes you've committed against us. It would not do to allow the general to see one of his officers mistreated in this way—barefooted, threatened with a cocked gun, gagged. We'll remove the gag and the gun. We'll give the lieutenant and his men their boots and weapons. If you will agree to these things, the general will see you."

The encampment rang, reverberated, echoed and trembled with the thunderous shouts, huzzahs, cheers and open weeping that went up from every corner when General Jackson and his aides finally appeared, coming out of the command center. Old Hickory came only when the area was at last policed and prepared, his imprisoned soldiers released, rebooted and spruced up. Lieutenant Catchpole was permitted to stand beside Locke. That he was allowed to hold his handgun at his side while Locke was disarmed was without apparent consequence in the overall design.

Watching the general approach, walking slowly and succumbing slightly to that nagging gouging pain in his side, Locke felt conflicting emotions warring inside him. His heart pounded raggedly. There was no doubt he was in the august presence of the most outstanding American alive, including the present and surviving past presidents. The weeping homage paid by Jackson's own troops testified to this. They not only loved him, they deified him. Despite President Monroe's doubts, it was difficult to believe at this moment that General Jackson had any intentions less than the loftiest toward the United States and its elected government.

A canvas chair was brought out by two smartly clad privates and placed with some ceremony under the gently furling flag. General Jackson slouched down in the chair and gazed at Locke in what may have been benign malevolence or merely habitual Olympic chill. His deep-pocketed eyes swirled with shadows of agonies that had long been erased from his conscious mind. His voice, high-pitched and strident, was nevertheless formal and polite, a courteousness somehow more disturbing than the threat of a handgun at one's head.

"Now, suh," he said in that whining, backwoods twang, "what's this all about?"

Locke repeated what he had told Major Reade. He laid

particular stress upon the fact that he had come from Virginia to volunteer for service with the general's army. Now that Jackson's lieutenant and platoon had been returned unharmed, the important matter was his dedication to the general's cause. He repeated that part twice, unable to find even one face in the least impressed.

"Virginny, eh? Manassas, eh? That where you come from?"

"Yes, sir."

"Lot of effete, spoiled people live east there," the general observed. He gazed at Locke. "You acquainted with President Monroe?"

Locke winced, seeing the other senior officers, including General Gaines, lean forward to hear his reply. "I am barely acquainted with the President, sir. He was a—casual—friend of my father. No more. I don't know him well."

"Come on, my boy. If you know the President, don't be modest."

"Only acquainted, sir. That's all."

"I see." The general waved his hand. "Now then, what's this about some kind of charges against my men? I best warn you, suh. Lieutenant Catchpole is a particular pet of mine. Eh, Lester? You all right, my boy?"

"I am now, sir." Lester's voice shook, overcome with emotion at being singled out like this by his general.

"Lester has been with me some spell. Since he was a pup. He fought well at Chalmette. Made us see he was officer material. Can't believe he'd do anything unmilitary. Now what kind of charge is this you're making against Lester?"

Feeling the tension stretching taut in the silent afternoon, Locke repeated what he had said to Reade. He kept his voice flat, unemotional. He told almost what he had written in his secret report to President Monroe, papers still in his possession.

General Jackson's voice remained polite. He said, "What you got to say about that, Lieutenant?"

"I was following orders, sir. As I am proud to say I always do, and always will as long as I've got a breath in my chest to serve you, sir."

Jackson nodded. "You're a good boy, Lester. Just relax now. Sounds like what we got here is an overzealous easterner making what he sees as an honest mistake."

"I couldn't believe Lieutenant Catchpole was ordered to

mutilate Indians," Locke said. "If I am wrong, I apologize. To Lieutenant Catchpole and to you, sir."

General Jackson's face reddened slightly. "Mutilate?"

"Those Indians were mutilated, sir. Their kneecaps shot away. That's why I put the lieutenant under arrest. I couldn't believe the military would tolerate mutilation."

"Of course we don't." Jackson's voice rose, shrill. "It's the last thing we will tolerate."

But Locke was not deceived. Jackson was enraged, but his rage was directed against him and not against Lt. Lester Catchpole. Jackson was reacting violently against the idea of mutilation, but Locke was not deceived about this either. For the first time he learned something that would remain foremost in his mind as long as he lived: What public figures say in public is not always what they believe privately.

Locke waited. General Jackson waved his arm tiredly. A one-star general stepped forward and reprimanded Lt. Catchpole. The reprimand ended lamely, "If the lieutenant misunderstood a direct order, then the communications between senior and junior officers should be reevaluated." The lieutenant was absolved from any further blame or from liability in further action. This was a closed matter.

Locke waited for the hearing to be adjourned, but Jackson was not through yet. He seethed with rage, but he remained polite, even conciliatory toward Locke. He said, "We can't always be squeamish in time of war, Mister Locke. We see many sad things which would outrage us under ordinary conditions, but these are not ordinary times. We are dealing here with savages. They are like children. They understand love. I give them love. They understand reprimand. When they stand against me, I chastise them.

"You come down here to the frontier from Virginia, with your ideas of how to deal with Nigras and Indians. Enlightened, that's what I hear Tom Jefferson calls it. Well, I think I know how to handle Nigras and Indians. You might hear 'em preach my funeral up around Washington. They is them that calls me a racist, suh. And that's the farthest thing from the truth.

"I respect Nigras in their place. Long as darkies know their place and keep it, I am as good to them as I can be.

"But I want to put a word in your good ear, suh, about

dealing with these here Indians. Everybody knows what to do with the devil 'ceptin' him that's got him. What do you know about Indians—you coming from Virginia where you ain't seen a real redskin, outside a sideshow, in a hundred years? Nuthin', that's what you know.

"Let me tell you. You talk about mutilation. Reason my men sometime strike hard at Indians is because of the scalpings and the killings by them red sticks. You think of an Indian as a human being. Well, that's what a fool you are. They are some Indians, right now, who flatten the heads of their infants by artificial pressure—until them heads are flat. Is that civilized? Or human? Or is that the action of wild half-animal beings?

"Sioux women, suh, find life so intolerable with red males that the Sioux women sometimes destroy their female infants within the hour of their birth, in the belief that it is better for them to be put to death than to live the miserable lot of their mothers. Suicide is most common among these Indian women—especially the Sioux."

Jackson waited. Several of his senior officers breathed out in what appeared to be a taut amen.

"Now, we got problems out west along the Mississippi and down on this southern frontier that we wouldn't have today if I'd not been restrained by effete easterners. I made a treaty at Fort Jackson with the Creeks, and then the lily-livered administration tried to nullify *my* treaty. Tried to say it was abrogated and made void by the Treaty of Ghent. Well, them whey-bellied nances in Washington might yield to the Indians under pressure from the British, but by hell, I won't. If they had let me go north, there'd be no bastard British in Canada today. I'd have driven them and their goddamn Indians into Hudson Bay. This would be our hemisphere—for our own white people. Well, at least I'll make the south secure for white people. I set out to and by God, I shall.

"Give lands back to savages? Never. They got more land than they need. A few acres to squat on, that's all an Indian needs. And let them savages hole up in Spanish Florida—that haven for rampaging savages, preached to and led wrong by half-breeds and renegade white men—for their own gain? Never.

"I'm down here now. I mean to march south all the way to

the Gulf. I'll take the Keys—and Cuba!—in sixty days, if the President gives me the word. The Spanish can't contain their Indians, can't guarantee rights of life and property for our people along the border. I can. I shall. I'll secure the safety of this land for white people. I'm acting with the President's knowledge and authority. He sent me here to punish the Indians and I shall. What does he expect me to do? Tap 'em on the wrist? No, by God. I've been patient with them savages. I know what the white people in America want—they want that no savage Indian inhabit one inch of land east of the Mississippi—ever again. I'm going to give them what they want. If we make some mistakes—if we return barbarism for savage barbarism sometimes in heat of battle—that won't stop me, either. It is the first wish of my heart to be in friendship with all good men. But when they violate all I live by, by God, I will strike them down. I know my men act in loyalty to me, because I act in loyalty to them. Loyalty in my men, and in me, is sacred to Andrew Jackson—prized above all things."

Locke sweated. The tongue-lashing Jackson had delivered to him was as well a rousing address to his men. When Jackson stood up and moved slowly toward his tent, the men in his command went wild again, cheering him, pledging their lives to him. The forest rang with their voices, and in the chaos Locke and his men stood, forgotten.

Soldiers crowded around Locke and his company. The men were quiet, but they muttered threats, promising castration as the least punishment for what they had done to Lester Catchpole and General Jackson's soldiers.

Locke and his men may have had to fight their way out, but a lieutenant, leading a detachment of sixteen men, arrived. The lieutenant was extremely polite, but his men held their long rifles at the ready. "The general requests that you and your men remain with us as his guests, Mr. Locke. A disposition of your case will be made soon. In the meantime, we are pleased to furnish you with quarters and rations." He smiled, but his eyes flared with suppressed hatred. "If you and your men will go ahead of us, please."

— *XXII* —

THE AFTERNOON waned. Long shadows encroached from the ancient oaks and sweet bay ringing the clearing beside the river. Silence lay heavily across the encampment and a strange lassitude affected the troops. They had been almost frantically active when Locke marched in; now they were unable to pick up the old tempo. It was as if the abnormal, effete and hateful charges Jeremiah Locke had leveled against these crusaders could not have come at a less opportune moment. These were men who saw themselves led by a man with the stature and soul of a god; they saw themselves as Christ-chosen patriots, sacrificing homes and families and fortunes and even their lives to help General Jackson achieve his holy cause. They had only recently crossed into what was undeniably Spanish territory to war on Spanish subjects in a region at peace with their central government. They didn't need the nobility and rightness of their selfless expedition questioned. This was like spitting in the face of Old Hickory himself—ill, wracked with cough, separated from his beloved Rachel, a true martyr. For the rest of the afternoon at least, the tensions and hatred hung on the bivouac like a choking miasma.

Locke prowled the compound to which his small company had been assigned. Pup tents, blankets, lye soap, candles and matches had been issued to them. They were not under guard.

"Not bad, eh?" Halsted said. "Better'n plowing the back twenty. Lot better'n I hoped when I saw Old Sharp Knife's face. He talked polite but he looked ready to chew you up and spit you out."

Locke shrugged. "He still may."

"I was truthfully expecting to be imprisoned."

"No." Locke shook his head. "This is worse than wires or bars. They can still smile at us this way. This is true Southern hospitality. We are free to roam the camp—though I don't think it would be safe to do that. We are free to leave—"

"Let's get to hell out of here then—"

"—only I believe they'd kill us if we tried to leave—until they're ready to let us go."

Halsted exhaled in a long low whistle. "You sure in hell don't leave a man much to hope for."

"In the military mind there is only one right side, Halsted. You were in the army, you should know that."

Halsted grinned tautly. "No, sir. I was always on the right side, until now."

Cato had not been allowed to enter the compound where tents had been set up for Locke and his company. The lieutenant who assigned their quarters told Cato to stay on the supply wagon. When Locke had protested, saying Cato was his body slave and stayed with him, the lieutenant only smiled and shook his head.

"No, sir. Not here. We have our own ways of doing things here. And I follow orders. Your man will be perfectly well taken care of, I assure you."

Locke had shrugged; there was no sense making an issue when he was helpless to enforce his desires. But as the afternoon waned, a sense of wrong settled over Locke. He couldn't explain it, but he couldn't shake it off, either.

"General Jackson probably don't allow Nigras in white areas," Halsted said.

Locke remained troubled. He could not say why panic nibbled at the taut-drawn nerves in his belly. He saw no sign of Cato, though he saw other black men in the encampment, and black women among the camp followers.

When supper was called and Locke was invited to eat in a mess tent with junior officers, he saw many body slaves serving their young masters. He also saw Lester Catchpole across the tables with a group of lieutenants. They spoke often and stared directly at Locke, but they did not speak to him.

He had no appetite. He pushed his plate away. He became

afraid that Cato had run away. It seemed to him that some of Jackson's people would report this to him if it had happened, yet he realized he was in a sense a prisoner—unshackled, unindicted, but under surveillance, and cut off from ordinary communications.

It had never occurred to him in his life before that Cato would run away from him, no matter the provocation. But Cato had never been mindlessly and passionately enslaved by a lovely female before—he'd never even met a woman like Isabella who could "drive you crazy with the things she does to you with her mouth and her tongue."

He got up from the table and left the mess tent. Silence spread out like carpeting ahead of him and whispered conversation resumed behind him. He did not glance back.

He wandered the streets, quiet in the late dusk, the first campfires glowing across the clearing. He saw blacks around him—body slaves, animal handlers, mess hall attendants, laborers—and he paused near an open fire where blacks had gathered to eat, without forks or knives, from tin plates, wiping grits and red-eye gravy up in their fingers and thrusting the runny globs into their mouths. Cato was not among them.

Damn Cato. If he had sobered up alone, denied the privilege of joining Locke, he may, in terror and longing, have turned in his mind to Isabella. Maybe Cato had been unable to stand the thought of living apart from Isabella and had run away to find her.

He sighed heavily. He could not blame Cato if the black youth were unable to resist the siren call of the Morisco girl. God knew, he of all people understood Cato's need. He was unable to forget Yolanda. But he had let considerations of a mission, of her family's objections, of the differences in religion, of his own distant but actual involvement with Mary-Stuart, come between himself and the true happiness he knew he could find with Yolanda.

Cato was nearer the earth, more simple and direct in his desires and passions. Once wildly aroused as Isabella had roused Cato, the black slave would not complicate a simple man-woman matter with complexities imposed by an artificial society. Cato would take what he wanted.

He sighed. God knew he envied Cato, one generation removed from the jungle where to need was to take, where there were no artificially imposed restraints and a man slew his enemy and climbed his woman where he found them.

How could he ask Cato to forget Isabella when he was haunted by Yolanda and unable to forget her? Her face flared in the red core of the campfires, her voice whispered in the breeze off the river, her unforgettable fragrance of faint flowers trailed after him in the spreading darkness.

Damn. If he were sure that Cato had run, trying to rejoin Isabella on the trail to Pensacola, he could wish him godspeed and relax. Though the hammocks were dangerous places where displaced Indians hid, killing first and questioning later, Don Castillo's caravan could not have made too many miles today. Running, Cato could overtake them in a few hours.

He knew he should turn back toward his own quarters, but somehow he kept walking slowly in the middle of the street, searching for some sign of Cato. He was aware of hostile gazes fixed on him. It seemed that every man, his supper eaten, now settled around a campfire cleaning and babying his Kentucky long rifle.

Locke paused, watching the men caressing, fondling, oiling and polishing their rifles. They were coldly aware of his presence but ignored him.

These men took better care of their long rifles than of any other possession, or even of their own offspring. A child grew away from a man, but his gun was part of him as long as he lived.

These years were the supreme moments in the history of what came to be called the Kentucky long rifle and its matching Kentucky hand pistol. The flintlock rifle was a man's personal weapon—as individual as a man could make it. Its sleek lines and burnished stock snugged sweet into a man's shoulder socket. If a backwoodsman needed a squirrel to feed his family, his long rifle never failed him; it had a deadly accuracy. Already almost one hundred years old, it had been tested in hunting, in battle, in self-defense and on guard on lonely farms. Seventy years at least had gone into unceasing experimenting with its barrel rifling to guarantee that accuracy and impact.

Though between two hundred and six hundred individual gunsmiths made the Kentucky, no two guns were ever alike, except in the loving care of craftsmanship. Caliber, length, decoration differed with each maker, each owner. A certain man would want his own gun to fit his own purposes.

The Kentucky was a backwoodsman's gun. A citified dandy might get by with a Charleville smoothbore, or even a breech-loader, using loose powder—most of them didn't know how to shoot anyway. But the backcountry man made the Kentucky the queen of all rifles. And at New Orleans, the Tennessee volunteers had proved the superiority of the long rifle over the British Brown Bess—named for Elizabeth I who'd ordered one of her personal regiments equipped with matchlock shoulder guns of browned barrels and fittings.

The Kentucky long rifle averaged nine pounds. It was a .45 caliber, with forty-two-inch, full-octagon barrel and curly maple stock. Its open sights front and rear were fixed to the barrel by grooved slides which permitted adjusting to individual taste—for hunter or warrior.

Several newly introduced alterations and accessories made the Kentucky more formidable than ever. A box for tallow-greased buckskin patches made loading quicker and easier—no more pounding the bullet down the barrel; the patches eased it into place. The new model percussion rifles added firepower. The percussion bullet with small metallic cap or cup containing fulminating powder was now used with a percussion lock. The lock struck the cap and set off the charge. Even the older flintlocks had been altered to the newer and more efficient firing system.

Locke heard the sarcastic whispers passed among the men working lovingly over their guns. "Gonna be hell when the flint hits the frizzen." This could be gun talk among men who loved guns and knew that when the flint hammer struck the frizzen—made in one piece with the cover of the priming pan—sparks would ignite the priming powder.

Locke sighed heavily, turning away.

"Gonna be hell when the flint hits the frizzen." Tonight these words had nothing to do with guns. They were talking about him and what was going to happen when Old Hickory struck down on him, as he would, as he would. . . . Andrew Jackson never forgot a wrong, nor forgave it.

* * *

He found no sign of Cato in the vast bivouac. When he returned to his quarters, he found one of Jackson's senior officers seated alone some yards from the company's campfire. He stood up when Locke approached. He said, "Locke, I am Colonel Jed Allan." He smiled. "Like to chew the fat with you awhile, if I may."

Locke shook his hand and smiled. They sat some distance from Locke's company of felons and away from the shadowed tents. "I too am from Virginia, Mr. Locke." He smiled crookedly, a tall, dark-haired gallant with a carefully trimmed moustache, jutting jaw and sharply hewn features, a handsome man somewhere in his thirties—and definitely first family Virginia.

Locke nodded and waited. After a moment Colonel Allan put his tongue in his cheek and said gently, "I am a friend of President Monroe. A close friend."

Again, Locke waited, feeling panic flutter like flushed coveys of quail in his belly. President Monroe had mentioned no contact in Jackson's camp. He was so low in spirit, so lacking in faith in human beings, that it seemed more likely that Allan had been sent here as some ruse hatched in the mind of a vengeful Jackson, or some of his cronies.

Almost as if reading his thoughts, Allan said, "I don't blame you for mistrusting me. You find yourself in an unfriendly—even perilous world. I want to be your friend, if you'll let me. . . . I may be the only friend you'll have in the next days. . . . There may be very little I can do for you, but I sincerely hope you will call on me."

"Why would you put yourself in jeopardy like that?"

Allan grinned, his mouth twisting wryly. "A good question. I'll answer it with a question. You have put yourself in jeopardy, haven't you? Another question. If we did have mutual friends—even a mutual friend—this would give us something in common, would it not?"

Locke sighed, troubled. "If we did."

Colonel Allan laughed. "I assure you that we do. But let me not waste time. I have come here to advise you that no matter why you came here to join Jackson—no, I'm not asking for any explanation from you—but no matter why, put that all from your mind. Whatever your mission, you cannot accomplish it now."

"Oh?" Locke felt slightly more at ease now with the colonel. "Do you advise anything else?"

"Yes. That's the reason why I waited for your return. Believe me, the fact I came to your compound will be well noted by the other officers. When you are in any army of backwoodsmen, you must learn to live with spying, lying and buying. They trust nobody—but each other—and they're not even too sure of them."

"And your advice?"

"Leave. Tonight. Tomorrow morning at the latest. Get out of here. Make polite excuses, praise Jackson and his army to the skies, apologize profusely to Catchpole and to his men. Prostrate yourself if you have to. Tell them you have realized you unwittingly caused dissension—and you feel you should leave, though it breaks your heart to go. And then go. At once. Don't delay. And don't look back."

"Even if I could do that—do you really think they would let me go?"

"I think they would. Right now. Your willingness to apologize and to remove yourself from them would take them by surprise and I believe they would accept what you say and let you go. Anyhow, it's the only chance to get out of here alive—for you and your men."

"They intend to execute my men too?"

"Listen, Locke. I can't say this too strongly. They mean to keep you and your eight men with them as guests, or as part of their army—they haven't decided yet. But they want you free to move around so they can catch you in some dereliction, some crime, some failure—so that when they wipe you out, they can also wipe out the stain your accusations have spread on them."

Locke sighed. He had not deceived himself. He had realized Jackson meant to nullify the effects of his accusations against Catchpole—but to kill him and eight men?

Again Allan seemed to read his thoughts. "What are eight men to these people? In New Orleans after the war, they jailed, executed or deported hundreds of people. Men were arrested and never heard from again. They opposed the general's military rule, and they were liquidated. If you are not provably one of them, then you are against them. If you are an enemy, God help you. Your life is forfeit."

"Why do *you* stay with them?"

Allan merely smiled and did not answer. His neglecting to reply was a reply. Locke sighed again. Allan spoke in the deadly quiet.

"Maybe you don't fully understand. Jackson hates you with a passion he once reserved for Judge Hall of New Orleans who questioned his integrity. Jackson hates bitterly and totally. He is a petty man as well as a tyrant, and you stand for everything he hates—the east, protest, dissent."

"I don't know if I can leave. I certainly cannot leave until I find out what has happened to my body slave Cato."

Allan shook his head. "You're putting yourself and eight men in jeopardy. Unless you get out at once, there may be no way out."

"Still I've got to find Cato."

"I don't know where your body slave is, but I'll make every effort to find out." Colonel Allan stood up. He was no longer smiling. "Believe me, you could not have picked a worse moment for barging in here making trouble for Jackson. Right now, everything is going wrong for him. He says he has authority from Monroe himself to enter Florida. He says that authority came to him from Congressman Rhea of Tennessee speaking for the President. He has Rhea's letter of authority. The only thing wrong is that President Monroe swears he never even talked to Congressman Rhea.

"That's bad enough. But it's worse. Rains and lack of supplies almost broke Jackson's back getting his troops down to Fort Scott. When he got there, he found the fort low on supplies—and his men were actually and literally starving. The fort was begging for help in feeding *its* companies. Jackson found out that several supply ships from New Orleans were in the bay at the mouth of the Apalachicola River—in Spanish Florida. They were denied access to the river. That's why we came south from Fort Scott. Jackson ordered the entire food stock of Fort Scott rationed to his men, all livestock slaughtered and issued to them—each man getting three meat rations and a quart of corn. That exhausts the food supply. He's headed for those supply ships—and God help anything—or anybody—who stands in his way.

"Now, you're like a thorn in his foot. I say leave—at once. If you stay, I'll do what I can for you, but I'm afraid you may not find it very much."

— XXIII —

A CHILL breeze raked the encampment, rattling dead leaves across the cleared, trampled ground. The army grew quiet, the sounds of bugles dying, and the campfires allowed to gutter and glow like small rubies winking in the infinite dark. At last, Locke heard his own men, troubled and fearful for their lives, settle into restless sleep. He remained taut and wakeful, listening to the baleful howl of distant wolves, the mourful whippoorwill, the persistent owl.

Locke forced himself to lie down in the chilled darkness. He shut his eyes but he could not blot out the sight, nor escape the horror he'd felt watching Catchpole and his soldiers mutilate those terrified Indians. And yet, there was no sense rehashing that sad scene, nor, in his depressed weariness, recalling the tortured faces of those victims flopping helplessly in that sinkhole clearing. He could not change it, nor even summon reprisal for its barbarism, but he could not get it out of his thoughts either. Then, suddenly, he went cold, an icy, sick chill that had nothing to do with the lowering temperature in the damp night. Each of those six Indians had the bronzed face of Cato. They were all Cato. Six heads, dilated eyes glittering with terror and unbearable pain—six heads—all with Cato's face.

Locke bit down on his lip to keep from crying out. It was a nightmare, but most senseless of all, a waking phantasm.

Locke gave up trying to sleep. He could not endure closing his eyes and seeing Cato's tormented face, anguished eyes, mutilated body. It didn't make sense and yet, though he could not escape the sight of the mutilation and torture of the Indians at the waterhole, the agony was a thousand times worse and more personal, more inescapable, because those six faces were all Cato's face.

He wanted to leap up and stride through this encampment until he found Cato. He could no longer believe Cato had run away to find Isabella. God knew, he could even *wish* now that he had.

He forced himself to remain where he was, crouched, hugging his knees in the dark shadows, an itchy blanket over his shoulders. He could not go seeking Cato in this silent camp. He would not find him. He would succeed only in getting himself killed and deepen the peril for the eight men of his company for whom he was responsible.

He sat unmoving in the darkness. Colonel Jed Allan had been right. There was only one thing he could do, get out of here. As soon as he recovered Cato, or got word of his whereabouts, he would do anything required to persuade General Jackson to release him and his company. They would ride away. Allan had not lied. He had not until now realized the depths of the jeopardy into which he had led these men, into which he had placed them all—at the mercy of back-woods men who knew no mercy, except to their immediate own.

He found himself haunted by despair. He tried to think about Hidden Brook, his mother, his sisters, Mary-Stuart, but every path led to the gallows. He decided he could take his company and try to find Yolanda, but this trail led only to ruin. He could find no glimmer of hope in the black, cold night.

He didn't know how long he sat there. At first, he thought he was suffering another illusion. A half dozen lanterns bobbed like corks on a lake in the darkness, moving, disembodied, toward him.

The squad of armed men and the sergeant and lieutenant came directly to his tent. The lieutenant nodded toward him. "Finding it hard to get to sleep, Mr. Locke?"

"I've slept better."

"General Jackson's compliments, sir. He would like to see you in his command tent as quickly as possible. We will be happy to wait and escort you there." The words dripped courtesy, concern and willingness to serve, but they left no margin for misunderstanding. This was a direct order. These men were not armed to protect him from hoot owls.

Locke stood up. His shirt was sweated, discolored. He touched his chin, found it thickly stubbled. He unbuttoned his shirt.

"What are you doing?" the lieutenant said.

"I'm going to look presentable," Locke said.

"Maybe you misunderstood me, Mr. Locke. It's three in the morning and the general is waiting for you in the command tent."

"And I have no wish to inconvenience the general. I hold him in the highest regard just as you and the rest of our country does. But I also know he is less than pleased with—the mistake—I made. He wouldn't call me at three in the morning unless it was important—to both of us. I'm going to look the best I can. It won't take but a few moments to shave and change my shirt."

He heard the lieutenant's sharp inhalation. He glanced up, waiting, but the lieutenant merely nodded, though his mouth had compressed itself into a gray line. The lieutenant had been warned against undue force. Military courtesy was the design here.

Two privates were ordered to hold lanterns aloft while Locke shaved. He did not waste time; the lieutenant was under the same pressures as he was. A junior officer who didn't execute an order on the double could suffer almost as certainly as the enemy; he became the enemy.

Locke washed his face, dried it and reached for a shirt. A glitter of light, reflected in his mirror, caused him to jerk his head around.

A second flotilla of lanterns approached. This time they decorated a flat cart. Locke stood with the shirt in his hand and the guard silently around him as the vehicle rolled, squealing drily in the dark, close to Locke's tent.

Two soldiers lifted Cato from the rear of the flatbed and half tossed him to the ground at the front of Locke's tent.

Locke fell to his knee beside Cato. Sickness gorged up from his taut belly. Cato lay, barely conscious, sprawled on his back. He wore no shirt, no shoes or stockings. At first, in the vague light, Locke saw only that Cato had been badly hurt. He did not see how until the lieutenant stepped closer, holding his lantern aloft. Locke's gaze struck Cato's feet. The slave's toenails had been pulled out.

Locke bent closer. He whispered. "Cato. You all right? Can you hear me, Cato?"

At the sound of Locke's voice, Cato stirred slightly. His swollen, raw lips moved. He whispered, whimpering, "Mastah?"

"I'm here, Cato."

The lieutenant tapped Locke's shoulder sharply, though his voice had no edges in its runny-grits courtesy. "I must remind you, Mr. Locke, the general is waiting for you."

Locke swung around, all his rage against Jackson, the inhumanity and bestiality of this lunatic militarism, swirling up and concentrating in fury directed at this officer. "Shut up, you son of a bitch. I'll talk to you when I can. I'll talk to General Jackson when I can."

His voice rasped, his face pallid and rigid.

"I don't want to have to put you under arrest, sir."

Locke stayed where he was, but his voice shook with his outrage. "Go ahead. Put me under arrest. Your men can drag me before General Jackson. But *you* won't be with us."

The lieutenant winced and retreated slightly under the cold lash of Locke's low-pitched voice. He straightened and spoke loudly. "You have two minutes, sir. You are then under arrest."

Locke ignored him. The young lieutenant had made the only compromise possible under the conditions. He understood this and relaxed slightly.

Cato writhed in agony. He cried helplessly, like a child in his pain. "They hurt me, mastah. Rifle barrels in the belly and across my back. Tore out my toenails. Oh God, mastah. I hurt . . . I hurt."

Locke felt his eyes burn; he was sick with helplessness. He said, "I'm sorry, Cato. I'm sorry."

Cato opened his agonized eyes. They glittered in the lamplight. "You got to stand up for me, mastah," he whispered. "You got to stand up for me."

Locke exhaled heavily. He nodded. "Yes, Cato. Yes."

* * *

Locke buttoned his shirt and stuffed its tails under his belt as he walked beside the lieutenant at the head of the squad of armed men.

The lamps burned brightly in the command tent. The lieutenant ordered Locke to stand with his sergeant, then he opened the flap and entered the large floored area.

The minutes ticked past. At last the lieutenant reappeared. He held the flap open. "Will you come in now, Mr. Locke?"

Locke entered the command tent. General Jackson sat at a pinewood table littered with maps, surveys and papers. The lamps glittered in the general's deep-set eyes, burning in the shards of pain, flaring in his wakefulness. Other men sat just behind the general, but he was unaware of them. They looked exhausted, but the general was unable to sleep; he lived in constant pain. He was disinterested in rest for others; they slept when they could, where they could. They had long since learned they were on call with General Jackson a full twenty-four hours a day. They revered him; they did not resent anything he asked of them. Loss of sleep was only one of the minor sacrifices they would have unhesitatingly made for this man to whom they dedicated their lives.

"Took your good time gettin' here, suh," Jackson complained. The backwoods whine added to the complaint for, as Locke found, the general was everlastingly harping on his grievances and personal slights, real and imagined.

"A little trouble," Locke said. "My apologies. And I did want to look presentable."

Jackson laughed with a whine of contempt. "You Virginians, huh? So effete you think always first of appearances, eh? How you're going to look. Why you think an ole country boy like me gives a damn how you look at three o'clock in the morning? Listen to me, Mr. Locke, I'm a country boy, came from a farm, two hundred acres of sour land. Born a few days after the sudden death of my daddy—who was then a young man of twenty-nine. Grew up scrabbling for a living. Had no time for the niceties. If I had a clean shirt for Sunday-go-to-meeting, I was proud. But if I didn't, I went anyhow. I learned what really matters in this life—honesty, decency, loyalty—and being punctual is a sign you are aware of your obligations and your responsibilities.

"Being punctual means you don't waste the time of these good men with me here. Men with more important fish to fry than your little mess. Don't matter about me. I don't need much sleep anyhow. And I've learned to expect a lot of showy manners, and a lot of fine talk, but not much guts from you fancy Virginians. Still, I *demand* more respect for these other gentlemen here. . . . When I send for a man, I expect him to come a-packin', not because he owes anything to ole Andy Jackson, but because by God, my officers have got a war to fight—a country to save—and no time to waste on namby-pamby appearances."

Locke straightened. In that flash of time he saw Andrew Jackson intimidating men and women, neighbors and strangers, supplicants and superiors, defendants and plaintiffs in his courts, savages and statesmen. Those unblinking eyes, like a falcon's eyes, fixed and terrible, glittering with shards of lamplight, that shrill voice, that imperious manner—everything designed to reduce his adversaries to pulp. He saw the general waiting now for him to waver, to cower.

Locke said, "I apologized for inconveniencing you, sir. But you will just have to accept my pledge that I was delayed for good cause." His voice remained level. He had learned on Amelia Island that any betrayal of weakness in face, hands, body or voice can be fatal. This fact had never been more true than in this place, at this moment, before this man who had been labeled a bully by his closest associates—and from boyhood.

Jackson leaped to the challenge, like a swordsman in a duel. "I don't have to accept anything, suh. You think your little problems, your little company of men—or what happens to you or to them—is important. But I can tell you it is not. We are engaged in a desperate struggle to ensure the safety of Americans on the southern frontier of our beloved nation. We are harried by savages—by renegades and half-breeds and prophets now inciting the Seminoles to acts of hostility. The Spanish cannot control their subjects. And the British—with agents like the reprehensible villain Alexander Arbuthnot—are supporting, encouraging, feeding and abetting the red sticks. Ain't that enough? Must we face, too, treachery and infamy and disloyalty from our own white citizens? I tell you this. We cannot be so troubled, delayed or disgraced—we'll deal with traitors as we will with Arbuthnot and any other sheep-killing dog.''

Locke felt the nerves twist and tighten in his belly. Jackson was accusing him of treachery, there was no mistaking this. For the first time he heard the general whine shrilly about Alexander Arbuthnot. There was a kind of irony and joke in his being linked with the skipper of the *Chance*. The absurdity of it kept it all in perspective. He had Colonel Jed Allan's warning, he heard the accusation in the general's high-pitched voice, he saw his life and those of his men were, as of this moment, forfeit. About all this there was a single reassuring knowledge that one could die no deader for standing up for one's principles than accepting death cringing and whining as General Jackson intended to see him do.

''That's all very interesting, sir,'' Locke said. He forced a faint, not unfriendly smile. ''But what has that to do with me?''

Jackson caught his breath. Some of the pain in his eyes ebbed, replaced by a new fire. Sharp Knife was enjoying himself suddenly. He had an adversary who would stand rigid to be broken. He would be broken, but not easily.

Jackson stared at him across the lamplit table. His thin, haggard face seemed hewn out of the darkness. ''I'll tell you right out, mister, what it has to do with you. Yore a goddamn spy.''

''Oh?''

''Coming in here all mush-mouth sweet, wanting to join us—''

''Would I have come, accusing Catchpole of mutilation, if I were an enemy—a spy as you say?''

''I'm talking, sir. And I'd appreciate you wait until I have spoken. I won't tolerate interruption. You want charges, evidence, by God, you'll have them.''

''Then they'll be trumped-up charges—''

''Don't play games with me, boy. You figure you're a learned, smart and intelligent Virginian, dealing with a pore ole country boy from the backwoods of Tennessee, huh? Well, maybe you are. But out in the open, in the fields and forests, we're close to our God. We got Him at our side to help us with the right. I learn what I have to know. I have friends where I have to have them. I have to protect the men who look to me for leadership. I know that you went into Washington to President Monroe. You want to deny that—before these God-fearing officers and gentlemen? Monroe sent you down here to buzzard-monger on me. He's given to me every authority to do just what I aim to do—but lily-livered like he is, he's afraid to trust either himself or his most loyal general. So he sends you to spy on me. . . . No use denying. Won't buy you a goddamn thing. Know what day you was with Jim Monroe. Know what time of day. Know what you wore."

Locke's head tilted. His voice lashed back. "If I'd known you were watching, general, I'd have worn my best cravat."

Jackson laughed sourly. "Monroe should have had better sense than to send you—no matter who you are. And you—no matter what Monroe promised—you ought to have had better sense than to come on to me like this."

"General, if you demand the truth from me, why don't you speak the truth with me?"

The general and half his officers lunged from their chairs. Jackson raised his hand sharply and his officers subsided, white-faced. "Mr. Locke, I've killed men for less an accusation against my integrity than that."

"I'm sure you have, sir."

"A man that calls me liar is no more to me than Injuns and niggers."

"You better shoot me down as I stand here. It'll wipe out the shame of what Catchpole did to those helpless Indians, won't it? A civilian called you a liar—after demeaning your men—and you shot him. That will go well—unless I really am an agent from President Monroe. I'm not. But you think I am. And if you—or any of your God-fearing gentlemen and officers—kill me, or even attack me, and I do represent the President, you're going to have to answer to him—and to Congress, aren't you?"

General Jackson leaned forward. He quivered with outrage. "I know you are from Monroe. You want to admit it, we can go on from there. These men heard you insult my integrity. If I shoot you, I'll have plenty of witnesses."

"But unless you shoot me now, sir, they are going to have to witness that *I* am telling the truth. You didn't find out that I had visited President Monroe because you have some clever spy network of your own—maybe you do, that's none of my affair. But I know you tortured Cato—until he told you what you wanted to hear."

Jackson shrugged and settled back in his chair. "I said it. I repeat it. I learn what I have to know."

"You brutalized my body slave. That's attacking me."

"Hell, boy. Calm down. You high-toned Virginians are too damn touchy."

"You tortured my slave."

"So? Jesus's dear name. What if I did? He's just a nigger."

Rage boiled up in Locke, but he reminded himself he was responsible for insuring the safe exit of his men from this encampment. *Keep your mouth shut, get out of here alive, and as quickly as possible.*

Jackson waited, but when Locke did not speak but stood in cold and silent fury, he said, shrilly, "You got your nigger back. Thank us for that. But you coming sneaking and spying in here, a traitor—"

"Sir. Make up your mind. You can't have it both ways. Not even if you are a god in this place. Not even if these men respect and revere you—as I do. Either I am a traitor and I deserve to be shot. Or I represent the President of the United States, and that puts a different view on who is *loyal* and who is *traitor*." Common sense warned Locke to keep quiet and try to emerge with a whole skin. But at Jackson's baiting tone, something erupted before his eyes like a fireball. Getting out of here alive suddenly was not as important as to make this backwoods redneck and his cronies see the principle by which self-respecting men lived—and died.

Jackson hesitated a long beat. Locke wanted to laugh savagely. Suddenly, ironically, his only true temporary safety lay in allowing, even fostering, Jackson's belief that he was a Monroe spy. One did not slay presidential agents with impunity—not even under martial law. In the long run, this would not save him. Jackson and his people had already sealed his fate; they would get rid of him. But afraid to alienate the President further just now, they would delay, and try to be clever in removing Locke; they would not dare summarily to execute him as they'd obviously decided to do when he was marched into the general's august presence.

Jackson spoke more deliberately, as he may have done from his judge's bench in the past, when, bowing to his prejudices, he nevertheless wanted to impress the witnesses with his impartiality. "Got no reason to want to break with Monroe—by eradicating you—if you do represent the President. But presidential agent or no—I won't have you coming in here spreading your attery and evil."

Attery? At first Locke had no idea what Jackson meant—except that it connoted something less than admirable. Then from somewhere he remembered the obsolete old word, which the President was mispronouncing, which had followed the Scots and the Celts to the hills of Tennessee—atter poison, corrupt matter from a sore.

"One must hesitate, general, to suggest that the President would want malignant and purulent evil spread among the soldiers of his general," Locke said.

Jackson waved his thin hand curtly. "Sometimes even presidents act without thinking. Without due consideration as to where their loyalties should lie, where the truth and the loyalty is. I admit I cannot defy my commander in chief, but I can tell you this, the welfare and security of my troops comes first with me."

There was a stirring, a whispered amen from the men in the shadows, as if only disloyalty would restrain them from demonstrating their support for the general in any decision he made here tonight.

"Still, even if I'm a spy, it'll look better if you have some defensible reason for killing me—it just might come to court-martial."

Now Jackson did laugh, a vicious sound, but certain indication that he was enjoying himself, his inner agonies for the moment overlooked. "Listen to me, son. Don't ever threaten me. I don't need no reason at all for killing you if I want you dead."

"That's your decision, general."

Jackson's Tennessee whine-and-twang chilled him. "That's right. My decision. I don't have to give you nor no other man no trial. I don't owe you nothing. Hell, all I got to do is wink at one of my marksmen out there—you won't ever even know which one." He laughed again. "It's a lot like gittin' lightnin' struck. You're dead. . . . Oh, we'll regret it. We'll regret it all to hell. Our letters to Washington will be filled with our regrets—" something like a savage surge of low laughter rose in a growl from the shadows and Jackson smiled, nodding, "but that won't bring you back among the quick, will it?"

"What do you want of me?" Locke seemed not even to have heard the threat.

Jackson's head came up. "I like your spunk, boy. You ain't plowin' with a full team, but you got guts. What do I want of you? What I asked you when you was brought in here. Are you a spy for President Monroe? You answer us that, and we'll go on from there."

"I'm afraid I can't answer that. I couldn't answer it if I did represent the President and he had pledged me to silence. You know that, sir."

"I've warned you. There are a lot of accidental ways to die down here in Spanish Florida."

Locke met his gaze levelly across the table. "I've seen many of them, sir. None is pleasant. On the other hand, maybe you're right. Maybe I am a little crazy—maybe I'd rather die than live sniveling and begging for mercy where I know none exists."

Jackson caught his breath. After a long beat he said, "All right. We don't need to talk anymore tonight. We'll just ask you—and your company—to stay with us awhile. Once we get to the nigger fort, food supplies ought to be better. We'll try to make you comfortable—as long as we can."

"That's very good of you, general. But I believe I've caused dissension enough. Perhaps I should take my men in the morning and leave."

"No. I told you. We want you to stay with us awhile. Maybe we'll absorb your company, brevet you a—a captain. That way we can keep an eye on you, eh? But you *are* remaining with us."

Locke exhaled heavily. "As you wish."

Jackson laughed now, more at ease. "Now you're beginning to see, boy. Things *are* as I wish. I am responsible to my country, my soldiers, my people and my President. I best tell you. I give commands that must be given. I do whatever is best—for my army, for my country. Your life, or the life of your nigger, or your company don't mean a goddamn to me.

But we want you with us—until we decide you can leave us. You'll do as I say, Captain Locke. Stay as I say. Leave as I say. *Live or die as I say.*"

Locke's gaze clashed against the pain-smeared eyes of the general. His voice matched Old Hickory's. "It's good to be with you, sir."

Jackson laughed suddenly and with such vehemence that his senior officers, grouped behind him, accepted the cue and laughed with him, briefly, coldly. "I like your style, Locke. I swear yore more a Tennessean than a pantywaist Virginian. My officers will tell you—you'll prolong your life by following my orders—and fast."

Locke nodded, sick at his stomach. There was something insidious about the unnatural attention, adulation, veneration and idolatry paid the military commander. He comes to use only the intensive pronoun. He comes to believe in his own divinity. He dreams of recreating former glories, accumulating to himself such sempiternity as rendered deathless the generals of ancient Rome. He erects his own pedestal, and comes to live for the ovation, the salute, the flourish of trumpets. He accepts it as his due; he even refuses to function without it. After his death, if such fate can be imagined for an admitted immortal, pigeons may smear him; but as long as he lives no man dares to, nor is permitted, such proximity. He is shielded, as far as possible, not only from every discomfort, disloyalty, despair, but also, most fastidiously, he is guarded from the truth. His world becomes an asylum and its inhabitants are this Napoleon and his sycophants.

Locke remained standing at attention. When Jackson said nothing more, the newly breveted captain, in terrible irony, saluted smartly and turned to leave.

Jackson allowed him to get all the way to the tent flap. Then the general's voice impaled him, stopped him cold. He turned and faced Jackson. The tall, lean man had risen and faced him with a terrible smile hacking at those rough features.

"Oh, and by the way, Captain Locke. Don't fret yourself no more about Colonel Jed Allan. Colonel Allan won't disturb the tranquility of my camps no more. He has been returned—under guard—to Fort Scott—there to await court-martial. Loyalty, Captain Locke. That's what I demand from my soldiers, because loyalty is what I give first to them. . . . A disloyal soldier—noncom or senior officer—I won't tolerate. . . . Like a bad apple in a barrel. . . . Yes, sir . . . like a bad apple."

— *XXIV* —

CATO'S TORTURED body and fevered mind racked him for more than a week. He cried out late at night and from his heartbroken, half-conscious sobbing, Locke recreated the fearful torment through which Jackson's men had run his slave.

Locke's eyes burned. Knowing Cato's unyielding pride, he saw that the process of torment had been extended, prolonged even more than his inquisitors wished. They had to destroy first his innate dignity, that monumental self-respect and consciousness of who he was under his dark skin, the inner high-minded self-assurance that often translated outwardly into insolence. In short, everything that Cato was—all that life had made him, all that Locke encouraged him to be, and even taunted and challenged him to become—all this had to be peeled away before his captors could get at the man buried inside.

As Cato, in his illness, relived the pain and terror of his inquisition, Locke recounted it in his own mind in agonizing detail. Cato had warned his captors, even including his highest-ranking interrogators—at first firmly and then in mewling cries—that his master would make them pay for their evil, would demand a strip of skin for strip of skin.

Cato rode in the flatbed of Locke's supply wagon. No one from Jackson's command objected as the cavalcade moved south toward the Negro fort. The five days passed slowly and every hour Locke felt Cato's eyes on him, accusing, sick with a sense of betrayal.

"You didn't stand up for me, mastah." Cato's voice rang, hollow with distress.

"I did what I could, Cato."

"What you could?"

"All right. Nothing. I'd only get us killed. All of us. They only want an excuse to execute us."

"A white mastah not man enough to stand up for his slave—he's not a man no more."

Locke sighed. "We've got to stay alive, Cato. Revenge won't keep you very warm in some open pit grave. . . . We've got to get along as well as we can—as long as we can."

"Why?"

Locke spread his hands. "We want to stay alive, Cato."

"To live without self-respect is to be already dead—mastah."

"Oh, hell, forget that Monticello talk. We're not in Virginia anymore. We're six generations removed from Jefferson's civilization."

Cato peered up at him, black eyes drowning in agony. "We could get out of here."

"How? Can you run—without toenails? Can you even walk fast? And get out—and do what?"

Now Cato sighed heavily. "Go to Pensacola. Join the Spanish. Hold up our heads like men."

"Joining the Indians or the Spanish in Florida is no way to stay healthy down here."

Cato stared at him. Sickness glittered in the slave's eyes. He looked abandoned, lost.

"Damn it, Cato. I'm doing the best I can."

"All right, mastah." Cato turned his head away. There was nothing more he wanted to say, nothing more he wanted to hear.

"You'll be all right, Cato. Hell, your toenails will grow back."

Cato nodded without looking at him. "Yes, mastah—everything gonna grow back—just like it was—exceptin' my trust—in you . . ."

Jackson marched his army with minimum delay south to the Negro fort. There was good reason for this strategy. The command was low on food supplies. He hoped to be able to feed his men when he got them near American ships in Apalachicola Bay.

The only delays countenanced by Sharp Knife were those occasioned by his deploying companies east and west of his trail to punish an Indian village, or to recover runaway blacks, or Negroes stolen during the fighting with the British. "This ain't just an Indian war," Jackson told his troops. "It's just as much a battle against defiant blacks. Runaway niggers have need to be punished severely, rounded up and returned to their rightful owners."

One morning, Major Theodore Drake came to Locke, his orderly leading a fine Tennessee stallion. "We figure you're from Virginia, Captain Locke. Used to riding to the hounds, eh?"

"I have ridden to them, sir."

"We want you to take out a company of hunters. Six mounted men—all chosen for their horsemanship as well as the ability to fire from the saddle. I'm sure by now I don't have to point out that we're low on food—fresh meat is completely gone. There's wild turkey, deer, rabbits, squirrel . . . well, I don't have to tell you, we want a meat supply—even if it includes a stray cow or two. We're not particular where fresh meat comes from—just so we have it. . . . I can say to you, here's an opportunity for you to win General Jackson's approbation and approval."

The men Locke took out in his command proved to be good riders, good hunters, excellent marksmen and pleasant company. He had no idea how far west they strayed into the wild, high forests and along strange rivers. They slew animals and two men who were professional butchers cut the meat into slabs which were wrapped in wet moss and croker sacks and thrown into a meat wagon which they met with at least three times a day.

Locke found it strange that men who could slay children, women and old people without hesitation, who professed hatred for all niggers and anything with a red skin, could, up close, be ordinary men, laughing, talking, in no sense walking monsters. They had families, homes, loved ones—they behaved in as grotesque a mockery Deep South chivalry as could be devised. Mounted, with guns, they became young masters of their trade, expert, proficient, skilled. They seemed to have no memory of Locke's accusations against Lester Catchpole, or if they did, no malice or interest. They followed Locke without question.

They were returning east toward the rendezvous with Jackson's bivouac when they heard a pitched battle south of them. Two of the men argued that they should continue east, deliver the meat to the encampment. This was their assignment. Anything else would be a breach of command.

Locke considered this, then decided to ride with four men south to reconnoiter, the others to continue east with the wagon. Once the decision was made, the company acceded immediately, the only dissension coming when no one wanted to miss the fighting.

Locke and his four men came to the sight of the battle within minutes. From the vantage point of an escarpment overlooking an Indian settlement along the riverbank, they had a full view of the fighting.

"Jesus," somebody whispered. "Them Indians and niggers are wiping us out down there."

Locke stared. The soldiers had marched into the village, expecting to find only old people, women and children. They had already killed many of them when the warriors struck from the hammocks. On tall saplings hung the severed heads of women and children. "Nothing takes the fight out of superstitious red sticks faster'n heads of their women on poles," one of the young officers said.

"Didn't seem to stop them this time," Locke said, sickness roiling in his belly. Every instinct in him ordered him to ride in on the side of the Indians, but he knew better. The soldier had not lied, the white men down there were being decimated; he could only get himself killed.

"Most of them is niggers—not reds," the officer said. "Runaway niggers down here—they revert—one hell of a lot more savage than the worst red stick."

Locke told them briefly his plan for a charge—they were mounted and this gave them an advantage over the blacks and Indians. "The river is our ally," he said. "That leaves three sides for us to ride in from. Two from the south, two from the north and I'll come in from the east."

He warned them to ride through yelling, to use rifles, handguns and sabers, to take every advantage of the element of shock, to wheel and ride back, even if their sabers were their only arms.

They moved in stealthily, cautiously in ambush, coming as close to the village clearing as possible. The backs of the Indians were to the hammocks, the bloody fighting was inching toward the river. At a signal, the five mounted soldiers rode into camp and directly into the chaotic melee above the riverbank.

The white soldiers saw them coming and screamed in salvation and celebration. They found renewed vigor and hope. When the blacks and Indians turned to meet the onslaught, the men on foot raged forward with bayonets.

The horsemen came across the encampment, yelling and firing. They drew the attention of the enemy long enough to give the beleaguered foot soldiers time to reload their long rifles.

The horsemen converged on the ragged savages, and when he was among them, swinging his saber, Locke saw they were half-starved wretches, with as many women among them as men, desperate, deranged people fighting without hope, but unable to surrender.

The first ride-through broke the back of red opposition. Blacks and Indians lay in the clearing, shot, their heads split open, their bellies ripped. Beyond them, at the river, the soldiers regrouped, reloaded and surged forward.

As soon as he made his turn, Locke stared at the bleeding, groaning and dying people standing as if in trance, awaiting the second run. He yelled at the top of his voice, ordering his men to stop killing, to take prisoners. None appeared to hear him. And he saw he was outranked by a major who brought his foot soldiers back from the river, finishing off the few reds who remained standing.

Locke was still yelling to take prisoners when the major grabbed his arm and almost yanked him from his saddle. "Captain! I'm in charge here."

"I just saved your hide," Locke yelled.

"I appreciate it all to hell, Captain. But I have my orders. We don't take prisoners."

In less than twenty minutes the battle was over. Locke withdrew his mounted soldiers and the major marched through the camp, making certain there were no survivors.

The major returned after some delay, leading a young private by the arm. The major was laughing. The private was covered with blood, his hands and clothing smeared with it. Stunned, Locke stared at the youth, recognizing Tavares in the U.S. Army uniform.

"Going to have to report this young fellow to the general." The major was shaking his head laughing. "Maybe get him a commendation, or a promotion at the least. This here private found a woman with her belly cut open. But she was still alive. He killed her." Raging with laughter again, the major slapped Tavares on the back. "He killed the Injun woman, but he did it his own way. By God, he fucked her to death."

Laughter spewed around Locke. He exhaled, staring at Tavares. At last, the youth had found his home, a place where his talents would not be punished, but would be rewarded . . .

After the triumphant return of the meat wagon and the soldiers sent to punish a village of reds, things were easier for both Locke and Tavares. Tavares was breveted a corporal and his fame spread through the camp.

Locke was commended for bravery and leadership by General Gaines and was assigned to evening meals with the senior officers. Locke did not accept this as a total sign of forgiveness and friendship. He knew he was being watched constantly, though with less overt suspicion than before the meat-finding expedition. He still had difficulty finding moments when it was safe to scribble additions to his report to President Monroe—a report he had no idea how he might transport to Washington. Because he was under surveillance, at first he wondered why Jackson allowed him to sit at table with him and his top officers. Then he saw why the move had been made—each meal comprised a civics lesson for him, a course in recent Jacksonian history, a presentation of Jackson's side of the general's unrelenting pursuit of glory.

As a matter of fact, none of the older officers overtly paid much attention to Locke. It was a table of middle-aged generals, colonels and majors—with General Jackson himself—that intensive pronoun—at its head. Locke felt almost like a beardless youth among military sages. He said little, speaking only when he was addressed directly—an extremely rare occurrence.

Suppers were dedicated to the exaltation of Old Hickory. Jackson was without modesty—and there was no call for diffidence in a man who had accomplished all he had, coming from the background he had. It was like seeing the sun in all its brilliance and magnificence rise blood red out of a dung heap. Jackson's name and his exploits were on every mouth—or bending every ear—or Jackson quickly lost interest and changed the subject. This painful exigency rarely arose.

The general, like a skillful choirmaster, led the chorus of acclaim in his own name. A smart and ambitious officer might inquire about Miss Rachel's health. For an hour, the table was regaled with stories about how Jackson had met Rachel Robards, married her first in 1791 and remarried her in 1794. This story inevitably included spiteful remembrances of the people who had opposed him and Rachel, the duels he'd fought in Rachel's dear name, the way she had assumed total control of the Hermitage in his absence and wrung profits from it as he never could. His laughter fluted, drowned in the appreciative guffaws of his guests.

Jackson made no secret of the fact that he was a man driven by ambition, that his temper was monumental and hair-triggered, that he'd been wild and reckless since childhood, that he realized his enemies in high places saw him as a dangerous man. He laughed such villains to scorn. He made light of his fights with the Benton brothers. He recounted his duels with Waightstill Avery, John Sevier and Charles Dickinson. "I'm a warrior," he laughed, lamplight guttering across his seamed face and sunken eyes. "I reckon a real warrior has to have his battles, whether there's a real war handy or not."

The general loved best recounting his fiery victories and his masterful handling of the red tribes after he defeated them and their half-breed allies and renegade white backers at Horseshoe Bend. It enraged him that many of those savages, rather than accepting the generous terms of his Treaty of Fort Jackson, had run away to join the Seminoles in Florida, where they were aided and abetted by the Spanish and British under such renegades as Alexander Arbuthnot.

"Well, now we'll chastise those red sticks properly. We'll hang their leaders and kill their lying prophets. They won't run again." This would launch him into a tirade against all his opposition, especially those in New Orleans—Judge Hall, Louis Louailler and their ilk—the scurvy lot who opposed his military law. "That bastard Hall, telling me we could have a nation of laws under him or a police state with authority invested only in Andrew Jackson. I tried to tell him—as I told every man—ordinary laws must be silent when necessity speaks. Well, they fought me. But I crushed them, too."

Angered, he might shout shrilly, his eyes going wild, his tantrum uncontrolled, uncontrollable. He never forgot a grievance, a hatred, or a slight to himself or his beloved Rachel.

Locke saw that while Jackson generally ignored him, he often pontificated on the traitors and lily-livered scum in the central government—traitors all the way in high places, up to that big white palace on Pennsylvania Avenue. Another man, any other man, would have faced censure, at least, for such slander. Jackson was totally sure of himself and his audience. As military commander, Jackson could be ruthless in action, treasonous in dialogue, and yet be absolutely certain that his men and his constituency approved everything he did, every word he spoke . . .

Five days after his troops entered Spanish Florida, General Jackson's army marched into the Negro fort on the Apalachicola. For Locke, entering the destroyed fort was like walking from outer desolation into walled hell. Only a shell remained of the fortified stronghold which once had served the British, Indians and finally a Negro nation. But Jackson seemed as pleased as if he'd found a winter resort. He strode about with his engineering officer Gadsden explaining how he wanted the fort rebuilt, renewed, restored—for American use. "Now it'll be a white man's fort," Jackson said.

Jackson enjoyed recalling how the Negroes had taken over the fort and a strip of land forty miles along the Apalachicola River and set it up as an independent black nation. Several hundred blacks occupied the fort. It was in good condition; there were guns, cannons, large amounts of ammunition in dumps. The Spanish didn't like the Negro fort because it was a target for white American hatred. But the Spanish hesitated trying to capture it because it was so strongly armed. So it stood as a symbol of Spanish weakness to Americans, who petitioned Andrew Jackson to do something about the huge stronghold manned by black men—most of whom were escaped slaves who should be returned to their rightful owners.

"I took the Negro fort," Jackson boasted, striding about the wrecked sanctuary, "just as I'll seize Florida and then Texas *and* Mexico—all Spanish North America. Hell, it belongs to us. We bought it from France."

"I wrote to them Spanish milksops at Pensacola in the spring of '16. I warned 'em what would happen if Spain continued to allow fugitive American slaves to occupy that fort and from it threaten and harass Americans on the border just sixty miles away. That fort stood as a threat to the safety and property of white Americans along the frontier. I told the Spanish—this fellow de Zuniga, the commandant—that the black menace would not be tolerated by our government and that if the Spanish could not or would not destroy that black fortress, then we would be compelled to act in self-defense.

"I had General Gaines send an expedition from Fort Scott upon the Flint River. Led by Colonel Clinch and Captain Loomis, the soldiers found the blacks had actually developed their own plantations along the river—like they were human white beings. My instructions were clear about the fort. I told General Gaines to blow it up and return the Nigras to their rightful owners. Colonel Clinch attacked the fort from the river for four days. Then a red-hot cannonball dropped into the fort's powder magazine. Less than one hundred of the nearly four hundred occupants of that fort got out of that holocaust alive—hell, only three escaped injury—and two of them, a red and a nigger, I ordered executed. That took care of the blacks—just as I mean now to take care of the runaway Indians and their renegade leaders."

Locke stared at him. Surely, unless Monroe had given General Jackson such orders—as Monroe swore he had not—taking this fort was in contemptuous disregard for sovereign Spanish rights and portended further Jackson conquests. Locke was forced to write all this in his report late that night in his tent.

From the moment Jackson arrived at the fort, his fortunes seemed to improve. A boatful of food was unloaded. The troops gorged themselves. Even this delay seemed to distress the general. Provisions no longer posed any problem. A flotilla of foodstuffs, meats and supplies arrived from New Orleans and was unloaded at the fort.

When that armada of supply ships was sighted, Jackson raged almost maniacally about one of his finest accomplishments. "I sent messages to that pantywaist governor of Florida, warning him that any attempt to interrupt the passage of my transports would be considered a hostile act—an act of war. I dared Castillo and Masot—all of them—to oppose me. I see they did not. If they are smart, they will sail for Cuba while they—and their women—are healthy."

The American flag flew over the fort despite the fact that it rested sixty miles into Spanish territory. Locke could not ignore the fact that General Jackson was boasting of removing reds, British and Spanish out of Florida—in whose name the general did not say.

Jackson left no doubt about his intent to clear the Spanish out of the Western Hemisphere forever. "In sixty days I'll have them in Cuba. Let them give me the word and I'll sack Havana."

More Creeks arrived to support General Jackson under Chief McIntosh, along with a new company of Tennessee volunteers under Colonel Elliott. With more than four thousand men directly under his command, Jackson was ready to strike out. He left only a work force to police the fort and marched east toward the Spanish town of St. Marks.

Cato was recovered enough to hobble about and perform simple tasks. He spoke to Locke only when addressed directly. He remained withdrawn, removed, despairing. Locke tried to laugh him out of his mood, saying, "See, Isabella was right. You should have killed me and run away with her."

But Cato did not lash back in reply. This was the surest sign to Locke how deeply the slave felt his hurt and loss.

As the cavalcade moved toward St. Marks, Locke began to pray that Cato would desert him. He even tried to talk to Cato about going to Pensacola. He wrote a letter, warning Yolanda of the danger she and her father were in, though he knew that if either he or Cato were found with that missive on them, Jackson would have a reason for hanging them that not even President Monroe could question.

Still, Locke saw what total destruction Jackson ordered done to the settlements, farms and villages on the trail to St. Marks. This seemed to Locke only an advance look at what would happen—under whatever pretext Jackson needed to justify his actions—at Pensacola.

As the army rolled forward, it burned and destroyed all hostile villages, trampling everything, leaving not a blade of grass or a child alive. Where there were cattle, the soldiers drove them into their own herds. In each ruined area, they left the bloodied heads of Indian women on poles as warning to the remaining savages.

Word of this campaign of annihilation spread ahead of them, like fire in a field. Terrorized Indians fled to St. Marks where they believed the Spanish garrison would protect them from the invaders.

Sickened, Locke gazed at the destruction of Indian towns and camps. Everything in Jackson's path was left in flames. When Locke ordered men under his command to take prisoners, he was hailed almost immediately before General Jackson.

"I was almost of a mind that I could trust you, Locke. I was losing my doubts. You've behaved with gallantry and bravery, and leadership. But I won't have my orders countermanded. If you are not with us, you are against us, and are our enemy. I don't want these savages taken as captives. My orders are clear: pursue those hostiles wherever they flee and make certain they fight no more."

"We are in Spanish territory, sir. Our captives need not slow us down. We could turn them over to the Spanish."

"Hell, boy. Are you that dumb? To the extent the Spanish *stay out of my way*, their rights will be respected. And only then. Now you listen to me. President Monroe knows my aims in Florida. He has approved them. All of them. My orders are to chastise the Indians and black brigands. To drive them—*and their supporters*—into the sea. Our actions are totally justified on the grounds of self-defense. My government will support me in everything I do. In the meantime, Spanish soldiers and savage hostiles are holing up in St.

Marks. I mean to burn and kill all the way there—and to raze that place to the ground if it opposes me. Now, you get back to command. You follow orders or I'll put you in chains. It's real simple, boy. It's that simple."

Locke nodded, saluted and retreated. The slaughter was not ending, it had only begun. He did not know how much more of it he could endure.

When he saw women slaughtered, their heads hacked off, or their bodies thrown to soldiers to use before they were slain, he kept looking ahead in horror to what could happen to Spanish women—and to Yolanda—in the months ahead.

It was less than fifty miles from the Negro fort on the Apalachicola to the coastal town of St. Marks, but every mile was a deeper step into hell for Locke. He no longer ate, even when he was commanded to a supper with the top echelon. When he did eat, or drink coffee, he vomited. He walked, or rode the horse assigned to him, in a daze of terror, a waking nightmare. All he really thought was that he had seen enough, too much; he was sick in his guts and he could not take it anymore. He wanted out. He tried to figure in his mind how he might steal away with Cato and make a run for it toward Pensacola. But there was not the slightest doubt—Jackson would send an army of executioners to run them down. There was only a small chance that he would make it to the Spanish capital alive, and if he did, there was little sanctuary there for him—or for Yolanda and the Spanish, for that matter. In his mind, he saw himself convincing Yolanda of the hideous dangers, of running with her to New Orleans, of finding a ship out . . .

Early one morning, the polished and high-stepping troops of General Jackson reached the gates of the Spanish garrison at St. Marks. The commandant came out, with much ceremony, to greet the great General Andrés Jackson. Jackson was curt. He had come, he announced, to garrison the fortress at St. Marks in order to "chastise the Indians and blacks warring against the United States." He would respect Spanish property as far as possibe—and this meant he promised nothing.

It did not matter, the Spanish commandant had only a few hundred troops. He capitulated and within an hour the Americans occupied the fort; the Spanish flag was lowered and the Stars and Stripes flew in its place.

Jackson was enraged to find that the hostiles who had fled ahead of him to St. Marks had vanished as he approached. He raged against the Spanish commandant for permitting this, and for a while placed the man under arrest. Finally it was agreed that the commandant, his family and his troops, would be permitted to return to the Negro fort, and from there, at the proper time be transported to Pensacola.

Jackson was making plans for pursuing the Indians east. He had heard that the hostiles were running to a town on the Suwannee River called Suwannee Old Town, or Billy Bowlegs's town. It was believed that Bowlegs would stand and fight. This was what Jackson wanted. He could not destroy the hostiles unless he could find them.

By supper hour that night, Jackson had reason to be elated. A Captain Isaac McKeever, a naval commander working with Jackson's expedition, came in from his ship, jubilant. By flying the English flag, McKeever had lured several of Jackson's old and most detested red enemies aboard McKeever's ship. Two Creek chieftans, Francis the Prophet and Himollemico, thought they could buy ammunition, powder and food aboard the friendly English ship. "I got 'em for you," McKeever chortled. "They fell for it like rats for cheese. And I got them in chains."

Jackson and his officers spent the night in celebration. The next day gallows were built outside the walls, from which place the winds would carry the message of the hanging of two traitorous Creeks—omen of what must happen to all who oppose Sharp Knife.

The next day all the troops were gathered to witness the hanging of Francis the Prophet and Himollemico. The thousands of red troops serving under Jackson were lined in military patterns, along with the white soldiers.

Jackson spoke briefly. "They have betrayed us. They have betrayed their own people. They have betrayed me who wanted only to be friend and brother. They will foment war no more."

When the bodies of the two chiefs had swung all day in the sun, Jackson was asked, "You want them thrown into the river?"

Jackson waved his arm. "They are no longer our enemies.

Let them be buried as decently as possible. See that it is done."

Jackson was barely able to contain his anxiety. Word had come that the British schooner, the *Chance*, skippered by Alexander Arbuthnot, was sailing toward St. Marks. "Arbuthnot thinks the Spanish are still in command. He expects to find hundreds of Indians—he's bringing ammunition and food for them," Jackson was told.

"That blackguard," Jackson raged. "Still fomenting war. Let him sail into port. McKeever and other ships will block his retreat. Gentlemen, I have my biggest prize—and I shall see him hung."

— *XXV* —

LOCKE STARED at Alexander Arbuthnot. The light was eerily luminous, a saffron-tinted and sallow green in the sour atmosphere of the garrison cell.

Shock charged through Locke. There remained little of the molten-lard captain he'd known on the *Chance* a few months ago. He hadn't know how old Arbuthnot was then; his age was indeterminate, an outdoorsman preserved by the salt of the sea. Now he knew how old the captain was: It was entered beside his name on the arrest record. And in this strange luminosity Arbuthnot looked his age, looked ancient. He had sagged into a corner of his straw-floored cell, disdaining the stool they'd placed beside the straw pad. An open slop jar fouled the air so one breathed shallowly, if at all.

Arbuthnot stared up at him. "Hello, my boy," he said. "What are you doing here?"

Locke winced. He'd expected outrage, a bellowing of accusations from the defrauded and victimized skipper of the *Chance*. But Arbuthnot was not one to live in the past, or to carry the burden of old grudges. Locke tried to smile. "I don't know."

Arbuthnot's seamed face pulled into a dour grin. "I could say I wish I didn't."

"Why didn't you run for it?"

"They gulled me, boy. Clean and clear. I'm too old for this. Too damned old—by twenty years. Smuggling, blockade running, Indian trading and warmongering is for younger men. With quick reflexes, and fast on their feet. They had me bottled before I had a chance to run. I can almost admire them for the way they took me. Old Jackson has hated me for a long time, you know. And for good reason. Aye, I stood for everything that old buzzard hates. I sailed into their trap and before I could haul around to run, they had me. I'm too old. I'm seventy years old. I ought to be smoking on the front porch of some rustic boardinghouse for retired seamen."

Locke tried to smile. "I don't think there is a pension for pirates, Captain."

Arbuthnot gestured tiredly with a spotted, thick-veined hand. "Ah, but they do, my boy. And this is it. A filthy jail cell. And sentenced to hang. And all for crimes I did commit, and for many they don't even know about yet. Were you there? Were you there in that summary court of old Jackson's?"

Locke shook his head. Arbuthnot smiled. "You should have been there, boy. Exciting, it was. A place bristling with lies and charges and half-truths and the verdict set in everybody's mind long before they ever dragged me into the docket. Aye. It was exciting. Almost matched the day you and that swaggering young Harmbrister fought off the privateer—and then had the gall to steal gold meant to feed and arm the Indians down here!"

Locke winced. "All I can say, Captain, is that I didn't know."

"Hell, boy, how could you know?"

"No way did I ever connect in my mind the Alexander Arbuthnot drinking in that Charleston alehouse with a man giving his life for the Indians."

"Well, we never know what life is going to do with us, do we, boy? You no more than me. . . . Right now, even seeing you with captain's bars, and in the uniform, I can't see you as a Tennessee volunteer fighting with Jackson . . . but you are an American, aren't you? That makes you different from young Harmbrister and me, aye."

"At least you believe in something. That makes you better than Harmbrister—"

"Eh?" Arbuthnot scowled, seemed about to speak, changed his mind and shrugged. "I'm better than nobody. Flotsam on the filthy backwaters of the sea, that's me. It wasn't till I started tradin' with the Indians and saw what you Americans are doin' to them that I got religion—and started on the road that brought me straight here. Almost as if God was on Jackson's side and led me, all unsuspecting, into that harbor out there.

"You ought to have seen Jackson's old buzzard face and his beady little eyes when he saw he finally had me. Went into a kind of ecstasy, he did. . . . I tell you people, you're worshippin' a madman. Under other conditions, he'd be rottin' right now in Bedlam."

He stopped talking suddenly and sighed. He leaned back against the rough texture of the wall. Locke bent down beside him. "Are you all right?"

"All right? For a man about to hang—and not used to it at all—I'm about as well as can be expected. Just figured I'd said enough, too much. I had my day—among the Indians. God knows I did what I could for them. And in Jackson's court, God knows I said what I believed had to be said. For all the good any of it's done me."

"I want to tell you I'm sorry. . . . You're an old hellion, but you're better than I ever would have believed, and I am sorry."

"Aye. And that and a shilling will buy me a mug of ale, eh?"

"That's right. What I think of you isn't worth a goddamn thing."

"I don't know. Tomorrow when they hang me, I'll need something to think back on. The land in Scotland where I came from. The ships I sailed. The men I met and gulled. Me wife and boys. Maybe I'll even think that a handsome young scalawag is sorry for me. I hope you're smart enough to learn from me. . . . You fight against the admiralty, the establishment or city hall . . . you'll end up like me . . . and that's a sorry fate."

"You did what you could. What you thought you had to."

"Aye. I did believe in what I was doing, lad. I met these ragged savages, and they trembled in fear of Andrew Jackson. He had threatened to exterminate them unless they lived by the terms of his Treaty of Fort Jackson. I suggested to the Indians the dangerous notion that Andrew Jackson's imposed treaty of 1814 with the Upper Creeks was abrogated and voided by the Treaty of Ghent. Aye, a lot of respected gentlemen concur with me on that.

"I had to laugh during the trial. And there was damn little to laugh about in that mockery of military court-martial. Jackson denied me all rights as a civilian or an alien because I was in front of a military tribunal. Then he set aside the more rigid aspects of court-martial that might have protected me—because I was a civilian and an alien. But the laugh came when he quoted from eastern newspapers—the same newspapers that send him into maniacal tantrums when they oppose him, but were now holy writ when they called me that 'unfeeling monster.' I laughed in his face. Monster. Perhaps. But unfeeling? I am a great bowl of anguish. I am undone by feelings this man would not even understand in his insensitivity to other human beings.

"Jackson's prosecutors said there were three charges against me, for which each one they would ask the death penalty, by hanging. First, that I excited the Indians to war. God knows, there was no way for me to deny this. I believed the aborigine better off dying for something—than being slaughtered where he slept. The second charge was that I acted as a spy for them. Now, how could I deny this and keep a straight face? I told them everything I saw, heard, read or bought. Then his prosecutors said that I had incited the red savages to kill two American traders, men named William Hambly and Edmund Doyle.

"Now, you're not going to believe this, but Jackson's own court refused to back him on this matter of murder. Finally, after much wrangling, the court said it didn't have jurisdiction in the matter and Jackson's lawyers were forced to drop it in favor of the other two. He practically foamed at the mouth, though I remarked loudly that hanging twice would kill me as surely as three times—in fact, in my case, that third one might be wasted anyhow. I thought your general would have a stroke. Like so many truly great men, he has not the faintest trace of a sense of humor.

"They started piling up the evidence against me. At first, because it was a Jacksonian court, hand-picked by the general, I thought I had no chance. But after the court had backbone enough to drop the murder charges, I began to hope, you know, as a man will, as long as he has life. The prosecution presented evidence that I had advised the Creek chief, Little Prince, not to comply with the Treaty of Fort Jackson. I asked how could a people comply with a treaty that had been declared null and void by the civilized nations of the world? My advising against compliance was the most heinous crime Jackson could imagine until that moment. He practically vomited at the idea that anyone would dare speak against *his* treaty. And in *his* presence. They said I supplied the Seminoles ammunition in their war against American settlers. I bowed to him and admitted this. Somebody had to, I told him. How could he slay the savages if they had neither the ammunition nor the will to oppose him? He warned me that I was making a mockery of his court. But I bowed again and told him he was accomplishing this quite well without my assistance.

"He wanted to run me through with a sword, but managed to sit there while they proved I had written letters to my son. That in my letters to my son, I included information on American troop movements which permitted the Indians to stay always just ahead of the invader. I told him if I truly had accomplished this, I died, if not willingly, at least with some content."

Locke prowled the Spanish town of St. Marks. The *Chance* lay at anchor in the harbor. From a yardarm the body of the skipper, Alexander Arbuthnot, hung by the neck, swinging in the wind all day. Locke felt sickness and revulsion rage through him, gorging up into his throat.

All he could think was that he wanted out of here. He wanted to escape Jackson's army, Spanish Florida, his obligations to the President. He had seen evil until he believed he could not look upon it anymore in sanity. Even General Jackson had evaded the actual hanging of Alexander Arbuthnot. Jackson had left the garrison at daybreak, resuming a campaign against the fleeing Indians. Jackson said only, "Arbuthnot is guilty of inexcusable crimes and his punishment is obligatory under frontier law and conditions."

Locke had learned that the Spanish commandant of the garrison at St. Marks, along with his soldiers and servants, were to be returned to Fort Gadsden—the Negro fort had been renamed in honor of Jackson's engineer and aide who had restored the gutted fortress, Captain James Gadsden. From the fort, after certain formalities were observed, and questions answered, the Spanish would be marched overland to the Spanish capital at Pensacola.

Locke sweated. If he could be assigned to command the convoy to remove the commandant first to Fort Gadsden and then to Pensacola, he could employ General Jackson's aid in escaping. There was no way he could be forced to return from Pensacola. Even if eventually Jackson attacked the city—and Locke was convinced he would, in the first leg of his crusade west to Texas and Mexico—by then he and Yolanda could be in Havana.

He used every shred of influence he had to win the convoy assignment. He talked about his horsemanship, his ability to lead, his willingness to accept responsibility for several hundred guests—spelled prisoners. But he had little clout anywhere; no one listened very seriously to him.

Whatever Locke's hopes, prayers and plans, they were totally disrupted when the entire garrison under Jackson was turned out ready to march the next morning at dawn. The next eight days were waking nightmares as the thousands of troops crossed snake- and alligator-infested swamps, canebrakes and almost impenetrable forests. Supply wagons and heavy guns had to be hauled through water waist-deep and clotted with vines and boles of long-dead cypress. Gray moss fluttered in the faint breezes like sad flags of surrender.

Locke was among the troops and did not encounter Jackson or any of the other senior officers during that forced trek. Rumor spread across the camp that Jackson was ill, worn down with fatigue, coughing constantly and spitting blood. But when advised to turn back, Jackson flew into a rage and required that the troops march until nightfall and camp where they stopped, wherever that was. The nights were infested with clouds of mosquitoes. Every man was bitten, his face swollen, often his eyes puffed almost closed. They were constantly wet to the chest, miserable and sour-smelling. They did not stop and covered the one hundred miles from St. Marks to the Suwannee River in eight hideous days.

Horses nearly starved for want of forage, and still Jackson drove men and beasts forward. Companies skirmished with hostiles, but the main force marched steadily onward.

The thousands of men marched into the vicinity of Billy Bowlegs's town on the Suwannee River. Jackson was coughing and spitting into a handkerchief when he came out and ordered his men into lines of attack.

He staggered, trembling with fury, when they found the town of six hundred buildings silent and deserted.

"Raze this town," Jackson ordered. "Don't leave a blade of grass for those demons to come back to."

Despairing, seeing that the Indians had been somehow warned in advance of his coming, Jackson ordered rafts built. Small companies of men were sent across the river to catch and punish any stragglers. This time they were ordered to take prisoners. Jackson was determined to learn who had betrayed him to the Seminoles.

Locke and eight men were sent upriver with orders to ford it and seek out any hidden hostiles. He and his men spent the whole next day searching but found no trace of Indians or Negroes. As they turned back they met a company of men under Lt. Lester Catchpole. It was the first time Locke had encountered the lieutenant since the army had started south for the Negro fort.

Locke was sick with chill, constantly wet and hungry. He listened with revulsion as his company talked among themselves of the "punishment" meted out to the fleeing Indians over the years.

Catchpole's face grayed at first, but when Locke managed to twist his swollen lips into a grimace of a smile; Catchpole smiled in return and offered Locke a drink of corn whisky from his canteen.

Locke said, in a terrible irony totally lost on Catchpole, as he had known it would be, "I want to tell you, Lester, after all I've seen down here, I regret making any charges against you—for mutilation."

Catchpole smiled, nodded and waved his arm. "Hell, that's

all right. I hated you at first, but I hear you've made a right good soldier for a fellow that ain't even from Tennessee."

Locke took another drink and thanked him. Catchpole laughed. "Hell, I knowed you was just ignorant. About war. About savages."

"That's right, but I'm not anymore."

"We all learn. I figured you'd come to your senses, once you saw what we were fighting for, what it's all about down here."

Catchpole decided to join forces with Locke's company for the return to camp, though this meant that as a captain, Locke would outrank him. Catchpole even laughed. "Do we come on some Indians, we'll see what you order done to them sneaking devils."

They had reached the rafts which Catchpole's men had pulled up the claybanks from the river, when they heard laughter, the sound of oars rattling in oarlocks, men's voices carrying on the water.

Locke ordered his men to conceal themselves in ambush above the banks. They waited. Shocked, Locke saw two large, fat-bellied whaleboats, manned by four oarsmen and a tiller and ferrying several men in unfamiliar uniforms.

"Hell almighty," Catchpole whispered. "Them's British uniforms. What's Britishers doing up here? My God, General Jackson will give us medals for this haul."

Locke stepped out on a high embankment. He could be seen clearly by the men in the whaleboats. He spoke loudly, keeping his voice calm. "There are twenty Kentucky long rifles fixed on you. You can come quiet to shore, or you can try to run for it and be blown out of the water."

A swaggering young officer stood up in the boat and doffed his hat. "Hold your fire, sir. We like your options and we have decided on the better side of valor. We'll come in to shore and never a protest."

Locke stood unmoving, unspeaking. He recognized the man who had waved his plumed hat and spoken with such brash disdain. Locke felt hot and cold at the same time, staring down at Robert Harmbrister, insolent and grinning in that boat.

"Who are you fellows?" Harmbrister inquired when Catchpole's men surrounded them and moved them up the clearing.

"Tennessee volunteers," Catchpole said.

"Oh, my holy God," Harmbrister said. He put his head back and laughed. "Old Sharp Knife. Jackson. Men, my deepest apologies. I've led you into another trap."

Harmbrister was the first to step out into the clearing on the cliff above the river. He stared at Locke, his eyes widening. Then he strode forward, both arms extended. "Jerry Locke! My dearest friend, comrade and one-time fellow conspirator! What in hell is a nice boy like you doing in a place like this?"

Locke smiled despite himself as Harmbrister wrung both his hands. He said, "Afraid I'll have to ask the questions, Robert."

"Of course, old boy. Of course you do. You're probably wondering about that sack of gold I took from your man. I do hope he recovered, with no ill effects. You see, I had to have that money—to finance the poor redskin in his battle against the invading Yankee."

Locke was aware of Catchpole and the other soldiers surrounding them, with the prisoners, their faces registering their shock at his fraternizing with the enemy. Locke said, "My God, Robert. You and Arbuthnot. Fighting together."

"Not really, old boy. He was too fat and old and slow for me. He did what he could, with his trading post in St. Marks and his ship. I'm more for the action. I used our money to buy goods and guns and ammunition—I got out where the fighting was."

"Arbuthnot is dead," Locke said. "Hung. Back at St. Marks."

"The poor old bastard." Harmbrister sighed, then shrugged and laughed. "Well, that's the tricks life pays us out with."

"That's about what he said."

Harmbrister smiled. "What else can you say when you're surrounded like this by mindless redneck hostiles—with loaded guns?"

"Not much, I'm afraid. I wish you had taken that gold in Fernandina and run to Haiti."

Harmbrister shrugged. "I thought about it. But not really. I get bored easy, and besides I figured my destiny was out here. . . . At least, maybe you'll forgive me for taking all our money. Now you can see I needed it twice as bad as you did, mate."

Locke smiled too. "I'm sorry, too, because you didn't get it all, Robert. I didn't trust you. I hid half of it."

Robert's head went back and laughter erupted from him, a wild unnatural sound in this silent forest and with guns fixed on him. "Did you, mate? And to think it never occurred to me to suspect your total honesty. That's first-rate, eh? I'm glad you did. No, really. I never did trust a man what was too honest, eh."

— XXVI —

THE RATTLE of muskets in the early morning reverberated across St. Marks, shattering the tense stillness and sending clots of gunsmoke through the sun-tattered sea mists.

Harmbrister's body was left where he'd fallen on the ground, executed by a firing squad of Tennessee expert marksmen. Cavalierly, he'd refused a last cigarette—"causes nasty coughs, you know, likely even unhealthy"—and a blindfold—"a man likes to see where he's going." The executioners had been ordered to aim for his head and they followed their instructions precisely. He was struck in the throat or above it, six times. There were no misses. Parts of his skull were blown away, his head a bloody mass of wounds, soon membranous with fluid and encrusted with blue flies.

Harmbrister's trial had been briefer than Arbuthnot's and less zealously pursued by the general. Harmbrister was in Jackson's eyes a "renegade white," but he was not a long-hated enemy like that "unprincipled and villainous old Scot."

Besides, Harmbrister's fate had been sealed since the afternoon on that cliff over the Suwannee when Catchpole had searched the British officer and found a letter in his own hand acknowledging that he had sent a party of Indians, well equipped, armed and fed, to attack the invading Americans. This letter doomed him; the second letter, from Alexander Arbuthnot to his son warning him of Jackson's approach, simply placed him beyond appeal.

Jackson read those letters and seethed. Now he understood how the Indians always managed to escape him, how they'd been able to slip away with their families and much of their supplies. Even worse, he saw in a blinding frenzy, that Alexander Arbuthnot—almost from his grave—had defeated him at Billy Bowlegs's town on the Suwannee. Alexander Arbuthnot, dead, still frustrated his magnificent design for American expansion.

Raging, Jackson stood with his officers while every building in Suwannee Old Town was put to the torch. Smoke and flames billowed against the rich forests of oak and bay and sweet gum. The sky blackened and plumes of smoke reached out vengefully in every direction.

The Indians had vanished. His war with the Seminole was over. No hostiles would appear to do battle. They'd simply disappeared into the unmapped depths of the wild Floridas. There was much to view with pride in Jackson's campaign to this moment. He had pillaged and laid waste Miccosukee, the largest Seminole town near the Tallahassi trail and had killed its chief. He had routed the Negroes on the Apalachicola and the Suwannee. He had executed Francis the Prophet and Himollemico. He had hung Alexander Arbuthnot to the yard-arm of his own ship. He had broken the will of the Seminoles to resist, or to stand and fight anymore. But he was not satisfied.

He returned to St. Marks, circumventing the swamps and making the forced march in five days, still obsessed and driven to destroy the last shred of resistance—from whatever quarter—in Florida. And he was determined to see Robert Harmbrister tried and shot—as an "awful example to the world of the final execution of unprincipled villains."

Arbuthnot had attempted to refute the charges made against him. He dismissed as hearsay the evidence that he had incited Indians against Jackson and the United States. He admitted sale of ten kegs of powder to Billy Bowlegs at Suwannee. "So that the Indians could hunt. If they did not hunt, they did not eat.'' The faces of the officers remained stern and cold against him. ''May it please this honorable court,'' Arbuthnot had said, ''I close my reply to the charges and evidence presented here against me, being fully persuaded that, should there be cause for censure, my judges will, in the language of the law, lean to the side of mercy.'' There had been no mercy shown for a man who trafficked with Indians, sympathized with them and tried to aid them.

Harmbrister faced his accusers almost insolently. The evidence against him was compelling. He offered little defense. He pleaded guilty with justification and threw himself on the mercy of the court.

His judges liked his rakehell manner, his admission of the strength of evidence against him, but rejected his justification in the name of humanity to offer his services to a savaged and harried, homeless people. He met their eyes, levelly, even Jackson's. The court found him guilty and sentenced him to be shot. Then, when the vote was reconsidered, the verdict was changed. He was sentenced to fifty lashes on the bare back and confinement at hard labor, with ball and chain, for one year.

Jackson railed at his court. He became violently ill, spitting blood and coughing helplessly. He had to be helped from the courtroom. The original sentenced was reinstated against Harmbrister and the next morning he was put to death in the open plaza.

Locke stood across the plaza from the sprawled corpse of Harmbrister. He wanted to claim the body, give it a decent burial, but the word was out. The cadaver was to rot in the plaza as a warning to the red sticks and niggers. Even the Spanish guests might read something of value in the lesson.

Locke leaned against the stone wall, feeling the rough bite of it against his shoulder. He had stayed beyond the limits of human endurance. He felt the wild need to cry out his rage and his agony at the inhumanity he saw around him. It was worse than inhumanity. It was brutality glorified as patriotism, atrocity cheered as self-defense. It was virulent insanity accepted as normality.

He wanted to escape to some place where he could wash himself clean of despair and vileness. He wanted to hold

Yolanda in his arms until there was no memory save of her gentle goodness and faint flowered fragrance.

As he stood there a commotion arose at the brink of the plaza. Under a white flag hoisted high on a peeled pole, fifty ragged, filthy, diseased and half-starved Indians approached. A young officer raced toward command headquarters. A chief and the remains of his tribe wanted to beg for peace and ask for mercy and food from the great father. The officer returned in less than half an hour. The Indians tried to head directly toward command headquarters, extending the flag, but the young officer, following orders, led them single-file past the bloodied body of their former ally.

Stunned, the Indians stood unmoving, struck dumb at the bullet-riddled body. The officer prodded at them, yelled at them, but they stood unmoving as if in a trance.

Across that plaza, Locke felt the sickness moiling in the Indians and unmanning them. He managed to stride into an alley where he found a barrel. He half fell across it, vomiting.

At five that afternoon, Locke faced General Jackson across a flat table in command headquarters. It seemed to Locke that the general had aged since that day a few months earlier when he met him for the first time. Though Old Hickory was fifty, he shuffled like an old man and coughed helplessly when roused to anger or even to infrequent laughter.

Jackson gave him the sharp edges of a smile. "What sort of a man be you, Locke?"

"I don't understand, sir."

"We believe a man to be what his actions show him to be. Eh? You've been with us for some months. Your actions have proved you to be as loyal as you swore you'd be when you joined us. For a man as is not a Tennesseean, you have been a good officer. I didn't trust you. And I came to trust you. Because of your actions. You made me trust you because you were a good soldier, a good leader.

"Yet, I'm forever hearing bad things about you. You do well and yet I hear bad. You behave with honor and yet I hear maledictions on you. Do you know that, of some five thousand men in my command, Locke, you and you alone visited Alexander Arbuthnot in his cell the night before his execution?"

"I knew him at Amelia Island, sir. I knew him very well. I merely said good-bye."

Jackson chewed this over for some time, shivering with chill in the humid afternoon. "I see. An acquaintance in the time before you came west? In the years you lived at Amelia Island. Is that where you knew Robert Harmbrister, too?"

"Yes, sir. It was."

"And despite how ugly it might look, you were in no way in league with them—trading secrets?"

"Sir. I haven't seen either of them—or heard of them—since I left Amelia Island."

Jackson coughed hackingly. "I'm inclined to accept that, Locke. I just want you to see how when a man behaves suspiciously, there are those who become suspicious of him. Remember what Shakespeare said about Caesar's wife—and being above reproach. I'm advised by my officers. We're engaged in a terrible struggle against vicious enemies. We cannot take chances. Sometimes, it's easier to shoot a man we suspect than to let him play out his rope—and hang himself."

"Is that what you think I'll do, general?"

"I don't know. And only because I don't, I'm giving you an assignment that will once and forever seal your fate with me. Tomorrow at dawn, you will take a small company of mounted soldiers and transport the commandant who once was in charge of this fort to Fort Gadsden. If you deliver them without loss, I will be disposed to look most favorably upon you. You will silence your critics. I might even decide to let you and your mounted company then transport these Spaniards all the way to Pensacola. It's up to you. You earn my faith this time, you have it against all who talk against you."

Locke walked out of General Jackson's command office feeling a sense of elation building deep inside him and erupting outward like static charges. His step quickened. He straightened his shoulders and tilted his head. Around him a garrison that had resembled a back street in hell, suddenly became what it was, a crowded, active army post in the wilderness. Men who had looked surly suddenly glanced up and returned his smile, put a friendly twist to their salute. The sun glittered brightly, spinning across the harbor and dancing off windows.

A breeze rustled the huge waxed leaves of the white cucumber trees, got tangled in the box elders along the river and lost itself in thick-growing hickory, hawthorn and flowering dogwood. He strode faster, suddenly aware that he was hungry.

At the mess hall, a mess sergeant prepared him a thick ham sandwich on freshly baked bread. He walked across the parade ground eating the sandwich, feeling a return of his old vigor, a sense of renewed hope.

He found Cato standing beside the narrow window in his quarters. Cato's gaze was fixed on some far distance in the west, on some poignant memory inside his mind.

"Pack, Cato," Locke said. The very walls of the room confined him, seeming to press in on him. There wasn't room to prowl, but this did not matter anymore. He was getting out of here.

Cato turned from the window. His black eyes were bleak, his dark face expressionless. When Locke laughed at him, blood suffused Cato's face and rage swirled like savage shadows in the depths of his pupils.

"Where we going now?" Cato said.

Locke laughed. "I've told you a thousand times, Cato. You're a nigger. A slave. You don't ask questions. You do what I tell you."

Cato no longer flared up answering him. He merely nodded, his wide shoulders sagging even more.

"All right. Jesus. If you're going to pout like a baby—" Locke began.

"You're right, mastah. It don't matter where we go. I your slave. I do what you tell me."

Locke waved his arm. "No. If you don't want to go with me, you don't have to. No. You stay here. See if you can find a master that you can respect."

Cato winced slightly. "Like you say, I your slave. I don't have to be happy about it."

"Pack for me. You stay here if you like." Grinning, Locke told Cato of Jackson's direct orders to transport the Spanish company to Ft. Gadsden, and from there west. "To Pensacola, Cato. They're going to send us to Pensacola. You and me. To Pensacola, Cato. You and me."

Cato almost smiled . . .

* * *

The rest of that day staggered past as slowly as a shuffling old man on aching feet. Locke prowled the garrison, the town of St. Marks. He could not escape the *Chance* bobbing at anchor in the harbor, or the closed, boarded and barred doors of Alexander Arbuthnot's trading post from which the old man had fed and supplied the Indians—often out of his own pocket. There was no way to close his eyes to the corpse of Robert Harmbrister, wet with flies on the plaza, but he could fix his mind on places removed from here.

He spent an interminable three hours at table with General Jackson and the garrison senior officers. Jackson talked about his battles with New England congressmen who had wanted to break him for his imposition of military law in New Orleans. He talked about Rachel. He coughed a lot and sagged in his chair, looking in the saffron lamplight like a fiery-eyed skeleton.

Afterward, alone, Locke prowled the fort. He was thankful to see that wiser heads had prevailed; Harmbrister's body had been removed for burial. For a long time he stood alone in the middle of the old plaza and watched the slow migration of stars across the cloudless sky. When he went to his room, Cato lay sleepless on a pallete. Their gear was packed, ready for the march in the morning. He heard Cato drag in a deep, raw breath. "We really goin', mastah?"

Locke smiled in the darkness. "We're really going, Cato."

He undressed and lay down across his bed. He was restless, unable to sleep. He thought about Yolanda, remembering all the excitement and sensuality of her. His belly grew empty and all the blood in his body seemed to congeal in his loins. He conjured up her face, her nude body, her rich old-gold blonde hair spilling acròss the ripe planes and rises. Once inside his mind, she spun there, and even when he fell asleep at last, he still saw her beauty, and he dreamed about her until Cato wakened him at dawn . . .

Locke knocked at the door of Duc Jesús Sanchez-Montova. The former garrison commander invited him in. He was an extremely dark man, slender, in his early forties, but what impressed Locke most about him, and disturbed him, was the distracted look in the officer's eyes—that disoriented, frantic light he saw in the faces of displaced Indians. A look of utter helplessness, of lost faith, of discarded hope, of fears unspeakable and inescapable, as if one could not even any longer turn to one's god because in this place there was no god.

Locke smiled and extended his hand. After a brief, distracted pause, Sanchez-Montova took his hand. "Sí, señor?" he said.

"I am in command of your convoy to Fort Gadsden. If we arrive there without loss, or incident, I may accompany you to Pensacola. I am sure from what you have seen and heard recently west of the Suwannee River, you will be pleased to reach Pensacola."

"I pray to God to reach that place alive."

"So do I."

"Señor?"

"I am on trial, Señor Sanchez-Montova. I am being watched. I have only one goal as of this day—I want you, and your men, every one of them, safely in Fort Gadsden. That is as important to me as it is to you or to them."

Sanchez-Montova frowned, puzzled, watching him. "Yes?"

Locke smiled tautly. "Let's just say, I cannot afford to lose one man on this march. For any reason. We are going first to Ft. Gadsden, but unless we arrive there an intact party—just as we leave St. Marks—it may well be the end of the line for me."

Sanchez-Montova nodded, but it was clear he didn't understand. "I'm sure I and all my men—loyal Spanish subjects—wish only to arrive safely in Pensacola."

"But your men also know what has been happening here. Every time an American force marches into an area, the Spanish flag is lowered, the American flag goes up. They have heard the rumors. Some may well be fearful for their lives. There may be many of them—including you, Señor Sanchez-Montova—who believe they will be safest if they run and hide in the forests, making their way as best they can to Spanish-held territory, who wait only until they are on the trail to make a break."

The ex-commandant's head tilted. "We want only to save our skins, señor."

"That's the point I'm trying to make. You can save your own skin by helping me save mine. The way to stay alive—

and safe—is to follow my orders, stay with me. If I can get you to Fort Gadsden, I believe I can then get you to Pensacola, and that's what I want."

"Why do you care what happens to us, señor?"

Locke smiled coldly. "That's it. I don't. Only that my own safety depends on getting you and your men—every one of them—to Fort Gadsden."

Sanchez-Montova sighed and relaxed. Once he understood that Locke had a selfish motive, he felt reassured, perhaps for the first time in weeks. He nodded. "I understand, señor."

"I hope you do. Tell your men. Make it clear. We will protect them, feed them, get them safely to Fort Gadsden. But if they run, they will be hunted down and shot. If there is rebellion from your troops, I will silence it with rifles. And you, sir, shall be the first to die. If I lose any of your men, it's all over for me and I may as well lose them all. And I will. I hope you will make that clear."

The Spaniard hesitated a long beat, finally he nodded and smiled. "My men and I want for one thing—to get back to our own people alive."

"And that's what I want, but it's all or none. That's what I hope you'll make them understand."

The entire garrison turned out to watch the departure of Spanish forces forever from the St. Marks area. Duc Jesus Sanchez-Montova put the best face possible on his abdication. He saluted the senior officers smartly from astride his white Arabian stallion. He and his men paraded, smartly attired, polished and gleaming in the sun. Their arms were stacked in wagons, one of which Cato drove. Locke sent half his mounted forces out ahead, then sat on the sidelines while Sanchez-Montova had his last moment of dignity. The duke rode out, his plumes catching the breeze, his features fixed and hatchet sharp, eyes straight ahead. In cadence marked by a single drum, his men filed out in his wake. When they went through the gates, Locke signaled his own men to fall in behind them, followed by the supply wagons.

He rode slowly, plodding in the sun. He stayed alert, taut. He had the duke's word that his men would cooperate and obey his commands. But he also was aware that even the dullest private in the Spanish forces knew that they were being driven out—with polite smiles instead of gunpowder, but still displaced. They had seen what happened to the Indians. They had seen that General Jackson proved a fearful, vindictive foe against whom the savages found only death, mutilation and confiscated lands. Desperate men were dangerous men.

The first day out of St. Marks was long and filled with unbearable tensions. Locke called frequent, but brief, rest stops. He did not want the Spanish to feel they were being force-marched, as prisoners might be. He did not want them getting sunstroke, heat exhaustion, or becoming prey to the fears that infest the minds of tired and fatigued men, already drawn taut and frightened. He fed them well. He wanted them all to understand they were guests, not prisoners. He warned his men to keep their guns handy but unobserved as far as possible. If there were arms, he wanted the Spanish to understand, they were for protection, not a threat. He treated Duc Sanchez-Montova with great respect and deference, letting his own men, and the duke's, see this courtesy. At night he placed Spanish soldiers on sentry duty along with his own men. That night he dreamed of Yolanda. He looked forward to Pensacola. He saw every mile bringing him nearer to her. His need for her gorged up, making his heart pound over his empty belly. He felt a new assurance. Every hour brought him closer to Yolanda, every step forward carried him slowly but surely up out of hell . . .

Three hours after daybreak of the third morning they came in sight of Fort Gadsden. He wanted to yell out his triumph. He had not lost a man. The Spanish soldiers were quiet, far less tense and more hopeful than when they had marched out of the garrison at St. Marks.

They found the fort remarkably restored, incredibly refurbished. Locke strode about briskly, getting the best quarters for Sanchez-Montova and his staff, food and beds for the Spanish soldiers. Inside, he roared with laughter. He had made it. General Jackson could find nothing to fault in his behavior. Hell, he was on his way to Pensacola!

To his astonishment, General Jackson and his troops arrived at Fort Gadsden two days later. The general had left St. Marks garrisoned with two hundred troops, and the American flag flying over it. Florida, as far east as the Suwannee River, was secured for white Americans, freed of hostiles.

Tensions built in the fort on the Apalachicola. There was no sign that Jackson intended to rest here, though he was noticeably ill, or to allow his men to do anything but prepare for new campaigns.

Locke went sick. No one confided in him, but they didn't have to. The path for the general's conquest lay to the west, toward Pensacola and West Florida. At supper, Jackson said, "I've secured St. Marks. Made it safe for white people. It was the hotbed of the war. But now I've removed the foreign influence on the Indians there. I can turn my attention to the greater interest, gentlemen—removing insidious foreign influence from all of Spanish Florida."

There were nods of approval, voiced approbation. Locke stared at the faces of Jackson's generals. They were looking west—to Pensacola.

He tried to learn General Jackson's plans for Sanchez-Montova and the Spanish troops. No one said anything about removing them to Pensacola. Locke could not ask. He had been commended for his convoying of the Spanish to Fort Gadsden, but any interest or anxiety about moving them out to Pensacola would be coldly and supiciously received. There was nothing to do but wait.

Wait and sweat. He waited and he sweated. He watched the preparations to move arms and ammunition, all the accouterments of war, west. He watched new shiploads of war materiel arrive daily from New Orleans and unloaded at the docks.

That old sense of helpless frustration settled over him. He saw that Duc Sanchez-Montova stayed drunk; he seldom shaved, and no longer even pretended to review his troops. The sick despair infecting the duke swirled inside Locke, a physical illness.

He was on duty as officer of the day when Cato came hobbling in, grinning widely. "Mastah—come outside. Come see who heah. The good Lord hisself done smiled on us today."

Locke followed Cato into the sunshine. Just outside the door, he stopped, stunned.

He stared at the mud-spattered coach and the accompanying flatbed wagon. First he recognized Uncle Oscar from the Randolph plantation. The aging butler had stepped down from the travel-blackened carriage. He opened the step and helped out Aunt Laura. By this time Locke was down the steps and across the stones. The black servants from Felicity Manor smiled widely at him. Aunt Laura spoke into the carriage, "Here he is, chile. We done found him. We done found Massa Locke."

Locke paused at the open door of the carriage. Slowly, Mary-Stuart edged across the seat. She reached out her hand for Locke to help her alight from the vehicle. "Come out," he said. "Let me look at you."

She laughed and came cautiously through the door to the street. "Afraid I don't look very good," she said. "Tired as I am. Fat as I am."

Locke gazed at Mary-Stuart. She was swollen, in the last stages of pregnancy. She smiled up at him, and stood there smiling.

PART IV

Home Is The Hunter

— XXVII —

GENERAL JACKSON was fascinated by Mary-Stuart.

As soon as word reached him that the young woman had arrived, with two vehicles and four black servants from northern Virginia, he invited her and Locke to his quarters.

Locke let Mary-Stuart enter the room ahead of him and saw General Jackson lunge to his feet and stride forward, smiling, to greet her. The other officers stood like attendants while Old Hickory caught her slender hands in his. "All the way from Virginia," he kept saying. "All the way from Virginia."

Mary-Stuart's presence reclaimed the aging officer from shuffling, debilitating illness to a gallant, attentive, spirited cavalier. There was about her—despite her very obvious condition!—a gentle beauty, an air of genteel breeding and elegant comeliness which inspired and entranced the general.

To the entire company Jackson expressed himself astounded that a protected, gentle young lady such as she, had undertaken and successfully completed so arduous, uncomfortable and wearisome a journey, much of it through wild and unsettled frontier country—"most especially in your delicate condition, ma'am."

"I rode with a handgun in my lap all the way, general." Mary-Stuart smiled up at him and the officer laughed with delight. She turned the full beauty of her eyes upon him and he was captivated. "I thought it time the father of my child learned of our condition, General Jackson. The best way, it seemed to me, was to tell him myself."

General Jackson laughed in his delight and bowed over her hand, unable to express his unbounded admiration for her, his pleasure in her courage and daring and bravery. "I've a lovely woman like you, at the Hermitage, Miss Mary-

Stuart. . . . Miss Rachel stood boldly against the outraged world for love of me. I know it to be one measure of my worth that Miss Rachel does love me."

As Mary-Stuart charmed and enslaved the general, Locke stared at her, himself incredulous. He had left her in Virginia, a sheltered, overly protected young girl, guarded from the unpleasant rigors of existence outside the boundaries of Felicity Manor. This lovely young woman seemed less than a distant relative of the girl he'd loved violently and left in anger all those months ago. Time had worked its force upon her. She no longer looked like a young girl—hardly, considering the girth at her waist. There was a beautiful maturity about her. Her skin glowed with that ceramic clarity peculiar to pregnant women and nursing mothers. Time had softened her violet eyes, saddened them somehow, yet left them aglow with those inner fires and unyielded dreams.

He sighed. Like General Jackson, he could not credit that the Mary-Stuart Randolph he had known could have accomplished this feat of marshaling four slaves, three animals and two vehicles almost a thousand miles across mountains, forests and wilderness. This Mary-Stuart was a determined, self-reliant and unrelenting woman who knew what she wanted, and would not be kept from it.

He winced. She was like a stranger to him; a lovely stranger, carrying his child, conceived in rage, and returned now, like a wraith from a world forgotten and almost lost to him.

"I knew Jerry would be as glad to see me as I would be to get to him," he heard Mary-Stuart telling the bemused general. "That's really what kept me going—no matter how bad things got."

The general went on holding her hand. "I cannot believe he would have left you—in your condition—to come away like this."

She laughed. "He didn't know about my condition, general." She bent forward, glancing around, and whispered in his ear.

His eyes widened, but he spoke without a hint of disapprobation. "You're not? Well, no one knows better than I that nature has a way of not always waiting for ceremony . . . we'll take care of that, as soon as possible."

She kissed the general's cheek lightly, though her deep eyes brimmed with tears. "Thank you, General."

"I want my men happy," he said. "And I've learned the best way to insure that my men are contented is to make certain their womenfolk are happy." He shook his head. "Though how any man could have torn himself away from you—I can tell you, men nowadays are not like they were when I was twenty."

Mary-Stuart sighed. "He—ran away, General."

"Ran away? From you?"

She bit her lip. "He was in trouble. He thought he was. Though time has proved to me that I was wrong—and the world was wrong—and that is another reason I braved everything to find him. I had to tell him that."

Jackson glanced at his fellow officers and laughed. "So young Locke absconded from Virginia, eh? And we thought some other—more devious matter—was at work."

"Jerry thought he would be arrested for murdering my brother," Mary-Stuart said. "But we know now that he did not do it."

General Jackson exhaled and patted her hand. "I can't tell you how happy you make me, Miss Mary-Stuart. We have held serious doubts and suspicions about your young man. But murder!" He laughed. "No. We never suspected him of murder. . . . In Tennessee, ma'am, we censure a man lightly—for crimes of violence."

"He's not guilty," Mary-Stuart stated. "I can attest to that."

"So much the better. Not guilty of murder. Not guilty of the disloyalty we imputed to him. You've done us all a great service here."

"I would never have let him go, general," she said, "except that I wrongly believed him guilty. My heart broke. Oh, he swore he was leaving on an errand so urgent and so secret he could not tell me what it was—but I know now, he was trying to avoid arrest."

Locke winced, glancing at the smiling faces of the general and his staff officers. Neither Jackson nor his generals seemed to notice the implication in what Mary-Stuart said. He stood holding his breath until the moment passed.

The general was bending close over Mary-Stuart. "This wild place is no sanctuary for a young expectant mother like you, Miss Mary-Stuart. There are no facilities here for caring either for you, or a newborn. No. Gentlemen, we must get Miss Mary-Stuart to our best physicians at Fort Scott. Do you agree?"

Every officer present nodded in agreement; not that it would have mattered if they hadn't—a fact obvious to each of them.

"Tomorrow—as much as we'll regret your taking the bright sunshine of your golden smiling from this place, Miss Mary-Stuart, I shall assign your Captain Locke to transport you—in all speed and comfort possible—to Fort Scott, where you will be provided every competent medical aid."

Locke hesitated. Jackson glanced up at him scowling. "What's the matter with you, Captain? Will you disobey a direct order?"

"No, sir."

"If you're concerned about getting those Spanish soldiers to Pensacola—put it out of your mind." Jackson glanced at his officers, then smiled at Locke. "I can tell you, we are not going to send Sanchez-Montova and his soldiery—impotent as they are—to join forces with those already at Pensacola. Why should we? We may ship Sanchez-Montova and his people directly to Havana. Anyhow, you don't have to concern yourself with it. You give your complete mind, heart, soul and body over to the protection and comfort of this dear lady of yours."

Locke bowed, smiled and nodded, but he was aware of a deep emptiness in the pit of his stomach, a sense of terrible wrong . . .

Locke and Mary-Stuart were married the next morning by the Baptist chaplain who served as General Jackson's personal religious adviser. General Jackson insisted upon giving the bride away. Colonel Ted Drake served as his best man. Even while the ceremony was being performed, wagons, supplies and animals were being readied for the trek north to Fort Scott. All the officers attended the ceremony. The post resounded with laughter and goodwill. Only Locke felt a troubling premonition of disaster that he could not shake.

General Jackson and his officers crowded around Mary-Stuart, laughing and talking, making all those jokes which, despite their poor taste, are considered a charming part of a wedding ceremony.

Someone touched Locke's shoulder. He turned and faced Duc Jesús Sanchez-Montova. The duke was attired in his most formal uniform, with battle ribbons and medals and fancy insignia. He was freshly shaven, erect. Only in his eyes were there the betraying signs of terror, frustration and distracted helplessness.

Locke winced. "Good-bye, Duc. I'm sorry I won't be going with you to Pensacola. I know I vowed you safe passage."

Sanchez-Montova managed to smile. "I understand. I harbor no ill-will toward you."

"Then you don't believe I lied—about getting you here first—and then to Pensacola."

"I am convinced, Captain Locke, that you spoke the truth as you knew it. It is your trust, your friendship, I shall treasure when I am far from this place. I have heard. I and my men—we will not be sent to Pensacola after all." He breathed deeply and looked about, distracted. There was no one to trust, no one to appeal to, no higher justice, no hope, in this place.

"I am sorry."

"I hold you in no way to blame. I have spoken to you only to wish you godspeed, to thank you for what you did for me and my men and to offer you the gift of my white Arabian horse. I won't be able to take him with me. I want you to have him. As demonstration of my respect and affection."

Locke watched General Jackson kiss Mary-Stuart good-bye, watched him stand like a loving, benevolent foster parent while his officers passed and kissed her cheek lightly. But despite all the goodwill generated around Mary-Stuart, it was that anguished distraction he saw swirling in Sanchez-Montova's eyes and in the eyes of the displaced Indians, that disturbed and rang in his mind like a warning bell.

Under the cover of the farewells spoken outside the chapel, Locke placed a bag in the carriage where Aunt Laura sat, awaiting Mary-Stuart and Uncle Oscar. On the boot of the carriage sat Odin and Minos, the black slaves who somehow had followed twisted, dim and poorly marked trails south from northern Virginia. Behind them, in the open-bed supply wagon, Cato slouched, lines gripped in his fist.

Still leaning inside the carriage, Locke placed the thick envelope containing all the reports he'd scribbled over these past months to President Monroe, on the seat. "Can you put these papers where they're unlikely to be found, Aunt Laura? Don't keep them on your person. If they were discovered, they would make trouble for you. I don't want that."

"I don't mind a little trouble for you, Massa Jerry. . . . Me and my Miss Mary-Stuart, we been mighty partial to you—almost as long as we've knowed you."

He squeezed her hand. "And I love you, Aunt Laura. I'm only glad Miss Mary-Stuart doesn't suspect how much."

The big woman laughed. "Such talk! And just married this minute. Go 'long with you. And don't you worry about your papers. No, suh."

A young lieutenant touched Locke's shoulder. When Locke straightened, the lieutenant smiled and saluted. "Congratulations, Captain. And the general's compliments. We would like for you to hold your party here until the general and his staff have left the area."

"Protocol?" Locke inquired, aware of the panic churning in his stomach.

The lieutenant only smiled and saluted again. From the steps of the chapel, the general bowed to Miss Mary-Stuart, saluted in the direction of Locke and then marched across the parade ground with his officers in his wake.

Mary-Stuart came to Locke, still carrying the bouquet of magnolias, roses and hibiscus the general had ordered prepared for her. She slipped her hand through his arm. "Can we go now, Jerry?"

He sighed and nodded. "In a moment. We have to let the general get out of the area first."

"Why, I never heard of such a thing," Mary-Stuart said.

"You've never been in the army," Locke told her. "That's the least of the weird customs. Eh, lieutenant?"

The young officer flushed slightly but he did not reply. He smiled at Miss Mary-Stuart in a reassuring, military smartness and saluted Locke again.

A half dozen soldiers surrounded the wagons and carriages as soon as the general and his officers were out of sight across the fort. "What is this?" Mary-Stuart cried. "What's the matter?"

Locke held her hand. "It's all right, Mary-Stuart. It's just part of being in the army."

The soldiers were expert, efficient, quick and thorough. They were also exceedingly neat. Everything was moved, in every trunk, suitcase, carpetbag and valise, and everything replaced precisely.

Locke stood sweating in the sun. Aunt Laura was ordered out of the carriage; it was completely investigated. Locke tried not to look at Aunt Laura, but his gaze involuntarily moved to her. She stood, relaxed, staring with infinite patience, waiting.

The inspectors stepped back from the wagons and carriage, reported to the lieutenant. The lieutenant saluted Locke and smiled once more at Mary-Stuart. She, however, was outraged. "I've a good mind to report this to General Jackson," she said.

"You may go now, ma'am." The lieutenant bowed. "We truly regret any inconvenience we caused you—and we wish you a pleasant trip."

Locke saluted. He stood waiting until the soldiers marched away with their lieutenant. Then he exhaled. "We may as well get out of here," he said. "And I want to thank you, Aunt Laura."

She laughed. "For what, massa? I hides somethin', ain't nobody finds it, less'n I want 'em to."

Indians and soldiers stood in the sun and watched the small caravan head north along the river. That sense of oppression hung over Locke. He had believed it would lift when they departed the gates of Fort Gadsden, but it pursued them along the trail like a virulent threat in the blaze of sunlight.

Mary-Stuart pressed close to him in the tonneau of the carriage. She touched the backs of her fingers against his cheek. "I had to come to you, Jerry. Do you forgive me?"

"Forgive you for what?"

"For everything. For all the mean and wicked things I said

to you that last day at Felicity Manor. For doubting you—and believing your enemies. For following you down here like a common camp follower."

He laughed gently. "You don't look much like a camp follower. You're too pregnant."

"That's your fault." She laughed and pressed closer, sighing. "I had to see you, Jerry. Had to be with you."

"Only more appropriate place for a lady in your condition than with her husband is someplace she can be cared for."

"You'll take care of me." She sighed again and sagged against him. He met Aunt Laura's eyes in the seat across from them and grinned. Mary-Stuart had relaxed; she had been brave as long as necessary, borne responsibility as far as she had to; now it all belonged to him.

"I'll try," he said. "I'll truly try."

She held up her left hand. Upon it, a diamond glittered, its richness almost obscene. "Where'd you get a ring like that?" he said.

"From Worthington Jennings."

He laughed. "I can't believe that old skinflint would buy a ring as expensive as that—for anyone."

She did not smile. "That's because you didn't know how devotedly, how passionately, how insanely—those are his very words—Squire Jennings has loved me all these years. Everything he has done, all he worked for, has been for me. He told me that."

"The squire is a hard man to fathom."

She straightened slightly, her voice hardening. "Not if you get to know him well enough—"

"I thought I knew him."

"No. You never knew him. Never. I began for the first time to know him when he told me with such pious hypocrisy that I must not wait for you. . . . I had just found out I was going to have your baby—thanks to your violent farewell—and, guiltily, I thought he had learned the truth too. But that wasn't what he meant at all. He said you were never coming back to Virginia. He said there was not just one murder warrant outstanding against you—for the murder of Harry—but that the Alexandria police had been looking for a man answering your description, believed to be the last person to see Anne Stoker alive. He said an anonymous source had sworn that that man was you.''

He sat, unaware he was holding his breath. The carriage limped and hobbled through the rough country, the creak of leather and metal and the cry of the driver intensifying the frontier stillness. The death of Anne Stoker, the brutal murder of Harrison Randolph, seemed remote, like something from another existence. Yet, Mary-Stuart brought it all back, wiping out the present, and hurtling him backward in time—to another life.

''Sometimes I almost forget,'' he said, ''that murder warrants wait for me in Virginia.''

''Maybe they don't,'' Mary-Stuart said. ''At least, I no longer believe you killed dear Harry. And I'm equally sure you didn't kill that poor woman in Alexandria.''

''What changed your mind?''

She clutched his hand fiercely in her chilled fingers. ''Time, Jerry. Time to think, to miss you, to remember what you're really like, what you are inside. Time to watch Worthington Jennings come apart—like a shattered doll—all for the love of me.'' She held up that ring again. ''You know he went out of his mind, the way he hoarded every dime, to buy a ring like that to prove his devotion to me.

''I would not say yes. If I lived to be a hundred I could not bear to let him touch me! But he seemed suddenly so unlike the family friend protecting your good name. He told me you were not worthy of me. That you had been the last person to see Anne Stoker alive. That *he* himself had been the anonymous source who revealed your identity to the police.

''I asked him why he would do this to you who trusted him above all men. He told me—sweating—that he would do anything to be sure you never came back to me. . . . He meant to have me, no matter what he had to do. He loved me so deeply that murder was the least of the crimes he would commit to have me.''

She shook her head. ''In time he almost became deranged on the subject. He gave me this ring, said I must keep it whether I wanted it or not. He came at last one day and told me I had to marry him—I no longer had a choice. He said he would foreclose the mortgage on Felicity Manor unless I did.

I almost laughed. He sounded like the villain in some cheap play. But he was not joking. With my father ill and barely conscious, Jennings had systematically cleaned out my father's holdings. He actually had ruined him.

"When I saw he was no longer joking, and not only quite serious, but quite mad, I told him I had only to get in touch with you and you would provide my family the money to save our home.

"It was then that I knew how deranged he was. He boasted to me that you were helpless—to help yourself. You could not even afford a good defense attorney to save your own neck from the gallows rope. He paced in front of me, stating in cold tones just what he had done to you—your mother and your sisters—and to Hidden Brook."

"The power of attorney," Locke whispered.

She nodded. "He boasted of how he had systematically looted your estate. He told me he would own it all and that you could never return to Virginia anyhow. Well, he went too far. He overplayed his hand. He gave me only two choices. I could stay in Virginia and marry him—or I could run away to you. . . . And what he didn't know was that I had been running away to you all my life."

Uncle Oscar laughed across the tonneau. "That's sho' nuff right. She been runnin' away to you, Mastah Jerry, since she was a scrap of a little girl. When she tole us we was going to Florida to find Mastah Jerry, the others didn't believe her. But I did. I knew in that minute we was coming."

Mary-Stuart laughed, clinging to Jerry. "That's right. I had seen the letter you wrote to your mother—from someplace called Cows Ford—that you were on your way west to join General Jackson. . . . All I had to do was to find out from President Monroe where the general was."

Locke smiled. "You make it sound easy." Inside he raged. He said, "My mother and sisters. Are they all right? Jennings hasn't dispossessed them yet, has he?"

"No. I don't think he dares. Both your sisters are marrying this summer. Very good marriages, Jerry. Best families. I suppose with what he has stolen from you, he can afford to let your mother go on living there—"

"Until I'm out of the way." Locke stared at the lustrous

whiteness of that dïamond glittering on Mary-Stuart's finger. Something about it nagged at the deep recesses of his mind like mice in an attic.

"But don't you see, Jerry? Jennings has talked too much. He used threats, boasting, everything he could think to convince me there was no hope for you and me—that my only salvation lay in marrying him. He even admitted that Harry's poor body was discovered by a worker, all right—but by a worker Jennings sent to that spot to examine the circling of a buzzard."

"He might have done that."

"But why would he have noticed the circling of a buzzard in that place? It might have been a dead animal. Why would he care? He was not the kind of man who cared—or even noticed things like that."

"You don't think he killed Harry?"

"I only know *you* didn't."

"Have the police found any clues at all as to who the killer might be?"

She shook her head. "There were no clues—except the stout piece of white cord clutched in Jerry's poor fingers when the sheriff's men found his body."

"White cord?" Something danced in Jerry's mind. He sweated, trying to clutch at it. The vague memory nagged at him, and then eluded him like a skittish moth. Hadn't Harry himself said something about a stout white cord? Locke caught Mary-Stuart's left hand in his and stared at the lustrous white diamond. He laughed, a sound half triumph, half growl. "A stout white cord. A two-carat diamond ring. You're right, Mary-Stuart. You have set me free at last. I not only didn't kill Anne Stoker or poor Harry, but I know now who did."

— XXVIII —

THE SCENTED night air whipped past Locke's face as he held the carriage lines, sitting on its boot between the slaves Odin and Minos, speeding the horses over the last miles into Fort Scott. Locke was thankful to have this responsibility to occupy his mind and hands and eyes. Both Odin and Minos—unafraid on the trip south—suddenly were childlike slaves with a white man along to assume command. They held on to the side guards, moaning and praying as if neither of them had ever handled fast-moving horses in their lives. In the carriage tonneau, the onset of regular pains struck Mary-Stuart and added panic to the other burdens of the long trip north. Locke ordered the carriage forward at full-tilt in the darkness, but both black drivers were fearful of breaking a horse's leg in the blackness, or of overturning the carriage and killing them all. Locke took over, watching constantly that small scrap of trail which was vaguely illumined in the dim carriage headlamps. Behind him, he heard the rattle of the flatbed supply wagon with Cato following faithfully and blindly in his wake.

Across the serrated horizon in the black Georgia night, he could see the reflected lights of Fort Scott on the Flint River, a wan gray against the clouds. He slowed the horses at the gates. Sentries ran out to meet him. For the first time he appreciated military efficiency. Stretcher bearers came running. Mary-Stuart was carefully lifted from the carriage and borne swiftly across the grounds to the camp hospital.

Locke presented his orders to the officer of the day. The lieutenant read them hastily and assigned Locke and his entourage to a log house in officer's country. Aunt Laura and Uncle Oscar declared everything satisfactory, polished, clean and amply provisioned. Cato found a straw pad in the pantry, fell upon it and was soon asleep, exhausted.

Locke was barely aware of his surroundings. As soon as the servants were settled, Locke headed for the hospital. When Aunt Laura insisted upon accompanying him, he slowed his pace to her waddling gait.

"Ain't never no Randolph chile been borned without'n me right there," Aunt Laura said. "Ain't likely I let's it happen to my own dear li'l Miss Mary-Stuart what I raised from a baby herself. Ain't goin' to happen less'n I right there."

Locke put his arm about her. "You're absolutely right, Aunt Laura."

" 'Course I'se right. I always right." She laughed and patted his hand on the thickly padded hip. "I jus' happy you an' Miss Mary-Stuart together at las'. . . . Thank God a thousand times a day, I do."

"You're as good as you are pretty, Aunt Laura."

She tried to wriggle free of his arm about her. "What's folks goin' to think—us walkin' along like this?"

He yawned helplessly and smiled. "Just a fellow and his girl out walkin', that's all, Aunt Laura."

"I declare. You is a caution."

Mary-Stuart writhed on the white hospital bed in mindless agony. The doctor gave Locke a smile intended to be reassuring. He said he'd given Mary-Stuart a small dose of laudanum to ease the pain, but not enough to interfere with nature. "Just a matter of time now. Just waitin' until the little rascal is ready to join us. Everything is just fine with the mother, and I never have lost a father yet, eh? Eh?"

Mary-Stuart gripped Locke's hand. "Look what you've done," she said, trying to smile. Her blonde hair lay plastered to her cheeks, sweated, her eyes stared, wide, and her lips were pulled taut and white. "If you say you're sorry, I'll kill you."

"No. I'm not sorry. I just wish there was something I could do."

"You can. You can tell me you love me."

He nodded and smiled, smoothing her hair back from her forehead. "I've always loved you."

"You—said once—oh, my God! Hold my hand. . . . You said you'd want no other woman made by God—other than me—as long as you could have me. . . . Do you still feel that?"

"Don't talk so much."

"Do you? Or did you marry me—because I was so pregnant you had to?"

He smiled and kissed her lightly. "I had to, didn't I?"

"No . . . I was cruel to you. I said enough to kill your love—oh God, tell me I didn't kill your love? I didn't. Did I?" Her voice flared to a keening wail. Nurses and doctors came running. The doctor made a hasty examination and looked up, nodding in satisfaction.

The doctor met Locke's gaze. "You better wait outside, Captain. This is what we've been waiting for."

But the moment had not yet arrived. Mary-Stuart continued in labor through the long silent hours of the night. Aunt Laura tried to calm Locke's fears. "It's always hard with the first one, Massa Jerry."

He smiled and nodded to reassure Aunt Laura. He paced the silent corridors, walked out on the parade ground, overcome with fatigue, though he knew he could not sleep. He yawned helplessly, staring up at the darkened dome of the sky, trying to find a glimmer of reassurance in the vast black cosmos, and finding none. He returned helplessly a dozen times to the door of that labor room only to be given the same answer, "Not yet, Captain Locke."

In the hour before dawn the doctor came out to where Locke sat with Aunt Laura. The doctor scrubbed his pink hands together and smiled. "You have a daughter, Captain Locke."

Locke nodded, unable to speak. Aunt Laura came up to her feet as lightly as a ballet dancer. "Anothen pretty little girl-chile," she said, smiling widely. "Praise be to God."

The doctor told Locke that Mary-Stuart would be confined to the hospital bed for two weeks. Childbirth, among the social and military elite, was not regarded lightly. Two weeks of bed rest was not excessive; it was a required minimum for recuperation, though the doctors saw slave women drop their gits and return the next day to their chores. They saw no relationship between the two conditions.

"Your wife had a very bad time," the doctor said. She would receive every attention and Captain Locke would be permitted to visit her each afternoon.

The time spent alone exposed Locke to the workings of the military machinery as he had never seen it before. Daily messengers rode sweated horses into Fort Scott from Jackson's headquarters in Spanish Florida. Daily, messengers rode out, evidently with orders forwarded from Secretary of War Calhoun, or with other vital military information. Too, messengers departed each morning for the long journey northeast to Washington, D.C. Until now, Locke had not realized how closely the field generals kept in touch with War Department officials.

His rank of captain placed him in that middle nowhere. He was not entitled to information beyond his "need to know." He learned what General Jackson's forces were doing in Spanish Florida only through the talk among senior officers at mess. These men considered him disinterested, removed from the decisions of command. He listened quietly, but with a sense of growing despair. The war in Florida had not ended when General Jackson drove the Indians east of the Suwannee River. The general now looked west.

Locke told himself he should be disinterested. His life and his responsibilities now lay north with Mary-Stuart and his daughter, and the restoration of his name and his fortune in Virginia. As the days passed, Mary-Stuart talked more and more of the time when they could start back home together.

Dutifully, Locke applied for discharge from the army. He would return with Mary-Stuart to Hidden Brook as soon as she could travel.

He shivered deep inside. The very thought of returning to Hidden Brook should have him yelling in exultance. Things would not be easy there, but until he returned and faced those charges—with his new evidence—his life remained in limbo. Yet, there was this sense of wrong that would not release him.

He could not understand the conflict raging inside him. His destiny lay in northern Virginia now. The world of Spanish Florida—the life and welfare of Yolanda Castillo y Martiz—

no longer concerned him. They had parted forever on the Tallahassi trail, and they had known it was the end for them. She would return to Spain, marry her royal fiancé, and in time he would forget her—the fire of her kisses, the glint of lights in the rich *oro antigua* of her hair, the faint fragrance of flowers. He would forget . . .

He learned much, piecing together the fragments of dialogue of the senior officers. He never questioned them, afraid to arouse suspicions. No matter how puzzled or troubled some bit of information left him, he had to accept what was offered, and let it go at that. No matter how concerned he was about some half-expressed remark, some unfinished statement, he must pretend disinterest. He must be patient. He must wait for other fragments to fall.

Jackson had sent word to Secretary Calhoun, through Fort Scott, that though ill, racked with cough, he intended to "make a movement to the west of the Apalachicola." He was going to strike at Pensacola, that last bastion of Spanish strength in Florida. His justification, Jackson said, was clear. Self-defense demanded that, since the Spanish could not control the Indians and blacks in Florida—in fact, encouraged and abetted them—he would drive the Spanish from all of West Florida along with the hostiles.

"The Spanish must go because Indians at war with the United States have free access to Pensacola—to the food, arms, ammunition and information there. From that quarter they are advised of all of our movements. They are supplied from Pensacola with ammunition and munitions of war. This cannot be tolerated," Jackson wrote. His intelligence reported Indians presently gathering upward of five hundred warriors at Pensacola—under the protection of the Spanish—to continue the war. American welfare demanded that Pensacola must be occupied with an American force. Citizens along the border would not be safe until the American flag flew over Pensacola. "And the governor must be treated according to his deserts or as policy may dictate."

This last statement troubled Locke deeply. He had seen enemy commanders and leaders "treated as policy dictated." He would never forget the sight of Robert Harmbrister with part of his skull blown away in that plaza at St. Marks, or of the aged Arbuthnot hanging from the yardarm of his own ship.

Then he heard that Governor Castillo had fled in the night and left José Masot as governor of Spanish Florida in his stead.

Locke sweated. Not his most carefully guarded questions could elicit any information about Governor Castillo's daughter—whether she had fled to safety in Havana with her father, or remained defiantly in Pensacola.

Quite by accident, Locke learned that Colonel Jed Allan was in the Fort Scott stockade—a prisoner. As soon as he heard, Locke went directly to the fenced area and requested to be allowed to visit Colonel Allan.

Permission was refused. The colonel was not permitted visitors. Only when Locke appealed to the fort commandant was he allowed to visit the colonel inside the compound.

Locke stared, incredulous, at the thin skeleton of a man. Col. Allan looked like an aged, tired and disillusioned relative of the young officer who had warned him of Jackson's deep hatred months ago.

"What do they charge you with?" Locke asked.

Allan's smile was twisted, sour. "In the army they don't *have* to charge you with anything. Disloyalty is the only charge I've heard. I'm actually, they tell me, in protective custody. If they charged me with the crime they hold against me—they would be forced to report to Secretary of War Calhoun that I am a spy. And spying for whom?" His laugh sounded tired and raging, impotent. "Spying for President Monroe. If I were spying for the President, that would hardly constitute a crime, since President Monroe is the commander in chief of the army."

"What will happen to you?"

"Nothing now. Thank God. Calhoun himself, acting on President Monroe's direct orders, has sent an order removing me to Washington—for final disposition of my case. I suppose once I'm safely in Washington, the whole thing will be dropped. Jackson's people don't want to let me go. But there is nothing they can do. They have been warned they will be held responsible for my *safe* arrival in the Capitol." He shook his head. "It would be funny if it were not so hellishly scary. . . . I can tell you. I live for nothing more than escaping this place."

"I wish you good luck."

"Don't waste your wishes on me. You're not out of this yet."

"Do you think they still suspect me?"

Allan laughed coldly. "They suspect their own mothers. They've exceeded all authority on every level. They've broken all laws—national and international. They have illegally crossed international boundaries, illegally claimed foreign territory. They have illegally executed British citizens. They know they have broken all laws, but they won't be headed. Still, they don't sleep well." He gazed at Locke a moment. "Do you have anything you wish to get to the President?"

Locke hesitated. Any doubts he may once have had about Colonel Allan were dissipated by the wasted, harried appearance of the young officer. He nodded. "I've written a report to President Monroe. I don't know what it adds up to. If anything. Maybe he would know. But I don't want to endanger you any further with it."

Allan shrugged. "This is my job. Once they clear me from the stockade, they shouldn't search me anymore. They may, but I don't think they will. If you can get me your papers, before I leave, I'll do all I can to get them to President Monroe. Though I can't guarantee you anything—even that I'll get there alive."

One day Locke heard that Jackson had notified Secretary Calhoun that he'd scoured the country west of the Apalachicola River, found it free of niggers and other hostiles, and because of his failing health, was inclined to return directly to Nashville.

Locke felt his spirits lift. If Jackson went home now to Nashville, this meant his adventuring south of the border of Spanish Florida was ended. Locke's discharge would be routine. He and Mary-Stuart could leave within days for Virginia. Pensacola would remain legally in Spanish control. The nightmare in Florida would be past.

His exultance was short lived. The next day brought word

that Jackson now commanded 1,500 troops, regulars, Indians and volunteers, and that with this massive force he was headed west toward Pensacola.

Next came the information that Governor Masot had warned General Jackson that the American general's presence was unwanted and would no longer be tolerated in the Spanish province. Masot ordered Jackson and his troops out of the territory. Jackson must move across the international border if he wished to avoid bloodshed.

Though this message came from Masot, to Locke it was as if he could hear Yolanda's raging voice dictating this fiery ultimatum. He prayed that Yolanda had forsaken the Spanish cause in Florida and found sanctuary in Cuba. Another letter from Masot was quoted in Locke's presence and again he felt as if Yolanda herself, in all her rage, were in the room. "If you proceed contrary to these expectations, General Jackson, you will be repulsed by force."

The senior officers at Fort Scott laughed, slapping their thighs at the effect these letters must be having on Old Hickory. They could see him raging. They knew Jackson found no legality in these letters. They were threats, challenges to the sovereign rights of the United States. As they knew he would, Jackson sent word that he was certain the Seminoles were gathered in Pensacola in forces up to one thousand, and he meant to seize the town and execute the hostiles to the last man. The Spanish would do well not to interfere.

Laughing, a colonel quoted a Jackson communiqué to the Spanish Governor Masot. Jackson said that he had been informed the Spanish forces at Fort Barrancas had been ordered to fire upon his troops seeking to obtain supplies from an American ship anchored in the bay. "Understand distinctly," the general wrote Masot, "if such orders are carried into effect, I will put to death every loyal Spanish subject found in arms."

Later that day, Locke received word that a detachment of soldiers—called an honor guard, rather than a prisoner convoy—was to remove Col. Allan north to the Capitol.

Locke strode across the grounds to the stockade. He went in to see Col. Allan, but found no way to pass his papers to the officer. They were too closely watched.

The general was bending close over Mary-Stuart. "This wild place is no sanctuary for a young expectant mother like you, Miss Mary-Stuart. There are no facilities here for caring either for you, or a newborn. No. Gentlemen, we must get Miss Mary-Stuart to our best physicians at Fort Scott. Do you agree?"

Every officer present nodded in agreement; not that it would have mattered if they hadn't—a fact obvious to each of them.

"Tomorrow—as much as we'll regret your taking the bright sunshine of your golden smiling from this place, Miss Mary-Stuart, I shall assign your Captain Locke to transport you—in all speed and comfort possible—to Fort Scott, where you will be provided every competent medical aid."

Locke hesitated. Jackson glanced up at him scowling. "What's the matter with you, Captain? Will you disobey a direct order?"

"No, sir."

"If you're concerned about getting those Spanish soldiers to Pensacola—put it out of your mind." Jackson glanced at his officers, then smiled at Locke. "I can tell you, we are not going to send Sanchez-Montova and his soldiery—impotent as they are—to join forces with those already at Pensacola. Why should we? We may ship Sanchez-Montova and his people directly to Havana. Anyhow, you don't have to concern yourself with it. You give your complete mind, heart, soul and body over to the protection and comfort of this dear lady of yours."

Locke bowed, smiled and nodded, but he was aware of a deep emptiness in the pit of his stomach, a sense of terrible wrong . . .

Locke and Mary-Stuart were married the next morning by the Baptist chaplain who served as General Jackson's personal religious adviser. General Jackson insisted upon giving the bride away. Colonel Ted Drake served as his best man. Even while the ceremony was being performed, wagons, supplies and animals were being readied for the trek north to Fort Scott. All the officers attended the ceremony. The post resounded with laughter and goodwill. Only Locke felt a troubling premonition of disaster that he could not shake.

General Jackson and his officers crowded around Mary-Stuart, laughing and talking, making all those jokes which, despite their poor taste, are considered a charming part of a wedding ceremony.

Someone touched Locke's shoulder. He turned and faced Duc Jesús Sanchez-Montova. The duke was attired in his most formal uniform, with battle ribbons and medals and fancy insignia. He was freshly shaven, erect. Only in his eyes were there the betraying signs of terror, frustration and distracted helplessness.

Locke winced. "Good-bye, Duc. I'm sorry I won't be going with you to Pensacola. I know I vowed you safe passage."

Sanchez-Montova managed to smile. "I understand. I harbor no ill-will toward you."

"Then you don't believe I lied—about getting you here first—and then to Pensacola."

"I am convinced, Captain Locke, that you spoke the truth as you knew it. It is your trust, your friendship, I shall treasure when I am far from this place. I have heard. I and my men—we will not be sent to Pensacola after all." He breathed deeply and looked about, distracted. There was no one to trust, no one to appeal to, no higher justice, no hope, in this place.

"I am sorry."

"I hold you in no way to blame. I have spoken to you only to wish you godspeed, to thank you for what you did for me and my men and to offer you the gift of my white Arabian horse. I won't be able to take him with me. I want you to have him. As demonstration of my respect and affection."

Locke watched General Jackson kiss Mary-Stuart good-bye, watched him stand like a loving, benevolent foster parent while his officers passed and kissed her cheek lightly. But despite all the goodwill generated around Mary-Stuart, it was that anguished distraction he saw swirling in Sanchez-Montova's eyes and in the eyes of the displaced Indians, that disturbed and rang in his mind like a warning bell.

Under the cover of the farewells spoken outside the chapel, Locke placed a bag in the carriage where Aunt Laura sat, awaiting Mary-Stuart and Uncle Oscar. On the boot of the flag flying over it. Florida, as far east as the Suwannee River, was secured for white Americans, freed of hostiles.

Tensions built in the fort on the Apalachicola. There was no sign that Jackson intended to rest here, though he was noticeably ill, or to allow his men to do anything but prepare for new campaigns.

Locke went sick. No one confided in him, but they didn't have to. The path for the general's conquest lay to the west, toward Pensacola and West Florida. At supper, Jackson said, "I've secured St. Marks. Made it safe for white people. It was the hotbed of the war. But now I've removed the foreign influence on the Indians there. I can turn my attention to the greater interest, gentlemen—removing insidious foreign influence from all of Spanish Florida."

There were nods of approval, voiced approbation. Locke stared at the faces of Jackson's generals. They were looking west—to Pensacola.

He tried to learn General Jackson's plans for Sanchez-Montova and the Spanish troops. No one said anything about removing them to Pensacola. Locke could not ask. He had been commended for his convoying of the Spanish to Fort Gadsden, but any interest or anxiety about moving them out to Pensacola would be coldly and supiciously received. There was nothing to do but wait.

Wait and sweat. He waited and he sweated. He watched the preparations to move arms and ammunition, all the accouterments of war, west. He watched new shiploads of war materiel arrive daily from New Orleans and unloaded at the docks.

That old sense of helpless frustration settled over him. He saw that Duc Sanchez-Montova stayed drunk; he seldom shaved, and no longer even pretended to review his troops. The sick despair infecting the duke swirled inside Locke, a physical illness.

He was on duty as officer of the day when Cato came hobbling in, grinning widely. "Mastah—come outside. Come see who heah. The good Lord hisself done smiled on us today."

Locke followed Cato into the sunshine. Just outside the door, he stopped, stunned.

He stared at the mud-spattered coach and the accompanying flatbed wagon. First he recognized Uncle Oscar from the Randolph plantation. The aging butler had stepped down from the travel-blackened carriage. He opened the step and helped out Aunt Laura. By this time Locke was down the steps and across the stones. The black servants from Felicity Manor smiled widely at him. Aunt Laura spoke into the carriage, "Here he is, chile. We done found him. We done found Massa Locke."

Locke paused at the open door of the carriage. Slowly, Mary-Stuart edged across the seat. She reached out her hand for Locke to help her alight from the vehicle. "Come out," he said. "Let me look at you."

She laughed and came cautiously through the door to the street. "Afraid I don't look very good," she said. "Tired as I am. Fat as I am."

Locke gazed at Mary-Stuart. She was swollen, in the last stages of pregnancy. She smiled up at him, and stood there smiling.

I almost laughed. He sounded like the villain in some cheap play. But he was not joking. With my father ill and barely conscious, Jennings had systematically cleaned out my father's holdings. He actually had ruined him.

"When I saw he was no longer joking, and not only quite serious, but quite mad, I told him I had only to get in touch with you and you would provide my family the money to save our home.

"It was then that I knew how deranged he was. He boasted to me that you were helpless—to help yourself. You could not even afford a good defense attorney to save your own neck from the gallows rope. He paced in front of me, stating in cold tones just what he had done to you—your mother and your sisters—and to Hidden Brook."

"The power of attorney," Locke whispered.

She nodded. "He boasted of how he had systematically looted your estate. He told me he would own it all and that you could never return to Virginia anyhow. Well, he went too far. He overplayed his hand. He gave me only two choices. I could stay in Virginia and marry him—or I could run away to you. . . . And what he didn't know was that I had been running away to you all my life."

Uncle Oscar laughed across the tonneau. "That's sho' nuff right. She been runnin' away to you, Mastah Jerry, since she was a scrap of a little girl. When she tole us we was going to Florida to find Mastah Jerry, the others didn't believe her. But I did. I knew in that minute we was coming."

Mary-Stuart laughed, clinging to Jerry. "That's right. I had seen the letter you wrote to your mother—from someplace called Cows Ford—that you were on your way west to join General Jackson. . . . All I had to do was to find out from President Monroe where the general was."

Locke smiled. "You make it sound easy." Inside he raged. He said, "My mother and sisters. Are they all right? Jennings hasn't dispossessed them yet, has he?"

"No. I don't think he dares. Both your sisters are marrying this summer. Very good marriages, Jerry. Best families. I suppose with what he has stolen from you, he can afford to let your mother go on living there—"

"Until I'm out of the way." Locke stared at the lustrous

whiteness of that dïamond glittering on Mary-Stuart's finger. Something about it nagged at the deep recesses of his mind like mice in an attic.

"But don't you see, Jerry? Jennings has talked too much. He used threats, boasting, everything he could think to convince me there was no hope for you and me—that my only salvation lay in marrying him. He even admitted that Harry's poor body was discovered by a worker, all right—but by a worker Jennings sent to that spot to examine the circling of a buzzard."

"He might have done that."

"But why would he have noticed the circling of a buzzard in that place? It might have been a dead animal. Why would he care? He was not the kind of man who cared—or even noticed things like that."

"You don't think he killed Harry?"

"I only know *you* didn't."

"Have the police found any clues at all as to who the killer might be?"

She shook her head. "There were no clues—except the stout piece of white cord clutched in Jerry's poor fingers when the sheriff's men found his body."

"White cord?" Something danced in Jerry's mind. He sweated, trying to clutch at it. The vague memory nagged at him, and then eluded him like a skittish moth. Hadn't Harry himself said something about a stout white cord? Locke caught Mary-Stuart's left hand in his and stared at the lustrous white diamond. He laughed, a sound half triumph, half growl. "A stout white cord. A two-carat diamond ring. You're right, Mary-Stuart. You have set me free at last. I not only didn't kill Anne Stoker or poor Harry, but I know now who did."

It was General Jackson himself who solved Locke's dilemma as to how to transport his papers to President Monroe. While he was visiting Col. Allan on the night before the convoy was to head north, he was summoned to the office of the fort commandant.

General Jackson's latest communiqué concerned Captain Jeremiah Locke and it was read to him in full: "Captain Locke's discharge from the U.S. Army is at this time denied for reasons of national security. Captain Locke will rejoin General Jackson's forces at Pensacola instanter. Mrs. Locke and her child are declared medically and physically fit to travel to northern Virginia under military escort."

Locke's idea was to secrete the papers where even Jackson's guards would never suspect them to be—among the possibles carried by black Aunt Laura.

Locke felt his heart sink slightly. Colonel Allan was right: the war was not over yet, not for him, and not for the Spanish. He grinned crookedly; it was a war neither of them had ever declared but which they must wage at General Jackson's convenience and on the general's terms.

The commandant said, "I know you will be anxious to rejoin the general. That's where the excitement is. Would God he'd permit me to go in your place—"

"I can see how you'd feel that way, General," Locke said.

"I'm going to expedite matters for you, Locke. A convoy leaves in the morning guaranteeing the safety of Colonel Jed Allan to Washington. We will increase the troop force to convenience your wife, child and her company."

"That's very kind of you, General."

"Always happy to oblige a good soldier, Captain Locke. You can be on your way to Pensacola by noon tomorrow."

XXIX

GENERAL JACKSON'S victory over the Indians and the Spanish at Pensacola was total and absolute by the time Locke and Cato rode into the outskirts of the Spanish town.

As soon as the general had secured the town and raised the American flag in place of the Spanish ensign, he issued his first proclamation. He had brought peace to Pensacola and to West Florida.

If it were peace, it was a troubled and fearful quiet in a devastated place. The citizens of the town, caught in the frenzy of contention between two flags, danced a frenetic fandango on the fissured rim of their own graves. As soon as the Spanish proved impotent against the invading forces of the Americans, civil law disappeared in riotous rebellion. There was no law, there was not even the promise of tomorrow, there was only this moment before the pillagers arrived, slaying and looting and raping and burning. Long before the first contingent of American forces arrived, the sounds of muskets and cannon heralded their coming, and with them the end of easy, unrestricted life under the Spanish. When the Spanish governor took refuge at Fort Barrancas, anarchy ruled in the town. Mobs, fevered and frantic, roamed the streets, looting and stealing, taking what they could before the Americans came in and grabbed it all. They discovered all egress closed, they found themselves trapped in a hell of their own making.

When Jackson and his army arrived at Pensacola, only a token force of Spanish soldiers challenged him. These abandoned and expendable troops were anxious to surrender. Most laid down their arms without firing a shot. They were marched to the quay and jailed there, awaiting disposition ''as policy dictated." What Jackson meant was, the fate of these soldiers depended on the reason and sanity displayed by the governor in opposing him any further.

Few of the privileged citizenry, the affluent or the members of Spanish royalty, remained in the town. Most had fled to Cuba, and those remnants of the crown's tattered glory in Spanish Florida ran in panic to Fort Barrancas in the wake of Governor Masot.

From the security of this massive fortification reared against the sky and overlooking bay and gulf, Governor Masot refused Jackson's demand for the immediate and peaceful surrender of Barrancas.

Masot replied, "Your Excellency has violated the territory of Spain by taking possession of the post . . . and by lowering Spanish colors there. I protest before God and man. . . . My ardent wishes . . . are to contribute to the peace and friendship of our respective nations. . . . If your Excellency will persist in your intentions to occupy this fortress, I am resolved to defend it to the last extremity, opposing force to force."

Jackson answered Masot's protest by aiming one nine-pound cannon and five eight-inch howitzers at the fort.

A single round, rising like cotton puffs against the azure sky, marked the only opposition. Immediately afterward a white flag of surrender was hoisted.

Masot's resistance ended after this token gesture of defiance. All reason dictated immediate capitulation to the overwhelming forces of attacking Americans. There were only a few hundred troops assigned to protect the fort.

The huge gates were opened in great ceremony. A rattle of snares and the pound of drum marked Masot's exit with his troops.

Jackson declared himself enraged at this pitiful display of cowardice. He had lusted for vengeance, he told his troops. An American family named Stokes had been recently slain by Indians or Negroes just above Pensacola. As an example to the world, Jackson said he wanted to capture the Spanish governor, charge him with the crime of murder of the Stokes family and hang him for the deed.

The general met with representatives from the crushed José

Masot. Jackson agreed to allow the Spanish garrison to retire from the fortress with full honors of war. He would transport them to Cuba and would respect Spanish rights and property. He stated coldly that the occupation of Florida would continue until such time as Spain could provide a military force competent to prevent criminal acts against the United States, until such time as Spain could or would enforce the obligations of existing treaties between the two countries.

All that really mattered was that the Spanish flag was gone and the American flag flew in its stead in West Florida.

Jackson's proclamation declared that he had "invoked the immutable laws of self-defense." His justification for striking at Spanish rule in Florida rose from those helpless women butchered on the mutual frontier and countless babies whose cradles were stained with "the blood of innocence."

The proclamation promised that all Spanish subjects would be respected during the occupation, that Spanish law would govern all cases involving persons and property. Trade with all nations would be encouraged, religious freedom warranted. Revenue laws of the U.S. would be immediately enforced and such taxes collected forthwith by American forces.

Not in the proclamation but enforced at once was the kind of martial law Jackson once had imposed upon New Orleans. There, the Americans chafing under British domination and curfew had gone wild when freed by Andrew Jackson, only to find his curfews and his laws far stricter than the British had ever been. There was an added difference. New Orleans was an American city. Pensacola was, in Jackson's words, a "hotbed of intrigue and war" deep in enemy territory. Military rule would be ruthless. No hint of defiance to Jackson's government would be tolerated, on pain of death . . .

It was into this military rule that Locke and Cato rode. Locke sat astride the white Arabian stallion which had been a gift of Duc Jesús Sanchez-Montova. At his side, Cato plodded along on a Tennessee army horse provided them at Fort Scott. Locke realized from the heads that jerked up, the gazes that followed them, that he cut a swaggering figure on the white horse and that this was likely to weigh heavily against him with General Jackson. Though Old Hickory lived for praise and pomp and circumstance, he spoke bitterly against any shows of ostentation among his men. Sighing heavily, Locke tried to calm the prancing thoroughbred, but the beautiful animal knew only one gait—a parade trot.

During the long ride south Locke had seen few human beings. He'd found certain signs that Jackson's army had marched through—burned settlements, destroyed fields, slain hogs, cattle and even dogs left for the buzzards.

It was little better in the town. Since the entry of the invaders had been peaceful, only one house was half burned, but there was a look of demoralization, of devastation in the streets. Locke saw a huddle of men and women wandering lost in the streets. In their faces he saw the distracted glitter of terror he'd seen in the eyes of displaced Indians, of Sanchez-Montova, of all people who attempted to oppose Jackson and then to abide by his laws. These people were of all ages, and all races except Indians; there were old men and elderly women, young men and children, loitering in the sun, hungry, frightened, homeless and afraid even to ask for alms. In the hopeless dejection of their faces, the anguished terror in their eyes, they were all one—the flotsam that bobbled always in Andrew Jackson's wake.

Locke became aware of Cato's increasing consternation. The slave said nothing, but at the sight of the wretches along the street, he grew more tense, troubled.

"We'll find Isabella, Cato," Locke said. "We'll do that first."

Every street of the Spanish town was under heavy guard of American soldiers, but because Locke wore a captain's uniform, they were neither challenged nor detained, but they were marked well by army officials.

The city sprawled along the northern shore of Pensacola Bay—a deep-water, landlocked harbor. Dozens of ships stood at anchor or moved along the channel toward the open gulf. The town rose from sea level with its irregular, tree-fringed bayous and ochre-yellow bluffs.

They rode the guarded streets—Zarragossa, Palafox, Tarragona—a jumble of Spanish architecture, of gables, pilasters, colonnades, long plank walks and flights of those steps so dear to the Spanish heart, leading up to second-story entrances, high balconies with wrought-iron railings and jutting balustrades. Everywhere people loitered in the shade of oak, magnolia and elm trees, as if hiding from the revealing glare of the sun.

Today, there was little sign of the lawless and disorderly city Pensacola had become by 1814 under lax Spanish rule, sanctuary for escaped convicts, runaway slaves, fugitives and agents. It was this lawlessness which Jackson had declared as justification for his invasion. Whatever unruliness there had been had been stamped out since the arrival of American troops.

Locke did not know why he believed Isabella would not be among the people wandering the streets. Somehow, he felt instinctively, if she still remained in Pensacola, she would be held as an enemy to American rule. He learned that Plaza Ferdinand VII on Palafox Street was being used as a concentration center by the Americans for the rebellious, the traitorous, the criminal. They rode to the plaza, dismounted and left their horses at tie rails.

Soldiers ringed the plaza and inside it, Spanish subjects were gathered, huddled together as if seeking anonymity in crowds.

"Cato!"

Isabella's frantic cry stopped both of them. Cato heeled around, searching among the clusters of people crowding the plaza. Locke felt as if ice slid along his veins. Though he'd promised Cato they would find Isabella, he had been praying they would learn she was safe, with her mistress, in Havana. There was no hope for that now. Locke stood for a moment, shoulders slumped round, as if afraid to take one step forward into hell. Cato pushed through a crowd of people to where Isabella had leaped to her feet. She threw herself into his arms, sobbing his name over and over.

There was about Isabella the wild look of an abandoned, homeless kitten. Her face was drawn thin, shadowed, her high cheekbones like prominent ridges beneath her distracted eyes. Her peasant blouse and skirt were wrinkled, grimy, streaked with dirt. A look of terror spread across her features, like a tinge of pallor, pulling down the corners of her lovely, voluptuous mouth and deepening the shadows of distress swirling in her black eyes.

People stared as Cato held the Morisco girl, wordless for a long time, his arms clutching her to him. Locke remained unmoving, watching them. At last, crying like a forsaken child, Isabella whispered, "Oh, Cato, please, take me away from here."

Across the top of her head, Cato stared at Locke in mute appeal. Locke nodded. With his arm protectively about Isabella, Cato walked beside Locke toward the sentries at the Palafox portico. A sentry stepped forward. "This woman is a prisoner. She cannot be taken from this place."

"I'll be responsible for this woman," Locke said. "Who's in charge? Who do I see? Are there papers to sign?"

The soldier shrugged. "It's all right to take her, I reckon, if you're responsible, Captain."

They bought her food—coffee, meat and Spanish bread—at one of the bodegas still open near the plaza. Isabella wolfed down the bread and meat as if she had not eaten in days. With one hand, she clung to Cato, as if, having found him again, she meant never to be parted from him.

In the quiet garden at St. Michael's Church, they sat on a limestone bench under a spreading magnolia. In the silence of this ancient edifice, the war and the killing seemed remote and removed.

At last, Isabella glanced at Locke and attempted a wan, gray smile. "I don't see how you were able to get me out of there. We who are imprisoned in the plaza are to be allowed to leave Pensacola only when we can make restitution for our crimes or prove our new loyalty to America. We all were arrested for some crime against your army."

Locke winced. "What was your crime?"

She gazed at him, her black eyes brimming with tears. She bit her lip. "I was with Doña Yolanda when they captured her. . . . I would not deny her."

"Yolanda? Where is she? Is she all right? Is she prisoner?"

"No, señor. No. It is too late for Doña Yolanda." Isabella sobbed, pressing her face against Cato's shoulder and digging her nails into his arms. Her body shook with her weeping.

Locke caught Isabella's arm. "Where is she?"

Isabella, unable to speak for the moment, gestured helplessly with her arm. At last she whispered, "They have killed her, señor."

Locke sagged as if struck physically. It took a long time for Isabella to recount what had happened. Doña Yolanda had squandered so many chances to escape Spanish Florida with her life. She could have gone safely with her father when he abdicated to Cuba. But she would not. She said her father ran like a coward, disgracing their name, and she could not go with him.

She had remained in the governor's mansion with the José Masot family as the most vocal advocate of resistance against the invading Americans. But when Masot took his family and fled to Fort Barrancas, again Yolanda threw away an opportunity to save her life.

The last moment came when Spanish loyalists, led by Yolanda and a deserting lieutenant from Masot's guards, opposed the onrushing Americans in the streets with guns. "I was among them," Isabella said. "I and Doña Yolanda." She gestured, her hands trembling. "We were quickly silenced; Lieutenant Hildalgo was killed almost at once. The rest of us were rounded up and taken before General Jackson."

Isabella covered her face with her hands. "Again, Doña Yolanda could have saved herself. When the General Andrés Jackson saw us, he said we were misguided fools, servants mostly, and if we would take an oath of loyalty to the new flag, he would release us, and let those of us who wished sail to Cuba when José Masot and the soldiers departed.

"I felt as if I had been given a reprieve. I was alive. I was to be allowed to leave with my people. He asked each of us our names and our occupations. All of us declared ourselves to be nothing more than servants in the homes of the affluent Spanish. The general appeared almost sorry for us. He said that while the privileged rich ran for cover, those of us who were loyal to Spain and Ferdinand had tried to fight. He believed first in loyalty, and though we were enemies, he was proud that we fought for what we believed.

"I clung to Yolanda's hand. I begged her to say she was a servant in the Masot house, as I was. I was called before the general first. He asked my name and what I did. When I told him, he waved me on. 'We are at peace now,' he said to me. 'Go in peace.'

"I walked across the room and leaned against the wall to wait for Yolanda. When the general asked her name, she replied that she was called Yolanda and she had been in the house of Masot most recently. He took this to mean she had been in service there—not that she was Spanish royalty—and I prayed that Doña Yolanda would accept this and live.

"I stood with my nails digging into my palms. I willed her to bow to the general, to thank him and to join me where we would be transferred to the docks and outgoing ships. We were so close to freedom. I could taste freedom. I could smell the clean air of the sea.

"But it was not to be. Perhaps there is some fate written for all of us. Except for what happened in that moment, Doña Yolanda would be alive at this hour.

"A half-breed Indian-and-Negro man was standing behind Yolanda. He had been a gardener at the governor's mansion, a huge man, but gentle always. When the general looked up and asked him what his name was, the man must have gone insane. He leaped at the general as if he would kill him. The general lunged to his feet. Before the man could get to the general, he was surrounded and beaten to the floor with gun butts. The general stood watching as if he enjoyed the sight. When the man had been subdued, he swung his arm and said, 'Take the half-breed nigger out and shoot him.'

"Yolanda in that moment went insane. She heeled around, like a tigress, screaming at the general. 'Is he an animal, that you kill him when he protests? Is that all any of my people mean to you?'

"The general told her that if she were smart she would shut up and get out of there. But she was not to be silenced. She screamed the truth at him, who she was, who her father was, what she had done to oppose him, how she had tried to rally the Spanish and their subjects against him. She called him a wizened animal, made ill inside by the evil of his own actions, by his own inhumanity. She screamed that he was bloated with self-importance, blind to humanity, deaf to the rights of other human beings. She told him that he had lied when he said there were five hundred Seminoles in Pensacola. There was none, she raged, but what mattered was, he had known there was none. He had wanted an excuse before the nations of the world for clutching Spanish property, for driving out the legal owners of this land. They tried to shut her up and she would not be silenced. There was the truth, she said, and the world had to hear it above his pious lies.

"The most objective person in that place could see in General Jackson's face that the things Doña Yolanda was saying to him were truths that he had closed out of his mind, shut his eyes to, refused to consider. She made him hear them, but worse than that, she made the world hear them. She screamed at him that he had no right before law, or before God, to be standing conqueror in this place.

"One saw the rages boil and erupt inside him. She said things he did not permit spoken aloud in his presence. She spoke the truth and this was what he would not countenance. Suddenly, raging, he waved his arm. He said, 'Get that greasy bitch out of here. Get rid of her.'

"I ran to her, and because I stayed with her until she was executed, I was arrested and taken to the plaza to await whatever sentence was handed out for me.

"I think had General Jackson been less violently angered by Doña Yolanda's outburst, he might merely have ordered her arrested and by morning would have cooled off enough to consider her position, her family, anything except the bitter accusations she heaped upon him. . . . But I think nobody knew better than General Jackson that he had no legal right to invade this territory or take over the city. He could not stand to have it put in words. He wanted her removed, effaced, gotten rid of as if she'd never existed. She was executed by a firing squad along with six others that same afternoon."

Locke bought an expensive casket and bribed a priest at the Catholic Church to accompany him to the United States military command to claim Yolanda's body. There, after much haggling, they found Yolanda's bullet-riddled body in a pine box, awaiting burial. He paid money, lied, signed papers, threatened superiors and finally was permitted to remove Yolanda's body for ceremony and burial in the cemetery at ancient St. Michael's Church.

For a long time after the priest, the mourners and the gravediggers were gone, Locke stood alone beside the raw yellow mound. But he could not make himself believe the vital, lovely Yolanda was in that grave. It was as if there was nothing left of her. The mound, the quiet graveyard, the old stones of forgotten beings, all of it was silent. She was gone and her world was empty for him. He turned at last and walked away.

Before nightfall, he found a freighter bound for Cuba. Cato looked ill with loss, but offered no protest. Isabella had to leave Florida as quickly as possible for her own safety. It was only when Locke bought tickets for two that Cato protested aloud.

"You're going with her, Cato," Locke said.

"I can't go without you, mastah."

"If you want to save her life, you'll go. And now."

"I'm your slave, mastah."

"Not if I say you're not. I'll put through papers of manumission, Cato. Meantime, you have my word. You are no longer my slave. You are free to go."

Cato stared at him, face bleak, rigid. "What will I do?"

Locke shrugged. "Marry Isabella. She'll know what to do. Hell, you can even become a preacher if you can work up a congregation somewhere."

Barely able to control her delight, Isabella clung to Cato's arm with all her strength. Cato seemed for the moment unaware of her.

Cato stared at Locke for a long beat. His eyes filled with unwilling tears. He looked away, blinked hard, but the tears welled and spilled along his dark cheeks. "I been with you—all my life, mastah. Long as I can remember."

"Too long. It's unmanned you. My father taught you, Cato, long ago. A man does not cry."

Cato sobbed suddenly. "If your father believed that, mastah, he was—an unfeelin' son of a bitch."

"There you go," Locke said. "Free for five minutes and already you're running down my family."

Crying like a young boy, Cato grabbed Locke in his arms. "I don't know where I go, mastah, what I do. But I know I loves you, mastah. Like a brother. Better than a brother. Like my own self."

Locke sighed heavily. He handed to Isabella the pouch containing the remainder of the gold he'd stolen from Arbuthnot's ship. "You better hang on to the money. It'll give you a start somewhere. . . . Take care of him, Isabella. He may be a good man yet. At least, he finally knows how to cry."

— *XXX* —

ROWS OF chairs were placed precisely at a long, highly polished conference table of burnished oak. Behind them, tall Spanish windows opened on the streets of the town, the dock and the bay beyond. Sunlight streamed in, lancing half across the silent room. At the middle chair General Jackson sat alone, a few military papers stacked before him; all the other chairs were empty. Locke stood at attention across the reflective surface of the table.

General Jackson looked debilitated, more like a fiery-eyed skeleton than ever, as if he were devoured by inner sickness. His shock of hair, graying, was streaked with memory of brown, the skull bones stood in sharp relief against the papyruslike flesh of his forehead. Perhaps it was the length of the table, the number of chairs arranged for his officers, or the very size of the chair in which he sat, but the general looked ill, desperately ill, and Locke felt a flaring of honest pity for him, mixed with his hatred.

General Jackson stared up at him for a long time, the discomfort of the "crick" in his neck causing him to hold his lean head at an odd angle. Dust pirouetted and glittered in the shafts of sunlight.

The general's whining, shrill voice crackled across that

silence like the swish and snap of a bullwhip. "You took your time getting here. When I order a man to my presence, I expect that man . . . on the double."

"My apologies, General."

The general waved a bony hand angrily. "Don't waste my time. We don't know each other well, Locke, but I think we know each other, perhaps as few others know us."

Locke tried to smile. "I'm afraid so, General."

Jackson's head jerked up, rage glittering in his eyes. "When I want jokes, Locke, I'll call in clowns."

"My apologies, sir."

Jackson peered up at him for a long beat as if searching for irony. He said, "I sent for you to come here because I don't know if I'll permit you a discharge from my army. There is a lot to be settled between us, Captain, before you're free to leave my service—if ever."

"I'm sorry about that, sir. I applied for discharge, and I'll continue to do it."

"You'll do not a goddamn thing unless I say you will, Captain. You don't seem to realize, man, you're in trouble. Deep trouble. The list of charges I have before me against you could get you a firing squad, or a gallows, long before it'd earn you an honorable discharge."

"I have been a loyal soldier in your service, General."

General Jackson's mouth twisted. "Oh, I know what that means. I've dealt with you lacy-pants from Virginia before. You've carried out my orders to the letter whether you agreed with them or not."

"Yes, sir. That about says it."

"Well, mister, that don't add up to loyalty in my book."

"I'm sorry about that, sir. But it doesn't add up to criminal charges in mine."

Jackson almost laughed in his rage. "You want criminal charges, Captain? You in a hurry to be hung? You'll just hear criminal charges pour out of my mouth. How is this for a start? You freed an enemy woman from a place of army detention without authority."

Those falcon eyes fixed on Locke, unblinkingly. At last, Locke nodded.

"You took—again without authority—the body of a belligerent from the army depot for private burial. That sounds so unimportant, don't it, Captain?"

"No, sir. I suppose it can be interpreted as defying orders, even of inciting the enemy against authority."

"You goddamn right it can and it does. You've gone too far now, Locke. Inciting the enemy against the lawful forces of the United States just sticks in my craw. I won't tolerate it, and I mean to make an example of it—before the disputants and before the world."

"I figured you might, sir."

Jackson hesitated a moment. "You knew what you were doing was going to get charges lodged against you?"

"Everything has its price tag, sir. Everything costs you. You figure the cost, you decide if it's worth it."

"And you decided it was worth your own neck to put the body of a greasy spic woman in a Catholic grave?"

Locke bit down hard on his underlip. At last he spoke in a very low tone. "I could not make you understand, sir."

"Well, you sure as hell better try. We're talking things over here, boy. It's me and you. But it won't be me and you when you come up before a court-martial."

"I did what I thought I had to do, General."

"What in the hell kind of defense is that? If you want to live to git back to Virginia and your lovely lady and new girl-child, you better do one hell of a lot better than that."

"That's my only defense, sir."

Jackson's grayed face pulled taut and he stared at Locke impassively for some seconds. At last, he spoke, reading from the report before him again, "You arranged immediate and illegal passage for a prisoner of the United States Army upon an outgoing vessel. Do I have to spell that out? You helped an enemy alien escape. That, sir. is aiding and abetting the enemy. You could have hardly done more if'n you'd worn one of Masot's fancy uniforms."

"I know you don't want to hear this, sir, but the enemy alien was a servant woman, loved by my slave."

"She was my prisoner."

"I am here, sir, to answer for whatever crimes I have committed."

"And you shall. You shall. Tell me, Locke, tell me one

thing, why is it always you? I got trouble inside my own loyal forces—and where does it come from? It comes from you, Locke. Why?"

"Either I am disloyal, and criminal, as you believe, General, or I am a loyal soldier who finds himself at odds at times with command—"

"A soldier don't *find* hisself at odds with command, Captain. He gits his goddamn orders and he goddamn well obeys them. It's as clear and simple as that."

"Because I find fault doesn't necessarily prove I'm subversive, General. No one accuses you of less than total love and loyalty for our country. But not everyone who loves this country—and even loves you, General—agrees with you all the time in all you do—"

"I never heard truer goddamn words in my life."

"Because I disagree doesn't mean I love my country any less than you do. Sometimes the dissenters are the true patriots—"

"Yore just fogging up the issue, boy."

"Am I, sir?"

"The issue here is right and wrong. There is right and wrong and you are wrong."

"Yes, sir, in this place and under this command, I am wrong. But those who find fault with what they see as wrong in their beloved nation, don't want to destroy that nation. The very opposite! They want to find what's wrong, what is bad and evil and diseased—and repair it."

"There you are. The theme song of the nice-Nelly Virginia sunshine patriots. Thomas Jefferson himself could have spoke those words. Words any subversive could hide behind."

"I'm not hiding behind them. You asked me and I told you. I agree that I bought passage for Isabella Mesablanca to Cuba. I do not dispute that charge."

"Even though you may well hang for it?"

"Even so."

Jackson went into a spasm of unrelieved coughing. He writhed in his chair, clutching at the pain erupting in his side and intensified by his coughs. He jerked out a handkerchief and spat into it, bloody sputum. But when Locke tried to aid him, he waved him away angrily.

"Stand where you are, Captain." Jackson sagged in his chair for some moments. At last, gray and shaken with fatigue, he got himself under control. "You know why I sent to bring you here, Locke? I heard—for hell's sake—you was reported consorting with Colonel Allan who was in restricted confinement at Fort Scott. Laws, rules don't mean a goddamn to you, do they? I sent you to Fort Scott to see to the safety of your wife in her labor—and that's the way you repay me."

"I deeply appreciate all you've done for my wife, General. I merely went to Colonel Allan to say good-bye."

"Consorting. A prisoner not permitted guests. But you went. Just as you went to see Alexander Arbuthnot on the night before he was hung—as you consorted with British agent Robert Harmbrister before he was executed. It's always you, Locke. You accusing a good soldier like Lester Catchpole of mutilating Indians. Helping an enemy prisoner escape. Spying on me."

"That's it, isn't it, General?"

Jackson's head jerked up. "What are you talking about?"

"All these charges. The only important charge—as far as you're concerned—is that President Monroe may have sent me and that I may live to report to him."

Jackson did laugh now, grasping the sides of his chair until his knuckles grayed, and coughing helplessly for some seconds. "No, boy. I don't have to worry about you ever getting back to President Monroe—unless I decide to let you go. . . . You've helped a prisoner escape. I can hang you for that and that's the only charge I need against you."

"But you and I will know, won't we? You're afraid I'll report to President Monroe—"

"I don't give a damn about your report to President Monroe."

"Yet you've ordered at least three searches trying to find it—if it existed."

"Oh, it exists all right. Do you deny, Captain, that you have written a long report to President Monroe—on my activities in Spanish Florida?"

Locke shook his head. "Sorry, General. You didn't find such a report. You won't find such a report. You have my confession on the criminal charge of aiding an enemy. You'll have to be content with that."

"Oh, no, I don't." With a gesture of impatience, Jackson shoved aside the reports before him and leaned, reflected, across the table. "I'll make a horse trade with you. You turn over that report, whatever it is, and I'll drop all charges. You'll have your dishonorable discharge from the army by morning."

Their gazes met across the glossy surface of the table. "I'm sorry, General, I can't do that."

"You won't? You're willing to die for some damn fool sense of duty—"

"You yourself, General, prize loyalty above all else."

"Listen, boy. Let's not talk abstract nonsense here. We're dealing with your life. Your life. I'll see you hanged as a traitor, and there's nothing Jim Monroe or nobody else can do to help you."

"I won't ask President Monroe's help, General."

Jackson stared at him, eyes growing wild. "Yet, you admit you came down here as his spy."

"I admit to helping Isabella Mesablanca—"

"Stop that slop. We know you kept a report. We don't give a damn. But we want to know what's in it. What lies you want to send to President Monroe about me."

"Why would I want to lie about you, General?"

"You charged my men with mutilation!"

"We can rage at each other until doomsday, that won't change. Those Indians were mutilated. Catchpole testified he was following orders—"

"Is that the kind of horseshit you're sending to Monroe?"

"I haven't admitted sending anything to the President. That's a charge you haven't been able to substantiate, General."

"Listen, goddamn it, that's a charge I never want to substantiate. It's a charge won't ever be made officially against you. And you know it. But you also know it's a fact. What does Monroe want to know about me that he can't ask me? What does he suspect me of?"

Locke shrugged. "You'd have to ask him."

"I'm asking you." He coughed violently. "I'm giving my life for my country—and I'm suspected of treason."

"It is not news to you, sir. There are men who suspect you of motives—"

"I know all about that. Those blue-bellied, weak-assed New Englanders. What in hell do they know the troubles we got on this border and along the Mississippi frontier? Listen to me, boy. Do you want to live?"

"At what price, sir?"

"Does life mean so little to you that you'd refuse to turn over a report to me to save your hide?"

"I don't know. I don't have that report."

Jackson's face grayed out. He coughed into his handkerchief, his face flushing blood red and then going whiter than paper. "You mean you've sent it to him?"

"I don't have it. Even if you execute me—for aiding and abetting the enemy—there is no way you can stop my report from reaching the President now . . . if there is such a report."

Jackson stared at him. "Oh, there's such a report, all right. We know that. But we don't know how you got rid of it. If you did. We still may rip your skin off to find it."

"That's your decision, sir."

"You're a true son of a bitch, Locke. But, by God, I can't help but admire you."

"May I say the same about you, sir?"

Jackson stared at him for a long beat, then shook his head. "Don't know why we had to be enemies, Locke. We could of worked well together."

"I've learned to admire you—for accomplishing your ends—at all costs, sir."

"And yet, you wrote against me. . . . What? That I mean to set up a republic of my own down here in West Florida?"

"No, sir. I don't know that. Your actions make it seem logical that you might—if pushed. If you don't get your way in dealing with the President and with Congress—you'd be willing to tear this nation apart."

"You wrote that?"

"No, sir. As factually as I could, I set down what you have done. Nothing more. If they draw the conclusion that you may set up an independent republic in Spanish Florida, it will come out of what you have done, not anything I might have said."

"Listen to me, boy. If they fight me, I'll do what I have

to. If that means setting up a republic to force the issues that must be resolved, then I'll do that. If they're willing to talk reason, to compromise with me, then I am willing to go on following orders. But if they fight me—if they try to return this land I've taken by military conquest, I'll set up a free nation before I'll give it back to Spaniards, Indians, niggers and white renegades—"

"President Monroe believes that would wreck this nation."

"Then I'll wreck this nation. If they can't see the right, then it's not worth saving. Better to wreck it than to let it go in the direction it's headed." Then Jackson laughed and waved his arm. "Hell, boy, I know politicians. And I know Jim Monroe. I sure hell ain't the only one says sometimes Jim Monroe acts like he ain't got brains enough to hold his hat on. None of that will happen.

"Hell, boy, what you don't know is that sometimes I have to take strong measures to deal with them New York bankers and moneymen. I have to make them white-livered New Englanders listen to reason, and get them fence-stradling Virginians off their high horses. I put the fear of God in them. That's all. And that's what I'll do now if they oppose me in this matter of taking these lands from Spain."

"No, sir. You won't get that far."

"What the hell makes you think it won't?"

Locke spread his hands. He spoke in a low, almost gentle tone of conciliation. "*President* Monroe will stop you, sir. If it takes the whole force and all the finances of the country, if it pushes the nation into final bankruptcy, he won't let you wreck this country—no matter how noble your cause may seem to you."

"Then, so be it. I am ready to face them all."

"But you have to face only the President. President Madison may have bowed to you and your threats. Maybe, in order to preserve the country, President Jefferson might have submitted to your demands. I don't know. But I know that President Monroe will not."

"Jim Monroe?" Jackson put his head back, laughing out his contempt. Then he cleared his throat loudly and spat into his handkerchief. "That gutless wonder?"

"Jim Monroe might knuckle under to you, sir. That's what

I'm trying to tell you. Jim Monroe might not have the courage to fight you, he might submit—but *President* Monroe won't."

General Jackson stopped laughing abruptly. He sat back in his chair, his bony hands gripping its ornate arms. Without speaking, he stared at Locke for a long time in cold silence.

"Think you've bought yourself an impasse, don't you, boy?"

Locke sighed. "I don't know, sir. I only know that even if you execute me, you can't stop that report from getting to President Monroe now."

Jackson cleared his throat and spat in his handkerchief again. He pushed the papers farther from him on the polished tabletop. He shook his head and almost smiled. "You are a son of a bitch, Locke . . . but by God, an admirable one."

Locke saluted. "So are you, sir."

— *XXXI* —

AFTER HIS long and enforced exile from Hidden Brook, Locke at first found himself unable to deal with the simple and wonderful fact that he was actually back home again. Hidden Brook! Laughter and pleasure sang in the name itself, filled with memories and dreams and love, with the very act of birth, becoming aware, of growing up. Hidden Brook! Those first mornings, waking up in his own bed, far from the rigors and discomforts and miseries of a strange and Spartan army bivouac, were more dream than reality. It took some getting used to! He lay in his own bed, in his own room, in his own home, overwhelmed by the inexpressible pleasure of familiar sights and sounds, plus the added wonder of finding Mary-Stuart lying asleep beside him, golden strands of hair clinging to his pillow. And he need only stretch out his arm to Hedy's

dealing with it? The law says this place must be sold to settle the leins against it. The law says the money in my accounts was removed legally, that the debts and losses accumulated in my name are lawful and must stand against me. The law says I may be guilty of murder. Though the law cannot prove it, I am their quarry. There is one way to settle this matter, Mary-Stuart—force the truth to the surface—and *force* it, I shall."

"We've been so unhappy for so long," she whispered. "Now, at last, we are together—and now we have our baby. We have everything, Jerry. We don't need any more. By trying to rectify wrong—outside the law—you may destroy us all."

He nodded. "I may. I've taken that into account, Mary-Stuart. I can let the law take its course. I can lose this home, these lands, everything my family built—"

"As my family has lost theirs, Jerry—"

"I can start over. I am young. Strong. But I have been robbed. My mother has been defrauded, cheated of everything that belongs to her. If I let this happen, there is only one thing I cannot do. I cannot live with myself."

She saw that he would not be turned, or headed, or dissuaded. She said only, "If you get your revenge—what about us? What about our baby? What happens to us then?"

He stared down at her. "You would not want to live with what I would be if I let them do this to me."

"Can't you wait just a little while?"

"No. I've waited too long now."

He rode into the sweeping grounds at Elms Head upon the white Arabian stallion given to him by Duc Sanchez-Montova. He had ridden that horse all the miles from the Florida frontier to northern Virginia. He had plodded along the trails, the traces, the broad roadways, staring ahead to that moment when he would come to the gates at Elms Head. It seemed as if all roads he had traveled, every act of his life, had pointed him toward this moment. When his father died, Worthington Jennings had come to him, with his pious smiling and honeyed lies, telling him his father was a defaulter, a liar, a cheat, a gambler, a wastrel who had squandered his savings and left Hidden Brook on the brink of bankruptcy. In that hour he had been robbed of his lifelong love and admiration for his father; he had believed Jennings, he had doubted his own father, he had learned to hate him. Something, he still didn't know what, had caused Jennings to hesitate to foreclose, and he had been able—through piracy, privateering, pillaging—in two years to accumulate money enough to repay the ruinous debts incurred during his father's last illness and death when Jennings had been acting as his administrator and executor.

Rage trembled under the civility of his tone when he asked for the master of Elms Head at the veranda door. "Tell Squire Jennings I am here and wish to see him at once on matters urgent to us both," he said. "Tell him I shall wait here until I see him."

The black butler's eyes widened, white-rimmed. He shook his head. The civility of Locke's tone did not deceive him; he had served Squire Jennings most of his life; he had seen too many men at this door, fighting to control inner rages that compelled them. "I afraid the squire, he cain't come out here, Mastah Locke."

"You tell him he'd better come, or I'll drag him out here."

"No, sir. You don't understand. He cain't come. . . . If you wish, suh, I be most delighted to lead you to where he is."

Locke nodded. He followed the servant across the foyer, the parlor and out upon a veranda where the morning sun struck full.

Locke stepped out upon the flagstones and then stopped, stunned. He had ridden here, the rages building, wanting to kill Worthington Jennings for evils the attorney had done him, but he saw he was too late. Time had already slain the lawyer. He was alive, but barely. He looked as if all the accumulated evils of his career and his hypocritical existence had spun and simmered and stewed to boiling and had erupted, destroying him. Staring at Jennings, Locke became almost convinced that the inner evils of a man show themselves in disabling, crippling and tormenting physical infirmity.

"Brain fever," the butler whispered. "Mastah Jennings done had what the doctor calls a massive stroke—blood vessels done burst in his head, doctor say."

Locke nodded, unable to drag his fascinated gaze from this human wreckage. Jennings slumped, tied with strips of cloth and supported by goosedown pillows in a wicker wingback chair. His head was twisted far off its axis, and his eyelids, cheeks and lips seemed pulled downward on the right half of his face. His right side was tortured out of shape and held in rigid paralysis. His right knee was permanently buckled up over his left and his feet were liver colored, bare and swollen.

"Jerry," this warped being managed to mutter, spittle oozing from the misshapen corner of his mouth. Flies swarmed about his face and the servant brushed at them with a palm-leaf fan.

Locke stared down at the lawyer. It was impossible to tell in the man's tormented face what he felt, or if he felt anything. Locke said, "I know you never expected to see me again, Jennings. But I am here. I came to square matters between us. But I see I am too late for that."

"Stroke," Jennings managed to whisper after a long, agonizing effort.

"Yes. I see. I wish I could say I feel sympathy. I don't. You're still alive—the people you tormented and twisted and destroyed are dead. Maybe they are better off than you are, I don't know."

"There's no use trying to talk to him," a man said from behind Locke. "He barely understands the simplest things."

Locke turned and faced the doctor. Locke exhaled. "Maybe he only understands what he wants to understand. Look at him. I think he knows why I am here."

They gazed, in revulsion, at the twisted man. His eyes were brimmed with tears. "With a power of attorney from my father, he robbed him of everything. A pious churchgoer, he sneaked secretly into the house of a whore named Anne Stoker. In a jealous rage, he killed her, expecting Harry Randolph to walk in and be blamed for the crime. Harry Randolph had given Anne Stoker a two-carat ring which she wore about her neck on a stout plain cord. When I went into Stoker's house instead of Harry Randolph, Jennings was afraid he might yet be exposed. He met Harry on the road. They argued. Harry found the greedy Jennings had taken the ring from about Anne's neck after he killed her. He knew then that

Jennings was the killer. Jennings killed Harry, cut the ring from the cord which was gripped in Harry's fist. He dumped Harry's body at the edge of my lands. Then, pretending friendship, he urged me out of the country until the matter was settled—he to handle everything with my power of attorney. Only, he gave that stolen ring to Mary-Stuart, not knowing that Harry had told me about it. And so I came back here, knowing that Jennings had killed Mary-Stuart's brother, defrauded my father, and then robbed me as well as Mary-Stuart's family, all the while piously proposing marriage to her. If you understand me, Jennings, save what's left of your life by nodding your head—confessing before these witnesses—or they will see me throttle you with my bare hand."

The twisted man gazed up at them, his head cocked awkwardly. His eyes filled with tears and they spilled crazily along his ruptured cheek. At last, with what seemed an unnatural and supreme effort, he nodded his head and then nodded it again.

— XXXII —

MARY-STUART stood rigid, icy with chill, feeling as if she were isolated in this lovely old sun-room at Hidden Brook, set apart in some invisible enclosure from the people around her. As if from some great distance, so remote they could neither hear her when she spoke, nor be heard by her, she watched the laughing faces—convinced they belonged to happy people in some far galaxy in time and space, unrelated to this darkling earth where she existed in her own private hell. Even Jerry's mother seemed improved by this gathering of friends and acquaintances of distinction. New color suffused the lovely woman's slender cheeks, her eyes glowed, her smile reached out to touch all her noted guests. One looked at her and realized her radiance and youthfulness had been only masked by tragedy and pain. She was still a young woman, one saw, in her earliest forties. Mary-Stuart was happy for her, but unable to relate to her pleasure. The spirit of conviviality rang in the room and only Mary-Stuart was removed from it, denied access to it, thrust in a vacuum of which only she was aware.

It was not as if these people were less than friendly. They were effusive in greeting her. They embraced her. The men swore she was even lovelier than ever in her new bliss of wedded life and motherhood. She smiled and thanked them, and prayed they could not see the confusion swirling deep in her eyes.

President Monroe's wife Elizabeth had known Mary-Stuart since she was a little girl, had always found her charming, and now held her hand reassuringly. Mary-Stuart shivered. Why must *she* be reassured in her own house? Am I the true stranger here? Do all these people belong at Hidden Brook, but I do not?

More than a dozen close associates of President Monroe had accompanied the President from the Capitol, in four splendid coaches. President Monroe kept assuring Mary-Stuart this was a festive occasion—one he was happy to be celebrating in the bosom of his closest friends, in a place where he'd always been happy.

The sociability and excited goodwill swept and eddied about Mary-Stuart without really touching her, or involving her. All she was capable of thinking was that Jerry had ridden in rage to Elms Head to confront Squire Jennings. Nothing else held an atom of reality. It was as if she waited on a time bomb and she was helpless to do anything except stand, waiting. Even when Aunt Laura brought the baby Hedy down for the exclamatory recognition of her beauty and perfection, Mary-Stuart was unable to respond. At another time, her pleasure in her daughter would have surged boundless, catching them all up in her enthusiasm. Today, she could only force herself to smile.

To smile and nod, to stand, smiling and nodding, and waiting . . .

* * *

A small brown hand tugged at Mary-Stuart's skirt. She turned, almost astonished to see one of the slave children assigned to watch the trace for arriving guests. She'd left word she was to be notified the instant Jerry was spied returning on the hard road.

The small, chocolate face was stretched wide in a grin. The dark little head nodded furiously.

Mary-Stuart felt her eyes blur with tears, and she was unsure whether they welled in relief or anxiety. She nodded vaguely at the child and touched his head in a gesture of gratitude. "Go tell Aunt Vera you're to have a double helping of blackberry cobbler, with lots of milk," she told him. His face gleamed with delight and, forgetting his manners, he ran shouting and dancing toward the manor-house kitchen.

The celebrated guests laughed, enjoying this byplay which underlined that happiness and familial love they always discovered anew at Hidden Brook.

Mary-Stuart excused herself and hurried from the room, her lace handkerchief knotted in her fist.

She ran across the foyer. A maid held out a sun hat, its bright ribbons fluttering, but Mary-Stuart only shook her head. She had no time to stop. Her long-suppressed illness surged upward and she was afraid she would be ill. She had kept her fears hidden from everyone but herself, but now the moment had caught her unprepared. She wanted to be sure that Jerry was all right; she dreaded to hear what may have happened at Elms Head.

She let the thick magnolia-wood front door close heavily behind her and hurried across the sun-patched veranda. She went down the wide steps and across the drive, walking faster and then running. She hardly knew if she were running toward Jerry, or from those happy and excited people who had come to welcome him home—honors that would be meaningless, ceremony turned to wormwood if he had slain the lawyer.

Her dress puffing around her ankles, her arm extended, she ran along the drive, illumined and then shadowed in the crosshatching of sunlight. From the gateway, Jerry saw her and booted the Arabian stallion, racing toward her.

He drew reins and leaped from the saddle. He was smiling,

but when he saw the gray pallor and rigidity in her cheeks, his own face went bleak. "Hedy," he whispered. "Is she all right?"

Mary-Stuart sagged against him nodding. Hedy was all right.

He held her fiercely. "Are *you* all right?"

She pressed against him, nodding. She tilted her head back, staring upward, trying to read his gray eyes. Her fingers closed on his arm. "Squire Jennings," she whispered. "Did you—you didn't—?"

He gazed at her, seeing that all her fears had been for him. Suddenly, all the shackles that had imprisoned him snapped like rotted hemp. He caught her hands in his and pressed his mouth against the backs of her fingers. He laughed, and it was as if all the evil that had plagued him in these last years was wiped out, totally erased from memory. His fierce and raging hatreds, his agonized sense of wrong, his thirsting drive for vengeance, lost all urgency and meaning. It was past, over and forgotten, as if it had never been. He was young again, in love with Mary-Stuart, the loveliest girl in all Virginia, his alone in all the world, whom he loved and cherished and would keep safe and close as long as he lived.

"Kill him?" He gazed at her for another moment and then laughed, truly laughed. "I would have. . . . I wanted to. . . . When I went there I meant to kill him. . . . But I was too late. . . . I didn't kill him. I didn't touch him. He wasn't worth it."

She laughed, a helplessly joyous sound. Relief flooded through her. Their world which had seemed lost was whole and secure and safe and full of promise. They were young, and there was nothing they could not accomplish, together, and this was all that really mattered.

She clutched him to her and kissed him fiercely, clinging to him, and not caring about the laughter that drifted out to them from the veranda. Without releasing her, Locke tossed the reins to the slave children.

The celebrated and distinguished guests lined the shaded veranda. They laughed and nudged each other though they were kept waiting, as the master of Hidden Brook and his lady walked close in each other's arms up the sun-dappled lane, like children again, like young lovers looking ahead in delight and anticipation to what they found inside their own hearts. They were together at last and they were back home. They asked no more.